Lord of the Bayou

by Bruce T. Jones

© Copyright 2022 Bruce T. Jones

ISBN 978-1-64663-591-7

This is a work of fiction. The characters are both actual and fictitious. With the exception of verified historical events and persons, all incidents, descriptions, dialogue and opinions expressed are the products of the author's imagination and are not to be construed as real.

REVIEW COPY: This is an advanced printing subject to corrections and revisions.

Published by

 köehlerbooks™

3705 Shore Drive
Virginia Beach, VA 23455
800-435-4811
www.koehlerbooks.com

LORD OF THE BAYOU

BRUCE T. JONES

VIRGINIA BEACH
CAPE CHARLES

CHAPTER 1

THE BLACK DENALI SLOSHED through the storm-soaked trail. Lined with moss-cloaked tupelos, cypresses, and the occasional twisted oak, the double-track path narrowed to a needle's eye, providing barely enough room for the large SUV to pass as it rocked and rolled deeper into the moonlit bayou.

Junior Tazwell and Colin Wells made jovial conversation as they shifted gently to the rhythm of the rutty, root-covered byway beneath the Denali's wheels. "Wow, we're really out there," said Colin as they forged through the submerged, disappearing trail.

"It's not much farther," Taz replied as he glanced into the welcome blackness of the rearview mirror. "Anyway, congratulations on your promotion."

"Thanks, Taz." Colin, who worked under Taz, beamed over his hard-earned achievement. "Do all the new guys eventually get to make a pickup?"

"Hell no. The boss don't trust too many guys with this much responsibility. But since I'm moving up, and he's obviously impressed with your work, this will be part of your new job. Looks like you're on the fast track, buddy boy."

Colin smiled. For nearly a year, his duties had been exclusively delved out by Taz. Outside of Colin's regular courier task of transporting countless mysterious parcels, his work could best be described as marginally shady—but to what extent, he did not know. He had never dared to open or tamper with any of the packages because he always felt the eyes of his employer's minions lurking in the shadows.

He was hoping tonight's work would begin to unmask the true nature of his employer's empire: Was it possible that his boss, the reclusive David LaRoux, one of New Orleans' wealthiest entrepreneurs and philanthropists, was in fact one of the world's biggest narcos? Such allegations had never been considered publicly, much less spoken. But that was the real reason Colin had been working with Taz—to uncover the answer for the Drug Enforcement Administration, his true employer. In all the time they'd worked together, however, Taz had never mentioned a thing about drugs. So, a part of Colin wondered if he and his fellow undercover DEA agents were tossing one of the agency's most dangerous Hail Marys ever. *One thing's certain,* Colin thought. *At this hour, in the middle of the bayou, we're sure not meeting a UPS driver for office supplies.*

"Pay attention to how I'm driving, Colin. When the road narrows, you've got to keep her dead in the middle, or you will slide right in the muck. And there ain't no getting her out after that. Trust me, with all the gators out here, you damn sure don't want to have to get out and push. And Triple A? You want to hear someone laugh their asses off?"

Colin maintained his sappy smile and nodded. He marveled at the natural beauty of the heavily wooded oasis ahead, illuminated by the headlights. Suddenly, the road seemed to dead-end at the base of a massive twisted oak, laden with dreadlocked moss.

Taz turned sharply to the right, and the Denali splashed into two-foot-deep water. Traveling about fifty yards, he unexpectedly turned left through a veil of moss. Once inside the island's naturally guarded perimeter, the staccato flash of countless fireflies played off the heavily wooded canopy to create a constantly evolving galaxy of insect delight. Across the island, through a small break in the trees, Colin could see the river, and just above the horizon, the haze-filtered sickle of the crescent moon. Beyond that, streaks of lightning illuminated the stream of cumulus clouds.

"Looks like we might get a storm," Colin reported.

"We'll be long gone before it gets here."

Through the heavily forested plateau, the road ahead sloped and abruptly ended at the water's edge. From the passenger seat of the SUV, Colin stared at a ramshackle wooden dock and a solitary, elfish-sized outboard motorboat knotted to a leaning pylon. With its algae-covered white-and-red trimmed paint and numerous fiberglass patches, this miracle of floatation physics had seen better days.

Taz pulled to a stop and killed the engine. "Let's go."

Colin's smile vanished. "Out there?" he asked. *Gators and snakes,* Colin fretted silently. He feared something was amiss.

"That's why I carry this." Taz proudly displayed his .357. "Killed three of those nasty handbag bastards this year alone." Taz gauged Colin's expression, then patted his leg. "I've been doing this for years. You'll be fine."

The two men climbed out of the Denali. Moments later, Colin stood at the water's edge and rested his hand on his holstered Glock to ease his anxiety. Taz, who stood next to him, checked his watch, then fixed his gaze down the river. "Won't be long now."

Silent as a Choctaw hunter, the shadow approached from the darkness. "Mr. Tazwell and Mr. Wells."

Although the voice was smooth and low, it startled the pair. It especially jarred Colin, because whomever it belonged to knew his real last name. Something was up.

"Mr. LaRoux?" Taz coughed as he and Colin spun around. "What are you doing out here?"

"May I see your gun, Taz?" LaRoux requested as he extended his hand.

Without deliberation, Taz passed the weapon over. LaRoux briefly inspected the gun before handing it to Colin. "Mr. Wells, when we hired you a year ago, what, pray tell, was priority number one?" LaRoux asked.

Colin hesitated. He glanced at his mentor before answering with a slight stutter, "*Tr-tr-trust*?"

"Precisely. And would you consider an unauthorized secret meeting with the NOPD a breech in that trust? Or worse yet, how about wearing a tracking device?"

Confounded by the sudden turn of events, Colin struggled to swallow the lump in his throat.

"Yes sir," Colin replied firmly.

"Kill him," LaRoux ordered calmly.

"Mr. LaRoux, I can explain," Taz pleaded.

"But, sir," Colin objected.

Within an instant of Colin's plea, LaRoux brandished a Sig 226, racked it back, and aimed it at the conflicted young man. "Kill Tazwell now."

"It's not like that, Mr. LaRoux," Taz frantically implored.

"Do it now, Colin," LaRoux insisted as he turned away.

Click.

No bang.

LaRoux turned to find the gun aimed at him.

Click, click.

Colin squeezed the trigger again. LaRoux stepped forward and put his Sig to Colin's head; Taz removed Colin's gun before retrieving his own, then he ejected the empty magazine and slapped in a loaded round before passing a scanner over Colin's body and removing the tracking device hidden in his belt.

"Colin, didn't anyone teach you to check a gun when it's handed to you?" LaRoux taunted. "Didn't I tell you, Taz? I knew this boy would piss his pants and blow my head clean across the bayou given the opportunity." Satisfied with his foresight, LaRoux smiled. "Mr. Wells, I know it was *you* who had the meeting with NOPD, just like I knew that you were wired tonight. The question is why you would choose to rat me out. Haven't I provided ample income?"

"*Ye-ye-yes*, sir," Colin stuttered as he considered his predicament. True, he was wearing a wire, but he had not been anywhere near the NOPD. Somebody had set him up.

"Needless to say, Colin, I am extremely disappointed with your behavior. Not as disappointed as you and your friends will be when I inform you that my Denali is equipped with the latest communications-jamming equipment. Nobody knows where you are. Nobody is coming for you." With Taz covering Colin, LaRoux retracted his gun and stepped back. "I don't know what the New Orleans Police Department accused me of to cause such treason, but believe me, not a word of it is true."

"Mr. LaRoux—"

"Don't," LaRoux snapped. "Your betrayal is unforgiveable. But don't panic—not yet anyway. You're going to have the opportunity to save yourself."

"I can tell you things, Mr. LaRoux," Colin pleaded.

"You should have told Taz when *they* first approached you." LaRoux took Colin by the elbow and ushered him to the dock. "I already know everything I need to know about our police department, which leaves you only two options. One: I leave you here with Taz and whatever happens *happens*. Me personally, I can promise you, that is a very bad option. Or two: you get in this boat and pray you find open water, and if you get there, you keep going. Never come back here ever again. If you do, there will be no warning and no options."

"But, Mr. LaRoux—"

"It's too late." LaRoux stuffed a bundle of cash in Colin's hand. "Here's two grand. Call it severance pay. The boat has more than enough gas. You've got two minutes to be gone from my sight, or I swear to God, I will shoot you myself."

Colin braced himself against the swaying pylon as the boat rocked. He sloshed the boat as he stepped in.

"Colin, I know you're pressed for time, but before you go, I'll take that tracker on your ankle as well," LaRoux insisted. "That is, unless you'd prefer to be shot right here."

Colin reached into his sock, pulled the device from his ankle, and held it out.

"Trust, Mr. Wells. Given the opportunity, you placed more faith in *this* and the people on the other end than one last opportunity to be straight up." LaRoux dropped the second tracker device on the pier and crunched it under his foot. The remnants barely made a *kerplunk* as they sank into the muck. "I was going to offer you a can of mosquito repellant, but given the extent of your treachery, I think a simple *fuck off* will suffice."

Colin pulled the rope, and, surprisingly, the small outboard motor easily smoked to life. He tossed the mooring line onto the pier and cast off. As the boat sputtered away, the moon reflected in the apex of its wake, pointing the way for LaRoux's personal Judas and his imminent price to be paid for betrayal.

CHAPTER 2

A DOZEN DEA AGENTS talking shop packed the drab, yellow cinderblock conference room. They'd been summoned from various districts across the country and now eagerly anticipated the arrival of the agency's deputy director, William Martin. In addition to the six male agents in the room, Martin had assembled five vivacious and highly ambitious female agents for this special task force, and the not-so-young or ambitious Rebecca Pearson. Hailing from Seattle, Rebecca had been an agent for twelve years and had scaled her way up the chain of command.

Drinking coffee and complaining of the oppressive Louisiana sauna just outside the window, the agents' speculation about today's gathering ran rampant. Rebecca sat silently, observing her counterparts. Their rambling conjecture amused her. Pete Jones, an electronics intelligence specialist, was the only agent in the room she recognized. Like the five other male agents, he was not chiseled enough to attract the female agents' attention. Rebecca mused about Martin's selection of players. *So predictable*, she thought.

Rebecca knew Director Martin *intimately*. Regrettably, there was history between them, which she wished she could wipe from her memory. She had been in love with Martin for three years, but he had played her just like all his other conquests. Her fall had been harsh and left her unwilling to get back in the game. What was he thinking, bringing *her* to New Orleans? Even though their affair had ended five years earlier, did he honestly believe she could be remotely forgiving and let bygones be bygones? Did he honestly think she would not rat out his playboy ways?

Silently, she critiqued her five female counterparts, trying to decide which of them would be *the chosen one*. Martin was completely obsessed with his ego-boosting, conquistador behavior and undoubtedly would attempt to bed them all. Near the top of the DEA food chain at forty-five, fit as a fiddle, gray-haired and handsome, he would be a fine catch for any woman—if only he weren't such a prick.

Rebecca had tried to refuse this assignment, but the edict had come down from Washington. Shit did indeed roll downhill. Forced to work with Martin, her biggest romantic failure, would be painful enough, but watching Mr. Slimeball in action would be downright brutal. She knew his MO. He would swoop into the room full of confidence, power, and charisma and immediately ensnare one—perhaps all five—of the naive junior agents. After the job was complete, emails full of praise and charm would begin. Martin was a jetsetter, and juggling three or five girlfriends spread across the country was easily manageable. He was Don Juan with a badge, and all on the taxpayers' dime.

Pete Jones strolled up to Rebecca and interrupted her memory-lane train wreck. "So, what's your take on all this?"

Rebecca looked up. "Did you ever see *Miss Congeniality*?"

Jones chuckled. "Are you standing in for Sandra Bullock?"

Before Rebecca could reply, Director Martin burst urgently into the room and slapped his briefcase on the table and removed several folders and manila envelopes. His ostentatious arrival did not disappoint. "Everyone, please take a seat," he commanded as if lives were hanging in the balance. With a remote in hand, the lights dimmed and a projector glared.

The first slide filled the screen with a man. *A damn fine-looking man*, Rebecca thought.

"This is David LaRoux—socialite, aristocrat, entrepreneur, philanthropist—and most likely the biggest marijuana and cocaine importer in the western hemisphere. He is the sole proprietor of Crescent City Imports. His lineage is completely immersed in the very foundations of New Orleans. David LaRoux is a direct descendant of Pierre LaRoux, a notorious smuggler in the mid-eighteenth century. LaRoux's ancestors were major trading partners with John Law's Company of the West, but they also engaged in illegal trade with the Natchez Indians, maroons such as Jean Saint Malo, and just about any enterprise that lined their family pockets with wealth and power, regardless of legality.

"From its very founding father, right through its current scumbag kingpin, CCI has been a front corporation for all sorts of illicit trade. It is quite possible that Juan Pablo Escobar's empire was nurtured to life by the LaRoux family's interest. LaRoux donates heavily to local charities, especially law enforcement, indigents, churches, and any cause to keep him one vote up on Mother Teresa for Saint of the Year. The people of New Orleans love David LaRoux, so taking him down is not going to be easy."

"David LaRoux? Are you friggin' kidding me? What's the source of our intel?" George Walker barked. Walker had been in the agency long enough to know Martin's propensity for tackling high-profile cases. He also knew that when cases imploded, Martin excelled in slipping the blame like a Teflon pan.

"Until two weeks ago, we had an agent, Colin Wells, on the inside. But he has disappeared without a trace. We've been taking a hard look at several of LaRoux's key associates who were Wells's contacts." Martin flipped through six slides of unnamed men. "When we nail the first bastard, LaRoux's empire will fall like dominos. But the LaRoux family has not stayed on top for two hundred and fifty years by being stupid. They won't go down easily." Martin slowly flicked through a dozen slides that showed LaRoux with a multitude of beautiful women.

"Anyone care to guess LaRoux's Achilles' heel?"

"He's gay?" Rebecca cracked, creating a rumble of snickers across the room.

Martin's eyes launched daggers of ire in Rebecca's direction. "Thank you, Agent Pearson. But with Agent Wells missing, it would be nice if you would keep your smart-ass commentary to yourself."

"Sorry, boss, but your rhetorical question distracted me from the serious nature of this investigation."

Martin stared at Rebecca long enough to question the wisdom in putting her back on his team. He knew her banter was nothing more than a personal attack—and that he'd have to put up with it. No other female agent was better skilled at grooming inexperienced female agents than Rebecca. Out of necessity, the five other women at the table were as green as they come, and Rebecca's skill was crucial to creating the perfect plant. Deciding his extended silent reprimand would sufficiently quash any further undo commentary from Rebecca, or anyone else, Martin distributed the sealed envelopes. As he did, he made eye contact with each agent to gauge the easy alliances versus the skeptics.

"These are your assignments along with a dossier on LaRoux. Please wait until after the meeting is over to review them. If anyone has a problem with their assignment, you will have twenty-four hours to make your objections known." Martin reassessed the attention and intent of his entire team before continuing.

"LaRoux fashions himself quite the ladies' man. Our objective is to plant one or more agents within his posse, or ideally, with LaRoux himself. The intel we gather will guide us to a much broader investigation into political and law enforcement corruption. Our objective is not only to take LaRoux down for drug trafficking, but I also want his entire network for extortion, racketeering, bribery, and murder." Martin looked back at the image of LaRoux, flanked by several women, on the screen. "If there are no questions, I suggest you go study your packets and be ready to deploy in forty-eight hours."

"Sir," Agent Walker began, raising a finger, "extortion and racketeering—aren't we stepping on the FBI's jurisdiction?"

"Fuck them. This starts with narcotics. We'll feed them the scraps after we're done with LaRoux. Any problem with that?"

Walker looked around the room. "Sounds like we're gonna take down half of the city. You sure you got the ammo for that?"

Martin sneered. "When the time comes, I'll have the additional resources. Anything else?" Martin waited, then nodded toward the door. "Let's get on it, people."

With no objections, the agents began to file out of the meeting. Rebecca, however, lagged behind, then approached Martin and stood uncomfortably close.

Martin took a step back to create a buffer. "Rebecca, it's good to see you again."

"Cut the horseshit, Will. I see where you're headed with this. Do you honestly think I'm going to play mother hen to a bunch of greenhorns, entrenching them with seasoned criminals? And if your accusations are right, criminals that think nothing of killing cops? I'm not going to let my career go down the toilet pimping those girls out for you."

"Easy, Rebecca," Martin said as he closed the conference room door. "Look, I'm not happy about how we ended things, but I really need you on—"

"Ended things?" Rebecca interrupted. "My displeasure with this mandatory bullshit assignment has nothing to do with your promiscuous behavior during our relationship. But since *you* went there, explain this one thing to me, Will. How did *'I love you, Rebecca'* translate into fucking every woman who was dazzled by your smile and badge?"

"Rebecca, I was going through some hard times back then."

Rebecca lowered her gaze to Martin's groin. "Hard times—going through cases of condoms was more like it. But you know, that's ancient history. You've forced me here, so as long as we can agree that you're a womanizing piece of shit and limit all conversation to the specifics of the job, we can talk."

Martin shook his head and sighed. "Fine."

"Now, tell me if I'm wrong, Will. You are expecting those girls to spread their legs as a means to gather intelligence. And you want me to be their den mother because I know the inside game, while simultaneously providing you with a buffer against any backlash for improper conduct."

"Nobody is asking, or ordering, anybody to have sex." Martin pointed an agitated finger in Rebecca's face. "You know, it *is* possible to entice a man and glean information without ever removing your pants."

Rebecca pushed Martin's finger away. "Dammit, Will, you and I both know the kind of info you're looking for will require a lot more intimacy."

"LaRoux and his crew are arrogant playboys. They're not accustomed to women who *just say 'no.'* The challenge your agents will present will make them much more desirable than their customary one-nighter bimbos. And just for the record, I'm not condoning any sexual liaisons for the sake of this investigation."

"But you're not forbidding it either. And when it happens—and, judging by those ambitious green probies, I'm sure it will—I know you'll readily accept the evidence all the same."

Martin could not contain his condescending sneer. "Are you certain this isn't really about how we ended things?"

"How *we* ended things?" Rebecca huffed. "Don't flatter yourself."

Rebecca's composure disappointed Martin. Apparently, she was not as emotionally fragile as he remembered. "This is a career-defining case for everybody. LaRoux will go down, with or without you, Rebecca."

Rebecca turned to La Roux's image on the screen. "This guy is loaded and connected. Screw this up, Will, and it will be a career-ending case." Rebecca turned back to Martin and again violated his space. She warned, "I'll do it, but those girls report to me, not you. And if you don't keep that peashooter of yours in your trousers around my girls, I swear to God, LaRoux won't be the only man going down."

Again, Martin retreated a step. "Why, Agent Pearson, is that a threat?" His tone was smug and his grin offensive.

"No, I would prefer to think of it as a small contribution to the human race."

Martin waited a long minute before continuing. "I can live with your terms." As he began collecting the contents of his briefcase, he cleared his throat and said, "I have added an additional member to your team. She is a NOLA native and NOPD as well. She's going in without cover. I figure if we put it on the table that one of your friends is a cop, LaRoux's crew will be far less likely to scrutinize the rest of the team."

Rebecca rolled her eyes. "Is she another pretty-faced rookie, or does she actually bring some talent to my team?"

"She's two years on the beat down here, so she's got *some* moves," Martin sighed. "I know what you're thinking, but it's not like that at all. It's true—I picked these women because they fit a certain . . . physical profile. By design, their seductive talents trump any actual law enforcement knowledge or skills, for now."

"And my NOLA cop?"

"She fits the team profile as well." Martin's tone reflected an increasing impatience with Rebecca's inquisition.

"I don't fit the profile."

"I need your experience, not your body. You've worked these stings in the past. And as I recall, you didn't wind up fucking any perps back then either."

Rebecca wanted to say something snarky about Martin being too busy getting laid and kissing ass to know the truth, but his blunt explanation wounded her pride. "So what? Back then I was good enough for you and the perps, but a few years go by and now I'm too old for you and too old for LaRoux?"

"There's nothing wrong with the way you look, Rebecca. It's just that your age doesn't fit the profile."

"Whose profile, Will? Yours or LaRoux's?"

Martin threw his hands in the air. "Jesus, Rebecca."

Recovering from Martin's perhaps unintended insult, Rebecca had scored a minor victory—she had rattled Martin. "Easy, Will. I said I'd do it. But until this job is done, you do not interfere with my team. I wouldn't want their—how did you put it?—oh yes, *their seductive talents* to cause you any undue disciplinary action."

Rebecca turned and stormed out of the conference room, slamming the door. With her back to the room, her smirk snowballed into a smile as she walked away. Will Martin had shown his hand; he needed her. Martin was completely unaware that his balls were on a serving platter, and Rebecca was holding one nasty carving knife.

CHAPTER 3

THE FRIDAY NIGHT SCENE at Bamboula's rarely varied. The key ingredients were all in place: ample booze, a kickass band, and a house packed with reveling patrons all looking to get their Big Easy groove on. David LaRoux and his crew were seated at their customary table, its premium location affording an opportunistic view of all that ventured in.

Regardless of who might be seated there, whenever LaRoux and his entourage rolled up, the table was immediately cleared for the city's favorite native son. Not every patron, drunk or sober, appreciated the courtesy afforded to the LaRoux clan, but any objections were quickly quashed by security.

LaRoux preferred the haunts of Frenchmen Street. Its lively night scene lacked the raunchiness of Bourbon Street, yet never lacked for an enticing *soup du jour* of available attractive tourists. LaRoux avoided the local fanfare like a rabid raccoon. The homespun talent meant reoccurring episodes of his least favorite drama: *Why Didn't You Call Me?*

"So, according to my sources, Taz's apprentice's sudden departure from our fair city was not appreciated by our friends at the DEA,"

LaRoux informed his party as he raised his glass of bourbon, "so much so that they have resorted to desperate measures, such as bugging this very table."

LaRoux's cohorts exchanged nervous glances before turning their attention back to their boss.

"If you happen to notice the three buffoons over there digging like they've got earwigs, that's because their bugs are malfunctioning," LaRoux explained with a smile. "Now that I've laid those rumors to rest, nothing needs to change. Our security is bulletproof, and a bunch of DEA dickheads will not disrupt business as usual. Any deviation in our routines would tip them off that we know they are watching. There is not a piece of technology they possess that I don't own a substantial share of the company that makes it. Therefore, like the table bugs, we will continue to know what they think they know, the day before."

"Any clue what stirred the hornet's nest, boss? Wells was with us almost a year."

"I don't know *the what* yet, but according to my sources, *the who* is a deputy director, William Martin. Seems he has acquired quite the boner for me. Now, I don't know what in the world is motivating this douchebag, but until we find out, assume every man you meet has an agenda and every woman is wearing a vagina cam."

"Not that we don't already trust nobody, but if you're looking for a volunteer to inspect all the fresh pussy . . ." Walt Allen snickered before wiping off his grin. All the men at the table—Ryan Patrick, Junior Tazwell, and LaRoux—stared at Walt until he squawked, "What?" Walt recognized his companions' restrained snickering. If any of these guys farted in an elevator, it was damn near impossible for all not to bust out laughing. But with Walt, they resisted laughing at anything *he* said or did no matter how funny. It was their latest game—withholding laughter to induce awkwardness. But in his typical style, Walt could not withhold his own comment. "Fuck off," he crowed.

Walt was LaRoux's *what if* man—his first right hand, hired by LaRoux's father eighteen years ago. At thirty-six, he was the eldest of the group. Always contemplating the risk versus reward, Walt kept the house in order by constantly playing the devil's advocate. Any and every activity, legal or otherwise, had consequences. Walt laid all the cards on the table, studied every possible play and the ramifications, then mapped out detailed strategies. Nothing ever took him by surprise. At six foot two and a rock-solid two hundred twenty pounds, he was always ready for a good barroom brawl whenever things got out of hand. But underneath his intimidating tattooed façade hid a dangerously brilliant and sophisticated mind.

LaRoux's second right hand, Ryan Patrick, an eight-year veteran of LaRoux's business, was the proud grandson of Stuart Patrick, a notorious IRA assassin. Ryan was well known as a full-blown lady killer. Women couldn't resist his Irish accent, lean and rugged physique, wavy red hair, and charming demeanor. While he preferred beautiful women and a good party to the violent ways of his grandfather, he remained an expert in his family's craft. Beyond his lethal skills, Ryan's IQ rivaled that of Walt's. Between the two of them, LaRoux was bulletproof.

Junior Tazwell, on the other hand, was as Creole redneck as you could get. His ash-brown, shoulder-length hair flowed in waves, and his blue eyes sparkled when he turned on his Cajun charm. Built like a lumberjack, his scruffy-bearded, unblemished face could turn most women's heads in an instant. In his natural habitat, he was unrefined as a jug of bayou moonshine, but in the presence of a lady, he was as smooth as a twenty-year-old Kentucky bourbon. Plain and simple, just like the man himself, Tazwell was LaRoux's muscle and security.

All three were LaRoux's unquestionably faithful employees and confidants. Rarely would LaRoux make a public appearance without at least two of *the boys*.

"So, boss, whatcha think about those guys?" Taz asked.

"Well, considering Mr. Wells's sudden departure, I see this as some sort of desperate attempt to learn something. I mean, look at them. They take square peg to a whole new level. Chances are the feds have been watching for months, but losing one of their playmates—I don't know. One thing I am sure of, they don't have a clue what they're looking for. But until something concrete surfaces, we have more pressing business." LaRoux's crew stared as their boss silently deliberated sharing the news. As if it were excruciatingly painful, he confessed, "I don't have a date for tomorrow night."

"Say it ain't so, David LaRoux," Ryan taunted.

LaRoux folded his hands behind his head and leaned back. "I guess it won't be the end of the world if I go stag. I just can't seem to find one single woman who's different or unique enough to invite."

"It's one night, not an engagement, for Christ's sake," Walt badgered. "This is David LaRoux's Annual Charity Mascarade du Bayou Extravaganza, and the *maître des cérémonies* must have a date. This will never do."

"I'm just not feeling it, guys. Honestly, I prefer to not have a date, you know, so I can mingle. Who knows, maybe I'll meet someone there."

"I disagree, David. In fact, I don't want to even think about all the gossip that would create. The Big Easy's most eligible bachelor goes stag to the hottest ticket in town? Hell no!" Ryan took a long draw from his beer as he surveyed the talent filing into the bar.

"I've tried, guys." LaRoux leaned forward, looking dejected. "This business with Colin and the DEA . . . I don't know. I've been thinking maybe I need something different, maybe a change in career paths."

"Like what? You want to open a woman's shoe store or something?" Taz scoffed.

"I don't know. Maybe I can buy a football team or something."

"Mr. Benson ain't got no plans to sell the Saints, and there ain't no other team worth owning," Taz taunted. "So you might as well just keep on doing what you do best."

"Shit, David, what you need," Ryan interjected as he scanned the bar, "is a flaming-hot redhead, like that one right over there."

They all followed Ryan's finger pointing to the table marked *Reserved*. Seven exceptionally attractive women, all dressed to the nines, sat there making small talk.

"*Shee-at*, would you get a look at that carrot top," Taz raved, singling out the redhead Ryan had mentioned. Her tightly curled strawberry-blond hair hung several inches past her shoulders and framed her tanned, delicate smiling face. Her curves contoured precisely in all the right places, complementing her short black dress. From across the bar, the vixen appeared like any breathing man's fantasy from a torrid wet dream.

"My friends, behold the bachelorette party straight from the gates of Venus," Walt announced.

"Dibs on the blonde in the red dress," Ryan barked eagerly.

"You know, I won't be picky. Any of them would fit me just fine, even the one in the tiara," Taz added with a devilish grin, surmising that she must be a bride-to-be. "Every girl needs one last fling, you know, to make sure she ain't making a mistake."

Ryan studied the seven. "You know, from here, I'd almost have to say I think they're models.

Even the older one looks pretty damn inviting."

Without as much as a word, LaRoux silently studied the new arrivals.

"I bet I know whatcha thinking there, buddy," Taz said as he leaned toward his boss. "You want that redhead, don'tcha? But you're worried you might hurt our feelings? It's alright. You go for whichever one strikes your fancy."

LaRoux's sliver of a smile turned up. "Ryan," he began, "see to it, unless the wedding is tomorrow, that those fine young ladies come to our little *soirée* tomorrow night."

Taz pulled on LaRoux's shirt, drawing him near. "You know, David, if you honestly hope they will come, then you might not want to send a man with a speech impediment for the job. Hell, I've known Paddy eight years, and I still can't understand half of what he says," Taz joked.

"Ryan will do fine, Taz. Because if he fails, he'll be on the next boat to the bayou." LaRoux smiled at Ryan. "Whatever it takes."

Ryan stood up and straightened his shirt. Looking at Walt and then at Taz, he turned on his best suave expression before flipping them the bird. "You got it, boss." Ryan left the table knowing his employer's instructions afforded him *carte blanche* tactics to accomplish his mission. He also knew, all too well, it would take months to recover from the verbal thrashing that would follow should he fail.

Ryan's laser-focused approach did not go unnoticed. As he drew near, the woman with straight, short brown hair elbowed another brunette with longer, wavy hair. They focused their charms in Ryan's direction. "Good evening, ladies."

Sarah Turner, the first to notice him, eagerly returned the greeting. "Why, good evening to you."

"I hate to interrupt your festivities, so I will cut to the chase. When's the wedding?"

Cassandra White, the second brunette, looked at Ryan suspiciously. "Next Saturday. May I ask why you're interested?"

Commanding all the women's attention, Ryan smiled. Victory was at hand. "Are any of you from New Orleans?"

"I am," answered Margo Carter.

"And praying that everyone survives tonight's festivities, will all of you still be in town tomorrow night?"

"Why, sir," Cassandra began with an exaggerated Southern belle accent, "before I elaborate on such intimate details, I think proper introductions are in order and the nature of your intentions should be revealed."

"Oh, I beg your pardon, ma'am," Ryan replied in a failed Cajun-Irish attempt to mimic Cassandra. "I am Ryan Patrick. And you are?"

"Cassandra, but my friends call me Sandy." She pointed around the table and continued, "To my left is Sarah. Beside her is our blushing bride-to-be, Mary; her sister, Rebecca; and our friends Cindy, Margo, and Sean, the redheaded homewrecker."

"Ladies, I am honored to make your acquaintance. As I promised, I will be brief. Are any of you familiar with the Mascarade du Bayou?"

"If you are referring to the thousand-dollar-per-ticket party at the LaRoux mansion, yes, I am," Margo replied.

"Ever been?"

"At that price, on my salary, not hardly," Margo complained.

"Well, ladies, tonight is your lucky night. I so happen to have exactly seven extra tickets to tomorrow night's gala."

"And what's the catch, Mr. Patrick?" In her wildest dreams, Rebecca never considered that LaRoux and his crew would take their bait so quickly. "For seven thousand dollars, you must be expecting some kind of *big* bang for your buck."

"There are absolutely no strings attached." Ryan paused before recalling her name. "Rebecca, accept my offer, and I promise you and your friends an evening you'll not soon forget. Tell me no, and I'll leave brokenhearted. Either way, I'll leave you to your fun tonight."

"As much as we'd love to accept, we'll have to decline. We're here for Mary's big sendoff, and besides, we didn't quite pack for some elaborate masquerade," Cassandra said.

"Ah, but what better way to celebrate than a mystical ball at Louisiana's most enchanting plantation. Come to the ball. I'll arrange for your costumes and transportation. The party starts at eight with a silent auction to benefit the Children's Hospital. Stay an hour or as long as you want. My driver will be yours for the entire evening. And seriously, there are absolutely no strings attached."

A young waitress stood patiently for the negotiations to end. As the women silently exchanged deliberations, the waitress jumped in. "I'm available, Ryan."

"See, ladies, even Sue knows it's a great offer. Here's my card." Ryan smiled as he extended his hand while giving Cassandra an extended visual coaxing. "Call me when you've decided. I'll send Enrique over at nine thirty in the morning to arrange for your costumes. What hotel should I send him to?"

"I didn't say—" Rebecca began.

"The Bienville House," Sean interrupted eagerly as she reached in and snatched Ryan's card. "And I for one would love to come to your party."

"Outstanding decision, Sean. I certainly hope the rest of you will decide to attend. If it will help to ease any concerns for your personal safety, even the governor will be there." Ryan gave a short bow and turned to the waitress. Speaking in a voice just loud enough to be overheard by the women, he said, "Mr. LaRoux will be paying their tab tonight." He turned his attention again to the bridal party. "Ladies, enjoy your night, be safe, and I hope to see *all* of you tomorrow evening."

CHAPTER 4

A KNOCK ON DAVID LaRoux's bedroom door threw off his third attempt to execute the perfect bow tie. "What is it?" he sighed in exasperation, his fingers tangled in the mess of fabric. Walt Allen stepped into the room. "You sound a tad irritable, boss."

"Do I?" LaRoux's sarcasm was intentionally obvious.

Walt checked the hall behind him then closed the door. "Honestly?" Walt waited for any sign that his opinion was truly welcome. When it never arrived, he prodded. "It's been pretty obvious for some time now. Like last night—you were so far off your game. It was like David LaRoux did not bother to even show up. What's eating at ya?"

LaRoux tossed his bow tie on the bed. "How long have we known each other, Walt?"

"I don't know. Let's see. I'm thirty-six. You're thirty-three. So, thirty-three years?"

LaRoux chuckled. "Your father worked for mine, and my father hired you right out of high school, right?"

Walt nodded, somewhat unnerved by LaRoux's peculiar emotional tone while recounting family ties. Considering the DEA's recent interest in the family business, Walt feared a question of his loyalty might be forthcoming.

"And your granddaddy worked for mine, so it's fair to say you know more about our family than anyone else in the organization, right?"

"Damn right."

"I've heard you tell stories about the family going all the way back to our immigration. So, being more or less the only aficionado of the LaRoux family history, tell me this—at thirty-three, what's missing from my picture?"

Walt felt relief as LaRoux focused the direction of the inquisition on himself. He retrieved the bow tie and began tying it around LaRoux's neck. "I don't know, David. You've got every toy under the sun. You've traveled the world, and most women line up for your attention. So, as far as I can tell, you've got everything a man needs."

"Do you know the one thing that all of my forefathers had before they turned thirty that has so far eluded me?"

Walt was relatively sure where LaRoux was heading, so he thought this was a good place to inject a little humor. "You've already nailed a few actresses . . . and models. I don't know, maybe bang a princess?"

LaRoux silently reflected while allowing Walt to finish his tie. Turning to the mirror for inspection, although the bow tie was perfect, LaRoux still fidgeted with it. "Is it any wonder with you clowns surrounding me that I've never come close to finding a wife?"

Walt presented LaRoux his black-and-gold paisley tuxedo jacket. "Oh, hell's bells, David! That's what this sad puppy-dog attitude is all about? You're still young. There's plenty of time to find the right woman."

LaRoux offered his left arm, followed by the right, as he backed into the jacket. "No, it's not just a time thing. It's the business. It's all I've ever known. It has defined me and dictated my decisions. Sure, there was a time I could have walked away, but I didn't. And you know what?"

Hearing a completely alien side of his boss and friend, Walt could only shrug.

David turned back to the mirror and began working the tie again. "This business, the things I've done, there's no fucking way on earth I would ever want a child of mine to do the same things. Hell, I wouldn't even want them to know the things that I've done. What were my parents thinking? Maybe it wasn't their intention for me to run all of this, but they're dead, and here I am. That's the reason I've avoided a steady girlfriend, or a wife, or especially a family. I wouldn't want any family of mine involved in this game."

"So, go legit. The import business rakes in plenty of dough. You know we'll follow you anywhere, even down *that* road."

"You know as well as I do that every time we've scaled back, even a little, the pushback up and down the supply chains has been dangerously relentless. It's like we'd have to kill off the majority of our partners just to make a clean break."

Walt leaned in and pushed LaRoux's hands away from the tie. He returned it to its previous form of perfection, then he dusted imaginary lint from the lapels of his boss's suit jacket. "So, spin off the illegal shit. Bring in new management, and gradually turn it over to them."

"I wish it were just that simple. Import and sales are not the issue. You know that you can't clean that much money without a corporation as big as CCI. And if the money isn't cleaned properly, people will wind up in jail."

"I guess you're right. But you've got enough money, David. Just let go of the reins, turn it *all* over, and move to Fiji." Walt picked a stray hair off the shoulder of LaRoux's suit.

"Three hundred years of family tradition down the drain, just like that. The ghosts of my ancestors would hound my ass into eternity."

Walt scrutinized his longtime friend's appearance. "Whatever and whenever you decide what you want to do, I know it will be the right thing." Having never seen LaRoux struggle with such personal issues before, Walt smiled uneasily. "So, on a different note, me and the boys have this little wager tonight. If you don't already have a strong preference, I think that redhead, Sean, could be just the elixir you need to break you out of this funk. Just saying." Walt winked.

"How much?"

"It isn't about the money, David, which is a measly grand. It's the braggin' rights."

"And you think I'll go for . . . Sean?"

"Well, take out the bride and her sister, and that leaves two blondes, two brunettes, and Red. Your track record hasn't been all that great with blondes, which leaves the brunettes and Sean. And once you've gotten up close and personal, particularly with Sean— well, you'll see."

LaRoux turned from the mirror and switched on his textbook public smile. "What makes you think I'll go for any of them?"

Walt snickered. "Enrique called earlier. I already know how much you dropped just to get them all gussied up for tonight. For a man with no interest, that was pretty damn extravagant." Walt poorly mimicked his boss's broad smile as he opened the door. "And as *you* already pointed out, I *do* know David LaRoux."

* * *

As Ryan Patrick had promised, Enrique had arrived at Bienville House at the uncomfortably early hour of 9:30 a.m. The agents had partied their undercover roles to perfection, not returning to the hotel until three thirty in the morning. So, regardless of their mission, the hungover agents had not been remotely prepared for, or enthusiastic about, Enrique's charismatic, flamboyant personality.

Arriving with a food and ball gown–toting entourage, Enrique had immediately set to his work, pairing the gowns and marking alterations. By ten thirty, he and the gowns were gone, leaving the agents to recover from their previous night's self-induced misery. By early afternoon, after naps and another round of food, they had begun dispersing to various French Quarter salons that LaRoux's people had arranged. Rebecca, Sean, and Cassandra arrived at Fifi Mahony's for their updos, manicures, foot massages, pedicures, and makeup. The excessive pampering had included Creole hors d'oeuvres and a variety of cocktails. Indifferent to their host's alleged illicit behavior, the agents had thoroughly immersed themselves in LaRoux's generosities.

Detailed to perfection by six o'clock, the women now headed back to the hotel. Excusing herself from Cassandra and Sean, Rebecca detoured into 801 Royal for a drink. She took a seat at the door-side table and allowed her mind to meander while she watched crowds pass on Royal Street.

"What can I get you, sweetie?" the waitress asked.

Before Rebecca could answer, a nauseating, suave voice interrupted from behind. "Are you drinking alone?"

Rebecca turned and smiled at the man. "Apparently not anymore." She returned her eyes to the waitress. "Gin and tonic, please."

Will Martin flashed his debonair smile at the waitress and said, "Bulleit Bourbon, on the rocks, please."

As the waitress sauntered away, Martin, pretending to be a stranger, asked, "Do you mind if I join you?"

Rebecca nodded yes. "Is this meeting really necessary? It seems a big risk if I'm being watched," she whispered.

Martin laughed boldly, as if Rebecca's remark was humorous. After checking the attention of the surrounding barflies, he turned his attention back to Rebecca. "I just wanted to check in, make sure everything is in place for tonight."

"Nothing has changed since this morning. Next time you feel the need to risk blowing my cover, you damn well better have a good reason."

Martin's pretentious laugh echoed across the bar. Leaning in, his jovial expression morphed into a sneer. "Look, this is my op, and if I want to call a meeting, I'll damn well do so." He leaned back in his chair and forced a smile. "I hope you ladies enjoyed your spa day on my dime. I'm surprised you all didn't go for the body wax session while you were at it."

With that, Martin's true intentions surfaced like a submarine emergency blow; he was jealous. Now it was Rebecca's turn to laugh out loud. Martin didn't know LaRoux was the one who had paid for the day's indulgences. She resisted the temptation to flaunt his generosity, but she still ground the blade in deeply. "If you think any of those girls are going to snare David LaRoux looking one hair less than model perfect, you are delusional, Will. So, when you get the bill for today, suck it up." Rebecca paused as the bartender delivered their drinks. She thanked him, then she continued talking to Martin. "And as if it were any of your business, there is not a hair on my body that needs to be waxed." Rebecca looked up at the smirking bartender. "What's your name?"

"Aubrey."

"Well, Aubrey, if you have a seat at the bar for me, I believe you'll be much better company than this jerk."

Aubrey tipped his cap as he snickered in Martin's direction. "I have just the seat for what ails you."

* * *

After Rebecca returned to her hotel room, she found her ball gown on her bed and a jeweled and beaded silk mask resting on her pillow. On her dresser, an open, blue-velvet box displayed a brilliant crystal and sapphire necklace and matching bracelet. Before she could take a closer look, Margo bounded into the room in a cream gown and twirled toward Rebecca.

Margo looked down at Rebecca's refinement and gushed, "Sandy says they're real diamonds."

Rebecca inspected Margo's ensemble before returning her attention to the jewelry.

Suspicious of LaRoux's connections and the hours away from their room, she cryptically asked, "Has anyone had a problem with palmetto bugs in their rooms?"

Understanding Rebecca's true intent, Margo needlessly crafted her reply. "Nope, I think they've done a good job with the bugs."

Somewhat surprised their rooms had not been bugged while they were out, Rebecca replied, "Good." She lifted the velvet box containing the necklace and studied it. "LaRoux's tentacles run very deep in this town. One careless word and the entire op is blown. Martin's already breathing down my neck about our spa day, so make damn sure all of the jewelry gets catalogued."

"But this is all LaRoux's stuff, and didn't *he* pick up the tab today—and last night?"

"Martin doesn't know that, and I'm not about to spoil his torment."

Margo snickered. "Word is, you and Martin have a history."

"*Had*," Rebecca snapped as she surveyed Margo's attire. Not wanting the conversation to go further, she said, "You look amazing."

"Thanks. I would imagine you will look equally bedazzling. Everything fits perfectly—even the lingerie. Too bad we can't take Enrique back home with us."

Rebecca inspected the silk undergarments on her dresser. "Don't you mean LaRoux's wallet?"

Margo fidgeted with her bracelet. "For tonight, he's fair game. Innocent until proven guilty—right? Or at least until we have one shred of evidence he's actually guilty of something."

"Margo," Rebecca snapped, "*that* attitude could get you killed. I shouldn't have to remind you that an agent *is* missing. And LaRoux, complacent or not, has enough money, and ties to people with even more money, to cost a careless agent their life."

"You're right. It's just hard not to fall into our parts, with all the partying and pampering. We're *all* just a little overwhelmed. None of us has ever experienced a man like LaRoux. He's quite extravagant and deliciously handsome. I'm sure once we're actually on the job, we'll be more focused."

This was exactly what Rebecca had feared—immature, green agents thrown into an environment most women would kill for. "You have all been warned. If I feel any of you poses a risk to our safety, I will pull the plug and send everyone back home. Nobody is going to die on my shift."

Margo knew Rebecca was right, and she bowed her head. "Okay, Rebecca. I'll make sure everyone understands." She stepped over to the bed and brushed her fingers down Rebecca's dress. "We better get you dressed. The limo will be here soon."

"Thanks, but I can dress myself."

With a sheepish smile, Margo lifted the gown and displayed the intricate weave of the corseted back. "Unless you're double-jointed, you're going to need some help."

Rebecca reflected on the task ahead. *It's going to take a miracle to pull this sting off.*

* * *

The Hummer limo arrived promptly at eight o'clock to collect David LaRoux's last-minute invitees. During the hour-long ride out to the LaRoux plantation, the six undercover DEA agents and the lone cop embellished their well-scripted bachelorette weekend cover story for the sake of the driver's all-too-eager ears or any potential eavesdropping devices. Fearful of blowing their cover this early in the op, Rebecca had insisted, and Martin had reluctantly agreed, to monitor the agents' activities solely through Instagram postings.

As the limo rolled through the delta plains outside of New Orleans, Rebecca stared at the majesty of the late afternoon's heavenly canvas as it slowly surrendered its pastel beauty to its nightly adversary. Mostly ignoring the fabricated banter between her subordinates, her focus drifted like the passing cumulus clouds between their idle talk and tonight's mission. Along this isolated road, there would be no battalion nor agents ready to storm the gates. Standing out like an aircraft carrier on Lake Pontchartrain, the DEA forces had been forced to hold back some twenty-five miles down the highway, and Rebecca and her crew were unarmed and ill prepared for trouble.

The sun cozied into the western horizon as the limo turned left off Highway 3127 onto Route 20. After a few miles, the driver eased the Hummer onto a long single lane of thickly lined, moss-laden twisted oaks, then it swayed side to side over the uneven oyster shell driveway.

"Oh my," Sarah gushed. She was the first to take in the spectacle of the monstrous antebellum mansion.

"This is like right out of *Gone with the Wind*," Mary added.

In silence, the agents craned to take in the grandeur of the LaRoux plantation.

Climbing skyward, twin, opposing granite stairs wound gracefully to the second-floor porch. Wrapping the house, and illuminated by gas-glow lanterns and chandeliers, the porch was framed by white pickets with black hand railing connecting a series of massive Roman columns that supported a third-floor balcony. The alabaster exterior glowed a warm peach hue against the star-filled night.

A tuxedo-clad Frenchman greeted them at the car. "Good evening, ladies. Welcome to Mascarade du Bayou and Manoir de LaRoux. My name is Marque, and I will see you to the house."

Knowing this might be her last shot to curb her agents' giddy enthusiasm, Rebecca reminded the crew, "Alright, ladies, try not to forget your manners, and remember we are trying to preserve Mary's virtue."

"Thanks, *sis*," Mary said with a squeeze of Rebecca's arm.

As Rebecca and her entourage followed Marque up the marble stairs, they marveled at the sprawling, torch-lit manicured lawn, the bronze alligator ceremoniously spouting golden streams into the marble fountain, and the twisted oaks illuminated by twinkling dragonfly lights. Then on the porch, the women were afforded their first views of the richly appointed parlor through the ten-foot windows. "I must say," Mary announced with a mischievous smile, "if I happen to catch his fancy, I am so calling off my wedding."

Sporting an Armani tux and donning a wolf-head mask, Ryan Patrick eagerly greeted the women as they entered the foyer. He removed his disguise and smiled broadly. "Welcome, welcome, welcome. I am so glad you decided to grace our little gathering. I trust tonight will be filled with memories not soon forgotten."

"Why, Mr. Patrick, after such lavish enticements today, there was no way we could possibly refuse," Sarah replied, once again in her finest Southern belle accent.

"As this is your first Mascarade du Bayou, if you will please join me briefly in the parlor, I will share the order of the evening." Ryan ushered the women into the seclusion of the parlor and pulled the French doors behind them.

In the dampened hush of the luxurious space, the women fanned out. "Oh my, this is magnificent," Cassandra gushed. The avocado-green walls were dressed with lustrous mahogany hardwood trim and windows framed with burgundy-colored crushed-velvet curtains. The solitary source of illumination radiated from a chandelier made up of twenty slender, green hot-wax candles seductively dancing in a phantom breeze. Portraits of visiting dignitaries from previous centuries accented the immaculate antique French provincial furniture.

Ryan moved behind the paisley embroidered sofa and cleared his throat. "I am so happy you decided to attend. Now, about tonight . . ."

Rebecca nudged Cassandra, who was busy inventorying the refinements of the parlor. Once Ryan had all seven women's attention, he continued. "First, I have to say, you all look ravishing." Collectively, in no particular order, the agents conveyed their gratitude, particularly Sean, who laid it on hot and heavy, as if she were vying for an Oscar.

"Now, this is not a requirement, but if you would be so kind as to attach these buttons to your gowns." Ryan distributed the numbered buttons and watched as the women complied. "These are for tonight's silent auction. You'll find that virtually every woman will be wearing one. At midnight, when the ball begins, you will discover that gentlemen have been discreetly bidding for the privilege of your hand on the ballroom dance floor."

"So, this is really some kind of sex-slave auction," Sean exclaimed with a wink-wink.

"No. It's simply just the first dance of the evening. If any romance should transpire between you and your gentleman, that is completely beyond the realm of our intent—or control. All the money raised from the dance, the casino below, bar tab contributions, and other auctions goes directly to the Children's Hospital. If you do not wish to participate, simply remove your button. However, I must tell you, over the vast history of the LaRoux family hosting this event, twenty-three couples have gone on to be married, including Mr. LaRoux's parents."

Sean stepped in front of Mary and waved her button in Ryan's face. "Why, Mr. Patrick, if my suggestion of the number eighty-three appears a little brazen, it is intended to be."

"Watch it. The tramp meter is about to explode," Cindy blurted as she grabbed Sean by the arm and pulled her back. "I'm sorry, Mr. Patrick. You'll have to forgive my lecherous friend. She hasn't been in the company of a man for at least two hours."

Ryan laughed heartily. "Please, all of you, call me Ryan. And there are no apologies needed for anything tonight. But as much as I would love to compete for Sean's hand, I do believe a gentleman of excessive means far beyond mine has already expressed interest in your . . . horny friend." Patrick maintained a stoic expression as the women waited for him to reveal the details. After fifteen seconds of intentional suspense, he broke into a jovial laugh and said, "Be that as it may, I will keep a sharp eye on the bids. Now, on with the party details. As I alluded to earlier, on the ground floor, you will find casino gambling. In the gardens, which are out the rear exit of our home, you will find Doreen's Jazz band and various performers. Food and libations are abundantly available on the first two floors and in the garden. Mr. LaRoux will be matching all gratuities collected by our waitstaff for the hospital charity, so please tip often. If there is anything additional you require," Ryan said as he signaled to the butler waiting just outside the door, "have James come and find me."

Sean flashed her button number to Ryan as James entered the room balancing a silver tray containing eight shot glasses. "Ladies, this is James. He will be your personal valet for the evening."

As they were being offered, Margo threw her hand out. "None for me."

"Why, Margo, it is tradition for all guests to begin the evening with a Louisiana Tulip," Ryan insisted.

"I'm a cop," Margo explained, "and if I'm not mistaken, a few of my bosses are here tonight."

Ryan smiled. "Margo, are you packing heat somewhere under that delightful gown?"

Margo shrugged. "No."

"Then I'm guessing you're off duty. And based on last night's performance, I don't think you have a medical condition for abstaining, and you don't have to drive anywhere either. So, I would ask that you honor our family tradition. It helps loosen the purse strings, so to speak. And trust me, your bosses are already several drinks ahead of you."

Margo stared into Ryan's chestnut eyes and flashed a playful smile. "Let's hope we both live to not regret this." Margo fired her shot back and set the glass on the tray. "Okay, ladies, you heard the man." Rebecca followed Margo's lead, and the remaining five agents followed Rebecca.

"Outstanding," Ryan chirped. "I'm sure our paths will cross many times tonight. But until then, please enjoy our hospitality." Ryan promptly exited the parlor. The women were now alone with James, who stood by the door.

Rebecca chose her words carefully. "Ladies, time to get to it." Just like the previous night, she knew if they were to get LaRoux's crew to take the bait, they'd have to break some rules. "Be smart," she said as she rolled her eyes and nodded toward James. Then the subordinate agents exited.

Alone in the parlor, Rebecca tensed over her game plan. *Inexperienced agents, an endless faucet of alcohol, and a job that requires them to party. One slip of the tongue, and our cover will be blown.*

CHAPTER 5

BY HALF PAST ELEVEN, Rebecca's sobriety had abandoned her. She and her tipsy, hormone-raging agents had toured the expansive mansion multiple times, which had put them in Ryan's and his shot crew's path several times too many. Rebecca had also encountered the governor, the mayor, and several prominent celebrities. But the *golden goose* had eluded her and her team.

As Rebecca roamed the lavish casino on the ground floor, she smiled at the liquor-induced festivities. Packed with gamblers succumbing to the effects of the free-flowing alcohol—thus involuntarily donating more to the charity than initially intended—most laughed off their losses without shedding a tear.

Leaning on the sweeping ebony wood handrail, Rebecca labored in her gown to return to the main floor. As she ascended the stairs, her head felt much lighter than desired, which forced her to remind herself aloud, "Just say *hell no.*" She passed Mary, who was on her way down, and at that moment realized she was not the only one lacking an acceptable level of sobriety. Rebecca pulled her agent aside on the mid-stair landing and exclaimed, "Hey, sis," before asking quietly, "anything?"

"Ryan and his buddies have been all over us—well, except for me. Apparently, the fact that I'm engaged has made me taboo. But overall, I think the plan is working. Those boys appear quite smitten. If everyone stays focused, particularly Sean, we should have at least one of us on the inside after tonight."

"Pass the word. Immediately after the auction, I want to get together in the garden. We've got to slow the drinking pace a little— that is, unless anyone makes contact with the goose."

"That sounds great. I'll pass the word. But Margo seems to have succeeded in attaching herself to Ryan Patrick. It's probably best if she stays on him. There are plenty of other sharks in LaRoux's pond. Sean and Sandy are trying to hook the one they call Taz."

Rebecca placed her hand on Mary's shoulder as she waited for a couple to pass.

"I know I don't need to remind you, but any one of them might be responsible for Colin's disappearance."

Rebecca checked her watch as Mary continued down the stairs. It was eleven thirty-five—just enough time for some fresh air on the back porch before the auction. Surely, LaRoux would put in an appearance for the highlight of the evening.

* * *

As Rebecca leaned on the rail of the massive back porch, she marveled at the storybook setting of the back lawn and gardens. White-wicker candlelit tables and chairs were randomly scattered about the spacious lawn. A massive magnolia stood sentry over the checkerboard Italian-marble patio, where many of the guests were twisting and turning to the high-spirited jazz laid down by a clarinet-playing woman and her band.

Lavender paper lanterns glowed beautifully, illuminating the twisted oaks with their mossy, mountain-man beards. Beyond the outstretched arms of the ornamental lighting, the moonlight cast fractured shadows across the lawn to create a foreboding mystique.

Suddenly, a Southern, intoxicatingly smooth voice startled Rebecca out of her hypnosis. "I love this view when the moon is just rising over the bayou and the light seeps through the trees. No matter the situation, *this* view is my magic elixir. But tonight, it pales in the presence of a beauty I do not know. What good fortune that the most enticing woman at my party has no gentleman on her arm."

Rebecca turned. The images Martin had provided did not tell the truth about this hunk of a man. Now that she was up close, she could see he was more than fine looking; he was gorgeous in the extreme. She looked right and left to ensure his brazen compliment had been directed to her. And as for his Pied Piper voice, she could listen to it for hours. His face was flawless and tanned; his vibrant sapphire eyes penetrated her armor and made her feel naked and filled with desire. Had the alcohol completely obliterated all sense and sensibility?

Trying her best to recover her faculties, Rebecca blushed as she forced a little Southern charm into her dialect. "Why, sir, is it proper etiquette for Southern gentlemen to offer such flattery without a proper introduction?"

LaRoux chuckled. "Why, I must apologize for my ill-gotten manners. But I was not aware the daughter of Venus had been invited to our little soirée. David LaRoux, at your service."

The pair exchanged awkward smirks for a mere five seconds before Rebecca first, and then LaRoux, broke into uneasy chuckles. "You are *David LaRoux*?" Rebecca paused. "Your party, this house— it's all so amazing, Mr. LaRoux."

"Thanks, but I can't take much credit. My ancestors are responsible for most of this decadence. As with many things in my life, I'm afraid I'm just a simple guardian." LaRoux's sigh and drawn expression beckoned the need for a more intimate conversation. "But tonight is not about me. It's for my guests, our city, and our charities, Ms.—" LaRoux cleared his throat and wordlessly prompted for Rebecca's name. Oblivious to his prodding, Rebecca stared with a besotted schoolgirl expression until LaRoux just flat out asked, "And you are?"

"Rebecca . . . Tracy, Mr. LaRoux. But after all of your indulgences today, I would have thought you might already know *all* of our names. Tell me, do you customarily spoil all of your female guests with such extravagant luxuries?"

Not accustomed to being called out so quickly by a new acquaintance, LaRoux smiled coolly. "No, never." Without breaking eye contact, he took Rebecca's hand and lightly planted a kiss on it. The sensation started out as a tingle on her hand and quickly radiated to an unexpected inhale, leaving Rebecca's lips parted and wanting. Ignoring her sudden consternation, LaRoux pressed on. "Ms. Tracy, it is my genuine pleasure to welcome you to my home. Tell me, is there a Mr. Tracy here tonight or back home?"

"No, Mr. LaRoux, there is no Mr. Tracy at all. And please, call me Rebecca."

"Only if you will call me David. And to answer your question in greater clarity, no, this is the first time I have ever stooped to such drastic measures—*bribery*, if you will—to entice you and your friends to attend. If you will indulge me one last compliment, I never imagined how absolutely ravishing you would look in that gown."

Suddenly, a light breeze stirred the wind chimes and helped cool the onset of Rebecca's uncontained blush. "I'm glad you approve. After all, someone in your organization did arrange for it."

"It was money well spent." LaRoux's eyes were systematically mapping the features of Rebecca's face as he spoke. "Are you and your friends enjoying yourselves?"

Unable to reel in her schoolgirl-crush giddiness and dodge the pendulum of awkwardness, Rebecca stammered, "No, no, not that I am counting, but I believe you just backdoored another compliment." Pausing long enough for LaRoux to consider his continuing use of flattery, she smiled. "And yes, we are having perhaps a little too much fun."

"Excellent." LaRoux looked back out over the lawn. "I would love to show you around the plantation, if you'd like."

Considering her younger, more armed-and-dangerous teammates, Rebecca was taken completely aback by LaRoux's proposition. She had studied his MO. The other agents were right smack in the heart of LaRoux's wheelhouse of desire. Knowing his alleged reputation, Rebecca calculated the possible scenarios for his sudden interest in . . . *her?* Her hastily drawn conclusion: *He knows.*

"Rebecca?"

Apparently, her deliberations were taking longer than she realized. "I would love—"

A sudden, methodical ringing of a handbell interrupted her. A white-haired, ponytailed butler clad in a black tuxedo slowly marched onto the porch. "Ladies and gentlemen, the auction will commence in five minutes."

Sensing something aloof in Rebecca's demeanor, LaRoux's charm faded. "Saved by the bell," he said. He retreated a step, then bowed. Amid turning away, he stopped. "If you are available after the auction, my offer remains on the table."

Despite her intuition, Rebecca flashed a mischievous smile. "As long as both your hands remain on the table, then I accept."

In a flash, LaRoux's boyish charisma reappeared. He placed his hand under her chin to brush the tender lines of her jaw with his thumb. "Why, Ms. Tracy, I will make no promises that we both might regret—later."

* * *

In the ballroom, guests were packed shoulder to shoulder. After minutes making her way through the crowd, Rebecca finally found her fellow agents. They were all between two to three sheets to the wind and clutching spirits. None appeared especially delighted by her sudden appearance. Tethered to their sides were Ryan, Taz, and several other newfound *drinking* best buddies, all looking to capitalize on the agents' loss of sobriety. Rebecca forced herself to appear pleased by the spectacle. Any opportunity to compare notes would have to wait.

"Look now, here comes our missing guest." Ryan beamed.

Mary extended to Rebecca one of her two drinks. "Here ya go, sis. You've got a lot of catching up to do."

Before Rebecca could refuse, Mary had thrust the drink into her hand. "I can't. I've already had too much."

"No, no, no," Taz objected. "You have to. We've all been waiting for this." Taz raised his glass. "To our new friend Mary, may your marriage be blessed with health, wealth, and bliss, and if it's not, may your lawyer be blessed with wisdom, friendly judges, and a mountain of bullshit."

"Cheers," Ryan chimed in.

Just as everyone fired their shots back, David LaRoux jumped on stage. Sarah elbowed Rebecca in the ribs. "There he is!"

LaRoux flashed his million-dollar smile as he looked out over the ballroom. "I would like to thank everyone for coming out tonight. On behalf of the LaRoux Family Foundation, CCI, and the City of New Orleans, I bid you welcome. We are honored by your presence and appreciate your support of Children's Hospital. Your generous contributions are greatly appreciated. As most of you know, I'm not one for the spotlight or long speeches, so I thank you again for joining us, and more importantly, for opening your wallets. Please enjoy your evening."

LaRoux jumped off the stage to boisterous applause, then began shaking hands as he moved throughout the crowd.

Rebecca watched intently to see if he would seek her out or at least acknowledge her with a playful eye. But he disappeared out the door without looking her way. Her spirit dropped. Alleged criminal activities aside, LaRoux had stirred long-suppressed emotions. The allegations made by Will Martin were competing with her natural inclination, wrangling her desire like a Texas steer. As her head swam in alcohol, Rebecca's attention drifted between the drunken gibberish of her agents and their admirers, her renewed anger over her past affair with Martin, and second-guessing what she should have said to LaRoux to coax his attention. Mired in conflict and wanton fantasies, Rebecca decided on another drink.

"Ladies and gentlemen," Leonne, the master of ceremonies, began, "the bidding is complete, and it is time to crown La Grand Belle."

Rebecca started to leave, but Ryan grabbed her arm. "Don't go. I think one of your friends might win."

Great. Rebecca forced a smile. *Just what I need. My youth and beauty have abandoned me in a wake of failed relationships, and now he wants me to suffer this insulting parade of debauchery.* Despite her feelings, Rebecca begrudgingly accepted.

Leonne continued, "Of our seventy-four contestants, sixty-three raised between five hundred and two thousand dollars." Applause echoed across the ballroom. Leonne put his hands together and bowed toward the crowd. "Yes, we thank you ladies and your admirers." Looking to his left and then to his right, at no particular individual, he said, "We have seven belles who raised between two and three thousand dollars." The applause grew more rambunctious. "Now, I know what you're all thinking. How on earth did they raise *so* much money? I must confess, if left to the imagination, then yes they do." Leonne raised a finger to his lips and snickered to the crowd's amusement. Raising his other hand, he hushed everyone. "So, you can only imagine what the next two lovely ladies did to raise between three and ten thousand dollars." The laughter and applause roared as Leonne again raised his hands high. "But apparently, that was not quite enough. Ladies and gentlemen, it is now my high honor to present the top three belles. Ladies, please come to the stage as your name is called. Raising twelve thousand dollars, Marie DuBois of New Orleans."

To the crazed applause, Marie DuBois, a local businesswoman wearing a red-sequined dress with a fox mask, made her way to the stage. Leonne handed her a small wrapped box and a bouquet of flowers. As the applause dissipated and Leonne continued. "Raising seventeen thousand dollars and drawing the most votes, may I present a newcomer from Baton Rouge, Miss Sean Taylor."

Answering the spirited call, Sean high-fived her fellow agents, pumped her fist, and headed up to the stage in her short, red-laced, low-cut dress. Leonne again offered flowers and a gift to the somewhat inebriated agent as she blew kisses to her many admirers.

"God, there will be no living with her now," Cassandra groaned.

"And now, your number one contestant, with seventeen benefactors, raising forty-nine thousand dollars—may I present the contestant enticing the most gentlemen to open their wallets, Miss Sybille Gardner of Biloxi, Mississippi." The catcalls and applause shook the halls.

Sybille Gardner sashayed to the stage in her black stilettos and long black satin dress, notable for its plunging neckline that exposed ample cleavage and halted just below her navel. It also stood out for its plunging back, which randomly covered her panty-less derriere. As she waved to the crowd, the drummer thumped a beat to the swaying of her hips, and with that, a burlesque inferno atmosphere exploded into being. Leonne handed Sybille the last of the bouquets and gifts but withheld the tiara displayed upon the podium.

Again, he hushed the crowd. "Ladies and gentlemen, tonight is indeed a most special occasion. Historically, the title of La Grand Belle has always been reserved for our top fundraiser, and tonight is no exception. But throughout this rich tradition, never has a top fundraiser neglected to register or removed her bidding pin as tonight's contestant has done. Ladies and gentlemen, drawing one solitary, unsolicited bid of two hundred thousand dollars, may I present your two thousand and twenty-one Grand Belle, from Monroe, Louisiana, Miss Rebecca Tracy."

The crowd roared as the band began hammering out "When the Saints Go Marching In." Rebecca stood frozen in shock, fear, and a quickly dissipating drunken stupor. Mary began nudging, then pushing Rebecca in the direction of the stage as the other agents yelled, *"Go, Becca!"* Rebecca cupped her mouth and blushed wildly as all eyes fell on her. As she made her way to the stage in a full-length emerald-green dress with a daring split up the thigh, she could not fathom what in the world she had done to draw the fancy of any man for such an excessive donation.

At the podium, Leonne took her hand and kissed it. "Mademoiselle."

Rebecca stared at the crowd, attempting to remain steady and not throw up. Feeling quite exposed, she smiled tensely as she waited for Leonne's instructions.

"Now, honored guests, as is customary, the gentleman whose bid won the fair hand of Miss Tracy shall now present the diamond tiara to our La Grand Belle. Ladies and gentlemen, once more, I give you our host, Mr. David LaRoux."

LaRoux waved as he hustled through the crowd and made his way to the stage. Rebecca cut an apprehensive smile as she studied his approach. *How can this be?* Every instinct of her training and experience told her something was amiss.

LaRoux took the tiara from Leonne and stepped behind Rebecca. "I wish you would have kept your bidding pin on. You would have raised a lot more money for the hospital," he said in a soft tone. Feeling the heat of his breath, Rebecca swallowed nervously. She was unsure of whether she wished she was sober or more intoxicated. After placing crown upon her head, LaRoux removed Rebecca's necklace, reached inside his jacket pocket, and produced a diamond Tiffany necklace. His fingers lightly brushed her neck, and Rebecca trembled.

"Your skin is incredible." With his nose near her ear, LaRoux inhaled deeply. "And you smell absolutely delicious."

Chills ran down Rebecca's spine, then down her legs, and she found herself wishing she weren't a federal agent. At a complete loss for words, the best she could do was turn toward the voice in her ear. And there he was, his lips so close she felt the heat, and she wanted nothing more than to kiss him—passionately. The fire glowing in his eyes would betray any attempt to deny his true intentions.

"I hope you waltz," he said. But manifested in Rebecca's eyes lay fear, reared by the truth of her purpose. Like a good poker player, she knew she had slipped the tell—and LaRoux had seen it. As he took her hand, she felt it in his grip.

"Why would I?" she said nervously.

"For starters, it's tradition. The La Grand Belle—that's you—always has the first dance, which traditionally is a waltz."

Rebecca stared blankly as LaRoux feigned confidence for the benefit of her lack thereof.

"This will be fun, you'll see. It's pretty simple. I lead, you follow." As LaRoux took Rebecca's hand and led her from the stage, the sea of regular attendees began to usher away the newcomers, clearing room on the dance floor. LaRoux leaned into Rebecca's ear and whispered, "Don't worry. Most of these people are so pickled they'll think you dance like Ginger Rogers."

"Most of these people probably don't know who Ginger Rogers is," Rebecca chirped nervously.

LaRoux took Rebecca's hand. As he waited for the music to cue, he read the spotlight-induced panic in her eyes and assured, "Nobody actually expects you to know how to waltz. But it's a simple three-count." He raised his left hand to eye level. "Take my hand." He placed his right hand behind Rebecca's shoulder blade and gently pulled her closer. "Put your left hand on my shoulder. When we start, you will step back with your right foot. With your left, you will step sideways and then bring your right foot to your left. Then repeat it all, but starting with the other foot and then repeat. When we run out of dance floor, I'll lead left into a turn. Got it?"

Exasperated, Rebecca groaned, "I don't know if I will ever forgive you for this."

"Oh, and one last thing. Look into my eyes like you've waited for this moment all of your life."

Rebecca gazed deeply into his pupils, and every lifelong unfulfilled desire forced a shudder in her breath. Failing miserably to conceal LaRoux's intoxicating effect, she tried, but failed, to remember her last orgasm. The thought of a naked LaRoux plunging into her evoked a shudder of ecstasy. She rolled her eyes and with a dreamy smile said, "Like that?"

LaRoux chuckled. "I was right about you." He looked at Leonne and nodded. On Leonne's cue, a string quartet began playing Johann Strauss's "Blue Danube." Without warning, in a sweeping motion, LaRoux led Rebecca through the first series of steps.

Immediately, she patterned her moves after LaRoux's, and by the first turn, her awkwardness disappeared. Her emerald gown flowed as if she were floating on clouds. If she could step back and observe herself, truly this moment was right out of some enchanted childhood fairy tale. David LaRoux in his tux, handsome and stately, was for *this* moment, *with her*. Assignment be damned. Criminal—who cares? This moment was unlike any fantasy she could have ever conjured.

What she had initially feared would last an excruciating eternity ended all too soon. After their dance, they took their bows and exited toward the French doors that led to the porch. Before they made it out, the DJ bellowed, "Okay, New Orleans, enough of that nonsense. It's time to shake it down Cajun style. Please welcome Creole Butta and the Gator Bites." The beat instantly switched gears as the band's rendition of the Ying Yang Twins' "Dangerous" began thumping and enticing the multitudes onto the dance floor. Rebecca looked back to the scene of the crime, where she had just finished her first waltz. The magic was gone—the rambunctious rhythm of the dance had wiped the vision clean. Rebecca looked for her agents, who were absorbed in the beat, and decided they must not give a damn, and frankly, neither did she.

"Would you like to dance again?" he asked.

"After *that*, I may never dance again." Rebecca laughed with glee.

The pair walked around the porch until it grew noticeably quieter. "So, are you ready for that tour now?" LaRoux prodded.

"If you will indulge me by answering a few questions first. After what just happened, I would love an explanation."

"Fire away."

Rebecca stepped in front of LaRoux, cutting into his path. "You are David LaRoux. That would make this your home?"

"Yes," he replied with boyish innocence.

"Okay. So that makes you rich. And you're handsome. Any girl in that room would kill to fill my ridiculously expensive, sequined green shoes, which you paid to put on my feet. And all of that overindulgence this morning." LaRoux confirmed it all with an easy smile and a nod. "Two hundred thousand dollars? For me? Please help me grasp exactly what is going on here."

"You do know you're quite beautiful, don't you?"

Rebecca was accustomed to cliché pickup lines in bars or coffee shops or anywhere a horny man found opportunity. A romp in the sack for a one-nighter was always their endgame. "I'll agree to *attractive.*"

"I was already in Bamboula's when you arrived last night. To be honest, when I first saw you and your friends, my sole motivation was to elevate the financial biddings of tonight's fundraiser. Your friends alone netted us an additional fifty thousand dollars." LaRoux turned to Rebecca, again with those soulful eyes, his smooth Southern voice selling every word. "But you, the more I watched, then studied, and even stared—which, by the way, you never seemed to notice even though I was willing you to notice me—the more I was captivated." LaRoux shook his head in disbelief. "Everything about you just made me *desire* you all the more. And I'm not accustomed to that kind of . . . weakness. Perhaps it was because you ignored me. Then there was this shyness, yet an ease about you. I kept asking myself, *How's she doing that?* And every time you smiled, I thought, *Oh man, she's really got it going on.* I have *never* so badly wanted to—" LaRoux wrestled with his confession with a clearing of his throat.

Unconsciously, Rebecca unleashed the very smile LaRoux had just spoken of.

"See, there it is again . . . that's the one." LaRoux looked quite serious, almost businesslike, as he continued to explain. "Either I have been completely blinded all of these years or, more likely, I witnessed something unique in you, so refreshing, so unpretentious that . . . I couldn't help myself. I knew you were someone I had to meet, regardless of my reputation."

"But seriously, two hundred thousand dollars?"

"I don't want to hurt your feelings, but we have a goal for the fundraiser, and every year I make sure we surpass it. I'm just glad you took your button off, otherwise I would have had to pay so much more for your hand."

"So, our waltz. I guess you do that dance every year?"

LaRoux chuckled. "Actually no. Tonight was the first time for me."

Rebecca threw her hands on her hips and once again conjuring a Southern belle dialect. "Why, Mr. LaRoux, is that horse manure I smell?"

"Honest Cajun, I know there's this rumor that circulates that I am some kind of ladies' man, a Casanova so to speak, habitually flocking to the younger female species, such as your friends. And if one were to believe those rumors, I can see where you might believe I would use the auction as a means to, well—"

"Do tell, Mr. LaRoux."

He sidestepped Rebecca. "Let's walk." He gently took her arm and waited until her feet began to move before leading her down the porch.

In the ensuing unnerving silence, Rebecca felt it was the optimal moment to pry the lid off David LaRoux, if that were possible. "I've never personally known a man who could ballroom dance. That was pretty amazing."

LaRoux smiled faintly before explaining, "You don't grow up in a house with a ballroom that has hosted many lavish parties and not learn how to dance accordingly." He paused and stopped walking as he reminisced about long-gone days. "One day, if you hang around, or come back, I might teach you to tango," he said stoically. With no reply from Rebecca, he continued. "My mother taught me. I have danced in that ballroom for as far back as I can remember, but tonight was the first time since my parents were killed seventeen years ago."

Having read his file, Rebecca already knew the answer, but playing her role, she stopped, turned, and inquired dramatically, "How'd they die?"

"Car accident." LaRoux's response was peppered with traces of bitterness.

"And who raised you afterward?"

Without a word, LaRoux resumed the stroll and they turned the corner. Soon, they were back at the location of their initial meeting. LaRoux checked his watch and sighed. "My father's business associates."

Rebecca waited. She sensed he was deliberating his next move. In a cooler tone, he said, "Come, I promised a tour." Slowly, they descended the granite stairs to the back lawn and gardens. As they threaded their way through the multitude of guests, LaRoux gave a very generic, abridged history of the house. Then they meandered away from the crowd, and just off the perimeter of the illuminated lawn, they weaved between the oaks as LaRoux shared the plantation's rich and jaded history: indigo, sugarcane, and slavery. In the fractured light of a seductive moon, they arrived at a black wrought-iron bench just beyond the reach of prying eyes and they sat.

Rebecca's earlier qualms had not eased. She knew LaRoux's smooth flirtations might be a charade, an attempt to romance her to bed, or worse yet, if he knew her identity, to kill her. But if the allegations were false, and his actions genuine—*holy hell*. Seated next to him, she squirmed as warmth stirred deep within. His words faded into an alcohol-induced, desire-filled fantasy. Yes—right here on this bench, if he asked, she would. Sex now—ask questions later.

Somewhere amidst the blossoming garden, an illuminated bronze clock chimed soulfully—*one o'clock*. The last half hour had melted away. Their largely one-sided conversation led Rebecca to conclude that LaRoux was lonely. His unexpected frankness only served to ignite her doubt about his guilt. Sitting closer to him than she ever imagined, the epiphany smacked Rebecca like a bucket of ice water. The task of infiltrating LaRoux's organization would fall squarely on her shoulders.

"Come, there's something I want you to see," LaRoux said as he suddenly stood. "Then I have to meet with the governor, and you really should get back to your sister and your friends." They walked across the lawn, and LaRoux took her arm in his, only this time he placed his other hand on her forearm.

His skin was soft and warm, and Rebecca's head spun in the fantasy of his hands exploring her body. Lost in her erotic thoughts, she nearly ran into the back end of the crowd that had gathered around the large wisteria-covered white gazebo. On the stage stood a statuesque, kilted violin player. And with the first stroke of his bow, Rebecca lost herself in the beauty of his haunting melody. The music spread out like an encroaching mist across the lawn as a woman in flowing sheer robes appeared on the stage. Seductively gliding, she contorted to each mesmerizing note as if her body were born from the cords.

Watching in spellbound silence, the music summoned Rebecca to involuntarily drift into David LaRoux. Glancing silently, he acknowledged the space invasion with a sly smile, and he wrapped his arms around her. He pulled his cheek against the back of her head and inhaled deeply.

As the performance ended, he took Rebecca by the hand and turned her toward him. "I feel I would die if I never did this." LaRoux's hands glided onto Rebecca's cheeks, his fingertips seducing her flesh. Her lips parted, and he guided her close and kissed her delicately before saying, "The governor is waiting. You should find your sister and make sure she doesn't get into too much trouble. I hope you'll still be here when my business is concluded, but if not, I know where to find you, Cinderella."

At a loss for words or action, Rebecca was not sure whether the trained agent or a scandalous vixen controlled her mind. Both alter egos possessed the same agenda—*Get LaRoux*. Without further deliberation, she grabbed him by the shoulders and kissed him passionately. Suddenly, Rebecca broke off the kiss and inhaled deeply. "Tell the governor you don't have much time."

CHAPTER 6

WITH SCARCELY ENOUGH LIGHT to discern her location, Rebecca's only reassurance was that, wherever she was, it was heavenly. She was in a bed, that much was assured. She would have liked to feel some sense of panic, or urgency, but it was a glorious bed, with linens so soft and fresh she had to consider the reality of her senses. She could be dreaming. But as the silk lightly caressed her skin, a panic-stricken reality hit home.

"Oh shit," she whispered. "I'm naked."

"Good morning."

There it was again, that mellow, soft, enticing voice, which apparently, at some juncture, had seduced her clothes off her. It was the song of a notorious scoundrel. She slid her hands away from her body, then searched left to right, but came up with nothing.

A click in the dark followed by the hushed whirring of an electric motor slowly eased a room-darkening drape skyward, which allowed filtered sun to illuminate the once lightless room. Rebecca marveled at the twelve-foot-high ceilings with intricate hardwood block molding, and pale-green walls accented by art deco Mayan walnut furniture. Amid multiple works on canvas, an original Chagall also hung. A few artifacts of hand-blown glass and pottery added to the ambiance of this five-star resort bedroom.

"This is *definitely* not my hotel," Rebecca said as she discovered LaRoux seated in the corner in a peculiar velvet Andy Warholish–like chair. Light struggled to push its way past the white linen, which shielded Rebecca's eyes from that morning after ocular explosion. LaRoux was wearing an undone white button-up shirt, loose khaki pants, and no shoes. He was the spitting image of at least one hundred dark-and-lonely night fantasies. Upon catching his eye, the cat smiled warmly—*too damned warmly*. Rebecca wanted her canary back, or at least to remember whether she enjoyed its demise.

"No, this most certainly is not your hotel." LaRoux flashed *that* smile, which at this moment, Rebecca did not appreciate.

If it weren't for the obvious fact that he had capitalized on her inebriation, his answer would have been acceptable. *God, I hope he used a condom.* "This is *your* bedroom, David?"

"Yes, Rebecca, it most certainly is."

If not for the big-picture scenario, she'd have him on a rape charge. "And why . . . am I naked in your bed?" Rebecca tensed. "Wait, before you answer, wipe that ridiculous grin off your face or I swear I'll gouge your eyes out."

David's smile exploded, unleashing what at other times would be irresistible charm. He glowed with a carnal familiarity that blushed Rebecca's cheeks. Under other circumstances, she would have been overwhelmingly smitten, but at this very moment, no dice.

"Before you commence with the gouging, how much do you remember from last night, after *you* kissed me?"

Would that be the same gazebo kiss that he initiated? Suddenly, remembering that itsy-bitsy detail, the awkwardness of the memory turned her blush into a fever-pitched inferno. Forced to consider that her current situation might be of her own accord, she swallowed the bitter pill. "I remember going back to the ballroom. My sister and friends were all dancing, and they were pretty trashed."

"And you joined right in?"

"Maybe," Rebecca replied sheepishly.

"And then?"

Rebecca sorted through the scrapbook of groggy memories. "We met this guy. I think his name was John. We went to some room. It was closed at first, but he opened the door. There was a piano. He started playing and singing. From what I remember, he was really great, or at least I think he was. Your friends showed up with a bottle of tequila, maybe two, and we all stood around drinking and singing. Then next thing I think I remember was that the room was filled with people singing really loud."

LaRoux leaned forward and chuckled. "John *is* awesome. So, go on. What happened next?" Rebecca tried to recall more, but she was at a loss. She'd simply been hammered last night.

After her long pause, LaRoux filled in the rest of the story, answering his own question.

"Well, Rebecca, when it became obvious to my friends, and *yours*, that a sleepover was in order, *they* all thought it would be hilarious to put you in my bed, naked. I do have to confess, when I came to bed this morning, I had the unexpected, hmm—*surprise*, of finding a naked woman, that being you, in my bed. And it would not be very honest of me to say that I didn't enjoy the view."

"So, nothing—"

"Nope, not from me. I can't say for sure that your friends didn't post any compromising pictures online last night, but as for me, I was completely innocent of any such shenanigans." LaRoux stood and took a measured step closer. "After discovering you had made yourself at home, which was around five this morning, I showered, got dressed, and helped the staff tidy up the place."

Rebecca forgot she was naked. She sat up, and in an instant, the sheets fell about her waist and just as quickly, she yanked them shoulder high. "It's funny. I don't feel like I'm that hungover."

"Probably Taz's magic cure-all for hangovers. I'm sure sometime before they showed you, or more likely carried you, to my room, somebody poured coconut water down your throat. It's not entirely pleasant, but it works."

Nervously, Rebecca said, "I probably should get dressed and go." She gazed around the immaculately clean and precisely detailed room to find her clothes nowhere in sight.

"Please, don't be in a hurry. Your gang all spent the night. I don't think anyone else has begun to stir. I'm going down to the kitchen to make you some breakfast. Please feel free to use my shower to freshen up. You'll find jeans, a blouse, and some lingerie in there, but I'd much prefer that you choose the bathing suit and cover-up."

"Are we going swimming?"

"Not where I want to take you. Are you okay with a boat ride?" With a cautious nod, Rebecca affirmed.

"It's going to take me about twenty minutes to stir up an omelet When I get back, you will either be dressed to go home or to spend the afternoon with me out on the bayou."

"Has Enrique been working his magic again?"

LaRoux chuckled. "Actually, I hope you enjoyed *my* taste. I chose your ball gown, and after I discovered you spent the night, I ran into Baton Rouge this morning."

Rebecca rubbed her head and asked, "Isn't it Sunday morning?"

LaRoux sat gently, then slid up the bed and leaned in. He lifted Rebecca's chin and softly kissed her lips. "You know something, Rebecca Tracy? I believe it is."

* * *

Rebecca showered and dressed, all the while debating her options. LaRoux's intentions as well has his guilt or innocence had to be determined. Rebecca chose the jeans and shirt—she considered the boat ride out in the bayou alone with LaRoux as too risky. LaRoux was thorough indeed; no way could Rebecca conceal a weapon or a wire in *that* bikini. Besides, the bikini was what *he* expected. She didn't want to appear overly anxious to impress. But if he found her dressed and was disappointed, the day and her opportunity might end abruptly. And who knew what David LaRoux's fickle taste might bring tomorrow?

Minutes later, the bikini fit perfectly, just as the jeans and lingerie had. *How in the hell did he figure my size so precisely?* She stared in the mirror as she applied makeup from the apparently newly purchased kit. Rebecca grumbled aloud, "I hope you know what you're doing, Pearson." She pulled on the cover-up, then walked through the bedroom, pausing briefly to scrunch her toes on the luxuriously plush area rug before opening the French doors to the veranda.

Basking in the warmth of the midday sun, Rebecca stood at the rail and breathed deeply as she studied the gardens from a new vantage. She panned her eyes left to right, then back inside. Every detail was precise and pristine in LaRoux's Disney World. This home was right out of a *Southern Living* magazine. Rebecca looked for a flaw—a fingerprint on the glass, a smudge on the furniture, or just a piece of simple lint on the floor. *Nothing.* If LaRoux was actually guilty of the alleged crimes, well, a man this meticulous would not be easy to catch. But even before she first laid eyes on him, she believed Will's evidence was, at best, thin and circumstantial.

As she glanced at her reflection in the French door, she almost understood his attraction. The cut of her bikini, combined with the cover-up that barely earned its name and a sassy pair of Krewe cat-eye sunglasses, were all so perfect that Rebecca couldn't help but think LaRoux's intentions might actually be honest.

Interrupting Rebecca's hypercritical, self-examination, LaRoux practically bounced into the room. "Here we go," he said as he appeared with a fully loaded tray. "You will not hurt my feelings if you only eat the fruit, but I hope you will at least try my Cajun omelet."

"What's in it?"

"Two hundred and fifty years of family lovin'."

LaRoux's enthusiastic, charming smile, coupled with his generosity and the fact he had been a complete gentleman last night, made Rebecca suddenly detest her deception. She'd seen this scenario too many times in the movies; the undercover cop falls in love with an innocent perp, and when the dust clears, all is made good and they ride off into the sunset together. *Bullshit. This is real life, and in real life, that crap doesn't happen.* This was Martin's case, and his promotion, not hers. As she peered into LaRoux's eyes, she was ready to end this deceit before things got out of hand, before any report was filed, before she learned the truth, if she even cared about the truth anymore. *Just roll the dice.* If this was just another weekend fling for LaRoux, she could make the most of it and go back to Seattle knowing she'd had a great time. She was several years past due for a carefree, crazy weekend, or even just one crazy day. *Screw Will Martin,* Rebecca mused, *just like he screwed me.*

"Hey, are you okay?" LaRoux asked as he wondered where Rebecca's mind might be drifting.

"I was thinking about that delicious smelling omelet. If I weren't about to get on your boat in this tasteful, but skimpy bikini, I'd love to try it. But one bite, and I'll have a food baby the size of Texas."

LaRoux laughed. "Why, Miss Tracy, if I didn't know better, I'd say you were worried about impressing me."

"More like trying not to embarrass myself. It looks quite yummy. What's in it?"

"Crawfish, Andouille sausage, some grilled gator, peppers, onions, mushrooms, cheese, eggs, and the LaRoux secret Creole sauce." David cut a small portion and offered it to Rebecca. "How about you try just a bite, and I promise to keep my eyes north of your neck this afternoon."

Rebecca's half-crooked smile telegraphed her skepticism. "Better be careful with those promises, David LaRoux. I don't take well to dishonesty."

"Fair enough. I'll do my best not to look."

* * *

"Are you hungry yet?" LaRoux asked as he eased off the throttle and steered his custom Chris-Craft toward a cluster of moss-draped cypresses.

"I'm starving, but you have failed miserably in your promise. So, I'm not eating a thing until I get some clothes back on."

LaRoux frowned. "I merely said I would *try* my best not to look. Besides, you ate half of that omelet this morning and still managed to make it impossible for me to not check you out." Underneath the thick canopy, LaRoux killed the motor and moved aft. "I'm hungry enough to eat roadkill right now, so if you will forgive me, I'm going to feed my food baby, and I don't care if you look." He raised the rear seat and tossed a small anchor overboard. From the other seat, he produced a picnic basket with two sandwiches, fresh fruit, and a bottle of wine.

That man could eat half a cow and still look amazing, Rebecca thought as she spun her chair to face the rear. "I hope that fruit is organic."

For the first time since boarding the boat, LaRoux looked directly at Rebecca in her bikini instead of glancing at her profile from the corner of his eye.

"Mr. LaRoux, didn't your mother teach you it's not polite to stare?"

"I won't apologize, Rebecca. I really wasn't prepared for everything about you to be so damn . . . perfect."

Rebecca tried to contain her blush as LaRoux uncorked the wine and poured two glasses. He set the fruit within Rebecca's reach and smirked when he noticed her attention was drawn to his body.

She gushed. "Looks like I'm not the only one who hits the gym." Suddenly, Rebecca turned her attention to a log teeming with turtles basking in the sun. She studied the reptiles briefly, then looked back at LaRoux and smiled politely. "Can I ask you something? And please, be honest." "Fire away," he said as he placed the fruit dish in front of her.

"Okay, between the boat ride, breakfast, and last night, we've known each other for about four hours, right?"

"Maybe five, if you count the time I spent sketching your naked body this morning." LaRoux sipped his wine with a most mischievous expression.

"Please, tell me you're not serious." LaRoux continued with his playful smile as Rebecca waited. "Fine. Have it your way, Rembrandt.

So, last night, your friends, they *love* to talk about you—particularly about this." Rebecca wiggled her finger, alternating between herself and LaRoux. "So, I kind of think I know your reputation." LaRoux's attempt to restrain his amusement was obvious. "I know I don't really fit the profile of your preferred," Rebecca cleared her throat, "*companions*. And with all of this extravagant doting, just tell me straight up—what's going on here?"

"This might come as a shock, but I know enough about you to make *this*," LaRoux said, mimicking Rebecca's finger wiggle, "dangerous."

Rebecca tensed. *How does he know? When did he find out? Does he have a gun in the basket?* To conceal her grave concern, and worse yet, her face, she glanced back at the turtles only to find a crocodile skimming the water. *One single bullet, my body tossed overboard, and it would be a perfect murder—a reptile smorgasbord, no body, and no evidence.*

Rebecca's consternation did not go unnoticed. It wasn't the first time she had become pensive in their brief association. LaRoux asked, "Are you okay?" He placed his hand on her knee.

She hesitated before saying, "I don't know how to do relationships, especially with someone like you."

"Me neither. It's no big secret that I've been running from relationships my entire life. But if you believe what you've heard about me, then you'll have to agree that I've been around the block so many times that, by now, I have to know what I want."

"And what would that be?" Rebecca looked for LaRoux to flinch, for him to reach for the gun and say something like, *For starters, it's time for you to die, bitch.*

He looked a little too relaxed as he leaned back and flashed that dastardly charming smile of his. "What do you want this to be, Rebecca?"

A career-enhancing bust with a huge promotion—but maybe just to rip your clothes off and do it just one time. Rebecca's mind was swimming in emotion. Trying to outfox LaRoux, she replied, "A weekend fling?" Her smile was awkward, and she covered it quickly by gulping her wine.

"Then this is a weekend fling." LaRoux turned away so she could not see the disappointment in his eyes.

Suddenly, a symphonic menagerie of wildlife began—birds, frogs, and crickets buffered the ensuing awkward silence. *Mating calls*, Rebecca mused. *How perfect.* On any other occasion, she would have greatly enjoyed nature's harmonious concert, but not today. She wasn't sure how to proceed with LaRoux. *This was never supposed to be my job. That's what the Barbie dolls were brought in for.* But LaRoux seemed unhappy with her answer, so she decided to roll the dice. "What if I said I wanted this—*for us*—to be something more?"

The man instantly brightened. "Then this, uh—we, would be something more." LaRoux leaned directly into Rebecca's face, and their lips practically touched. "I know you must have reservations about me, and I know they are well deserved." He kissed Rebecca softly. "I know this sounds utterly insane, but I am one hundred percent sure that I want you in my life." He placed his hands around Rebecca's head and kissed her passionately.

Career and assignment be damned. Rebecca's libido triggered, and she couldn't fake it. She ran her hands through LaRoux's thick, wavy hair, then her right hand began to slowly caress its way down his muscular shoulder and back until it ran across his thigh. As her hand worked its way into the leg of his shorts, LaRoux abruptly pulled away.

"Whoa, I hope you don't mind, but I didn't bring you out here for *this*," he explained against the tide of a pounding heart. Rebecca's expression of glistening anticipation did not falter as she reached behind and fumbled for the double-knotted bikini string. LaRoux pulled at her determined arms. "No, seriously. I did not come prepared, and given my reputation, I hope you appreciate that."

"So, you don't take that twenty-four-hour Viagra?"

"No," LaRoux snapped. "I don't need that stuff. And that's not what I was talking about."

Rebecca's smile exploded. "It's alright, Romeo. I'd never do it on a boat less than thirty feet anyhow. What kind of girl do you take me for?"

* * *

The sun had already receded below the lines of cypresses and tupelo trees when the lights of the plantation crept into view. As Rebecca navigated the boat according to LaRoux's directions, her mind was filled with romance and wanderlust. Her original intentions for LaRoux were so completely removed from her mind that all she could visualize was their naked bodies entwined in passion.

"Okay, ease off on the throttle some more. If you hit a stump here, we'll be gator food."

"Speaking of food, I can't wait to get back to my hotel. I'm so hungry. And once your back is turned, and I've actually got some clothes on, I'm going to eat half of the city."

"Speaking of hotels, I have to fly to Vegas tonight for a meeting tomorrow morning."

Rebecca's sulky expression was exactly what LaRoux had hoped for. "So, how about if you and your friends join us in Vegas? Think about it—a private jet, a suite at The Palazzo, food, maybe a show . . . whatever. It's all on me. Call it my wedding gift to your sister."

"I would say yes, but I need to talk to my sister first." *Innocent until proven guilty.* At this moment, LaRoux was no criminal, and Rebecca was anything but a DEA agent. "Here's the deal. I'm already way behind schedule, thanks in part to you." Rebecca shot a dubious glare at LaRoux.

"True, it's partly my fault, but I did not foresee any of this, which for me is completely out of character. But seeing as how we are in The Big Easy, I'll make it really *easy.* Everyone just needs to throw a few things in an overnight bag and leave the rest. Don't worry about checking out. I'll make sure your hotel rooms here are covered until we get back. When we get to Vegas, all of you can go shopping and get whatever you need. It's all on me. What do you think?"

"I think that's a skosh extravagant."

"That should be an indication of just how badly I want you to say *yes*."

Rebecca rolled her eyes in the direction of the mansion. She already knew her answer but was not about to let his charm and money win out so quickly. David LaRoux needed to be schooled in the art of being sweated.

When Rebecca did not immediately accept, LaRoux said, "Ms. Tracy, when I set my eyes on something I want, I can be vulgarly extravagant."

"I can't let you—"

"Allow me to explain." He reached over Rebecca and killed the throttle. As the slosh of the wake washed past the boat, he turned Rebecca's eyes to his. "My family has been in New

Orleans since there was a New Orleans. Right before the French ceded the territory to the Spanish, my family almost bought the whole damn thing. Not one major business deal was made that does not have LaRoux DNA. John Lafitte, John Law, Bienville, the dukes, and every governor this fine state has ever known have all done business right here at my home. My family's wealth is far more enormous than you or anyone could ever imagine. But you know what?"

Rebecca shook her head slowly.

"All of that wealth has not brought me a damned thing that I have ever been able to love." With their eyes interlocked and their lips enticingly close, LaRoux fumbled for his best explanation. "My instincts are unparalleled, at least that's what I like to believe. So, whatever the next few days might cost, ten times that amount wouldn't be too much to find out if you are truly what I think you are and who you might be to me."

Rebecca's jaw dropped. *Where in the hell did the wham-bam thank-you ma'am playboy go?*

LaRoux's crazy-assed confession blindsided Rebecca. She stared at him as if he had three noses.

"Say something, *chérie.*"

Rebecca shrugged. "Can we at least stop at the store before we leave and buy some condoms?"

CHAPTER 7

WITH NO PHONE CONTACT for almost twenty-four hours, followed by an unauthorized departure to Las Vegas by three of his agents and the hired-hand cop, Will Martin seethed. By the time Cassandra, Cindy, and Sarah had returned to New Orleans and reported on the event, the other half of the team was already wheels-up *en route* to Sin City.

The three agents had divulged info on the major aspects of the night, but they omitted minor events such as the excessive alcohol consumption and the state in which they had deposited Rebecca into LaRoux's bed. However, they let Martin know that Rebecca was the agent who had successfully set hooks into LaRoux. He desperately wanted the plant, but his stomach turned when he learned Rebecca had stolen the show.

Victor Hanson was equally displeased. Hanson, a retired twenty-year vet of the CIA, had worked advanced security exclusively for LaRoux for the past ten years. Hanson was a ghost, known only to LaRoux. At one time, he'd been a shining star in the agency and had specialized in manipulating third world governments by whatever means necessary. Eventually, his various associations in the underworld had led him to the doors of CCI. Off the CCI payroll books, Hanson was LaRoux's highest-paid employee. His job was to protect LaRoux from any formidable threat.

* * *

Just as LaRoux and his entourage entered The Palazzo, Ryan handed his boss the phone.

"You go ahead. I'll meet you at the elevator," LaRoux instructed. Ryan gave him a cross glare.

"It's alright. We're in the lobby. I'll be fine." LaRoux turned to Rebecca and kissed her quickly.

"This won't take but a second. Try not to get lost." As soon as they had moved out of earshot, LaRoux dialed a number and put the phone to his ear as he meandered behind his entourage.

"Victor."

"How is it you expect me to do my job on such short notice? You should have made me aware of your intentions much earlier," Hanson growled.

LaRoux smiled. He never grew tired of his protector's incessant ranting—or the magnificent and immaculate grand entrance of the hotel. The mainstay of the lobby was a frosted glass-sculpture fountain sheltered beneath a glass-domed rotunda garnished with frescoes and ornate Venetian plaster. Encircled by eight ornate marble columns surrounded by palm trees, the lavish variety of greenery and fresh exotic blossoms created a visual feast that greeted the masses of new arrivals. LaRoux soaked it in.

"One day you will be the death of the both of us." Hanson's protests yanked LaRoux back from the realm of daydreams. "No thanks to you, things are back under control." The phone went dead, and Hanson was gone. It was Hanson's duty to make sure his boss never got compromised. He stayed in touch with his former CIA associates in the electronics industry to stay abreast of the latest spyware technology. With virtually unlimited financial resources, Hanson was always the first kid on the block with the coolest toys.

Local law enforcement—FBI, CIA, DEA, the casino itself, and the most ruthless of all, Homeland Security—all had eyes and ears everywhere. Even with advanced planning, staying a step ahead in the security world was not simple. In tonight's scenario, LaRoux had added four long-legged trump cards to the mix.

He rejoined his party at the concierge desk and handed the phone back to Ryan. "Would it kill ya to get one of these for yourself?" Ryan quipped as he tucked it back in his sport coat.

"I already own one. Are you tired of carrying it for me?"

"Are you tired of carrying it?" Ryan bantered.

"Mr. LaRoux," a flamboyant voice interrupted, "we are so happy to see you again."

"Charles, it's great to see you," LaRoux replied. "You already know my associates, and these fine ladies are Rebecca Tracy, her sister, Mary, Margo Carter, and watch out for this one, Sean Taylor."

"I shall keep two eyes on her," Charles said with a wink in Sean's direction. "As we are a little pressed for time, unless you gentlemen require anything, I shall take the ladies to their room and prepare them for the party."

"Party?" Mary said.

"Yes, Miss Tracy. We are having a party in your honor, sort of a bachelorette shindig." Excessively animated, Charles appeared to have had two or three energy drinks too many. "But don't you worry one hair on that beautiful head. Enrique arranged for your evening attire, and I'll have room service send up a gallon of espresso. It is going to be such fun. Just wait. You'll see."

"David?" Counting on a good night's sleep, after perhaps something a little more intimate, Rebecca objected softly.

"Charles, please take the ladies," said LaRoux. "I'll send Rebecca in a few minutes."

Charles clapped. "Come, come, ladies. No time to dawdle. Just wait until you see what we have selected for you." Ryan, Taz, and Walt all followed.

Alone for the first time since the boat ride, Rebecca forced a smile. "A party?"

"I had to improvise. I had already planned a social, of sorts, for tonight, which included some of what you'll experience shortly. After you threw a monkey wrench into my plans, I had to—"

"I threw the monkey wrench? I was supposed to be back at work in Monroe tomorrow, but instead I'm in Las Vegas, which is exactly where you were supposed to be. It seems to me it was you who did the wrench tossing."

"Okay, I may be partially to blame. But according to your preconceived notions of my jaded reputation, I should have woken up with Sean in my bed this morning—not you. Goodbyes would have been exchanged, and I would have arrived here several hours ago." LaRoux took Rebecca's hand and began a leisurely stroll toward a bank of elevators. "I have never brought a date to a business meeting, but that's exactly what *you've* somehow managed to accomplish."

Rebecca stopped suddenly and was about to respond, but LaRoux's charming smile prevented her from getting one word out. "I know what you want to say. *I never asked for this.* That's what's so fascinatingly odd. So, go to your room, get changed, drink some coffee, and try to act your sister's age." LaRoux pressed the elevator call button and attempted to conceal his amusement.

"*My sister's age?*" With her hands on her hips, Rebecca's iceberg-melting glare burned into the side of LaRoux's skull. He ignored her menacing antics and remained focused on the elevator's progress toward their floor. "Stare all you want. Those buttons are not going to save you now or later, David LaRoux."

The elevator doors opened, and LaRoux quickly entered the car. He resumed his silent appreciation of the floor buttons while Rebecca deliberated her next move. She was firmly planted outside of the elevator, but with a huff, and several agonizingly slow steps, she entered and stood next to LaRoux. He beat back his chuckles and pressed *32.*

"Don't think I can't see through your pathetic attempt to conceal your amusement, David," Rebecca stated as the elevator chimed their arrival.

"This would be you, Miss Tracy."

Rebecca threw her chin in the air, let out an exaggerated "humph," and strutted into the hall.

"Don't you want to know your room number?"

Rebecca turned with a flourish. "You must think you're pretty darn funny about now."

"Thirty-two sixteen, and it's that way." LaRoux chuckled as he pointed in the opposite direction. Waiting for Rebecca to disappear before pressing the key, he took the time to enjoy the view of her fading silhouette. Upon reaching the thirty-third floor, he headed toward his customary accommodations. Just shy of his suite, a door suddenly swung open and a forceful hand pulled him inside. "What the hell?" LaRoux growled as he struggled to acclimate to the sudden darkness. Across the room, a series of laptops provided the only illumination.

"It should be me asking that question," the voice whispered.

"Vic?"

"David, what the hell is going on? Two hours ago, a DEA tech team rolled your room. They even have eyes in your shit can."

"What the hell. Is nothing sacred?"

"Exactly. Maybe that little boat trip today wasn't such a good idea."

"That was my idea, and there's no way that she or her friends are involved."

"Shit," Hanson grumbled. "Nobody is clean until I say they're clean. *Nobody.*"

LaRoux walked to the window and stared out to the blackened outline of the shadowed mountains. With Hanson's disclosure, and Rebecca just one floor below, he felt the weight of the game returning. Hanson joined him by the window. "Are we cool in here, Vic?"

"Of course we are. Besides, I have no desire to make that midnight boat ride to Mississippi, if you get my drift."

"How much time do I have?"

"Enough. I've looped you walking the lobby talking on your phone. Unless they put a live body out there, you're good to go."

LaRoux stared out the window a minute. "Suppose I told you I was thinking about shutting down operations? I've got enough investments to live ten lives and still pay your outrageous salary."

Hanson placed his hand on LaRoux's shoulder. "You know I don't give a damn where the money comes from. And while going legit is admirable, look where it landed your parents. Unraveling your business is too damn complicated. Too many people count on you for their livelihoods. Too many of them are within your own house, David."

LaRoux turned to Hanson. "Do you know something you're not telling me, Victor? Do I have a mole at CCI stirring the DEA's pot?"

"There's nothing concrete yet. Disposing of that little undercover gator bait, Colin, probably wasn't our best move. I can't believe those DEA dumbasses still have not uncovered the paper trail I left for them to chase. But the fact that they knew you were coming on such short notice, I have reason for concern. Are you sure your crew is still solid?"

"Solid as Gibraltar."

"What about these women you brought for your pajama party?"

LaRoux handed Hanson an envelope. "Here are their names and where they're from. I already know Margo Carter is a cop, NOPD. Pay particular attention to Rebecca Tracy. She might be hanging around a little while longer than normal." LaRoux smiled devilishly as he reflected on how he had discovered her this morning. "But I doubt you will find anything hidden on her. Lord knows I didn't."

"Do tell," Hanson replied sleazily as he checked the video loop of LaRoux pacing the lobby, chatting on his phone. "Here. You're gonna need one of these." Hanson handed LaRoux a compact silver box. "It's the same little gadget that was under your table at Bamboula's, only this one is portable. I guarantee whoever prepped your room, they're gonna be trying to listen to every conversation you have out here."

LaRoux studied the tiny device. "Do you think this has something to do with the Louisiana casino project?"

"It's DEA, not FBI. But I'll know soon enough. And I know what you're gonna say, but for the time being, please take this as well." Hanson extended his hand to reveal a burner phone. "I know you hate them, but until I get a handle on who's in our business, I must insist."

LaRoux took the phone and tucked it into his pocket. "Emergency only. Got it."

"Good. Now, it's time to get you back to the real world." Hanson headed to the door. "On my cue, exit the room and go on to your room like everything is normal. Once you've been in your room awhile, wash your face, but leave the faucet dripping, like it won't cut off. Call for maintenance. I'll make sure it can't be repaired tonight, and then they'll have to get you a new room. That should flush our little friends into action, and out into the open."

"And then?"

Hanson grinned. "The game begins."

* * *

On the thirty-second floor, Rebecca knocked on her suite door, not having a house key. Margo swung it wide open and swept her arm as she bowed deeply. In an excessively effeminate tone, she mimicked Charles's flamboyant behavior. "Welcome to the Lago Suite, over two thousand square feet, two bedrooms, two baths, and stocked to the hilt with everything we need to *par-tay*."

"Oh my," Rebecca groaned. She gazed at the spacious, elegant accommodations and slowly stepped in. She spotted Sean and Mary lounging in the sunken living room. They raised their glasses in honor of Rebecca's accomplishment.

Margo followed Rebecca inside. "Here, you're gonna need this." Sean handed Rebecca a Red Bull and vodka. "Wait till you see the bathroom, makeup, shampoo, and perfume. It's like Saks Fifth Avenue stocked it. And our dresses and shoes for tonight, holy hell. The vodka is Crystal Head. It's like fifty bucks a bottle. What the hell did you do to that guy?"

Mary and Sean edged closer, eagerly anticipating the sordid details. Rebecca took a sip and stepped down into the living room. "Nothing."

"*Nothing*?" Mary drilled. "There's a Ralph Lauren dress on my bed and an Alexander McQueen on yours. Do you know how much your dress cost? I do. I Googled it. Over two thousand dollars' worth of . . . *nothing*."

"Really, nothing happened." Rebecca sipped from her glass to conceal any smile that might escape.

"That kiss *I* saw at the party, by the gazebo, that looked like a little more than nothing." Sean stepped up to Rebecca and pulled her glass down. "Two hundred thousand dollars, for a dance? I'm thinking it must have been one hell of a blowjob."

Sean's innuendo returned Rebecca to reality. "A kiss—that was the extent of it. I had no idea until the auction that he was even interested in me. From that point, I just followed his lead, which wasn't as promiscuous as I was expecting. As for anything else, it sure wasn't my fault that I woke up naked in his bed."

Sean choked on her drink and coughed out the sticky beverage on the carpet. "I believe that was Cassandra's doing, if I recall correctly."

"I really don't care whose idea it was. Careers have ended for much less," Rebecca snapped.

"You didn't object to the *undercover work* at the time."

Not sure whether Sean was simply being playful or testing her leadership, Rebecca checked each agent's expression for a hint of disrespect. "I was drunk, and it could have put me in harm's way."

Sean, staying true to her reputation, continued to press. "How do you think Director Martin would feel about our tactical initiatives? Is it true he's got a jealous streak as long as the Mississippi?"

"Longer," Rebecca recalled. "Look, we've got to watch each other's backs—no more stunts like that. And honestly, I would have preferred LaRoux had chosen one of you. But that being said, don't let Vegas, or their Southern charm, dull your edge. We've got a job to do, so let's ease off the vodka and get dressed. We're not on the plantation anymore, and if Martin and company are not here already, they will be soon. So, assume every action you take will be seen or heard."

"Easier said than done," Mary defiantly blurted, finishing her drink. "Eyes or not, those guys are hardcore partiers." She swirled her ice cubes and continued. "If we don't play their game, they might lose interest—or worse, get suspicious. And I for one don't plan on winding up like Colin Wells."

"Fair enough," Rebecca sighed. "Which bedroom is mine?"

"You're in here, with me." Pleased with her victory, Mary cheerfully led Rebecca to their room. Rebecca eyed the simple, yet gorgeous black dress stretched out on the bed. Beside the dress was a Victoria's Secret bag and a pair of black leather pumps. "Don't worry. I'm sure everything will fit," Mary reassured. "Ours appears to be perfectly sized. Apparently, Enrique has been a busy little fairy godmother."

"Two thousand dollars?" Rebecca groaned.

"Over. But don't worry. Seeing as how there's only one bed in our room, I'm guessing LaRoux is planning on justifying his outlandish expenses in a more intimate manner later." Mary pulled her T-shirt off, wiggled out of her jeans, and fished through the lingerie bag. "Damn that little fruitcake!" Mary held up the panties for inspection and exclaimed, "Not only did he get the right size, but it's pretty damned sexy as well." After Mary finished stripping, she brought the lingerie to her nose. "You might know it—they've already been laundered."

Rebecca continued to stare at the dress. *Does David LaRoux expect sex in return for all of the opulent pampering? The audacity of that man.* She stared at the bed. It was a king-sized, after all. She glanced at Mary. *Bunkmates?* It didn't matter; Rebecca had already made her mind up about where she'd be sleeping tonight.

"Hey, better get cracking," Mary said as she stepped into her deep-plum-colored dress and pulled the sleeves over her shoulders. "What do you know? It fits perfectly. Imagine that." She took notice of Rebecca's obvious reservations and placed her hand on her colleague's shoulder. "It's okay, Becca. We've got your back. Mr.

Overindulgence will have to settle for Spank-it dot com and a tube of K-Y tonight." Mary disappeared into the bathroom to begin doing her makeup and hair. "You know, I can't believe that son of a bitch expects us to get all glammed up for a party without a hairstylist. What a cheap bastard."

Rebecca smiled momentarily as she slowly removed her clothes and folded them neatly on the bed. As she inspected the lingerie, she knew *he* had picked it out. He would know exactly what she was wearing under that dress. Rebecca reached back to the dresser for her drink and gazed in the mirror at her naked silhouette as she finished the vodka. Then she looked into the bathroom and watched as Mary's model-perfect form reminded her of her aging body's shortcomings. *I'll bet she eats everything she sees and never goes to the gym.* She looked back in the mirror and knew she wasn't twenty-five anymore—but for thirty-five, she looked pretty damn good.

First one leg and then the other, Rebecca slid into lacy panties. "Why bother?" she whispered as she inspected the nearly transparent fabric. And yes, the bra matched. As she put it on, thoughts of LaRoux's silky hands cupping her breasts ever so firmly wrecked her concentration. She visualized his charming, boyish eyes raking her over. Feeling aroused, Rebecca cursed LaRoux's absentee power of seduction. She dropped the Alexander McQueen over her head, and it instantly conformed to her curves oh so perfectly. *The nerve of that bastard.*

Rebecca returned to the deserted living room in her bare feet and made herself another drink to settle her *sex with LaRoux is on the menu* nerves. She slipped into the pumps, and damned if they didn't slide on like velvet slippers, so comfortable she barely noticed the five-inch heels.

Five inches—that would leave her about a half inch shorter than LaRoux. The perfect height to stand behind, wriggle the dress above her hips, and enter her from behind. *Of course he would.* As she reluctantly gazed into the mirror, Rebecca discovered how LaRoux had transformed her into his ideal desire. Feeling intimidated and aroused by his ability to craft not only her reflection but her thoughts as well, Rebecca muttered, *"Oh, you are a son of a bitch."*

* * *

Rebecca and her team arrived at TAO Beach to find the party in full swing. "Here we go again," Sean moaned.

"It's Sunday night. Don't these people have to work tomorrow?" Mary added.

"Personally, I don't care. I'm going to play this up to the best of my ability, and tomorrow, I'll be sleeping in," Margo announced happily as she grabbed Mary's hand and pulled her toward the bar. Before Rebecca and Sean could follow, Junior Tazwell intercepted the foursome.

"Well, there you ladies are and looking *so* fine, I might add. If you'll come with me, except for you, Rebecca." Taz's hand cut off Rebecca's path like a train-track crossing gate. "Mr. LaRoux is expecting you over there." He pointed to a large cabana across the pool where LaRoux and three men were seated around a table stocked with food and drinks.

"Thank you." Rebecca walked tentatively toward the table, acutely aware that LaRoux's guests' attention was focused solely on her. A warm desert breeze whispered through the palm trees and lifted her hair from her shoulders. Still a good distance from the table, she smiled nervously. LaRoux rose, and his laser-beam focus locked on her approach. He excused himself from his party and walked eagerly to greet her. In black pants, a white knit tee, and a black sport coat, LaRoux appeared dressed for a poolside fashion shoot.

"I'm not sure what to say. The minute I saw this dress, I thought it would be perfect for you, but this," LaRoux said, inspecting Rebecca from feet to head, "exceeds all of my expectations."

"Thank you, I think." Rebecca was irritated by her sudden complete loss of confidence and control of her emotions in the presence of the King of Smooth.

LaRoux smiled. "Come, I'd like you to meet some of my friends."

He ushered Rebecca in the direction of his table. "Rebecca Tracy, I'd like to introduce our fine governor, Marcus Brown, district four senator, Ralph Backus, and George Thomas, CEO of Las Vegas Sands. Gentlemen, my very good friend, Rebecca Tracy."

"You must be a very special friend, my dear," Backus said as he took Rebecca's hand and kissed the top of it. "You see, I have known David LaRoux for most of his life, and if memory recalls, this is the first time I have had the honor of meeting any of his—how did you phrase it David—*very good friends.*" Pudgy yet polished, sporting a white suit with a pale-green shirt and a white fedora, Backus looked the part of old-school Louisiana counselor and lawmaker.

"Thank you, Senator."

"My dear, such formalities are for politicians. Please call me Ralph."

Thomas interrupted. "I hate to rush off, Miss Tracy, but I am running late for an engagement," he began. Looking the part of big-money Vegas with his off-white linen pants and his strategically unbuttoned white shirt, his tanned, hairless chest and well-oiled demeanor would surely land the attention of the multitude of poolside vultures. "I hope to have the opportunity to get to know you better in the near future." He kissed her hand and turned to the others. "Gentlemen, as always, it's been a pleasure."

"David," the governor began as soon as Thomas had cleared earshot, "this is a great day for Louisiana. This project will bring many jobs, careers, and tourists back to our state. You have done the LaRoux family name proud, son." Governor Brown shook LaRoux's hand vigorously. "Miss Tracy, although I have not known David nearly as long as my esteemed colleague, I think it's safe to say you have landed one fine young man." The governor's smile was broad and genuine as he picked up a bottle of champagne. "Now, I think it's due time to celebrate."

Over the next half hour, details of the proposed casino and resort were discussed as well as fishing and the Saints. On occasion, as Brown and Backus would get into friendly debates between themselves,

Rebecca and LaRoux would sit back and take in the night's splendor. By one o'clock, the Thunder from Down Under boys had arrived for the bachelorette festivities.

Mobbed at the far end of the pool by frenzied, lustful females, the dancers did not disappoint.

"You should go join your sister," LaRoux suggested.

"I'm quite content right where I am." Rebecca patted LaRoux's thigh and smiled. "So, you did all of this craziness for Mary?"

"Not all of it. I already had the pool reserved for a small celebration for the people instrumental in getting this project done. Once I knew you were coming, I made a few modifications." LaRoux nodded at the half-naked male dancers and crazed women surrounding them.

"Can we talk?" Rebecca asked timidly.

LaRoux playfully replied, "Uh-oh, this sounds serious." He looked at Brown and Backus, who were waist deep in a debate concerning the Saints's playoff prospects, even though the season had yet to begin. "Gentlemen, if you will excuse us."

"Of course," Brown said, keeping one eye on Backus as if he were going to slide a poker card from his sleeve.

Rebecca walked over to the edge of the terrace and gazed out across the vastness of lights illuminating The Palazzo property. "This is amazing."

Trailing her path, taking in a different visual splendor, LaRoux concurred, "Yes, you most certainly are."

Rebecca went to turn but found LaRoux's arms wrapping around her waist and his lips exploring her bare shoulder. Trying her best to remain focused, she trembled. "Okay, playboy, it's confession time. Why am I here? I Googled you. Do you know how many images of David LaRoux I found on the internet?"

"I wouldn't begin to know," David whispered in Rebecca's ear. He moved directly behind her and raked his cheek and nose through her hair.

"I stopped counting at one hundred. And did you know, although I'm sure you don't, there was not a single picture of you with a woman older than—let's say for argument's sake, twenty-five. There are tons of paparazzi-type pictures where you are having way too much fun."

LaRoux moved to Rebecca's right ear and nibbled gently. Lacking any serious effort, her attempt to turn was unsuccessful. "Please stop. You're making this most difficult." LaRoux guided Rebecca around until their eyes met. With hers a half-inch below his, she looked up at his soulfully innocent expression. *Son of a bitch. I'll bet he had my shoes custom made just for this moment.* "David, why are you doing this?"

"Let me ask you a question, detective."

Rebecca's heart skipped a beat as she tensed at LaRoux's choice of words. Surely, he would not push her off the balcony with so many witnesses—witnesses that were completely engaged in the semi-naked Thunder across the pool. *The man truly knows how to plan a murder. Dammit, somebody look this way.*

"While you were conducting your internet-based investigation, did you see a single picture where I look like this?" And there it was again, summoned at will like an On Demand movie—his eyes reached inside her soul, soothing her fears and filling her heart with longing.

"No." Rebecca's reply was infused with lustful, long-unfulfilled desire—and guilt. Could she ever get past Will Martin's allegations? As she looked at LaRoux, her lips parted, beckoning him.

LaRoux kissed her passionately, short-circuiting any remaining objections. In the shadows of the poolside cabana, surrounded by aromatic blossoms, they kissed like new love, or love parting for all eternity.

The romantic spectacle, sure to be envied, was mostly lost in the presence of the wicked festivities across the pool. As their lips finally parted, LaRoux gently held Rebecca's face. "Why you? Since I first set my eyes on you, not an hour passes that you're not on my mind. I look at you, and I want nothing else. You have this adorable quirk," he explained as his fingers caressed her lips, parting them. "Yeah, like that, and when you do that, I can't stop obsessing. I have never needed to kiss a woman so desperately." He stroked Rebecca's cheek.

"I need to know you can feel the same way." His hand slipped from Rebecca's cheek and delicately settled over her heart.

God, he's going to feel that, Rebecca mused as her heart erupted to the sensation of his touch.

"I'd love to know why I feel this way, but I don't. I wasn't looking for this. But as each hour passes, everything I've known loses meaning in the shadows of this blinding desire. I'm falling in love with you, Rebecca. That's my *why.*"

"Oh my," Rebecca murmured. This was certainly not the confession the DEA was looking for. She studied LaRoux's face waiting for the *just kidding* punch line. "David, I'm not sure if I know how to be in love with someone like you. You're rich, and well . . . just look at you. Would you settle for going to your room for something a little less intimidating for the time being?"

LaRoux's instincts said, *Hell yes.* Fortunately, before he screamed his answer, he remembered his room was bugged and his second room might be under surveillance by now. Quickly, he inventoried his options: One, sex anywhere but his room. *Been there, done that.* And while he knew how hot spontaneous, risqué sex could be, Rebecca had to be more than that—at least the first time. Two, get yet another room. But if tonight was the cornerstone of his new life, he didn't want to start it with a lie. There would be no quick explanation for the condition of his suite. Three, just say *no.* He could make provisions for tomorrow night and map out a full, well-orchestrated confession—perhaps not a complete disclosure just yet, but cover the major points of his existence that she might find objectionable. He looked into Rebecca's eyes and realized option three was not voluntary—it was a mandatory.

His silence forced Rebecca to question her tactics. The man had just bared his soul, and her response was probably not the one he had been looking for. But honestly, *this* was the one scenario she was completely unprepared to face. "Well, don't you know how to make a girl feel awkward? I haven't offered myself for quite some time—like really long. Did I misread your intentions?" LaRoux's silence continued to baffle Rebecca as a couple of options stampeded through her mind: *Will Martin's allegations are complete bullshit. I could leave the DEA and run away with this handsome, wealthy, virtual stranger. Either way, my true identity will eventually surface and fuck up everything.*

LaRoux was lost amidst his dilemma, so Rebecca's angst barely registered. Her fragile expression tasered back his attention. "If you knew just how badly I want to say *yes*—to sex *right* now—but tonight is for your sister. I don't want to be selfish and take you away from her anymore than I already have. But tomorrow night, whether it's here, or back home, you're going to have to deal with me for hours, maybe days, or even weeks."

Aroused and frustrated, Rebecca asked, "How can you just turn it off, just like that?

Is it some kind of control thing or is saying and doing the right thing simply scripted in your DNA?"

Laying into his Southernize, LaRoux stepped back and crossed his arms. "My dear Miss Tracy, whatever are you talking about?"

"Oh, you know what I'm talking about, David LaRoux." Rebecca placed her hands on her hips and mimicked his accent. "The precision in which you executed this weekend right down to the waltz, my omelet, the afternoon on the bayou, this dress, the shoes, and practically everything you say—are you always going to be so damned perfect?"

LaRoux chuckled; after all, the answer was *yes*. He inspected Rebecca's attire, starting with her shoes. Returning to the height of her eyes, she was perfect. "So, I trust everything fit just fine?"

Rebecca sighed as she dug into her clutch. "I tried to wear these, I really did. But *they* were not perfect." She placed the sheer panties in LaRoux's hand.

He drew the silk fabric to his nose and inhaled. "So, you did try them on."

"Think about that—hard—when you're back in your room tonight, alone." Rebecca kissed LaRoux on the cheek. She turned to the festivities across the water and shook her head. She looked back over her shoulder at LaRoux and said in her Southern belle accent, "Maybe when those sweaty Thunder boys are done working, I might be able to persuade one of them to help me with my zipper on this incredibly perfect-fitting dress. What do you think, Mr. LaRoux?" She strutted away, using her hips as an instrument of torment and revenge.

Now alone, LaRoux brushed the lingerie against his face as he took in Rebecca's scent again. "Oh, Miss Tracy, whatever am I going to do with you?"

* * *

Staggering, stumbling, and laughing all the way back to their room, Rebecca and her fellow agents had proven their alcohol-induced performances Oscar worthy. "Holy crap," Sean said as she unsuccessfully navigated the card reader. "I think it's broken."

"That's your Visa, ya ditz." Margo cackled as she gave Sean a gentle nudge that made her tumble out of her way. Laughing wildly as she fell from her heels, Sean said, "Hurry up. I gotta pee."

Just as the door cracked open, Director Martin's angry voice greeted the unsuspecting agents. "Just what in the hell do you think you've been doing? The four of you are drunk, and I haven't heard a single report from you all since Saturday. You were sent to get inside of LaRoux's organization, and thus far all you have done is turn my investigation into your personal spring break."

"And just how do you suggest we infiltrate his organization when all he has done thus far is party? What did you expect—that after one meeting he'd invite us into his office and confess all of his wrongdoings over a line of cocaine and cupcakes?" Rebecca's lack of respect for Martin was obvious.

"I sure didn't expect you to jump in bed at the first opportunity."

"You're out of line," Rebecca snapped. "A word in private, Director." Rebecca stormed into the bedroom and waited at the door for Martin to follow. As she closed the door, Mary, Sean, and Margo silently stepped down to the sunken living room and sat on the couch. They turned their heads toward the bedroom, and Mary whispered, "Better her than me."

"I don't think this is going to end well for any of us." Sean grabbed the bottle of vodka. "If I'm going down, no sense in doing it sober." As she dispersed the shots, they sat eavesdropping in silence, attempting to ascertain the depth of their trouble.

"Will, this is bullshit," Rebecca fired off. "First, I have *not* slept with LaRoux. Second, if we don't play his game, how in the hell do you expect us to get close enough to earn his trust?"

"So, that kiss on the terrace, that was just your way of—"

"Grow up, Will! What the hell did you expect? He'd settle for a handshake goodnight?"

"I *expected* it would be one of the others."

Rebecca shook her head. "Oh, so this isn't about my team's behavior. It's about mine."

Will stepped away from Rebecca's wrath. He stared across the lagoon at Treasure Island and sighed. "I thought I was over us. But over the last week, it's been painfully obvious how much I've missed you—how big of a mistake I made."

Rebecca remained planted by the door. She folded her arms tensely across her chest.

"So, this tirade, disrespecting me in front of my team, is about childish jealousy?"

Will turned back to Rebecca. "Won't you let me admit I made a mistake and think about giving us another chance?"

"Mistake? What happened between us was you being true to your nature. As far as mistakes go, outside of sleeping with you, the only mistake I see is your suspicions about LaRoux. Not one member of my team has discovered a single trace of evidence to indicate illegal activities. LaRoux is here with the *governor* and a *senator* to make some kind of deal to bring a huge casino to Louisiana. That's all. And that party last night? Not a trace of any illegal substances. Personally, I think you're barking up the wrong tree."

"Exactly. He's too fucking clean. And how do you explain Agent Wells's disappearance?"

"For all we know, he could be deep undercover somewhere. It wouldn't be the first time that an agent has gone dark, would it? I read his reports. Wells was mixing it up with a lot of dealers, trying to find a connection to LaRoux. If it were my investigation, I'd be focusing my resources on those dealers."

Martin hadn't heard a word of Rebecca's theory. He stared at his vision of desire, fantasizing about removing his former lover's dress. Instantly recognizing *that* expression, and repulsed by his habitual caveman mentality, Rebecca took a step back. *The son of a bitch will never change.*

"You are leaving, and I'm going to bed." She took him by the arm and ushered him back into the living room. Aggravated beyond reason, she declared, "And, Will, try not to fuck any of my roommates on your way out."

CHAPTER 8

MANY HOURS LATER, WALT found his boss.

"Where'd you disappear to last night, David? When you never showed, we organized a search and rescue party." Walt spread a towel on the mesh poolside chair and sat on the edge facing his friend. "The problem is, when you vanished from the hotel security cameras, you never resurfaced."

Thanks to Hanson, LaRoux knew practically every conceivable blind spot in the hotel security system. "Actually, I've more or less been right here—all night."

"What the hell?" Walt reached over and tugged LaRoux's sunglasses down his nose so he could gauge his boss's disposition through his eyes. "Is everything alright?"

Still clutching Rebecca's silk panties, LaRoux rolled the concealed fabric between his fingers. "Walt, do you think if my pops could have done it over, outside of getting himself and Mom killed, do you think he would have made different choices?"

Walt stared intently at LaRoux. He knew the correct answer, but he was not sure if it was what LaRoux needed to hear.

"Do you think I'm living the life my parents would have wanted for me?"

"Okay, I think I know what's going on now." Walt sat back and signaled the passing waitress. After he and LaRoux placed orders, Walt said, "This whole thing with Rebecca, she's older, definitely more mature than your normal *flavor of the week*, and she's obviously planted some kind of notion in your head that guys your age should be settled down. If you're asking me if that's what Pops would have wanted, I'd say, as long as you're happy, he would've been too."

"And do you think if I wanted to walk away from all of this, the family business and all, Pops would have been fine with it?"

"Walk away, David?" Walt leaned into LaRoux. "With her? How much does she know?"

LaRoux rolled his head away.

"David, you don't even know this woman. One wrong word from her could bring your entire empire down and take us with it. Her sister's best friend is a cop, for God's sake. If you've told her anything, then you've got to know . . . she's gotta go for a little boat ride down on the bayou."

"You don't get to make that call, Walt. Besides, she knows nothing— yet. But the time may come that she might. I'm ready to settle down, maybe even have a family. I've known it long enough to know it's not just some passing fancy. But there's no way I would ever want my children to do the evil that I have had to do in this business."

"What, do this?" Walt gestured to the sunbathers lounging by the poolside. "Or that?" He pointed to three bikini-clad women passing by. "You and I both know this business will all be legal one day. And we both know the difference between *legal* and *illegal* is measured by whose pockets the bloody fucking dollars fall in. Every success story, legitimate or not, has its victims." As LaRoux's expression eased, Walt scanned for any eavesdroppers. "Are we cool?"

"Yep."

"And victims, specifically ours, given the opportunity, would have done the same to us. How many times have I heard you say we don't go to war expecting a bouquet of roses from our enemies?"

"Trust me, I hear you loud and clear, Walt. It's not what we've done, and I'm okay with every decision that's been made. But it doesn't mean that I would want to put a loved one in harm's way just for the sake of money." LaRoux pushed his sunglasses up and eased back. "So, tell me, Walt, do I continue on with business as usual until I'm old and alone, or do I make a change, maybe even disappear? I could always trade places with my brother. Hell, he's been hiding all over Europe for far too long. Isn't time to find some real meaning in my life?"

"David, we're gonna have to finish this later. Here comes Ryan and the girls."

Just as LaRoux's tractor-beam gaze locked on Rebecca, the waitress reappeared. She set their drinks on the table, blocking LaRoux's field of vision. In a huff, he stood from his chair for an unobstructed view.

Walt punched his thigh. "Damn, son, it's not like you've never seen a woman before. You are completely ate up with her."

The waitress realized she was the source of LaRoux's irritation, and she said, "Oh, I am so sorry."

"Oh no, baby," Walt pleaded, "don't you apologize to mean ol' Mr. LaRoux. You see, my friend has led a very sheltered life up until now. He has never seen, never even attempted, to look at a woman over thirty in a bathing suit before. The thought actually terrorized him." The waitress smiled as Walt continued his sarcastic banter. "And now, after years of such a shallow existence, he has suddenly awoken to the error of his ways. So, please forgive my rude friend, and as punishment, put everybody's drinks on his tab." The waitress looked at LaRoux, who quickly nodded his affirmation. Walt placed a one-hundred-dollar bill on the girl's tray. "That's for you, and if he dares to pull any more of that crap, you have my permission to *spill* the next round on him."

Walt rose to meet the approaching entourage as the waitress scampered away. "Ladies, ladies, ladies, I must say, everyone is looking quite fine this afternoon, considering the condition you were in when we parted last night. And those bathing suits . . . ooh wee!"

Mary stepped in front of LaRoux and hesitated briefly. "David, Taz told me how much you hate this, but I have to thank you anyway for everything you've done for us. There's no way I can ever begin to repay you or express how much fun we've had. And I know it's no big deal to you, but there's no way we could have ever afforded anything this extravagant."

They all stood in silence waiting as LaRoux's attention appeared to be lost in some distant memory. Throughout his childhood, his parents had taught him that generosity is the simplest expression of gratitude. And at this moment, he was, perhaps, more grateful than ever. But for the first time, his emotions were tethered to a twelve-thousand-pound elephant, and it was dragging him to an unexplored territory. Suddenly, he found himself saying, "It's not that I hate the expression of gratitude, but in situations such as this, *thank you* has ordinarily been closely followed by *goodbye*. Until now, that has *always* been a comfortable routine. But you ladies have provided my friends—and me—with hours of delightful companionship. I feel we've been taking advantage of you for putting up with us this weekend. What little money has been spent—it pales to the experience. So, actually, I need to be thanking all of you."

LaRoux continued. "As a result of my parents' tragic deaths, I have avoided all possibilities of any sort of relationships involving . . . attachment. That has always been a most hollow, empty place to be. And now—"

Ryan interrupted. "Whoa, do I hear the *David's had too much to drink* alarm ringing? I think it'd be a good idea to let Walt and David finish their conversation. Come, girls, the bar is calling." As they left for it, Rebecca passed LaRoux with a bashful smile. She glanced to find his attention intently following her.

Walt punched LaRoux in the thigh a second time. "Are you kidding me? TMI, David. What in the hell was that all about?"

* * *

Later, LaRoux and Rebecca found themselves alone while the rest of their party lounged in folding chairs by the main pool.

"I know I haven't known you nearly long enough to gauge your typical behavior, but I'd have to say you've been unusually quiet this afternoon. Is everything alright?" Rebecca asked.

With the sun receding, the shadows had begun encroaching on the lounge chairs. For the first time all day, LaRoux removed his sunglasses. The action revealed weary, troubled eyes. He turned in his chair so that he could face Rebecca, and just as quickly, he removed her sunglasses too. "If I ask you to take off with me, to leave everything behind, would you go?"

Rebecca was completely unprepared for the implications and ramifications of the question set before her. A tidal wave of confusion slammed her, but her heart screamed *yes*. Her brain said *maybe*. And the logic of the career agent explained that *this* was the opportunity Martin had scripted—for one of the other agents. From the core of her very being, guilt over her deception was the riptide pulling her under. "I have a job," was all she could manage.

"I can offer you a better one."

"We really don't know each other."

"Run away, and we will."

"What if it doesn't work out?"

"I'll put you on a plane to anywhere you desire, and you can keep the new job with the obscene salary."

"What about your company?"

"I have highly skilled people who can run it just fine."

Rebecca was absolutely dumbfounded. Nothing, not a single scintilla of evidence, indicated that this man had committed any crime. *Will's intel has to be wrong.* She looked at LaRoux, so easy on the eyes, and her heartbeat intensified. If this were a movie, the happy ending would have her running away with LaRoux.

"Yes," she replied like a timid child, "I'll go with you." LaRoux's eyes were piercing—plunging deeper than she knew possible. *Back away,* she thought, *or he will see the deception in my eyes.*

"When I say run away, I mean precisely that. Disappear with me, cut loose of all ties—until we find out who we really are, what we are meant to be to each other."

Rebecca blinked. "Can I call my mother first?"

LaRoux looked side to side, appearing nervous. "There's something I've got to tell you now, before it's too late to turn back." He paused, then looked about uneasily. "The only obstacle to our happiness will be the truth." He looked deep into Rebecca's eyes. "My company is dirty. It has been for centuries. We import drugs more than any other entity in the country. We are so deeply immersed in the narco culture that ending those relationships will be like severing my spinal cord. My only option is to run and never look back."

Oh shit! Rebecca cast her emotions to the side and found herself probing LaRoux for more information she could take back to the agency. "Have you tried?"

"CCI has always been involved in the world of contraband. From slaves to fabric, booze, raw materials, guns—my family has always had a hand in the world of illegal supply and demand. The drugs actually started with Pops. He made a few bad business decisions, which forced him into undesirable partnerships. When he decided to make a clean break from the cartels . . ."

LaRoux looked away briefly before concluding, "That's why my parents were killed."

Rebecca experienced a mental whiplash—she empathized with the man. It wasn't his fault that he'd found himself in the criminal underworld. Suddenly, she was the woman who had fallen for LaRoux again, not the agent. She replied, "Oh my God, David. Can't you go to the DEA and get witness protection?"

"Witness protection? Honestly, Rebecca, I *am* the big fish. My connections are vast and much smaller, and the others are mostly un-extraditable. The only way out for me is to run, disappear, and never look back. I can do it—but not without you."

Rebecca's emotions were spiraling out of control. Whether for professional or personal reasons, she had to go. But if she were to forsake her life and career, she would have to tell LaRoux the truth, right now.

"I don't know what to say, David. This is crazy. I really care about you, and yet I hardly know you. You're generous, charming, funny, and apparently more honest than any man I've ever known." She paused to reel in her emotions. "I knew your reputation, and honestly, I expected all of this indulgence to eventually lead to the bedroom— and I *was* more than ready for that. But I wasn't expecting love, or especially crime—and then your offer to give up everything—for me? I just don't get it."

LaRoux could see the raging debate and confusion in Rebecca's eyes. "Give me the opportunity to prove what you've done to me, now that you have changed me. You can always leave tomorrow, or the next day, or the day after. I'm willing to give up everything just for that chance. I promise you will never know another day without love."

Walt arrived just beyond the hedges and called out to the pair. "Hey, guys, I hate to break up your private time, but we've got to boogie. Our dinner reservations are just over an hour away. If we miss them, we'll likely have to wait until after the show to eat."

"An hour? There's no way I can get ready sharing the bathroom with Mary."

"Grab your stuff, and go up to my room and shower." LaRoux carefully inspected the key cards in his pocket and handed Rebecca the non-bugged one. "It's thirty-five twenty. I'll need about fifteen minutes to chat with the boys, so that should give you ample time." Rebecca took the key and stared at it before looking back at LaRoux.

"Thirty-five twenty?" She'd received intel that he was in a room on the thirty-third floor and had not been informed about the room change.

"Yes," LaRoux answered without hesitation or suspicion.

"Again, the answer is *yes*. I will go with you." She planted a quick kiss on his cheek before scampering off.

As soon as she cleared the pool and disappeared from view, LaRoux picked up the phone Walt had deposited on the table. He dialed Hanson.

"Where in the hell have you been, David? We've got to talk—right now."

"I'll be up in ten minutes. In the meantime, Rebecca is going to her room to get her things and then going to shower in my safe room. Make sure the feds don't see her leave her room or go into mine." LaRoux hung up and headed over to Walt, who was waiting with Ryan near the bar.

"Sorry, boss, the time slipped away." Ryan smirked. "Great call on bringing the girls. They've been a blast."

"College graduates with careers, my friend. Different maturity skill sets to be sure." LaRoux craned his neck skyward to look toward the thirty-fifth floor. "If we don't make dinner or the show, don't wait up."

"Yeah, buddy," Ryan cheered. "David LaRoux is back on his game. I told you he'd come around, Walt."

LaRoux ignored Ryan's juvenile boasts. "Are you gonna be able to resurrect Taz in time?"

"Your boy was on a mission last night. Apparently, you're not the only one the love bug bit." Ryan chuckled.

"Please tell me it's not the cop," LaRoux groused. "That's all I need right now."

"Me and Walt, we've got our suspicions, but ol' Taz was trying to play coy," Ryan explained. "I checked on him about a half hour ago, and he was stirring. That'll be the last time that son of a bitch forgets his coconut water."

"Okay, guys, I'll see you later, or maybe I won't. But either way, have fun and *do not* come knocking on my door."

Ryan smiled. "You too, boss. If you need any help—"

LaRoux waved off Ryan's insinuation and walked away. As he left his friends behind, a sudden bout of anticipation struck; Rebecca would be in *his* shower, warm, wet, and soapy. Suddenly, he had no desire to see Hanson. He glanced at his watch. She should be in his room in five minutes. Whatever Hanson had to say could be relayed in that time. That was a far better option than the shitstorm that would ensue if he were to blow off the meeting.

* * *

The elevator doors slid open. As LaRoux turned the corner, his room beckoned. Just thinking about Rebecca being in there, a dozen doors away, naked, and anticipating his arrival, filled him with warmth. Meanwhile, just ten doors away, Victor, who had moved floors to be near LaRoux's new room, was waiting—boring-ass Victor, who was certainly about to ream him a new asshole over his disappearing stunt last night. With the weight of his future on his shoulders, he had needed to be alone—consequences be damned.

As he neared Hanson's room, he noticed its door was ajar. Cautiously, he stepped inside to find Hanson sitting in a chair beside the bed. On the comforter lay a handgun with a silencer.

"Vic?"

"We've got some major issues, David." When David said nothing, Hanson went on, "A Colombian crew with several reputable hitters rolled into The Palazzo this morning packing some heavy artillery. They've shown no interest in venturing outside the hotel. We've encountered one of their guys before—in Miami. My facial recognition software picked him up. I don't know who the bastard is, but if he acts anything like he did in Miami, it's not good. If someone sold you out to the DEA, maybe they've tipped off these mutts at The Palazzo as well."

While staring at the gun, LaRoux asked in a deadpan tone, "Next issue?"

"Nothing major, just that William Martin arrived here yesterday." He tossed out a picture.

LaRoux knew better than to ask—Hanson was never wrong. As anxiety festered, LaRoux bottled it while appearing to remain calm. "He looks familiar."

"He should. A little over a year ago at the House of Blues, completely by pure fucking bad luck, you were dancing exceptionally close with one of his little fucklings. He shows up drunk—"

"And I knocked his ass out cold."

"You need to let me run full background checks on any woman you are remotely interested in before you ever open your mouth—or unzip your pants. Martin is a territorial prick. Once he found out that David LaRoux had put him down, he began an investigation—a very personal vendetta. Allow me to reintroduce you to Rebecca *Pearson*." Hanson tossed out a second picture. "I believe you already know *Agent* Pearson. She is a twelve-year veteran in the Seattle office, a former fuck buddy of Martin's, and, if I'm not mistaken, is currently in your bedroom." Victor tossed three more pictures on the bed. "Agents Sean Peterson and Mary Sampson each have less than a year in the agency and apparently were chosen because they fit *your* profile. Margo Carter is NOPD and was most likely chosen to deflect any suspicion about the others. You know the cover: if *they* admit one is a cop, then the others must be clean."

LaRoux studied the image of Rebecca as feelings of betrayal seared his heart. "She knows too much."

"I thought that might be the case. I've already worked out our exit strategy. I'm going to invite our little friends in The Palazzo over for a little *got caught in the crossfire* party with the DEA. The Colombians will take care of the DEA, and I will take care of the Colombians. You don't need to be involved. After I make sure all of our friends no longer pose any threat, you and I are going to have a long talk about my position and your behavior. Understood?"

LaRoux looked up from the gun, unable to conceal his pain. "What's with that?"

"I borrowed that lovely Sig from the Colombian's room an hour ago. It actually has your boy from Miami's prints all over it. I'll be using it to make sure the aggression escalates."

LaRoux stared back down at the gun. "I think your odds will be better with one less agent to deal with. Ms. *Pearson* is personal, and I always take care of my own."

"I knew you would. There are gloves in the drawer. Do make sure you return the Sig." Hanson rose from the chair and placed his hand on LaRoux's shoulder. "I'm sorry, David. I know this one was different. I know you had aspirations for something more. The Raven will be ready, if you need it."

"How about a heart surgeon? That's what I need." LaRoux wriggled his hand into a surgical glove and picked up the gun. Then he draped a towel over his hand and nodded at Hanson. "If this goes south, it may become necessary to call in my brother." As he slowly closed the door behind him, LaRoux suddenly realized just how much he hated the game.

CHAPTER 9

LAROUX SAT RIGID IN the bedside chair and listened to the cascading water as he tapped his foot incessantly. He envisioned Rebecca's shimmering body as the water cleansed her—and the kill shot about to transpire. Ten minutes ago, he was anticipating caressing her silky flesh in the shower. Now, he fidgeted with the silencer, twisting it again to ensure it was tight. LaRoux had been betrayed, and Rebecca's judgment would come swiftly, her sentence served without prejudice. His action would not be impulsive, avenging her own deceit.

The water stopped, and the shower door creaked open. Then the towel rack rattled. LaRoux steadied his foot as he realized that at any second, Rebecca would emerge and they would be face-to-face. His heart pounded like a pile driver, methodically slow, callously deliberate. He grasped a throw pillow to conceal the cold messenger of his wrath. *Don't let her speak*, his conscious warned, *she'll only make you weak.*

The door swung open, and Rebecca emerged in a terrycloth robe with her hair wet and untamed. At the sight, a lump rose in LaRoux's throat, and a silent, unnerving expression cast a shadow on his face. Startled by his look, Rebecca recoiled briefly.

"I kept expecting for you to join me. Is everything alright?"

Conflicting emotions instantly overwhelmed LaRoux's resolve. "Please sit." Rebecca feigned a smile as she toweled her hair and headed toward him.

"No. On the bed, if you please . . . *Agent Pearson.*"

Rebecca froze as fear launched a wave of dread through her. LaRoux's confessions of love and then crime had been so tenderly and freely offered. Had he done so just for the sake of some demented superiority mind game?

"David?"

LaRoux slid the pillow from his lap to reveal the Sig clutched in his gloved hand. He pointed the nine-millimeter at Rebecca with a surgeon's steady grasp as he repeated, "Please sit."

On the bed, her dress was neatly laid out for tonight. She sat between the dress and a small box. Neither had been there when she arrived in the room. Rebecca clutched her bathrobe out of fear. Perhaps if she could stall LaRoux, Martin's crew would storm the room. Though he had changed rooms, surely they had seen her arrive. But LaRoux's foreboding expression told her it did not matter; he was ready to die as well.

"I can't begin to imagine what you're thinking, Rebecca. So, why don't we begin by clearing the air of all your deceit." With his left hand, LaRoux reached for the glass of bourbon on the table beside him. "Customarily, I don't drink alone and would offer you a glass. But under the circumstances, I hope you will forgive my ill manners. Likewise, I never drink in situations such as this. But tonight's predicament dictates I break protocol."

Where are they? Rebecca fretted. *The door should have been demolished five seconds ago.* But not even the slightest footfall could be heard from within the suite. Those eyes, which not even an hour ago held such passion, were now dark and soulless.

"David, despite the agency's preliminary intel on your organization, I honestly believed they had it all wrong. Before our poolside chat, I was struggling to find a way . . . to tell you what I was. And even after you told me the truth, I still wanted—" Rebecca looked down at her lap.

Is this her shame? LaRoux studied every aspect of her performance.

"I came up here . . . wanting you so badly . . . despite the truth. I would have gone with you."

The desperation in Rebecca's voice did nothing to deviate the focus of the Sig's barrel. "I guess I'm not such a good judge of character after all."

Gone was the endearing, soothingly calm tone that LaRoux had grown so fond of. Without lowering the Sig, he took a swig of bourbon. "Apparently, neither am I. How about for the next minute or two we agree the jury is still out?"

Rebecca could not return the smile; in her twelve years at the DEA, she had never found herself the target of a loaded gun. "From where I'm sitting, it would appear as though the verdict is in and I'm on the way to the gallows."

"I apologize, Agent Pearson, if this is awkward for you. You cannot begin to imagine how stressful this is for me."

"Stressful . . . for you? Isn't this what you do? You orchestrated this entire production. How long have you been playing *me*?"

LaRoux finished his drink and began pouring another. With his eyes locked on Rebecca, he partially missed the glass and the bourbon pooled on the table. "Played you? From the moment I laid eyes on you, I have been nothing but honest about my feelings. I was ready to give up a billion-dollar empire just for you. But just minutes ago, I got a harsh reminder of how love can rip your heart out. Not since my parents were killed have I felt so utterly demolished. This was *not orchestrated*." LaRoux waved his drink between them, sloshing bourbon on the carpet.

"This, Rebecca, is why I've never let a woman get close. This sucks!"

Rebecca felt the truth of his words and the pressing burden of shame. "I know you will never believe me, but I'd rather none of this had happened than hurt you like I have."

The crushing weight of LaRoux's raw emotions yielded a tear from the corner of his eye. "I'll tell you what, Agent Pearson, let's put love or death to the test. But before we do, you should know that only one of us gets to walk out of this room." LaRoux took another drink. "This is actually good stuff," he said as he peeked at the glass beneath his lips. "It's a shame I'm not in the mood to share. I'm going to lay the rest of my cards on the table, just so you have a complete understanding of your situation. We knew back home that the DEA was watching us. If you're wondering why your buddies have not come to your rescue, it's because we knew they had bugged my room. Ergo, they have no idea we're in *this* room. We—I—just didn't know that *you and your friends* were also DEA."

The reality that she had no backup instantly registered on Rebecca's face.

"That's right, Agent Pearson, you are all alone this time. Not even your roommates will find you. Here's the true tragedy. If I had known two hours ago about you, neither of us would be sitting here." LaRoux finished his glass and poured another. "But sadly, fate has fucked the both of us. I'm not going to entertain any promises or potential deals, so there's no need to worry yourself about what to say that might save your ass. This is going to be pretty simple. I'm not worried about the future of my empire. My people have prepared for this scenario long before I took the reins at CCI. I will not trade my freedom on the backs of those who have trusted me, nor will I ever do one day in prison. Are you with me so far?"

With her throat parched from fright and barely audible, she replied, "Yes."

The tear that had formed now ran the length of LaRoux's face; the bitterness in his words rang out. "I fell in love . . . with you, Rebecca. Beside that dress is the first, and last, piece of evidence that you will ever see. I bought it this morning." LaRoux finished the glass and set it down. He pointed to the small box on the bed. "Open it," he insisted.

"David, please." Rebecca's hands trembled.

"Open the damn box!"

She reached for the box and flipped the top to reveal a stunning diamond ring.

"I would have married you, Rebecca."

Rebecca beheld LaRoux's agony that *she* had inflicted. She had lived with that same devastation, courtesy of her current boss. In the face of that raw memory, the consequences of her fate no longer mattered.

"I have always warned everyone who gets in this game that death is an intricate cog that sooner or later turns on us all." He wiped away another tear and stepped back. "Stand up, Rebecca."

"David, I'm sorry."

With lightning precision, LaRoux ejected the magazine and held it out for Rebecca to inspect. He slammed it back in the grip and racked the Sig. "The game has worn me down. You brought love into my life and then ripped it away. I will not go to prison." He grabbed the barrel and offered the grip to Rebecca. "Only one of us gets to walk out of this room."

Rebecca took the cold gun. This was no test; she knew the gun was ready to fire. As her finger slid to the trigger, a sea of emotion relentlessly pommeled her logic. She had never pulled the trigger on a perp. But this was kill or be killed. LaRoux had already confessed his intention.

"There's no going back. If I let you live, my associates will know I've gone soft. They *will* kill us both. Pull the trigger." Rebecca stared at the gun.

"Only one of us gets to leave. I can't . . . I can't kill you . . . not now," LaRoux said.

As she raised the Sig and mindlessly aimed at his chest, their eyes met. She took a final inventory of LaRoux's face and in that moment understood she would never again witness the love that hauntingly stared back. She shook her head and placed the gun on the bed. She picked up the ring and slid it on her finger. "I love you, David LaRoux." Slowly, she unfastened her robe and let it fall to the floor.

Bound by the promise of death, their absolute love was irrevocably uncaged; the two desperate lovers were left with nowhere to hide.

* * *

"At the risk of sounding cliché, that was absolutely amazing." Rebecca pulled the dampened sheets over her as she nuzzled into LaRoux's arms.

"I would say the feeling is quite mutual, but then I expected nothing less. I've waited a long time for you." LaRoux grinned with content as he pulled the sheets back and took in the visual delight of Rebecca's shimmering body.

"Three days—that had to be some kind of personal record for you, Mr. LaRoux." She snatched the satin sheets back up again, clutched them below her chin, and rolled to her side.

LaRoux pulled the sheets from the bottom of the bed and flipped them over Rebecca's head to expose her every delicacy. "On the contrary, Ms. Pearson, I'd say more like my entire life." He lightly kissed her pelvic bone and slowly migrated south. Rebecca rolled on her stomach and attempted to recover herself. Underneath the sheets, LaRoux's lips explored the length of her hamstrings and the crease of her knee while his hands kneaded her calves.

"Stop that this instant, or I will have you arrested for sexual misconduct."

LaRoux's hands slipped back up her inner thigh and found his intended target. "*Arrêtez-moi, si tu peux.*"

"Dammit, you speak French?" Rebecca moaned.

"*Oui, mademoiselle,*" LaRoux replied seductively. As his lips painstakingly explored the tender flesh of her thigh, Rebecca's resistance crumpled in a series of ecstatic moans. Flustered by the twisted sheets, she flailed her arms to free herself of the entanglement. She rolled onto her back, then pulled LaRoux up until his lips met hers. "If you don't stop, my legs will become completely useless and you will have to carry me to dinner."

LaRoux nibbled her lips softly before kissing her deeply. "It's quite alright. I can call for a bellman to bring a luggage cart to deliver you."

"That would not surprise me." Rebecca chuckled.

* * *

LaRoux made the short trip down the hall while Rebecca showered for a second time.

"David, what the hell is going on?" Irate with LaRoux's two-hour disappearance, Hanson paced the floor like a rabid dog in a pen.

LaRoux and Rebecca had blown dinner with Walt and the others.

"I'm improvising," LaRoux claimed boldly as he placed the Sig on the bed.

"You're fucking her is what you're doing."

"Can you blame me?"

"If she doesn't make an appearance soon, all hell is going to break loose. Martin is getting frantic over not being able to locate his favorite ex-piece of trim." Hanson studied the monitors again. "He needs to see her."

"Relax, Vic. We're about to get some dinner."

"Please do," Hanson said as he cut a stern glare at LaRoux. "David, I don't know what the hell you're up to, but it seems to me quite reckless. Are you trying to get busted?"

"Relax, Vic. I'm formulating a masterpiece." LaRoux smiled with reserved confidence. "What are our little Colombian friends doing?" LaRoux asked as he peered around the bank of computers.

"Anything you care to share, Sherlock?" Hanson stared at LaRoux with contempt, but got no response; LaRoux was immune to his best scowls. Hanson sighed heavily before reporting, "They are being too quiet. Something's going down, and I think that something is you. There's no chance this guy from Miami just happened to be in Vegas the same weekend as you, and stay in the same hotel. I've been monitoring their phones as best as I can, but for now—*nada*. Either someone in your organization or the DEA tipped them off." Victor opened an image file. "Emilio here, or whatever his name is, comes to

Vegas about three times a year, but never in the heat of summer, and he always stays at The Cosmopolitan. And what's really pissing me off is that outside of that, he's a damned ghost. I know every major South American player, but he is totally off the grid."

"For a ghost, you sure seem to know some pertinent details."

Hanson's scowl persisted. "He's a big-time gambler, except for this trip—at least so far—which means he's in the gaming system, but under an alias. But outside of that, *this* Emilio Lopez does not exist anywhere else on the planet. Anything else you want to know, like how many rolls of shit paper he's used since he arrived?"

LaRoux placed his hand on Hanson's shoulder. "When we go down for dinner, how about putting a clean gun in my suite. And you might want to wipe the Sig. Agent Pearson's prints are all over it." Hanson's scowl broadened as he inspected the Sig.

"How the fuck . . . never mind. I don't want to know." Hanson stood and leaned over the monitor bank. "David, are you going to let me in on what you're planning?" LaRoux did not respond.

"Dammit, David! Do you honestly think that just because you gave her an orgasm she'll fall in love with you and forsake the bust of a lifetime?"

"Got a new phone, Vic?" LaRoux held out his hand, already knowing the answer. As Hanson deliberately withheld the new phone, LaRoux gave in to his intentions with a sigh. "Victor, what little she knows is barely more than her boss. And there's no way in hell they can prove any of their suspicions."

Hanson rolled his eyes. "Bitch probably faked her orgasm." He slapped the phone in LaRoux's palm and warned, "Mark my words, David. She's going be the end of you."

LaRoux smiled confidently as he tucked the phone into his pocket. "Some things, Vic, are inevitable."

* * *

Upon returning to his room, LaRoux found Rebecca dressed and applying the finishing touches to her makeup. "I hope you don't mind the express version. I only grabbed a few things from my room, and I'm so hungry."

LaRoux inspected her work. "Express is quite beautiful." He moved behind Rebecca, slid his hands over her thighs, and firmly explored her muscles while he kissed her neck.

"I know it's early in our relationship, but I'm getting a vibe that if I want to wear pants, I'll have to buy them myself."

LaRoux's hands slipped higher. "Pants make it awfully hard to do this."

Rebecca arched her head onto LaRoux's shoulders. "Hmm, and if you keep doing that, we're never going to get out of this room."

"My mistake. Apparently, at this early stage of our relationship, you lack the ability to distinguish between a sexual advance and my simple appreciation for the closeness of your razor work." LaRoux withdrew his hands. "That being the case, I'll be right out here."

Rebecca huffed. "If you're fishing for an apology, it's not coming. My abstinence over the past few years has left me exceptionally vulnerable to stimulation overload. So, regardless of your intent, keep your mittens to yourself, or deal with it."

"Mittens," LaRoux purred. "We'll have to see if we can find a furry pair for later." LaRoux dodged the makeup brush Rebecca launched in his direction. Five minutes later, she emerged ready for dinner. As LaRoux's neck snapped in her direction, he jumped to attention. "You look absolutely breathtaking."

Rebecca's smiled slyly. "I'll bet you say that to all the girls—you almost kill."

"The last thing I remember, darlin', it was you who was pointing the gun." LaRoux stared until her expression relaxed. "That being said, that was a first, and a last, for me." Gauging her mood to be playfully reserved, LaRoux continued. "We need to put in a cameo appearance in the room your buddies are watching, or they'll know something's up. And I think they are getting rather anxious to learn of your whereabouts."

"Is that what you were doing while I was showering? Checking up on my coworkers?"

LaRoux knew he was treading on thin ice. "I was checking in with *my* people, who just happen to be checking up on *your* people."

"And what do *your* people say?"

With eyes full of longing, LaRoux stepped up to Rebecca and put his hands around her waist.

"That I'm wrong. That I'm making a big mistake."

"Apparently, your security detail is much more knowledgeable than we gave them credit for."

Minutes later, as they rode down two floors in silence, Rebecca questioned her sanity while LaRoux pondered his destination beyond Las Vegas. Then, out in the hallway on their way to his suite, LaRoux explained, "This is it, but you probably already knew that." He opened the door.

"After you, baby."

Baby? Rebecca had never been anyone's *baby*. The notion evoked an impish smile. "You're absolutely sure this room is still under surveillance?" Rebecca whispered.

"Absolutely."

Quite unexpectedly, Rebecca grabbed LaRoux's hand and pulled him to the bedroom. She shoved him forcefully on the bed, hiked her dress around her waist, climbed on top of his thighs, and began passionately kissing him. Nibbling his ear, she whispered, "Let's give them something to talk about."

* * *

"Holy hell, guys, you need to see this! I'm not sure where she came from, but she's back. And I think she's about to bone LaRoux," Agent Tyson barked gleefully.

Agents Mathews and Jones, flanked by Martin, scrambled to the monitor.

"There's no way," Jones objected. "She knows we've got eyes on the room—doesn't she, Will?" As Jones got his first glimpse of the monitor, he cried out, "Damn—Agent Pearson!"

Will cut a contemptuous glare at Jones but did not respond. He raised his right arm to his shoulder harness to squeeze his Glock.

The four watched intently as the passion escalated. "Damn, look at those hips. I'll bet she can grind coffee beans better than my Cuisinart," Tyson proclaimed as he turned the volume up until every breath, kiss, and moan echoed across the room.

"You grind your own beans?" Mathews asked in a deadpan tone as his eyes remained glued to the action on the screen.

"Fuck the coffee. We need some popcorn," Jones added.

Will Martin was livid; his fingers stoked the semiautomatic. No longer thinking with reason, he commanded, "We need to get in there before it gets out of hand."

"Oh, hell no," Mathews objected. "It will blow the entire operation. Pearson knows exactly what she's doing."

"Damn right she does," Tyson exclaimed. "There goes LaRoux's fly."

Martin wheeled around and made for the door with Mathews in pursuit. "Will, if you can't handle the situation, step down. We've got too much riding on this for some ancient, personal bullshit to screw this investigation. You wanted an agent close to LaRoux, now you got it! Deal with it."

"Oh man, he's in," Tyson announced perversely. "If it weren't for that damn dress, we'd have some serious X-rated shit going down."

Martin grabbed the doorknob and twisted it hard.

"Go out that door, Will, and I'll make damn sure it's *your* ass that gets hung out to dry when DC wants to know why the investigation went south." Mathews wheeled around and returned to Tyson and Jones. "Kill the monitor feed, but maintain a full recording. We know she's not in danger. When this is over, if there is no pertinent information, you make damn sure the video is erased."

"But, Matt," Jones objected with a huge smile, "without the video feed, I can't tell whether she's climaxing or he's killing her."

Mathews was not amused. He reached over Tyson and killed the feed. "Give Pearson her dignity, guys. She's doing exactly what needs to be done to bust this prick. And if I hear one word about any of this outside of this room or find out that a video recording magically survived, I'll make damn sure even Radio Shack won't hire you."

* * *

LaRoux stood by the elevator as he studied Rebecca's subtle smile. She whispered, "I'm glad you weren't camera shy."

"Would you care to explain what that was all about?" He grabbed Rebecca's shoulder before she stepped in and added, "That is, after we get out of the elevator."

"Don't worry," Rebecca replied. "I know where our surveillance is set up."

"But you don't know where ours is."

The elevator doors opened, and the two walked in relative silence to the restaurant. As they did, LaRoux noticed Rebecca's glow of deep-rooted satisfaction. He mulled over its possible source. Perhaps it was the bliss of a newfound relationship, or maybe it was the sex; or was it simply an undercover agent's confidence in her success?

In the restaurant, the maître d' instantly recognized LaRoux and whisked him and Rebecca past the line of diners awaiting their tables. He seated them at a cozy table for two. "You know, there was a time, like only a week ago, where it really irritated me to see people do what we just did," Rebecca said from her luxurious leather seat.

LaRoux snickered. "You might want to get used to it. But just so you know, we didn't steal anybody's table. I knew that in all likelihood we wouldn't be dining with the others tonight, and I didn't know what time we would be eating—if we would eat at all. So, this *courtesy* is afforded to anyone willing to pay the net value of the table to reserve it for the evening. I hope you agree that I was merely being practical, not rude."

"How about extravagantly impressive?"

LaRoux chuckled silently. "Tonight is far too important to me to be waiting in the back of *any* line."

"If you are truly giving up your life for me, you're going to have to learn to live on a budget, Mr. LaRoux," Rebecca lectured playfully.

With a stern expression and a nod, LaRoux concurred. "I'll take that into consideration. Now, before your associates arrive, why don't you tell me what just happened up in my room."

"Mr. LaRoux, your drinks, sir," the waiter announced as he set a gin and tonic in front of Rebecca and a bourbon in front of LaRoux, who nodded without breaking his eyes away from Rebecca. The waiter got the hint and quickly departed.

Rebecca stroked the side of her glass. "If I tell you, you'll tell me about Wells?"

LaRoux clenched his jaw before replying. "I can see our relationship is going to be a series of negotiations. I *think* that might be refreshing." He slid his hand into his pocket and switched on his signal-jamming device.

Rebecca took a sip and cleared her throat. "You said we needed to make an appearance. As you probably already know, or maybe you didn't, I had an affair with Director Martin over five years ago." LaRoux nodded in confirmation. "I thought as much," Rebecca said. After taking a much deeper swallow, she set her glass on the table and fingered the beads of sweat forming on it. "He's the reason I have avoided relationships and a significant factor involving some deeper personal issues, which we *might* discuss some other time. He brought all of us to New Orleans for *this* very purpose—that would be you. But definitely not for this." Rebecca's index finger flickered between the drink glasses on the table. "I tried to refuse the job, but he pretty much demanded I take it. Refusing would have been disastrous to my career. *I* was to be the mother hen for the younger girls." With a tinge of bitterness, Rebecca took another drink. "*I* was never supposed to be the one sitting here tonight. And to add insult to injury, the jackass actually had the nerve . . . he actually thought I would sleep with *him* again. I was so infuriated. I knew *he* would be watching tonight."

"So, it was a show—for him?"

"In the very beginning, yes. But I never intended for us to go *that* far. But when I felt *your*"—Rebecca cleared her throat—"*attention*, I didn't care anymore. I wanted you, and I didn't give a damn about any of them."

LaRoux leaned back and sipped his bourbon. Rebecca's wild-eyed passionate expression was pretty darn convincing. "If you don't stop looking at me like that, we may never get to eat."

"I don't care. We can go back up there right now. My career is over anyhow. I just hope you understand how I feel. You wanted me to fall in love with you. Well, I have." Rebecca finished her drink and looked for a waiter before returning her attention back to LaRoux. "But amid all my euphoria—and orgasms—this still scares the hell out of me, David. I have allowed myself to be vulnerable, which I swore would never happen again. And to top it off, all of Will's allegations, which I had completely dismissed, well, now you tell me they are true."

LaRoux wanted to believe Rebecca. He leaned back across the table and took her hands in his. "I looked past your physical beauty, the one I think you no longer recognize, or perhaps no longer care about. I've watched how you guard your confidence and enthusiasm. But when I look beyond the visible, behind those magnificent eyes, I sense a soul that's been waiting, and it calls to mine. That makes you the rarest of women, Rebecca Pearson, because I know there is no other who can fill this void in my life."

Those words played a beautiful symphony in Rebecca's heart, but deep in her subconscious, a warning echoed: *This man is a masterful architect of deception.*

She made love to me, twice now—once, literally right in front of her colleagues. That has to prove something, LaRoux's subconscious debated. *But perhaps she is driven for success beyond the boundaries of cruelty or shame.*

Despite the consequences, LaRoux was ready to relieve his burden. "I've already told you, in this business casualties happen. It is a war."

LaRoux uncharacteristically finished his drink in two swallows and eyed the waiter. "As you came from Seattle, I'm guessing you didn't know Colin Wells. It only took my people two days to discover what he was. From that point, we played him. That little shit made *our* politicians look like Abe Lincoln. When he couldn't find a single scrap of incriminating evidence, twice he manufactured circumstantial evidence, all for the sake of Martin's investigation. It took some brilliant manipulation to contain the damage he was attempting to fabricate. Not only that, but he was skimming cash to the tune of one hundred thousand and change and banking it offshore. What Colin failed to realize was that I have a separate security detail whose sole purpose is to watch all my employees, new and old. If *any* of them do something remotely out of line, I hear about it."

"Whoever is running your security must be amazing," Rebecca replied with genuine admiration. "I can't wait to meet him."

"Trust me. The one thing you don't want to do is meet Mr. Hanson. He and I have an exclusive arrangement, and if you ever do meet him, it will be the last conversation you ever have."

"So, Colin met Mr. Hanson?"

LaRoux's disposition grew dark. "No. Betrayal is intimate— and unforgiveable. I deal with betrayal personally—with extreme prejudice. I think you must understand that now. But enough of that talk tonight. By tomorrow, all of it will be fading far behind us."

"I'm sorry. I know I still sound like an agent, but I'm fascinated. And it's not just occupational curiosity anymore. You're in my life now, and I don't want your past to ever get between us."

"I understand completely, and one day you will know it all." LaRoux's mood was still solemn. "Speaking of occupational, the cavalry has just arrived." He nodded in the direction of the bar.

Rebecca glanced up as the agent took up a barstool. "That's Paul Jones. Undoubtedly, our conversation will no longer be private. But you probably already know that too," LaRoux confirmed with a smirk. "Is there anything your organization doesn't know about our ops?"

"For the immediate future, about the only thing is how your boss is coping with your little performance upstairs." As soon as LaRoux finished speaking, he knew his words were a lie. Hanson had bugged the DEA suite where Martin and the others had watched the video feed and pretty much knew everything that was said behind their door. *Details for another day*, LaRoux mused. Rebecca smiled as he signaled to their waiter, who had been attentively standing by. "I've got to be honest here, *chérie*. I'm feeling like you used me up there to make a statement." LaRoux failed to maintain a scowl. "But I'm pretty damn sure I'll recover from the hurt . . . if you need to do it again." Laughing as their waiter approached, LaRoux scanned the bar for additional agents. "Taylor, this is my fiancée, Rebecca Pearson. Impress her, please."

Rebecca blushed and fidgeted with her new ring. Three short days, and suddenly she was a fiancée. Mired in her post-Will misery, she had banished the thought of ever being married from her dreams.

As Taylor began to recite several gourmet Italian creations, all off menu, LaRoux's attention strayed. He was inspecting every attractive woman in the restaurant. His openly deliberate distraction drew Rebecca's attention and ire. "David?"

"Taylor, please order for us both. I'm sure it will be delicious," LaRoux stated as his attention was clearly anywhere but his table.

Rebecca waited for Taylor to depart before taking exception to LaRoux's rudeness. "I guess some habits die hard," Rebecca said sharply. "I'll bet she's no older than twenty-four."

"What did you expect? It's been at least thirty minutes. And did you see her rack?"

Rebecca was flabbergasted. "Are you totally mental?"

"About you, absolutely." LaRoux cradled his cheek and jaw, shielding the view of his mouth. "Did you know Paul Jones can read lips?" Rebecca shook her head *no*. "To clarify my bad behavior, I'm doing exactly what is expected of me. So, please, continue to look irritated." Rebecca crossed her arms, leaned back, and scowled. "By the way, your boss has been watching us from the terrace for almost five minutes. I think he's royally pissed and would desperately love to get something off his chest. So, with the assistance of our artificially busty friend over there, I'm going to give him the opportunity. She and her friend just paid their check. When they leave, I'm going to play the scandalous David LaRoux that I'm notoriously famous for. That should give you and Will a little quality alone time."

Rebecca continued to stare with disapproval while sipping at her ice cubes to extract the remaining gin. "I'm going to need more of these," she announced as she stared at her empty glass. "You scare me, David. You're too damn good at this business."

LaRoux watched as the two ladies began to leave. "They're getting up. I need you to be annoyed with me."

Rebecca pointed. "If you find her so damn attractive, maybe you should join them!"

With his face turned away from all the agents, LaRoux winked at Rebecca. "You know, I think that you will excel at this game as well. I love you." LaRoux walked with a deliberate stagger as he stalked his intended prey.

Just as LaRoux cleared the restaurant entrance, Martin stepped up to the table. "What the hell was that all about?"

"David LaRoux is a pig. Apparently, he has grown bored and wants to invite his new fancy to join us—for sex." Rebecca kept her eye trained on the door. "You need to go. He's going to come back."

"Don't worry. I'll know when he's heading back." Martin forced Rebecca's chin to face him. "What the hell were you doing up there?" he snapped in an angry whisper.

Rebecca allowed Martin to continue to cradle her chin as she explained, "I was losing his interest. Call it a last-ditch effort."

Martin muted his comm device. "Don't *ever* do that again!"

"Do what, Will?" Rebecca's mind quickly considered a series of replies. "Have sex with a perp or force you to watch?"

Martin released Rebecca's chin. "Both, dammit. I've told you how I feel."

"I know how you feel, Will. But I've already heard about your failed hookup with Cassandra back in New Orleans, so don't even start that shit." Rebecca slurped at her ice again before searching for their waiter. "I did what I had to do for the sake of the investigation. No different than what any male agent would have eagerly done with an attractive female perp." Catching Taylor's eye, Rebecca held her glass high and rattled the ice cubes. "But the manner of how I fucked David LaRoux, that was explicitly for you."

Martin scowled. He attempted to take Rebecca's hand, but she snatched it away. "Have you learned anything?"

"If you want to put *this* in your report, David LaRoux is great in the sack. I had an amazing orgasm." Rebecca watched with great satisfaction as Martin's entire body tensed.

Seething, he cast his best glare of intimidation. "That's enough, Rebecca. I get it!"

"Three years of my life, Will, wasted on your bullshit. And the last five? I haven't been able to have anything remotely close to a relationship since. I'm not sure if *that* or whatever else follows will *ever* be enough, Will."

Martin's expression softened. "It wasn't all wasted."

"After what I've just experienced upstairs, I can honestly say, *yes it was*." Rebecca nodded at Taylor, who was waiting nearby with her drink. Keenly observing Rebecca's consternation, he silently swept in with the drink and immediately returned to his watch.

Martin leaned in. "I'm gonna pull you off the assignment. Apparently, your objectivity is compromised."

Rebecca leaned in closer. "I'm *not* going anywhere, Will. I'm pretty sure Mathews has my back on this one. I'm exactly where you wanted an agent. You might regret who LaRoux chose to fuck, but I've got to be honest, I am enjoying every minute of his attention. And I do mean *every* minute. Secondly, when LaRoux goes down, I will be the one to take him there. And last, seeing you like this has finally given me a reason to smile."

Martin recoiled. "I've made some terrible mistakes. I know I have. But when this is over, I want to take you somewhere nice. You'll see. We can fix things."

Before Rebecca could reply, Martin touched his earpiece and turned away. "Shit, he's on the way back. We'll finish this conversation later."

"Will," Rebecca called in feigned regret.

Martin turned.

"You might want to back off the surveillance while you're at it. I don't know how, but LaRoux has already made you and Jones. He knows who you are and that he's being watched."

"How?"

"How? How in the hell did you ever make field director, that's what you should be asking yourself."

Martin's jaw practically dislodged as he scrambled for an appropriate reply. He growled, "When LaRoux goes down, you'd better hope you're nowhere near."

Rebecca smiled. "When LaRoux goes down, you'll know exactly where to find me."

Martin quickly made for the terrace just as LaRoux reappeared through the entrance. LaRoux set a single rose on the table, and his smile exuded his quiet confidence. "I'll wager whatever you want that you had a visitor while I was gone."

"You cheated," Rebecca said as she sniffed the flower.

"No, ma'am, I never cheat. But I did happen to see someone leaving, who resembled a certain director, nearly tripping as he ran out the terrace door. And look, even our good friend, Agent Jones is leaving now. I would have loved to be a fly on the wall to hear your last conversation."

"Would you now?" Rebecca's hand groped underneath the table in search of any electronic devices. "Are you claiming that nobody is listening to our conversation?"

"My dear, from the moment you laid that gun down and dropped your robe, I knew that trusting you was going to be the least of my problems."

"And what would be the most?"

LaRoux kissed Rebecca on the cheek. "Getting a good night's sleep."

CHAPTER 10

"WHO WOULD HAVE EVER thought to disguise a shopping mall like Venice?" Rebecca marveled the next day. "Honestly, gondolas, the blue sky, St. Mark's Square?" "If you see anything you want—" A ringing phone cut LaRoux off.

"Are you actually carrying a cell phone on our first real date, David LaRoux?" Rebecca covered her mouth as if she were shocked.

LaRoux looked at the number and grimaced. "This is important. Please excuse me for just a minute."

Rebecca pointed to Victoria's Secret. "I'll be in there, but don't take too long or you will be sorry."

LaRoux checked his surroundings and moved away from the main flow of pedestrians. He leaned against the façade of a store as he answered softly, "Yes."

"The Colombians are on the move, and it's not looking good. I didn't have time to put my plan into action, so they are not after the DEA." Hanson sounded rushed. "You are in front of Victoria's Secret?"

"Yes."

"Well, David, you've got a hit squad, and they appear to bearing down on *you*."

LaRoux checked to his right and then left. "Are you sure?"

"Sure enough to tell you it's time to get the hell out. Vegas is over. Somebody is feeding them intel. For now, just keep going to your right. When you get to the parking garage, there is a stairwell on the opposite side—"

"I've got to get Rebecca," LaRoux interrupted. "She's in the store."

"Fuck the girl. She's a fucking fed. Let her people worry about her. These thugs are not going to let the mall cops or anybody else get in their way. They are going to put you down the minute they lay eyes on you."

"Gotta go." LaRoux shoved the phone into his pocket. As he walked briskly into the lingerie store, he glimpsed three Hispanic men crossing the canal bridge. He darted between the rows of lingerie in a frantic search for Rebecca. "Tall, attractive brunette in a blue dress?" he asked the first clerk he encountered.

"Try the changing rooms," the girl replied with a flirtatious smile.

There, he called out softly but urgently, "Rebecca."

"I'll be done in a minute."

LaRoux followed the voice, pulled the changing room door open, and stepped in.

"Hey," Rebecca protested.

Even in a moment of imminent danger, LaRoux couldn't help but make a quick study of Rebecca in a sapphire silk negligee. "Goes great with the shoes, but we've got to go right now. Get dressed, please."

"Want to help me change?" Rebecca pulled him close.

LaRoux pushed back. "I would love to, but apparently, we have a group of assassins closing in on us." Rebecca watched in disbelief as LaRoux redialed his phone.

"In the back of the store there is an emergency exit that leads to a service hallway," said Hanson. "I've just disabled the alarm. Go now. Once you're outside the door, turn right, then take the first left and follow it to the parking garage. Once you're there, about twenty yards to the left is a stairwell up. I'd tell you to call your guys in, but there's no time for that. I'm counting at least six possible hostiles. Get your ass moving, right now."

* * *

Martin was pacing in the DEA command center in the hotel when his phone rang. He was still irate from his encounter with Rebecca and his blown cover. He snapped, "What?"

"Boss, you still watching Pearson's movements?" Dawson asked.

"Yes."

"To the left of the storefront, see the three Colombians? They just passed the store for the second time. I think they're looking for LaRoux."

"Shit! I see them. Drop back. I'm sending backup." Martin hung up.

With a sense of urgency, he turned his attention to a group of agents on the couch. "Parker, you and Lawrence get down there *pronto*." Martin looked back at the monitors. "Ben, I need some IDs—now!"

"Already on it, boss."

Martin directed his attention to Donald Mathews. "I told you LaRoux was dirty."

"We're a long way from dirty, Will." Mathews sighed as he lifted his radio. "Units one, two, and three, I need checkpoints at all the exits around Victoria's Secret. Suspects are three or more Latino men, mid-twenties to mid-thirties, high probability of being armed and dangerous. All other units stand by for immediate response. Uploading images your way now.

Do not engage without direct authorization from me or Agent Martin."

After a brief silence, a voice broke back over the radio. "Roger, home. I've got three more potential bogies entering the field from the escalator in St. Mark's Square matching your profile. Sending new intel your way."

"Hey, Will, I've got a probable match on one perp," Ben announced. "We've only got an alias—Juan Marco. He was a person of interest, involved in that massacre outside of Mexico City last year. Nothing before that date, and he's been off the radar ever since."

"Dammit." Will tensed. "What the hell is going on?"

Donald studied the image. "Somehow, I don't think this animal is interested in ladies' lingerie. This is your op, Will. How do you want to play it?"

"Send a pair of agents into the store to shop. One needs to be female. I want everyone else keeping the perps within a clean kill-shot range. If we see one gun, I want all those fuckers taken down immediately. We'll play this like a sting for Juan Marco there," Martin said as he pointed to the monitor, "and hope we don't totally spook LaRoux. Who knows, maybe we can *use* these guys to sell LaRoux on our reason for watching him." Martin tapped the top of the monitor with his right hand as he adjusted his vest with his left. "Ben, give hotel security a brief, and remind them to stand the fuck down."

* * *

Just as Rebecca emerged from the dressing room, LaRoux made eye contact with one of the three Colombians just outside the entrance of the store. Appearing unconcerned about the man's presence, LaRoux looked at the perfume display. His first thought was for Rebecca's safety. *They* had to know she was with him. There would be no surrendering or leaving her behind. In either scenario, there was a high probability they would not survive.

LaRoux ignored his potential assailant from across the store as he kissed Rebecca on the cheek and reported quietly, "Don't look, but we've been made. Our little Colombian goon squad has taken up position just outside the store, and my guys are not going to get here in time. We have to make a run for it." LaRoux picked up a bottle of perfume, took Rebecca by the hand, and continued to casually browse as they made their way to the rear of the store.

"Let me call it in," Rebecca whispered.

"Your people can't help us now." As LaRoux continued to browse, he peeked back at the storefront. Three more Colombians had arrived, one prompting two of the goons to enter the store. "There's no time. These guys are about to turn this entire store into a bloody massacre to accomplish their agenda, and they don't mind dying to do it. See that door?"

"Yes."

"We're going out it. When I say go, you go quickly, Rebecca. Do not stop for *anything*."

LaRoux looked back one last time. "*Go, now.*"

As LaRoux and Rebecca broke for the stockroom, the Colombians moved in. LaRoux heard a bullet ricochet off the cinderblock wall, and within a second, he and Rebecca cleared the stockroom and made it into the service hallway. As Rebecca's shoes clicked on the concrete floor, LaRoux demanded, "Lose the heels." Closing the distance quickly, the Colombians gave chase. Turning left, the door to the parking garage appeared as if it were a mile away.

LaRoux and Rebecca sprinted down the forty-yard corridor, but suddenly the patter of their feet was broken by the thud of the bullet as it entered LaRoux's left shoulder. The impact threw him against the wall and then to the floor. He screamed out to Rebecca, "Go!"

"No," Rebecca cried out.

Before LaRoux or common sense could rebut her, suddenly three Colombians were upon them.

"I am a federal agen—" Rebecca's words were abruptly halted by a backhand to the face that sent her tumbling to the floor.

Then two more Colombians appeared at the end of the corridor. The one the DEA had identified as Juan Marco called out to the pair, "Watch the hall. Nobody comes in or out." Juan found the door of the mechanical room locked, so he kicked the door open.

The noise from the electrical turbines filled the hallway with a conversation-deafening roar. "Put them in here," he ordered his associates. "Get rid of that security camera," he yelled to the two that remained down the hall.

Once inside the mechanical room, he pushed the door shut and blocked it with a chair. "David LaRoux, I've waited long for this day." With LaRoux restrained by a muscular henchman, Juan launched a thunderous, roundhouse blow to LaRoux's jaw. The hit knocked him back to the ground. Rebecca broke from the grasp of the other henchman and rushed to his aid, and Juan backhanded her a second time, sending her careening down. Juan pulled LaRoux by the hair up to his knees, grabbed an extension cord off a workbench, and wrapped it around LaRoux's neck. He handed the reins to his associate and pulled the cord tight. "If he moves, kill him."

Juan pulled a length of cord off a metal shelf. Then he grabbed Rebecca by the hair and dragged her unmercifully to the workbench, where he pulled her across the tabletop and tied her hands to a vise. He stooped down to her eye level and crowed, "That's more like it, *chiquita*." He returned to LaRoux to dig his thumb into his blood-covered bullet wound. As blood gushed, LaRoux gritted through the excruciating pain. "Yeah, I almost forgot—you a tough guy." Juan looked at his watch. "We don't have much time, *amigo*." Juan leaned in closer to LaRoux. "I have always admired your style, but one lesson you don't know—never leave a witness alive. That boy you spared in Miami, he is the son of a very influential man."

"*Those* assholes, they set me up," LaRoux said as he winced. "I spared that kid because he was the only one not pointing a gun at me."

"*Sí*, but the boy you spared saw you kill another boy. And that boy was David Antonio, the nephew of Miguel San Domingo."

"*What?*" The epiphany hit LaRoux like a freight train. Miguel San Domingo was his most trusted associate in Colombia. LaRoux had not seen the boy in years—or so he thought. San Domingo had sheltered his nephew from the family business. *David Antonio. How?* LaRoux was the boy's godfather and namesake.

"My employer tells me the boy was simply setting out to start his own empire. He said the old man had grown lazy and careless. He had no idea what his own family was plotting." Juan Marco gazed back at Rebecca and flashed a brown-toothed smile. "Miguel's son, Armando, did not like what you did to his cousin."

"Armando is responsible for this?"

"*Sí*. You can ask him yourself. He's waiting for you out in the desert." Juan used LaRoux's injured shoulder to push himself up. "Too bad we don't have room in the car for both of you." Juan looked over at Rebecca and grinned. "Tell you what, *amigo*, I'm going to have me some fun with your pretty little girlfriend before we go. If you misbehave, my buddy Choppo will splatter her pretty little face all over the wall." Juan stepped behind Rebecca and smacked her butt. "What are we going to do with you, Miss Federal Agent?" He lifted Rebecca's dress, exposing her barely covered buttocks. "Hey, Choppo, check this out."

Choppo pulled the gun from Rebecca's head and walked around the bench. "I like the panties."

Juan ripped them off. "Here, they are yours." Juan grinned devilishly as he began rubbing Rebecca's buttocks. "Hey, LaRoux," he yelled above the noise of the turbines, "you wanna watch me and Choppo fuck your girlfriend *fifty shades* of black and blue?"

With her lips and nose bleeding, Rebecca wailed, "*No*" as she struggled against his weight and her restraints.

As Choppo began to drop his pants, Juan leaned over Rebecca's back. "Play nice, *señorita*, or you will watch me cut out your boyfriend's eyes."

LaRoux's face didn't flinch as he stared into Rebecca's fear-stricken pupils.

* * *

"Hotel security just received a call from the lingerie shop. They reported a man and a woman leaving the emergency exit being pursued by five armed men who identified themselves as FBI. They want to know what you want them to do," Mathews said as he and Martin watched the floors count down in the elevator.

"Shit." Martin pulled his hand through his hair. "What do our guys see?"

"They are standing by," Mathews replied as he listened to the reports rushing in on his comm. "Possibly one perp remains in the store; surveillance cameras in the auxiliary corridors have gone blank."

"Have hotel security contact the store and get whoever answers to quietly round up the customers and employees and get out, *pronto*." Martin listened as Mathews relayed the instructions. "Teams one and two, do you copy?"

"Roger that," Mike Fuller confirmed.

Knowing that Rebecca's time might be up, Martin changed his plan. "Mike, if Charlie can make it happen without substantial risk, send him in to take the perp down. Then get Palazzo security to clear all the civilians and then lock down the mall. We'll be there in five minutes." "We're on it, boss," Mike confirmed.

"Teams five, six, and seven, let's secure all exits leading in and out of the parking garage. Ben, get Vegas PD to secure the perimeter of the casino." Martin wrapped up with, "Let's move it, guys. We've got a deal going down."

When the elevator hit the floor, Martin and his four agents sprinted through the casino in the direction of the Grand Canal Shoppes.

* * *

As Juan stood butt naked behind Rebecca, LaRoux's blood-covered face offered her no hope of survival.

"Hey, Choppo, which end do you want?" Juan taunted.

"I don't want the end with no stinking teeth." The men laughed callously.

In their moment of hedonistic distraction, LaRoux pulled down on his assailant's gun with one hand as he grabbed a screwdriver from under the workbench with the other. Fighting through excruciating pain, he thrust the screwdriver deep inside his captor's groin. He yanked the gun from his hand, turned, and fired a shot into Choppo's face, blowing half of it away. Choppo's dismembered body catapulted backward against the wall and slumped to the floor. Simultaneously,

LaRoux turned the gun and fired point-blank into the jaw of his impaled adversary.

With his pants around his knees, Juan stepped back and threw his hands in the air. "*Amigo*, don't do this."

"I'm not one to repeat a mistake, Juan. How was it that you put it? I believe you said, *no witnesses*." The thud of the silenced muzzle was the last sound Juan Marco would ever hear. The bullet struck him square in the forehead, launching skull fragments and brain all about the room. Thanks to the roar of the turbines, Juan's crew just outside the door was oblivious to LaRoux's assault. LaRoux struggled to his feet and retrieved a razor knife from a toolbox. Then he cut Rebecca's bindings and pulled her dress back down. "Oh God, look what he did to you," LaRoux protested as he tossed the knife and cord away.

"Me? What about you? We have to get you to a doctor." Rebecca wiped the blood from her mouth and nose with trembling hands. "Let me see that," she insisted as she tried to get a better look at LaRoux's shoulder.

"I'm glad it wasn't a hollow point. I think it went straight through." LaRoux handed Rebecca Choppo's gun. "There are more of them out there. We've got to go now. We'll head toward the parking garage. Are you ready?"

Rebecca nodded. LaRoux pulled the door partially open. Lunging low from the room, he targeted the pair of men at the end of the hall. LaRoux fired the silenced Glock, hitting the tallest one. The other ducked back around the corner in the direction of the stockroom door. "Go now!" LaRoux demanded as he kept his gun trained toward his assailant's position.

With her gun aimed forward, Rebecca hastily made her way. As soon as she disappeared around the corner, LaRoux fired four cover shots down the hall before breaking for the parking garage. Just as he cleared the corner, two earsplitting shots rang out and fractured the concrete wall just behind his back.

"I'm here," Rebecca called to LaRoux in an unexpectedly calm tone.

Within seconds, LaRoux found Rebecca standing between two cars. He pulled her by the hand, and they sprinted across the garage. Three rows down, he found a classic, green '68 Chevelle. "This will do." He fired a single shot into the backseat roll-down window and apologized to the car. "Sorry, baby." He reached through the shattered glass, unlocked the door, and tipped the bucket seat forward. "Be careful of the glass. I don't want anyone to see that you're still with me, so I need you to get down on the floor." As Rebecca began to climb in, LaRoux took her purse. "Is there anything in here you can't live without?" Before she could reply, LaRoux tossed the purse over three cars. "Never mind. I'm sure the damn thing and half the stuff in it is bugged anyway."

LaRoux reached under the dash and yanked the ignition wires down. Torqued under the wheel, he grimaced from the pain as he hotwired the ignition. Within seconds, the engine rumbled. LaRoux sat up and slowly backed the car out of the space. As he steered toward the exit, he glanced in the rearview mirror and saw two assailants emerge from the hallway. But they were a safe distance behind, so he pulled away casually. As he rounded the corner, he found the security gate was closed, most likely in response to the events now behind them. He made a call as he continued to monitor the rearview mirror. Suddenly, the Colombians came into view. LaRoux thumped the steering wheel as he mumbled, "Come on, Vic." Finally, Hanson picked up. LaRoux snapped, "You see me in the Chevelle?"

"Gotcha."

"I'd love to leave this party now, but somebody closed the gate."

"I'm on it. If you've still got the princess with you, I suggest you dump her now."

"Hurry, please. I've got two angry Colombians closing in. If they get here, I'm sure they'd love nothing more than to put a bullet in my head," LaRoux exclaimed as mentally he counted his shots off. He ejected the magazine and counted the bullets.

"Say the magic words," Hanson replied.

"Shit, Vic—what—*open sesame?*" Right on cue, the gate began rising.

"You've got thirty seconds before LVPD has the entire street blocked off. Haul ass straight out of the garage, and I mean punch it."

Just as LaRoux nailed the accelerator and the Chevelle's tires burned plumes of rubber, several shots rang out and shattered the rear window. "Dammit," LaRoux barked as he crouched his head and kept his hands on the steering wheel.

But LaRoux and Rebecca were safe. The Chevelle had rocketed out onto the surprisingly quiet service road.

* * *

Upon reaching the stockroom door, Martin lowered his shoulder and plowed into it. Then he lunged onto the floor and found the rear-entrance door ajar in the back left corner. After checking to his left and right, he yelled back across the store, "It's clear." Without his reinforcements, he moved to the rear door, stuck his head out, and rapidly checked to the left and the right. To the right, Martin thought he saw a pool of blood. As he pulled back and waited for his team, he tried to calm his heart.

After everyone gathered, Martin asked frantically, "Ben, you got anything?"

From the command suite, Ben searched the monitors and security feeds for any movement. "Shit, Will, we've lost all the video feeds." Martin grimaced in the prolonged silence. "Wait, the parking garage gate just opened. I've got no video confirmation, but that has to be them. Go right, then take the first left." Just as Ben finished reporting, multiple gunshots reverberated from the direction he had indicated.

Martin turned to his team. "Shit, guys, we've got to go. Agent Pearson is out there."

* * *

Hitting a few jarring bumps *en route*, Rebecca slammed against the hard floor. "Ouch! Easy on the bumps. I don't need any more bruises than I already have."

Before LaRoux could say anything, Hanson broke in over the phone. "Go easy as you turn right on Koval. You'll see why."

Just as LaRoux reached Koval Street, three police cruisers came screaming down the block. With tires squealing, they turned the corner and barreled in the direction of the casino's parking garage. Then two more cars raced in from the opposite direction.

"Don't worry about them. They still think the garage is locked down."

"Damn, Vic, there must be some serious shit going down back on the ranch," LaRoux replied. Realizing he was not entirely clear of the danger, he decided to shelve his banter for better times.

"Damn right there is. And as soon as I get you out of here, I've got to bug out as well. It won't be long before they come looking for the twidget who hacked into all their shit."

"So, where to?"

"Take the first left on Westchester Drive. There's a parking lot on the right. Green F-150. The combo is 3-2-2-5. The keys are on the visor." Hanson was looking at his monitor, and he chuckled at the scene playing out in the garage. The DEA guys appeared pissed as they frantically looked for LaRoux, or the Colombians, or especially their missing agent. Still chuckling, Hanson reported, "There used to be a traffic camera on the block, but somehow it got irreparably damaged three nights ago."

"Damn vandals," LaRoux replied with a smirk. This was the exact reason why Victor Hanson earned the *big bucks*.

"The GPS is programmed to take you straight to Raven. If you still have the princess with you, which I will reiterate is a really bad fucking idea, keep her out of sight until you hit the desert. This town's got more traffic cameras than illegal immigrants."

"I'm here," LaRoux reported as he pulled into the parking lot.

"I'm sending the boys to clean sweep my room and then back to Louisiana for lockdown. I'll be in touch."

LaRoux hung up as he pulled next to a Ford truck and watched three more Vegas PD cruisers fly by. He ripped his blood-soaked shirt open to use the clean, tucked portion to wipe his prints.

He reached over the seat and touched Rebecca lightly on the shoulder. "Let's go."

Rebecca grimaced as she unwedged herself from the cramped space between the seats.

"What the hell was all that *princess* crap?"

"Oh, you heard that? Victor says that *all* girlfriends are a royal pain in the ass. And as you are the first one he's ever had to deal with, considering the extended nature of our relationship, and the consequences as a result, well that makes you a double pain in the ass in Victor's book."

* * *

Lying in the backseat of the Ford, Rebecca noticed the lights of Vegas had faded mostly to darkness. "Is it safe for me to sit up?"

"You got so quiet back there, I thought you'd fallen asleep."

"After all of this, I may not sleep for a week."

"It's alright. We should be clear of the traffic cameras by now." LaRoux watched in the mirror as Rebecca, her face bruised and bloodied, struggled to rise. Had she been a civilian, his guilt would have been compounded. But she was a player, and this was the punishment their adversary had dealt. He glanced back in the mirror at his own injuries. The pressure he had been applying had stemmed the blood flow. This was the second time in two years the game had nearly claimed his life. Between Rebecca's involvement and the origin of the threat, this one was too close to home.

"Where are we?" she asked.

"Headed out to the desert."

"Am I permitted to know why?" she asked softly as she leaned between the bucket seats.

Before LaRoux could reply, she took note of his appearance. "God, you look rough."

LaRoux reached across Rebecca's head and pulled her near. He kissed her cheek and smiled.

Rebecca leaned back and stuck one leg through the gap in the seats and began to pull herself through. Despite his pain, LaRoux seized the opportunity and stroked the exposed flesh of her inner thigh.

"Hey," she shrieked as she tumbled into the front seat. "That's personal property, Mr. LaRoux."

"It most certainly is." Even though it hurt to smile, he managed to grin.

"So, what's our plan?" Rebecca asked as she pulled her dress back down and buckled herself in.

"Our plan? That will depend on you. In about twenty minutes, either we will get on a plane and start a new life, or we will say goodbye and you will take the truck back to town and go back to your life."

"Just like that? After all that has happened today, you still plan on disappearing?"

"As I said, it all depends on you. But if you get on the plane, then yes, just like that."

"So, if I go with you . . . all of this, it's done and over? But if I stay, what then? Revenge?"

LaRoux propped his hands over the steering wheel and leaned forward, staring out into the beacon of the headlights. "If I'm still in the game, then I play my hand."

Rebecca frowned. "You said you would leave it behind and start anew."

"As I said, my destiny is bound to yours." His voice was solemn, as if he anticipated an unhappy outcome.

"I just witnessed you methodically kill three men, like you were putting on a tie or brushing your teeth. Somehow, I never envisioned you to be quite so ruthless." Rebecca's tone was sullen as she studied the darkness from the side window.

"So, that changes everything?"

Rebecca was silent as she weighed her answer. "You know what scares me? It's that I really don't know the answer."

"I'm sorry you had to witness that. What they did, what they were about to do—to you. I have no tolerance for barbarians. They got exactly what they deserved."

In the ensuing, unwelcome silence, the pair contemplated their options in the dim light of the truck's cab, its headlights illuminating two parallel lines painted down one path. Like their lives, they knew the two should never intersect, save for some egregious error of fate.

CHAPTER 11

AGENT PHILLIPS LOCATED LAROUX'S associates, Walt, Taz, and Ryan, via Margo and Sean. He flashed his badge and requested they follow him to the DEA command suite. Upon entering the suite, Martin immediately moved from the computer and monitor banks to intercept the new arrivals.

"I'm Special Agent William Martin. I apologize for interrupting your time with your lovely friends, but we have a situation here that I feel may be of great concern to you."

Walt shook Martin's extended hand with reserved caution.

"David LaRoux—he is your employer?"

Walt nodded.

"It appears that a group of Colombians we have been monitoring have either assassinated or abducted Mr. LaRoux and his companion. I need to ask you some questions."

Calmly, Walt turned to Taz and Ryan. "You know what to do. Go now."

"Not so fast," Martin ordered.

"Are these men under arrest?" Walt asked stoically.

"No."

"If what you say is true, we have protocols in place for scenarios such as this, which we must initiate *immediately*. Additionally, these men are not authorized to divulge any information concerning Mr. LaRoux or his affairs, so they would invoke their right to counsel *immediately*. And unless they have committed a crime for which you can legally detain them, I must insist they be allowed to return to their duties."

Martin knew he had no legal cause to detain any of them, yet. "Go."

Ryan and Taz briskly departed, leaving Walt and Martin in an irate stare down. "Is there any purpose for me being here, Agent Martin?"

Martin tensed as he attempted to conceal his frustration over being out manipulated by LaRoux's lieutenant. "You don't seem very concerned that your boss is missing."

"I get paid a lot of money to be calm in the storm. That affords me the opportunity to spot the elusive details many people overlook. Details such as *how did you know who we were and where to find us*?"

Martin cleared his throat and spoke with the bearing of an evening news anchorman. "Your employer's name surfaced during our investigation of a Colombian cartel." Hoping Rebecca's cover, as well as his other agents' had not been compromised, Martin continued. "In the course of our surveillance, it appeared as if they kidnapped Mr. LaRoux and his friend. Once we realized it was him, it wasn't hard to find his crew. Now, I understand your hesitation to share any information about your employer, but is there anything you can tell us about his lady friend?"

Walt now understood that Martin believed his undercover agents' identities remained secure. "Here's what I believe, Agent Martin. You don't give a rat's ass about that girl. But you're hoping her identity might give you some clue about what really went down. I also believe that in addition to the Colombians, you knew Mr. LaRoux was in Las Vegas and have had us under surveillance from the get-go." Walt paused to ensure he had everyone's undivided attention. "I warn all of you, you are treading on very dangerous ground. Mr. LaRoux has numerous legitimate business dealings in South America and across the world. If Agent Martin has you thinking *big Colombian distributor, big American importer, there's got to be a connection,*" Walt said as he made eye contact with each man as he spoke, "then you have made an egregious error. If any of you want to know the true nature of your boss's grievance with Mr. LaRoux, you should ask him."

Martin appeared befuddled, unsure of Walt's intentions.

"Please don't play the village-idiot card with me, Agent Martin. I remember the night David LaRoux knocked your drunk ass out. I'll bet none of these guys have heard that story." Walt sidestepped Martin so all of the agents could see him clearly. "If any of you had been there that night, you would've kicked his obnoxious ass too."

Dumbfounded, Martin assessed his damage-control options.

Walt stared back at Martin. "My best advice to you, Agent Martin, is to take your beatdown like a man. You earned it. Mr. LaRoux is an upstanding citizen, and any investigation into his affairs is a gross misappropriation of power. If you had been focused on these perpetrators instead of my employer, your pants wouldn't be around your ankles right now. If you have any legitimate information *you* need to share, here's my number." Walt took Martin's hand and stuffed his business card in it. Then he flung the door open and whisked out into the hall, leaving a room of stunned agents in his wake.

* * *

As the truck approached, its headlights slowly illuminated the shadowy silhouette of oddly shaped mounds against the flatness of the desert. Upon drawing nearer, a half-dozen corrugated domed buildings became recognizable.

"Where are we, David?" Rebecca asked as she strained to make out details.

LaRoux pulled up beside the nearest structure, parked the truck, jumped out, and opened the passenger door. "Area Fifty-One."

Rebecca's heart skipped a beat. "Seriously?"

"Come, you'll see. But we need to get a move on."

Rebecca turned in the seat and propped up her feet on the doorjamb. "Would you be seriously upset if I confessed I have some reservations?"

"I'd be really concerned if you didn't. After all that's happened, you'd have to be pretty loony to trust me." LaRoux extended his hand, but Rebecca did not take it. "What are you afraid of?"

She looked directly into his eyes and answered meekly, "You."

He withdrew his hand and stepped back. "Why?"

"In all of my years with the DEA, I've never experienced anything that intense—back at the mall. You killed those men before I even had time to process what you were doing, or what I would have done." Rebecca struggled to maintain her contact with LaRoux's eyes. "Even after you told me the truth about yourself, I guess I pictured some dark, sinister person taking care of the dirty work—*not you.* I'm having a hard time purging those images out of my head."

"It shouldn't go away easily. It never does for me."

"I *thought* I was ready."

Rebecca's cracking voice warned LaRoux that their fragile romance was in jeopardy.

"Rebecca, it's alright to be confused and scared. But our time is short. You have to know this is equally difficult for me. But if I wasn't willing to risk *everything*, I would have abandoned you back at the mall and let our Colombian friends take the blame for whatever happened." LaRoux chuckled. "But damn—after our day on the bayou, I came to realize that everything I did going forward would have to be with you in my life. Yes, I have secrets, like this airstrip. And in time, you will know them all." LaRoux detected no change in her demeanor. He stepped exceptionally close. "You still have the gun. Shoot me now, and you'll get one hell of a promotion—or you can take the car, tell them I got away, and go back to the life you knew. Or you can get on my plane and leave now. And some day down the road, when you are ready, I hope you will marry me. All of this other crap—we can sort it out, one day at a time." Rebecca's face softened. "Baby, you have to shoot me right now, watch me leave, or get on that plane. But whatever you choose, it needs to happen right now."

"Did you say *marry* you?"

"*Nothing* has changed for me. But that option is only going to work if you get your ass on the plane." LaRoux extended his hand.

Rebecca took it and slid from the truck. "Where are we going?"

"That, I'm afraid, must remain a secret."

Rebecca planted her feet. "What kind of trust is that?"

LaRoux sighed. "Nobody, not even Hanson knows about this place. I have never taken anyone there. It is my greatest secret. You are the first and only. That's going to have to be your trust for now."

"Will you tell me if I give you the gun back?" Rebecca forced a nervous smile.

"Nope. Besides, after a week of me, you might decide you want to use it."

Rebecca relented. Her smile provided the only proof LaRoux needed. "Trust me, if you get out of line, I will."

* * *

"Where's LaRoux's crew?" The irritation in Donald Mathews's voice was abundantly evident.

"They had nothing to offer," Martin deadpanned. "So, I let them go."

"Nothing?" Mathews furiously paced the rear of the suite and checked the monitors. "So, we've lost Pearson and LaRoux, who could be dead, courtesy of a Colombian hit squad, who are also mostly dead, who were camped out in the same hotel, right under your nose. We've got injured agents, a shootout in a crowded mall," Mathews said as his face glowed red, "and with agents all over LaRoux's crew, you could not even collect one useful piece of evidence to detain anyone?"

"So far, we've got nothing." Martin's tone was uncharacteristically submissive.

Mathews's cherry-blossom face grew a frightful scowl. "Oh, you got something, Will. You got your dick handed to you. From day one, after I received your brief, I thought this was some kind of fishing expedition—a huge waste of agency resources. Minus one missing agent, LaRoux's file was, and still is, spotless. You sent Wells poking around the most dangerous part of New Orleans, asking all the wrong questions, to all the wrong people, and then you're surprised when he went missing?"

"And you think today was some kind of random coincidence?" Martin countered.

"What do I think? How about one of the wealthiest men on the globe just got fucking kidnapped right from under our nose. How about now you've managed to lose two agents. Jesus H. Christ, Will. Maybe LaRoux got snatched because he refused to do business with the very people you accuse him of being in cahoots with. How about if he hadn't kicked your ass at the bar, you never would have opened a file on him. Or maybe, just maybe, how about if he wasn't fucking the daylights out of your *ex-girlfriend* you might be ready to admit you were wrong."

Mathews took exception to Martin's shocked face. "Don't even fucking try to play ignorant, Will. I know every goddamned detail."

Martin glared over Mathews's shoulder at the agents who had witnessed his conversation with Walt.

"Dammit, Will, don't blame them. The thin ice you're treading on is about to collapse. If we lose Pearson and come up empty on LaRoux, your career is over. If it weren't for Pearson's possible abduction, or worse, I'd turn this clusterfuck over to the FBI and walk away. As it is, we'll be damn lucky to keep those pricks out of your mess once the news about LaRoux breaks."

Martin's cell phone rang. "You better have something for me." He listened intently, knowing he desperately needed a break. "Got it." He slid the phone back into his pocket. "Somebody inside the hotel plugged a socket into The Palazzo's security system. Ben's tracking down the hack as we speak. So, whatever went down today, it was orchestrated well in advance. The cameras and security gate in the garage were all hacked by the same IP address. Ben found one camera with its DVR recording intact. It was across the parking garage, and from that distance, it's impossible to tell who's in the car. But it's a late-model Chevelle with blacked-out windows. It left the garage when the gate was opened. A dash cam on one of the Vegas PD's cruisers caught it turning on Westchester Drive. So, we've got a BOLO out for the car."

Mathews's expression softened ever so slightly. "I'm not gonna tell you how to do your job, Will, but you might want to find some connection between LaRoux and these Colombians, and fast. If your personal details get out before you make any progress, you may be mopping peepshow floors while somebody else closes this clusterfuck."

"The connection is there, Don. I know you think this is personal, but I know LaRoux is dirty. I'm going down to try to interview the injured suspect. How about taking the lead on the Chevelle? Find out where it got off to."

Mathews sighed deeply. "My mouth is shut about your business until somebody asks. But if LaRoux's people leak your history with LaRoux, I'm not taking *that* bullet. And one more fuckup, and I'm yanking my people out."

* * *

Walt returned to his suite in a huff. Taz was on the phone, and Ryan was pacing impatiently. "What do we know?" Walt asked.

"Not a damn thing," Ryan replied. "Do you think David set this up? I mean, he did waste some pretty pricey show tickets. Maybe it was his plan all along—to waste the bitch."

"Who is Taz talking to?" Walt asked.

Ryan handed Walt a glass of bourbon as he looked back at Taz. "Our inside guy who works in hotel security here."

Swirling the glass, Walt headed for the window across the room. "We've got about eight hours."

"I say screw that. Let's get back home and tighten shit up. Our intel here is too limited. Besides, the feds are all over it."

"The feds are the idiots that lost them in the first place." Walt drank the entire glass down. "We stick to protocol."

"Shit!" Taz barked as he hung up the phone. "It sounds like David got nabbed by some Colombian goon squad. They found three of those guys dead in a mechanical room and another wounded in a hallway. Apparently, they were wired into hotel security for several days and knew exactly where to find the boss."

Walt turned a keen eye on Taz. "Wounded and dead? How?"

"Shot," Taz reported.

"Where'd the boss get a gun?" Walt looked at Taz first, then at Ryan.

"Not me," Ryan said defensively. "Maybe he took it from one of them."

Walt looked back at Taz, who shrugged. "So, those Colombians knew we were coming to Vegas?" Walt poured another glass of bourbon.

"The only possible leads the DEA has is a late-model Chevelle that left the parking garage, and one wounded Colombian."

Taz grabbed a glass and followed Walt's lead, pouring a tall drink.

"The feds are going to be all over him like ticks on a deer," Ryan added.

Walt stared out the window. "Taz, get in touch with our friends at the DEA. I want to know everything about those Colombians. We need to see if they are connected with any of our businesses, or if they have ever tried to be, like those fucking yahoos down in Miami last year. Find out when they checked in. Ryan, start a list of everyone that knew we were coming to Vegas. Include our DEA girlfriends, and have everyone's cell traffic checked from the moment they knew we were coming here. List all the gaming connections concerning the casino deal, our own people, and our other business associates. Somebody sold David out, and I want to know who the fuck did it."

"What about David?" Ryan asked.

"He's either kidnapped or dead. Either way, because of Agent Pearson, the feds will be all over that. *If* David resurfaces, he's gonna want to know how this happened."

"What about the girls?" Ryan asked.

"For now, let's assume they don't know that we know they are agents. We may be able to use them to our advantage. I'll go down to their suite and offer them a ride back to New Orleans and see if they have any information."

"Maybe you should send me," Ryan offered. "I'm much better equipped for knowledge extraction from three ladies in need of a ride."

Walt fired back his bourbon. "Your equipment is exactly the reason I will be going. The clock is ticking, guys. Let's make something happen."

* * *

Rebecca stood frozen as she studied the oddly shaped aircraft. "Exactly what kind of plane is that?"

"It's a carbon-fiber custom Cirrus SF50. I call it the Raven. It's fast, fuel efficient, and great at eluding radar. So, when we leave, nobody will see us." LaRoux opened the fuselage door. "Please climb in. I have no way of knowing for sure that we are not being tracked or if your DEA buddies are *en route*."

"Where is the pilot?"

LaRoux smiled broadly. "If I can remember where the keys are hidden, then you are looking at him."

Rebecca took two giant steps away from the plane. "Okay, now I'm really scared."

"Aw now, *chérie*, don't let a little thing like a novice pilot and a night flight scare you."

Rebecca crossed her arms and dug her heels in. "Seriously, where's the pilot?"

"This plane was built for me. I know her body better than I know the curves of yours. And if you like the way I handled yours, just wait till you see what I can do with hers." Rebecca climbed in with great trepidation.

"Trust me," LaRoux said as he kissed her cheek, "you're gonna love this."

He climbed into the cockpit seat, buckled in, then pulled Rebecca's strap tight. "We have to fly very low to stay off the radar, which means there will be a few *aggressive* maneuvers. Do you like rollercoasters?"

Rebecca's jaw hung loosely as she groaned, "*Great.*"

LaRoux punched the combination on a keypad and flipped a toggle switch, and the engines roared to life. In the overhead panel, he pressed another button, and the hangar door began to open.

"Should I be wearing a helmet?"

LaRoux patted Rebecca's leg as he chuckled at her nervousness. "I have something that will help. At first, I was just going to sneak one into your drink, but rather than royally piss you off before our journey even starts, I decided to give you the option."

"What would that be?" Thinking the time had passed to change her mind, Rebecca's ire was evident.

LaRoux continued without undo concern. "There's a small fridge right behind you with water and some protein bars. There's also a pill bottle in there. If you really think you might get airsick, now would be the time to take one. But it might knock you out."

"Stop the plane." Rebecca crossed her arms and launched a menacing glare at LaRoux. "You were planning on drugging me?"

"Initially, I thought about it. The pills have *been* there for anyone sitting in your seat that might have motion issues, or if I needed to keep any given destination secret, I could use them," LaRoux explained as he released the brake and taxied the jet out of the hangar.

"And our destination is where?"

He sighed. "That's why I almost snuck you a pill. I'm not going to answer that." He flipped two knobs, and two separate monitors illuminated. He pressed the overhead switch a second time, and the hangar door began to close.

"What happened to trust?"

"I told you, not even Mr. Hanson knows of this place. And you know how much I trust him."

"Are you sleeping with Mr. Hanson too?"

LaRoux chuckled. "Can you tell me with absolute certainty that you will not change your mind tomorrow or the next day? I believe I've already promised you that if things don't work out, you'll be free to leave anytime you want. That is why I'd really prefer that you not know the exact location just yet."

Rebecca's crossed arms, pursed lips, wrinkled forehead, and silent treatment did little to dissuade LaRoux's resolve.

"Trust is a two-way street," he said. "If you don't do well on thrill rides, you should take the pill. Besides, you really could use the sleep." Rebecca's stern face had not abated in the least. "Trust me, Rebecca, I could take you anywhere on the planet. I have many homes. But in the morning, you'll understand why I initially prefer you not know, but you'll also understand just how much you mean to me."

"And if I don't?"

"Ever see the ejector seats in James Bond's car?" LaRoux reached for a toggle switch in the overhead. Rebecca scowled again. "We can always take option two, which is to fly to my cabin in Montana. But I'm sure the DEA already knows about that one. We can stay there until my people sort this mess out."

"So, if I don't play by your rules, I get what, a tin-roof shack with an outhouse? That's not fair."

"Of course it's not, but inside this plane I could tell you that's the only deal on the table. But I won't. I hope you understand my reasoning. Once we are there, I'll let you make all the deals *you* want." LaRoux pointed out the window. "Or you can still get off the plane."

Rebecca unbuckled her seat and slid out. She reached into the fridge and grabbed a bottle of water and the pill bottle. Then she returned to her seat, plopped down, snatched her seat belt, and clicked in. "I hope you don't expect me to be all lovey-dovey when we get to wherever it is we're going."

LaRoux laughed. "Life's full of disappointments. Imagine mine when I learned you were a fed."

"That didn't turn out so bad, did it?"

"And neither will this." LaRoux pulled back the throttle, and the jet roared.

"This is crazy. I can't believe I'm doing this."

"You might want to take that pill now. If you've never flown high speed, low altitude through the mountains at night, it can be a little scary."

Rebecca swallowed the pill and chased it with water.

After a brief taxi, LaRoux asked, "Are you sure you're ready for this?"

"I took the pill, didn't I?" Rebecca could already feel its effects.

LaRoux pulled back on the flaps and eased the jet off the ground.

Rebecca could barely discern the desert beneath passing at two hundred miles per hour. "This is not so bad," she reported.

"The first couple of minutes are cake. It's not till we go over the mountains that it gets hairy."

LaRoux banked the plane to the northeast and set his bearings for a small airstrip just outside Dryden, Ontario. Bringing his speed up to three hundred twenty miles per hour, the first leg of his journey would last just under five hours. With tonight's marathon flight on the horizon, he reached back to the refrigerator and grabbed an energy drink. He popped the top, took a deep swallow, and looked at Rebecca, who was already conked out. He smiled. "Sweet dreams, baby. I sure hope to hell all of my friends are wrong about you."

CHAPTER 12

AFTER NEARLY THREE THOUSAND miles in the air, the last being one hundred eighty over the Gulf of St. Lawrence, Rebecca's restlessness was apparent. To help distract his curious, and at times, sarcastic passenger, LaRoux had resorted to teaching Rebecca to fly.

As they neared the island of Cape Breton, on the northern tip of Nova Scotia, Rebecca begrudgingly relinquished her pilot's wings. In the cloudless blue of the August sky, she fixed her attention on the larger landmass off to the left. "What's that land over there?"

So close to home, LaRoux knew she was referring to Newfoundland. Between fatigue and finally relaxing into the relationship, mindlessly, he nearly blurted the answer. "Nice try," he said as he recovered his wits.

Rebecca smiled. "That wasn't intentional. I know I have to be patient." As LaRoux banked the jet right and continued to descend, her focus switched to the rugged coastline. "I'm guessing that's where we're headed?" Still twenty miles out, the few houses she saw remained a mere speck.

"I really wish I could tell you all about it. In a few days, after I've answered all your questions, if you still choose to stay I will be your personal tour guide."

As the jet crossed the coastline, Rebecca noticed LaRoux's attention fixed below. "I don't think I want to know anymore. I know who you are, and I know the kind of things that life entails. I understand that's the only life you've ever known. I can't promise I won't ask questions from time to time, but for now I want us to be like two normal people who've fallen in love and spend their days looking forward, not to the past."

LaRoux glanced at Rebecca before inspecting his landing strip. As the jet recrossed the shoreline, he turned and gazed into Rebecca's eyes. "This is Nova Scotia," he proclaimed. "And it's not only what you just said, but it's how you said it. That's the very reason I know I love you." LaRoux banked hard left, bringing the Raven perpendicular to the coast.

As the jet's airspeed dropped, Rebecca tried to decide exactly where they were supposed to land among the scattered homes, hilly terrain, and trees. "I don't see an airport."

"Right there," LaRoux said as he pointed to a clearing.

"You're landing *this* plane on *that* patch of grass?"

"God, I hope so, or this may be one of the shortest love stories in history."

* * *

As LaRoux followed the coast along Meat Cove Road in an old Chevy pickup, Rebecca squinted as the sun gleamed off the Gulf of St. Lawrence. "So, I have to say, as beautiful as this is, I'm surprised you didn't pick a country without extradition."

"Oh, I have a place for that." LaRoux pulled his sunglasses off and handed them to her. "But up here, privacy and simplicity are treasured. Besides, it would take an elite team of Seals to extract me from here."

Rebecca put on the shades, then patted the well-worn leather seats of the Chevy. "I guess that's the reason for ol' Betsy here?"

"Outside of the jet, I prefer a nonexistent profile. With the exception of a few acquaintances in town, I am a nobody here."

"So, are we to be Mr. and Mrs. Nobody?"

LaRoux turned left onto a crushed shell driveway. With her view of the house obscured by hedges, natural vegetation, and trees, Rebecca paused her curiosity. First, she glimpsed the ocean, followed by a gazebo, and then a quaint white and green Cape Cod cottage. The meticulously landscaped, sprawling lawn, contrasted against the blue of the sea and sky, forced Rebecca to sigh. "This is your home?"

"*Ours*," LaRoux replied with great satisfaction.

After leaving the pickup, Rebecca stepped onto the wraparound porch with LaRoux trailing close behind. As she made her way to the rear of the house and took in the panoramic coastline, her face glowed with childlike jubilation. She eased into the Adirondack chair, leaned back, and inhaled deeply. "Can we just stay out here for a day or two, David?"

"Even with the fire pit, it can get a little chilly at night. But I'm sure we can make do."

Rebecca laughed. "To think, a week ago, I was sitting in a conference room plotting your demise. And now, I'm here on your porch thinking how badly I need you to make love to me."

LaRoux took Rebecca by the hand, and she rose from the chair. "Let's see if we can fix that."

He led her to the back door, and she couldn't help but gawk. Practically the entire back side of the cottage was glass. As she stepped in, she marveled at the brilliant openness of the expansive room.

Her attention narrowed in on volumes of books filling the wall to her right. "Somehow, I never took you for much of a reader."

"I rarely watch television, so at night it's either read or go to bed. There's a workout room in the basement, but outside of that—"

Rebecca scanned the walls. The artwork appeared, she believed, to be native to the surrounding area—wood bowls and various carvings accented by contemporary furniture, giving the room a spacious, uncluttered feel. "Who's your decorator?" LaRoux took a small bow. "It figures. It's nice, but it needs a woman's touch."

As she gazed over the kitchen, she noticed how meticulously clean and organized it was. Hanging neatly on the utensil tree, spatulas and spoons appeared matching and practically new. Wineglasses and several pans hung beneath the cabinets above the granite counters. "I'm guessing you eat out a lot. It doesn't appear as if the kitchen has ever been used."

"If you're hungry, I can stir something up." LaRoux kissed Rebecca's cheek. "I had my caretaker stock the fridge."

"Is the bedroom through here?" She did not wait for an escort. She flipped on the light and stood bewildered by the view. After experiencing the richness of his plantation bedroom, she was somewhat surprised; the room was rather sparse, almost minimalistic. The queen-sized bed was draped with a light-gray comforter, and the furniture was maple with clean, straight lines. Two pictures hung on the walls, one was a Chagall, and the other was of a bayou sunset.

"I'm sorry. I know it's not much. But it's functional—for my purpose of sleep. I never really thought I'd be bringing anyone here."

Rebecca turned into LaRoux's waiting arms. "It's more than enough. But if we're going to spend a lot of time here, I might want to cozy it up a bit."

"Anything you want. This is as much your home now as it is mine." LaRoux began to fidget with the zipper hook on Rebecca's bloodstained dress. "How about we get you into the shower and cleaned up."

Rebecca twisted, looked into the dresser mirror, and frowned. "We've looked this way long enough for it to almost feel natural." Laughing lightly, she said, "We kind of resemble a pair of serial killers fresh from a hot Friday-night date." Fidgeting with her hair, she turned back to LaRoux. "Oh well, I guess this means we have to stay naked until our clothes are washed and dried."

"Baby, there's no washing and drying that's going to help these clothes." LaRoux opened a door. As he stepped into a large walk-in closet, Rebecca's jaw dropped. She gawked at the rows of jeans, pants, blouses, T-shirts, and dresses. Sneakers to high heels and every style of shoe in between filled the shoe cubicles.

"Okay, this closet looks like a miniature Macy's. Care to explain this to me?"

LaRoux stood behind Rebecca and slid his arms around her. "Bergdorf's, if you want the facts. When I asked you to leave with me, I arranged for clothes and toiletries to be shipped to Halifax. My caretaker picked up the shipment and brought it here. If there's something you don't like—or all of it—I can have it returned."

Rebecca checked the price tag on a pair of skinny distressed denims. "You can send these back. I think they cost more than all my jeans put together."

LaRoux unfastened the hook, then slowly pulled the zipper down to the small of Rebecca's back. "Baby, I've got ten lifetimes of family money to spoil you with. You don't ever need to look at a price tag again."

Rebecca turned in his arms. "But, David—"

LaRoux kissed her neck before sliding the dress off her shoulders and guiding it to the floor. "There are no *buts*. The sum of this wardrobe pales in comparison to the money I give to charity each and every year. I buy what pleases me. It doesn't matter whether it's inexpensive or exorbitant." He unfastened her bra, leaving Rebecca naked in his arms. "And I will do the same for you. Not because I think money can buy your love or happiness, but because you make me want to spoil you rotten."

As Rebecca worked at LaRoux's buttons, his black-and-blue bullet wound was no longer concealed. "Oh my God, I forgot. We need to get you to a doctor."

"First order of business: we both need to get cleaned up. Then we can talk about a doctor."

"We?"

He kissed Rebecca lightly. "The shower is big enough for two. That is, unless you're shy."

Rebecca looked down at her naked body. "Why yes, I am very shy. Maybe you should go wait on the porch."

LaRoux backed away and blatantly perused Rebecca's curves. "I'm afraid, Miss Pearson, although I'm inclined to adhere to your wishes, that body of yours is insisting I ignore all of that nonsense."

* * *

As Rebecca applied gauze to his wound, LaRoux grimaced from the edge of the bed. "It seems as though your Percocet is wearing off. Can I get you another?"

LaRoux pulled Rebecca into his lap. She straddled his thighs, still warm and moist from the shower, and their naked bodies stuck as if magnetized. "Only if you're done with sex for the day," he replied.

"Ha! Any more sex like that, and I might need a wheelchair."

LaRoux spun Rebecca down on the bed. "I wouldn't mind, as long as you stay naked. I don't think I will ever tire of this view."

Rebecca pulled LaRoux beside her. "You know, before I met you, I would have never pegged you to be such a romantic."

"How so?"

"Everything I saw and read said that David LaRoux was a cavalier playboy—Mr. Wham Bam Thank You Ma'am, an uber-successful, self-serving businessman, with no time or desire for anything like this. I could go on, but it seems rather pointless now."

As he propped himself up, his fingers caressed Rebecca's shoulder. "Outside of gathering evidence to arrest me, what changed your mind?"

Uncomfortable with the reminder of her deception, Rebecca gave LaRoux a stern eye as she stopped his exploring hands. "When I first met you, on the porch, I was quite intimidated by your wealth and power," Rebecca said, chuckling, "and devilish charms. And then, with that infectious Southern accent, you talked to me like some old acquaintance. Your laugh was so at ease—and that damn smile. Every time you smiled, your eyes twinkled like some hopeless hero from a sappy romance novel. You were nothing like I expected. And honestly, you came damn close to charming my dress off me that night, right there on the porch." Rebecca's gaze was lost in the memory. "I guess—no, I know—it was then that I started falling for you."

LaRoux's hand slid up Rebecca's neck and kneaded into her scalp. "Had you been *any* other woman, you would have met my evil twin at the party. The twinkle *you* saw, it was nerves. You had my head spinning at Bamboula's that first night I saw you across the room. Then the next day, I spent the better part of the afternoon and night debating about what to do about you at the party. You see, up until now, I have always categorized people. There are employees, business associates, and acquaintances. Acquaintances are never privy to my intimate emotions, and I never have sex with employees or business associates. But for some strange reason I knew, even before we officially met, I wanted both intimacy and sex. But I had no category for that." His finger traced down Rebecca's forehead, then down her nose and across her lips. "Among my three categories, people are considered either a friend or an adversary. You can guess where the DEA fits into this blueprint. But even enemies are acceptable, as long as they understand the rules and abide by them. My rules are black and white. There is no room for gray. If you cross the line, you pay the consequences." He reflected momentarily as Rebecca kissed his fingers. "And then comes Rebecca Pearson. When I first saw you at Bamboula's, I wanted you, badly. But I knew if I succumbed to my caveman desires, Saturday morning would have been the end of it. And I *knew* there was something special about you, something that I needed to discover. Had I had known it was your *job* to seduce me, I would have tossed you into the adversary camp and gone for the one-nighter. But thankfully, I didn't know—and I *was* right about you, and now here we are."

"That doesn't sound like the same guy I met on the porch."

"Tell me about it. Can you imagine my dilemma? If I had a legitimate day job that I was proud of it would have been so easy to walk up, introduce myself, sweep you off your feet, and fall in love. But I knew eventually I would have to tell you the truth, and then all of this would end. You see, you rocked my world long before you ever said a single word." LaRoux brushed his hand across Rebecca's cheek and stared deeply into her eyes. "How on earth did you accomplish that?"

Rebecca's eyebrows arched in clueless response as she softly smiled. "You're asking me? But now I know the truth, and I'm still here."

"Then marry me." LaRoux's face was intense, almost unnerving.

"I already told you I would." Suddenly Rebecca understood. "You mean now?"

"That is the basic idea."

"What's the big hurry? In a month or two, I might really be grating on your nerves. And then you'll regret it, because I know some really expensive lawyers."

LaRoux remained somber. "Something about knowing that you'll be my wife makes this feel like we're going to last."

Rebecca's expression hardened. "If I didn't want it to last, I would have shot you back in Las Vegas." Her pensive expression expired quickly, and she broke into a snicker. "When you first said *marry me*, I envisioned a church wedding with my parents, our friends, the fancy white dress thing."

"It will be a while before we go back home. We can always have a grand wedding later, but I want you as my wife now, not in six months or a year. Hell, I would have married you in the Elvis Chapel back in Vegas if we'd had the opportunity."

Rebecca laughed. "Somehow, I doubt that."

"You're right. Only a ceremony on the plantation will do, with a second line parade right through the Vieux Carré. But nonetheless, I want to marry you, now."

"Why, so I can't be compelled to testify against you?"

LaRoux frowned. "You're still talking like an agent."

Rebecca rolled on her side to face him. "I'm sorry. All of this, this . . . my world's been turned upside down. When you mentioned marriage, I wasn't expecting it to be so urgent. Is there something you're not telling me?"

"No. But in all likelihood, we won't go back home until the spring. And apparently, there's a contract out on me. And if anything should happen to me—"

"Nothing's going to happen."

"If it did, as my wife, everything I own would be yours."

Rebecca rolled on her back and stared at the ceiling in momentary silence before smiling. She turned her head to LaRoux and asked, "If I agree, do you promise I can still have a big New Orleans wedding?"

Sensing a deal in hand, LaRoux smiled. "Of course."

"And you promise to *always* gawk at my naked body?"

"Every time I see you naked, even when you're eighty."

Rebecca beamed as if she had just hit the Powerball Lottery. "Can I keep my last name?"

"You've got to be a LaRoux to get all that LaRoux owns."

Emphasizing every syllable, Rebecca called out her new name. "Mrs. Rebecca LaRoux. It kind of rolls right off the tongue, doesn't it?"

"Like a thunderstorm rolling across the bayou."

CHAPTER 13

LAROUX GENTLY CARESSED REBECCA'S hair as they lay face-to-face, basking in the morning sunlight that streamed into the bedroom. It had been eight blissful months since their escape to the Canadian coast, and their passion was still flaming. Married five months earlier by a pastor he had befriended in the local pub, LaRoux knew to be truly free, he had to bring closure to the life left behind.

"I've been avoiding something for a while now, but I really need to address it," he explained tenderly. "I need to return home and settle up my business affairs."

"Settle up?" Rebecca propped herself up on her elbow. "That sounds like a lawyer's way of saying *dangerous* or *criminal* activity."

"Are you happy living here?"

"With you, of course. Not to say I didn't love our weekend in Paris last month or wherever else we might venture."

"Well, time is running out. I have to close out my business affairs in New Orleans before everything is liquidated." He went on quickly. "Should I ever disappear or be killed, I made provisions for how my company was to be run—and dissolved."

"You mean *our* company."

LaRoux smiled broadly. "Careful what you ask for, Mrs. LaRoux."

Over their time together, LaRoux had rarely referenced anything concerning his company and *never* mentioned returning to New Orleans.

"*What* exactly do you think I'm asking for?"

LaRoux rolled his eyes as he ignored her question. "These last eight months, our lives have not existed by accident. All of *this*," LaRoux said, gesturing his hand about the room, "was painstakingly planned—except the part where I brought you here."

"And married me," Rebecca snickered.

"Yes, *that* too. I developed an intricate strategy to disappear, whether due to personal danger or, say, a potential DEA investigation. All illegal activities were to be suspended, with the exception of our purchases. That was to be continued to protect the integrity of our supply chain. If they have followed the plan, *we* will have amassed an inventory large enough to purchase several third world countries."

"I'll bet prices are astronomically high by now if you are sitting on an eight-month supply," Rebecca surmised.

"*We*. And one would be inclined to believe so. At the end of a year, if I was still missing, legal documents would automatically trigger the dissolution of *our* company to my chosen successors. So, if I don't go back and liquidate the inventory, the vast majority of *our* wealth, including the family home, all goes to somebody else."

"How much are we talking about, David?"

LaRoux swallowed hard. "Street value? Somewhere in the neighborhood of a half a billion dollars or so."

Rebecca sat up, her naked body glowing gold in the early morning light. "You know," she said, "for the past eight months you've made it so absolutely easy to love you without ever once thinking about money, or crime, or even my old job. I might prefer to simply live here and just be poor—just maybe."

"I was *so* right about you, baby." LaRoux pulled Rebecca close, the warmth and silkiness of her body instantly breeding desire. "Well, we wouldn't be absolutely poor." He paused to kiss her forehead. "But more importantly, I have to resolve the issue of who sold me out to the Colombians. We will never be completely free and clear until I find the SOB that nearly got us killed."

Rebecca slid from the bed and walked to the window. She stared in silence at the Gulf of St. Lawrence. "What if I told you I'm pregnant?"

LaRoux jumped from the bed like it was on fire. As he turned Rebecca in his arms, he smiled broadly and then cradled her face in his hands. "Are you?"

"Probably."

He looked deep into her eyes. "Then I have no choice. I cannot chance something ever happening to you or our child."

Rebecca grabbed LaRoux by the shoulders. "I'm coming with you."

LaRoux studied Rebecca from head to toe. "Not dressed like that," LaRoux chuckled. "But we both need to put our affairs to rest. We've got to go back home, discretely. I hope you don't get seasick."

* * *

Rebecca maintained her course on their fifty-foot sailboat. She headed for the buoy on the horizon. The exhilaration of navigating the boat across the waves, then cutting the wheel tight to the breeze, had yet to fade. In all her dreams, she had never envisioned such a life, or a love. She watched LaRoux on the bow, his hair blowing in the wind. He was everything she had ever wanted in a man—and quite a bit more. Rebecca knew that the days ahead in New Orleans would be treacherous, so she silently contemplated possible scenarios that might mitigate the risk. Watching LaRoux as he pulled a phone from his pocket, she called out, "Hey, where'd you get a phone?"

"It came with the boat." LaRoux punched in the numbers and listened to it ring with a sense of apprehension.

"Hello?" The voice on the other end was uncharacteristically gruff. "Walt."

"David? What the hell, man?"

"I had to do it, Walt, for more reasons than one." LaRoux looked back at Rebecca propped up on the wheel and smiled.

"It was because of *her*," Walt snapped.

LaRoux inhaled the cleansing salt air slowly and smiled at a host of memories that made him want to scream, *Hell yes!* Had he not met Rebecca, he would have gone back to New Orleans and dealt with this business immediately. "A small part."

"Damn, David, you should have rid yourself of her the day you found out about her career ambitions."

"That was never an option, Walt, so let it go. I know there's no need to ask, but are you sure this line is secure?"

Walt paused to allow the insult to his expertise pass, then he continued in his annoyed tone, "You've been gone over eight months, and believe it or not, your loyal band of idiots has not sunk the ship or forgotten protocol."

LaRoux realized he had insinuated that his trusted friend was incompetent. "I'm sorry, Walt. The circumstances behind Las Vegas forced my hand. I'll be heading home very soon. But in the meantime, if you haven't already figured it out, we need to look into that plumbing problem I left behind. We've got to find the source of that leak in the office and plug it permanently."

Walt defended his crew. "The office plumbing has always been tight, David. I think you might need to check a little closer to your fly."

LaRoux looked back at the horizon; Rebecca's course remained good. "One thing I can promise you, Walt, is she is the least of my problems."

Walt forced his anger to abate just a tad before continuing. "You want me to brief Taz and Ryan?"

"Not yet."

"Is there a problem, David?"

"No, I trust them without question. I just don't want to answer to anyone else right now."

"Yeah, you know Taz and Ryan are going to rip you a new one when you get back home.

That fed in your bed is going to be the death of us all."

"I'll let you know when I'm close." LaRoux hung up and crossed the deck.

"Is everything alright, David?"

"Apparently, my crew is a little upset that there's a *fed in my bed.* Outside of that, there's nothing to report." He stood behind Rebecca and wrapped his arms around her. "Are you doing alright here?"

"I may never step foot on shore again." Rebecca glowed with the innocent enthusiasm of a child. "I'm really loving this whole boat thing."

"Just wait till we reach the Florida Keys." LaRoux rested his head on Rebecca's shoulder and savored the scent of her flesh and the crisp breeze in his face. Then suddenly, he said, "I need to check in with Mr. Hanson." He headed back to the bow and timed his steps to the pitch of the waves as he listened for Hanson to pick up.

"If you wrecked my plane, you'd better be calling from the afterlife."

"*Your* plane?"

"You might have paid for it, but I built it." The silence on the other end left Hanson to contemplate his employer's disposition. "I see you disabled my tracker."

LaRoux was preoccupied, enjoying the wind and sun in his face. "I told you, Victor, I needed to disappear. That meant from you as well, my friend." For the second time today, LaRoux experienced guilt for leaving his friends behind without notice. Once again, an uncomfortable silence lingered, this time of Hanson's making. "How are you?" LaRoux asked.

"In your absence, very busy. It has taken a lot of effort to fill in the blanks. I gave up trying to find out if you were still alive or where you were after the first thirty days and doubled down on my efforts to find out what happened and who was behind it."

"Go on."

"The Colombian you wounded is Renaldo Sanchez. He wound up in the custody of the DEA. Somehow, Mr. Sanchez disappeared somewhere between his discharge from the hospital and his return to the DEA office. I would have loved to have seen the look on that fucknuckle Martin's face when they lost him. Mr. Sanchez was destined to remain in federal custody for the rest of his life. But by some miracle of fate, he wound up enjoying deluxe concrete kennel accommodations in the Louisiana bayou, complete with some very unpleasant information-extraction sessions."

LaRoux knew that Victor's kidnapping of the DEA's only potential witness had to have brought down a gale-force shitstorm on both his employees, and Will Martin. "So, any luck?"

"Here's the shitkicker. I didn't nab Sanchez. Somehow your crew of amateurs got the jump on me. But apparently, Mr. Sanchez was more willing to be eaten by a nasty-ass gator than divulge the information your crew was attempting to extract. As a result, his leg already resembled a gator chew toy before I arrived."

"So, is that all we have?"

"Not hardly. Now enter the professional," Hanson boasted, speaking about himself. "I found my access to your crew's prisoner unacceptably easy. Upon my further interrogation, and a touch of sodium pentothal, I got the names of his Vegas comrades. This proved utterly useless, as you had already disposed of them. And sadly, much to the chagrin of your employees the next morning, they found Mr. Sanchez had abruptly expired."

"Damn, I can't believe my guys weren't more on top of it. Maybe I have been gone too long."

"Honestly, David, they weren't that bad. They sprung him from the DEA and got him to Louisiana without breaking a sweat. It's just that I am that much better, which is why you pay me the big bucks." Hanson waited for a reply, but without one, he continued, "So, on with the story. I flew down to Colombia to pay Señora Sanchez a visit in her hometown of Ocaña. Seems her son was going to Bucaramanga to do business, although the nature of that business was unclear. But whenever he returned home, he was always flush with cash."

"Bucaramanga?" LaRoux's shoulders tensed as Hanson's report sunk in.

"Yeah, I know," Hanson sighed.

"Are you sure?"

"Absolutely. I verified as much as I could without raising any flags."

"Miguel knew that if something like Vegas ever went down, that as part of our contingency plan we'd continue to purchase, but not take delivery for an extended period. Do you think maybe he planned this fiasco with intentions of keeping our product?"

"Hypothetically, let's say he's developed problems of his own. I could see him cashing out with you and selling our product to another client. With you gone, there's nobody in your company that could force him to honor his commitment."

LaRoux's spirits sank. Miguel San Domingo had been one of his most trusted business associates for years. Immediately, he made a connection between San Domingo's son, Armando, and this current situation. "I can't see Armando orchestrating this from Bucaramanga without his old man's knowledge. Shit, I've got to go to Colombia." LaRoux looked back at Rebecca, who puckered up and launched an air kiss back at him. He knew this new development would not sit well. He pondered his options briefly. "Book me a public flight for Sunday, with one of my compromised aliases, from New York to Colombia. I want to make sure the DEA thinks they've found me and has discovered where I'm headed."

"You know, David, if the Vegas hit was San Domingo's play and not Armando's, chances are you won't be leaving Colombia without someone dying."

LaRoux gritted his teeth. "It's time to flush out the roaches, all of them, which is probably going to reveal a big ass rat on our end."

Seconds later, LaRoux hung up the phone, gazed out over the horizon, and tensed his shoulders. Then he relaxed with a great cleansing breath. He turned and looked at Rebecca steering the boat through the churning seas with an eye of deep-rooted compassion.

Not waiting for him to return to her side, Rebecca called out, "What did Mr. Hanson have to say?"

LaRoux shuffled back to the wheel slowly, calculating his new plan of action. "We have a change in agenda, we're going to New York. I need you to catch a flight to New Orleans and report in with your boss. You need to inform Will, if they didn't fire him already, that I'm headed to Colombia to personally secure a large purchase with Miguel San Domingo."

"*San Domingo?*" Rebecca's appalled expression extinguished the tranquility. "You have done business with *him*?"

"He *can* be a dangerous man in a dangerous business. You don't think I could have gotten this rich doing business with two-bit smugglers, do you?" David was calm and his tone matter of fact. "As I've already told you, if you know the rules and play within them, anybody, even San Domingo, can be as benign as a kitten."

"Somehow I doubt that," Rebecca scoffed. "The agency always suspected he was dirty, but we could never find one shred of evidence to initiate a case. Anyone who has ever talked has disappeared."

LaRoux took in Rebecca's words, then he kissed her on the cheek. "Let me show you something." He flipped a switch on the console and the autopilot indicator lit up. "We've got maybe an hour before the seas get a little rocky." He took Rebecca by the hand and led her below.

"It's that simple? A computer can do it?"

"Not entirely, but I'll explain that later." He cradled Rebecca's face and lightly kissed her brows and forehead before he moved down the side of her head to nibble her ear while unzipping her jacket.

Although she moaned in approval, she was not about to concede to LaRoux's plan without an argument. "You promised me that you were done."

He pulled her jacket off her shoulders and dropped it to the floor. Slowly and deliberately, he began unbuttoning her shirt while intently staring into her eyes. "I am." He kissed her lips again, softer, while nibbling and tugging gently on her lower lip as his hands reached the last button.

"This certainly doesn't sound like you're done. Send somebody else down there."

LaRoux slid his hands around Rebecca's waist and slowly worked his way up. "The black lace bra?" he asked without ever looking. As his fingers began working between the fabric and her flesh, Rebecca shuddered and moaned. "It would appear that someone in my company is in cahoots with San Domingo—and possibly someone inside the DEA. I'm going down to flush them out under the pretense of a deal." LaRoux spoke in hushed tones so he could enjoy the exhilaration in Rebecca's breath.

"That's . . . too . . . dangerous," she croaked through her state of arousal. "Let's turn the boat . . . around and forget all of that, that . . . nonsense."

LaRoux unbuttoned Rebecca's jeans and slid his hand inside. She trembled at his touch. He dropped to his knees and tugged at her jeans as he kissed her belly. "That's why you're going to invite your DEA buddies to the party—for added security."

Rebecca arched and grabbed LaRoux's hair as his lips explored deeper. "Dammit, David, let's turn this around. I don't care about the money."

LaRoux scooped Rebecca from her feet and lay her across the galley table. He dropped his pants, pulled her legs over his shoulders, and slowly closed the distance until he was inside her.

As Rebecca arched in ecstasy, he lifted her head to his and kissed her passionately. "This is why I can't turn away. This is why the time has come to finish this."

CHAPTER 14

IN THE LOBBY OF the New Orleans airport, Rebecca fretted over making the call. She had no desire to deal with the onslaught of bullshit Martin would be dishing out. But she knew it had to be done; she only wished it could be with any director other than Martin. Maybe things had changed. Maybe somebody else would be in charge of the investigation. She dialed the number.

As a familiar voice answered, she cringed.

"Will, it's Rebecca."

"Rebecca? Where in the hell have you been?" Martin screeched.

"I've been undercover. Remember, that *was* my assignment, Will."

"Not a damned word for eight months! Are you fucking kidding me? We had no idea if you were alive or dead."

"Back off, Will. I've been in an area so prehistoric that phone access was impossible. LaRoux had no landline phone or cell in his home, and I didn't want to risk trying to use one in that Podunk village. The man had eyes everywhere."

"Where the hell were you?"

"I'm not sure. Maybe Scotland. He drugged me for the trip there and back, but I remember glimpses of flying over water. The few people

I talked to had Scottish accents. And it was cool when we got there and damn cold and gray over the entire winter."

Will's tone remained agitated, but softer. "Where is LaRoux now?"

Rebecca swallowed hard but knew she had to follow her husband's instructions. So, she gave away his location. "He's heading down to Bucaramanga, Colombia. Apparently, he needs to secure a large buy in person. I hope you're ready to mobilize." The silence on the other end led Rebecca to contemplate her boss's situation. "You are still in charge, aren't you?"

"Don't worry about that right now. How soon can you be in New Orleans?"

"I'm at the airport here now. He expects me to be back at the plantation when he gets back from Colombia."

"Why is that?"

Rebecca picked up on Martin's shifting tone, which was now pregnant with concern. "Gee, Will, I don't know. Maybe I've been his nightly piece of ass for the last eight months and he's going to expect more."

Martin's spirits plunged. "I'm so sorry, Rebecca."

"Don't apologize, Will. It's not like I haven't enjoyed the sex." She visualized Martin's face cracking. That made her smile. "He *is* pretty amazing in the sack."

"Are you going to bust my ass forever?"

Pity for Martin was not in Rebecca's playbook. "Only until this case is over. Once I'm back home, I won't have any need to talk to you. But until that day, you deserve every bit of it. Now, as I have no money, please make sure that they have continued to deposit my paychecks."

Martin knew if there was any hope of repairing the damage he had done, he'd have to play nice and be agreeable, perhaps even submissive. "I'll arrange for a room for you, just in case."

Rebecca knew her room would be uncomfortably close to his accommodations, so she said, "No thanks. David will be expecting me at the plantation when he returns, and that's where I'll stay until he's busted." She didn't wait for another barrage of questions. She snapped, "I'll be in touch," and then hung up.

* * *

Upon exiting a cab an hour later, Rebecca grimaced as she stepped into the oppressive late-spring humidity. Immediately, a sticky blanket of dampness enveloped her.

Within minutes, she entered the DEA field office. The sound of shadows traipsing across the bayou could easily be heard in the deathly silence of the squad room. She held her head high as she headed for Will's office, traced by a multitude of prying eyes.

Rebecca opened Will's door. An unfamiliar face greeted her.

"Oh, I'm sorry. I thought this was Director Martin's office."

"Agent Pearson?" the burly man inquired.

Apprehensively, she replied, "Yes."

"This *was* Agent Martin's office. Please, sit down."

Rebecca complied as she looked about the room suspiciously. Noting softball trophies, fishing memorabilia, and numerous other personal effects, she realized the change in command didn't happen recently.

The big man walked around the desk and extended his hand. "I'm Director Cutchins. This office was vacant until Martin arrived and created the task force to investigate the LaRoux family. I was transferred here in the wake of that debacle, which cost two men their positions. Director Thompson got transferred to Kansas, and Martin—well, he's damn lucky he's still got a job. He got demoted and sent to Atlanta. Until you resurfaced, I was closing the books on this investigation so that I could go home to DC. In light of your unexpected resurrection, Agent Martin is inbounded to assist in your debriefing. But I'd like to get started with some preliminary intel. After that, we'll get you in for a medical and psych eval."

"Director Cutchins, I don't mean any disrespect, but I *don't* need a physical or psych exam."

Cutchins held his hand up. "Relax, Pearson. It's protocol. You've been under deep for eight months and, from what Martin tells me, with recurring intimate contact. We need to make sure LaRoux has not infected you with any creepy crawlers. And although we all despise the psych eval, the very nature of your assignment has been proven to inflict some psychological duress. So, I'm afraid I must insist you will undergo both. Understood?"

Rebecca cut a cold stare of defiance. "If he or I had any creepy crawlers, I would know it by now. Secondly, if I give you any reason to suspect I need a psych eval, I'll reconsider your offer—after this investigation is concluded. I'm expected at LaRoux's home soon, and if I'm not there shortly, his people will become suspicious."

Cutchins ran his hands through his dark, wavy hair. "Fair enough, though if you ever feel you need to move to a safe location, we'll make it happen." Then he switched the topic. "Outside of the brief intel you shared with Agent Martin, what else can you tell me?"

Rebecca checked her watch. "I don't know where LaRoux is at this moment. I haven't seen him in almost a day. But I know he's heading to Bucaramanga, Colombia, to personally close a big deal with San Domingo. You might want to get a jump on it, but he may be there already." Rebecca checked her watch again. "I really need to be going."

Cutchins put his hand on the doorknob and snickered. "Between all the man-hours and money logged on this investigation, not to mention your disappearance and the clusterfuck in Las Vegas, I'm sure you'll understand your *former boyfriend's* demotion." Cutchins's snicker intensified. "And in the end, it appears as if Martin's methods and instincts might have been right all along."

Rebecca cringed inwardly, not at Martin's demotion, but at Cutchins's knowledge of her affair with him. "Is there anything else, Director?"

Cutchins turned the knob and cracked the door. "You'll have to forgive me if I reserve my praise for your *deep* undercover work. Until it proves to bear some tangible evidence of a major drug crime and not just a personal vendetta against Louisiana's favorite rich boy, I don't have any intentions of getting demoted over wounded egos."

"Understood, sir."

"Tread carefully, Agent Pearson. There are going to be many eyes on this investigation until it's resolved." Cutchins swung the door open and watched as Rebecca passed.

Rebecca breezed through the office and silently rejoiced. *Damn. Will got demoted. Served the arrogant prick right.* As the eyes of her fellow agents continued to stare unabashedly, she quickened her pace. She dreaded the obvious:. *They all know.* The validation of her rank, which had taken years to earn, had been instantly obliterated in the spotlight of sexual scandal.

Leaving the office in a state of emotional turmoil, Rebecca suddenly felt the eyes of a stranger upon her. Quite possibly LaRoux's security staff was running counterintelligence measures against the DEA. Or was it Hanson? From what she knew about the man, if LaRoux had not forewarned him of her purpose, he might take exception to her meeting.

* * *

After answering on the second ring, Rebecca's moment of overdue relief finally arrived.

"Hi," LaRoux said to the deadly silence on the other end. The lack of a reply unnerved him. "Are you there?"

"Yes," Rebecca replied coolly.

"Is everything alright?" LaRoux tensed, knowing the tempered reply was forestalling the unwanted lecture to follow.

"You never called."

Her tone is so lifeless, LaRoux thought. "It's only been a day."

"For twenty-four hours, I have endured not knowing if you were alive or if something bad had happened to you. I haven't slept since I got here."

"Darling, I didn't want to call too early and wake you up. But I'm sorry for stressing you."

This is why I stayed single, LaRoux reminded himself, even though he knew Rebecca was right. "Look, after I finish business in Colombia, I'll be home on Thursday."

"Is someone else going to die?"

"Amidst the instances of lies and treachery, somebody usually does."

Rebecca suddenly felt vulnerable. "Was it all a lie, David?"

Without the luxury of time or relationship experience, LaRoux sifted for the words to set things right. "Nothing has changed for me."

"Then what are you doing in Colombia? You said that if I left Vegas with you, you would be done with this business. Going to Colombia to make a buy—it makes all of this feel like a big fat lie."

Her objections were leading LaRoux to entrapment. Any verbal acknowledgment would incriminate him. Hanson's persistent warnings echoed in his mind as he formulated his response.

"Like I said, I'll be home Thursday. We can sort it out then."

"David, I won't be here Thursday. Without you, I don't belong here. Without you, this is not my home."

LaRoux heard her pain but knew he had no other option. With San Domingo—and most likely someone in-house—conspiring against him, he knew his life and Rebecca's would never be safe. "You should do what feels right, baby. I'll find you when I return."

Do what feels right? Rebecca had felt the eyes of distrust upon her ever since returning to New Orleans. She already knew LaRoux was the most calculating, intuitive criminal she and the DEA had ever encountered. He had managed to make Martin look like an idiot, leading to his demotion. The DEA had barely avoided a major publicity nightmare. And *if* LaRoux had orchestrated the entire Las Vegas scenario, Rebecca knew her safety was in peril. *I'll find you when I return.* His words sent a sudden chill across her flesh.

"Rebecca?"

"Yes," she said timidly.

"I love you."

Reality dealt an openhanded slap to the face. David LaRoux, drug lord and killer, vowed his love. Rebecca had to force her reply. "I love you too."

CHAPTER 15

THE OUTSKIRTS OF BUCARAMANGA were a menagerie of old world and new. As the modern urban sprawl that had migrated to the east drove up real estate prices, redevelopment had now returned to the once forgotten outskirts. It was from there, perched atop the eighth floor of a modern office building, that Miguel San Domingo ruled his empire.

Much like David LaRoux, his business was forged on a robust import-export endeavor, as well as on agriculture and metal industries. And much like LaRoux, he was a good shepherd to the poor and needy, which were many. His tentacles were wrapped tightly around the politicians, police, and military. In Bucaramanga, nothing transpired without his blessing, and a criminal's lifespan could pass in the blink of an eye.

David LaRoux paced off the last two blocks anxiously as he made his way to the main entrance to San Domingo's office. He hated feeling this way. He wondered if his old friend had been warned of his imminent arrival. Not much passed in Bucaramanga without San Domingo's knowledge. Flying on a commercial flight, under a false identity and disguised, LaRoux hoped he had avoided detection by facial recognition software during the journey.

He could feel the imaginary crosshairs on his back. The shadow of death had become an all too familiar companion, stalking him in Miami and Vegas. He could feel the weight of the shadow. Would today be the day LaRoux became death's overdue prize?

One block to go. Just ahead on the right, San Domingo's office rose above its neighboring structures by five stories. Across the street was Hotel Bucaramanga, a hostel, brothel, and dump.

This was old-school Colombia in its finest form.

Outside San Domingo's building, David LaRoux spotted a familiar face—Hector Lopez, henchman and *killer* supreme. Just inside the door, a mere breath from Hector, fifty armed and exceptionally bored mercenaries awaited his command to kill. If LaRoux's unannounced arrival was not welcome, this would be one short and ugly reception.

One block ago, LaRoux had dumped his disguise of a wig and sunglasses and now was easily recognizable. Hector spotted his approach, touched his ear, and spoke into his comm device.

Then he said, "Señor LaRoux, I was not told we were expecting you."

"No, Hector, I am not expected. But I need to see Señor San Domingo all the same."

"Please, step inside." Hector ushered LaRoux into the lobby, where the entire staff scrutinized him. "This will take just a minute." Just as Hector began patting down LaRoux, a reply came through his earbud. "I understand," he answered. "I have been instructed to tell you Señor San Domingo is not expected until afternoon. Please tell me where you are staying, and we will send a car for you when he returns."

LaRoux studied the lobby staff's demeanor; most had returned to their ordinary business. "If it's all the same, Hector, I would prefer to wait in his office."

Hector tensed; he was displeased with LaRoux's reply. Although LaRoux had been allowed free range in the past, Hector's orders were quite clear. "I'm sorry, Señor LaRoux, that will not be possible today."

"Hector, I know Miguel is here. I saw him when he entered the building this morning. What's going on?"

"I don't know, Señor LaRoux, but I have been instructed to send you away."

"Hector, you know how far back Miguel and I go. Should I call him and ask why you won't let me into his building?"

"I'm sorry, Señor LaRoux. I have my orders."

"Unless your orders are directly from Miguel, then I must insist." Hector rolled his eyes and sneered. LaRoux grew impatient as Hector displayed no intentions to capitulate. "Whoever is giving you orders, he is going to be in a world of shit. I'm going up."

"*Sí*," Hector replied into his comm. Then he moved to draw his pistol.

The struggle that ensued was short-lived; LaRoux grabbed Hector's wrist, twisted it down, and snatched the gun away. He wrapped his arm around Hector's neck, pulled him against his chest as a shield, and put the gun to his head. Backing quickly into the elevator, LaRoux said, "I don't know what the hell is going on here, Hector, but I told you I really need to see Miguel."

Hector pushed the elevator call button without being asked. "*He says,*" Hector squeaked out as he struggled to speak with LaRoux's arm around his neck, "that you are here to kill Señor San Domingo."

Just as the elevator arrived and the doors began to open, ten heavily armed men came rushing to Hector's aid. "Have them stand down, Hector, or nobody, and I mean nobody, leaves the building alive." LaRoux pressed the gun to Hector's head.

"Easy, *amigo*," Hector replied. "*Alto el fuego.*" Seeing that they were obeying far too slowly, Hector repeated his order. "*Alto el fuego.*" Begrudgingly, Hector's crew slowly lowered their weapons. LaRoux backed into the elevator car as he held Hector tightly against him.

"Press it," LaRoux ordered.

As the car began to lift, LaRoux released his grip on Hector. "Jesus, Hector! You know Miguel is like my own flesh and blood. *Who* says I'm here to kill him? *Who* says I can't see him?"

"Armando."

"*Armando San Domingo?* Since when?"

"I don't know. He just told me."

"Trust me, Hector, I'm not here to kill Miguel. There have been attempts on *my* life, which appear to have originated from Bucaramanga. That's why I'm here, and that's why I need to see Miguel."

The elevator opened to a sprawling loft with a panoramic view of the city and countryside. Across the polished cement floor sat Miguel San Domingo behind an antique Victorian cherry desk. As soon as he recognized his old friend, he rose immediately. "David LaRoux!"

LaRoux handed Hector his gun back. "Sorry about your wrist, Hector. You know I wouldn't have done it unless I believed it was absolutely necessary."

"It's alright, *amigo*. I thought something was wrong. That's why I *let* you take my gun." Hector winked and stepped back into the elevator. "I will go calm the nerves of my friends."

"What are you doing here? Why didn't you let me know that you were alive or coming?" San Domingo eagerly crossed the office toward LaRoux.

LaRoux scanned the expansive loft to ensure they were alone. "Miguel, we need to talk. Something is completely fucked up."

"I know. That shit in Vegas was crazy. Nobody knew if you were dead or alive. I guess you did that thing—that plan of yours." San Domingo gave LaRoux an overbearing grizzly hug. "I am so relieved that you are alive, my friend."

"Are you, Miguel?"

San Domingo took two steps back. "Why would you ask that, my brother?"

"Why did Armando refuse to let me see you?"

"I don't know. Why don't we call him and ask?" He walked to his desk and picked up the phone.

LaRoux cupped his hand over San Domingo's. "Don't bother. Something tells me he'll be here soon enough."

San Domingo released the phone. Concerned with LaRoux's strained expression, he reached into his desk and pulled bourbon from the bottom drawer. "I have been saving this for you. You know, I am a tequila man myself, but whatever this problem is, we'll find the answer somewhere in this bottle."

LaRoux looked at the twenty-five-year-old bottle of Pappy Van Winkle and grimaced. "I'll enjoy that a lot more once we get to the bottom of this, Miguel."

"I bought this after your last visit. It cost me three thousand dollars. I was saving it for a special occasion. You being alive is special enough, but the look in your eyes makes the price meaningless. So, for better or worse, today is that special day." San Domingo poured two glasses and handed one to LaRoux. "My brother, here's to being alive."

"I'm married, Miguel."

"Oh shit." San Domingo choked on his drink. "I'm afraid we don't have enough bourbon for that."

"She is—*was*—a DEA agent." LaRoux was nonchalant, as if San Domingo should have already known.

"Holy shit! I'm afraid there's not enough liquor in Colombia to resolve that problem. I had heard rumors about the two of you and saw on the news that you both might have been abducted. I assumed at least she had met with some unpleasant ending." San Domingo took a long swallow. "Being married to you, maybe she would be better off dead." He smiled and refilled his glass. "This is going to be a very long night, my brother."

LaRoux reached into his pocket and removed a photo. "Do you know this man?"

San Domingo studied the image. "I've seen him. When I heard the suspects were Colombian, I had my people looking into it. This man is the suspect the DEA lost last year."

"He was the only surviving player of the hit squad that tried to take me out in Vegas. They called him Little Dillinger. According to my sources, he traveled to Bucaramanga to earn his money."

"Trust me, my friend, there is no death squad that operates out of my city without my blessing. If he is a player, Armando would know it."

San Domingo studied LaRoux's suspicious expression. "Say, you're not accusing Armando of being involved in that Vegas business, are you?"

"I don't know anything for sure, but his name did come up. And for some reason, he sure as hell tried to prevent me from seeing you today." In the ensuing awkward silence, the pair buried their concerns in the bottoms of their respective glasses.

Miguel topped the glasses back to the brims. "My sources tell me your wife's employers arrived in town yesterday and are looking at *my* organization. This timing appears a little coincidental, no?"

"*Former* employer. And it's not the first time you've been looked at, is it?" LaRoux stared down his friend. "You think I brought them here?"

"No, my friend, but this wife—how much does she know?"

LaRoux downed his glass. "*Everything.*"

"Holy Christ, David! Do you think it's possible that maybe she married you just to take us down?"

LaRoux turned, walked to the window, and gazed out at the mountains off in the distance. He said aloud what he had not wanted to admit to himself. "Every time she says *I love you.*"

The momentary silence was shattered by frantic pleadings as the elevator doors opened and Armando rushed into the room with a gun aimed at LaRoux. "Father, this man is a traitor! He is with the DEA and is the one who killed David Antonio."

"Armando San Domingo! Put that gun away," San Domingo yelled.

"Father, this is the man that killed my cousin. Let me avenge David now!"

LaRoux stared at Armando, who he thought he had not seen in ten years—until recognition hit him.

"Miami." LaRoux recognized Armando from that altercation. At the time the deal had gone bad, he had no clue about the identities of the dealers who had tried to rip him off and kill him. "That was David and you?"

"You're damn right that was David." Armando raised the gun a second time.

"Armando, I'm not going to tell you again—put that damn gun away!" San Domingo demanded.

"But he's the one," Armando pleaded. "He's the one that killed David."

"Shut the hell up," San Domingo ordered, "and give me that gun." He took the gun from his son and turned to his friend. "David, is this true?"

LaRoux stared at Armando. Vividly, he remembered the face of the boy whose life he had spared. It was Armando's. LaRoux explained morosely, "My people set up the buy with a new supplier. You know me, Miguel, I personally oversee all new transactions. I went to Miami to meet with this new distributor. I hadn't seen David, or your boy, since they were kids. I had no clue who they were. But there never was a deal. It was a setup."

"Bullshit," Armando cried.

"Shut your mouth, boy," San Domingo shouted. "I'm not gonna tell you again." He looked back at LaRoux suspiciously. "So, tell me how my sister's son died."

"I thought the deal was airtight. We were at the Miami Hilton—and unarmed. As soon as David checked our money, and we discovered he and his crew had no product, David and some other guy drew down on us. You know me, Miguel—I took David's gun, killed the other guy—and then David."

"So, it was *you* who killed my nephew?"

"Dammit, Miguel, I hadn't seen those boys in ten years. I had no idea. And you and I are alike—you know how we deal with thieves."

San Domingo clutched the nine millimeter and looked at his son in disbelief. "Tell me the truth, boy!"

The lack of an immediate response told San Domingo all he needed to know. With the gun gripped tightly, he swiped away the tears. "David, you held my nephew at his baptism—"

"Dammit, Miguel. I never would have gone to Miami if I had known it was your boys. What in the hell were they trying to accomplish?"

Another bout of silence brought more unspoken speculation. Finally, San Domingo said, "It is my fault. I knew these boys were trying to break out of my shadow. I had refused their proposals too many times. I should have seen it coming."

"Father, you didn't pull the trigger. He did." The enraged young man pointed an accusatory finger at LaRoux. "You cannot let him get away with this."

"Shut your mouth, my son." San Domingo's anger was not restrained. "You and your cousin went to Miami with intentions of ripping off and killing my biggest customer, one of my closest friends—behind my back?"

"It was David Antonio's plan. He said a man came to him for a very large buy. But he said we had to get Uncle David out of the way before the deal could proceed. It was supposed to be just a setup. The DEA was supposed to be there to arrest him. Nobody was supposed to die. But the deal got moved, and the DEA and the drugs weren't there. When Uncle David realized there were no drugs, David Antonio panicked."

San Domingo nodded. "Who is this man? And do not lie, or I swear." Sliding the picture across his desk, San Domingo studied his son's face.

Armando did not have to study the image. He hung his head lower. "We call him Little Dillinger."

"And you sent this man to Las Vegas to kill my good friend?"

"Him and others—to avenge David," Armando answered proudly.

"Dammit, son. In this business, we do not kill the few trusted friends we have. Have you learned nothing from me? David LaRoux *is* family." San Domingo handed the gun to LaRoux. "David Antonio was an idiot and deserved to die. My son has betrayed us both, twice. You decide his fate."

LaRoux studied the gun, then looked at a shocked Armando. "You should have gone to your father or come to me. David's blood is on your hands as much as mine." LaRoux ejected the magazine and the expelled round in the chamber before handing it back to the boy.

"I might be a stranger to you, but your father will attest that I would die before I would knowingly bring harm to, or betray, your family."

"You see this man," San Domingo said to his son. "This is what honor looks like. I should insist that he kill you. You have disgraced yourself and our family. You have lost the privilege to bear our name. From now on, I will call you Armando the Fool. Now, go home to your mother and confess your sins. If she or your aunt Marie do not kill you first, pray that my anger is tempered before I return home."

As the boy turned to leave, LaRoux grabbed his arm. "Who told you I'd be in Vegas?"

The boy didn't answer right away. Then LaRoux squeezed his arm tighter, and he spilled the beans. "His name is Geno, the same man that was with you and set up Miami. He said the time had come to avenge my cousin's death. Initially, only David dealt with him. Then last year, he contacted me . . . about Las Vegas. He knew many details about your travel." The boy was speaking of no other than Geno Harper, LaRoux's stateside drug-empire lieutenant.

LaRoux released the boy's arm. "I am truly sorry about David."

The anger had not entirely dissipated from Armando's eyes as he looked into LaRoux's. "No, it is my fault. I listened to David. I should have gone to my father. I am lucky to still be alive."

"Armando, our families will get past this," LaRoux said.

Racked with guilt, the boy turned and left. LaRoux turned back to San Domingo, who was filling the glasses again. His distress was painfully obvious. He handed LaRoux his glass. "Apparently, we both have problems within our families. But first, you are going to have to face Marta and then her sister. So, you must come to dinner *tonight*. I will pray that neither of them cuts your heart out before the meal."

LaRoux took several sips before shaking his head. "Dying twice in one year would be rather unpleasant."

"If one of those sisters kills you, you will be staying dead, that I promise." San Domingo smiled, then took a measured sip.

LaRoux smirked, then placed his hand on San Domingo's

shoulder. "This is it for me, Miguel. After this shipment, I am out. Maybe it's time you consider retiring as well, so we can live to spend our money in peace."

San Domingo nodded. "No shit. You know it's going to take you two years to sell all this coke. And you're retiring on me?"

"I've already made arrangements, and yes, I'm ready . . . and married now."

"Yes," San Domingo said, thumping his finger into LaRoux's chest, "but to an agent of the DEA."

"Don't get any ideas, Miguel. She is my wife."

"*Sí*. So, tonight you will come to dinner. We will drink tequila and discuss this wife and my nephew."

"And let's not forget your family-sanctioned assassins."

San Domingo sighed. "*Sí*. And my family's attempt to kill you."

"Twice," LaRoux said as a sneer crossed his lips.

"*Ay ay ay*. I think I'd better stop by the tequila store on my way home. It's going to be a very long night."

CHAPTER 16

REBECCA STARED AT THE seedy, musty motel room. *Shag carpeting, dark wood paneling, and furniture from the thrift store dumpster? Shouldn't all of this have disappeared with tie-dye, bell bottoms, and hippies from the seventies?* As unappealing as it sounded, she considered going back to the plantation. But that would be a moral victory for her drug czar husband. He deserved to be punished, so she had taken up the DEA on its offer to relocate her to a safe place. He had lied. He was right back in the heart of the very business he had promised to abandon. All of his rationalizations had evaporated during their three days of separation. Besides, when was it ever *just one more deal*?

She had been forced to swallow her pride to teach her husband a lesson. But in this dump? This motel room was not a reward for a job well done; it was a token of disdain from her superiors for the insubordination she had displayed upon her return. Without a paycheck or any credit cards, she was helplessly dependent on the agency, or LaRoux. Jazzfest was the DEA's excuse for dumping her in the *only* vacant room in the city. *More like fuck-you fest, you little defiant bitch.*

She looked at her watch and then her cell phone. Martin would be arriving at any minute. She hadn't heard from her husband in two days. If he was dead, Rebecca was certain Mr. Hanson would be coming for her. The cell was her lifeline to LaRoux or a tracking hotline for quite possibly the most lethal employee in LaRoux's empire. She considered pulling the battery. After all, if everything went south from this point, she had done her job. She had delivered the biggest drug lord in the country and his South American connection. She would be an instant DEA legend, and all she'd had to do was fall in love with the son of a bitch.

A sudden knock at the door interrupted her musings. She looked from the corner of the dingy drapes and spotted Martin, who looked obnoxiously anxious. She unlocked the door, cracked it open, turned her back, and walked away.

As Martin entered the room, the smell and decor took him aback. "Jesus, Rebecca. Not quite the Palazzo, is it?"

"You think? Apparently, this was the only vacancy in the state. So, if you just got to town I guess you'll be sleeping in your car."

"It would beat the hell out of this place." Martin forced a conciliatory smile. "I'll see what I can do about your accommodations."

"Between your demotion and my unreasonable attitude, I won't hold my breath."

"That's all about to change. You did it! We got LaRoux and San Domingo's deal."

"David? He's still alive?" Rebecca's tone hinted at relief as she sat on the bed.

"*David*, is it?" In a wounded, snarky tone, Martin replied, "Yes, *David* is still alive."

"Don't give me your shit, Will. Thanks to you, I had to marry him and spend the last eight months with that man between my legs. And now, I think I'm pregnant. Eventually, undercover or not, I'm going to have to answer for all of this. So don't even start up with your bullshit!"

The rage and angst in Rebecca's eyes forced Martin to turn away. "Pregnant?" he murmured as he cracked open the drapes. He was clueless how to broach the issue, so he didn't. "So, you've had no contact?" Martin inquired as he turned and ran his fingers across the comforter. He inspected his hand with great apprehension and asked timidly, "Is it safe—to sit on?"

Rebecca ignored his concern for sanitation. She replied, "I haven't talked to him in two days."

Martin sat, pulled photos from his briefcase, and passed them. "He ain't dirty—much. That one's my favorite." He gloated.

As Rebecca thumbed through the photos, her heart sank. She knew the purpose of LaRoux's trip and was relatively certain he wanted Will to get these photographs. But the man in the picture looked nothing like the man she had spent the last eight months with. He did not look like a man ready to retire. Instead, he looked exactly like what he was—a drug lord. "So, what's the plan?" Rebecca's tone was almost shameful.

"He met San Domingo at his office yesterday, then spent the entire night at San Domingo's compound. Much more than your average business partner, you know. These were taken this morning."

Rebecca paused at the image of LaRoux standing beside a mountain of packaged cocaine. He had told her there was a stockpile, but this surpassed any rational expectation. *There's no way he's getting out of the business.*

"Now, we know where all the coke has been hiding these last eight months. Apparently, the market shortage is about to be resolved."

Rebecca could feel a tear forming, so she rubbed her forehead to disguise her attempt to wipe it away.

"They started moving it out today. It won't be hard to follow a shipment of this size. I will personally select the task force that will take LaRoux and his people down when they attempt to take delivery." Martin stepped closer to Rebecca as he proclaimed, "You know, when he and the cartel go down, there will be a couple of big promotions due." He placed a hand on Rebecca's leg. "I'd like a chance to make things up, to show you just how good I can be for you."

Rebecca didn't flinch. She just stared at Will's hand. Suspicion, doubt, and her jaded past romance began to fertilize the notion that she had been burned for a second time. She had never encountered anyone possessing LaRoux's moxie and intricate shrewdness. And to get her pregnant? *The ultimate fuck you. What a fool I've been.* "Will, please drop it. I've got to get my head on straight and deal with this pregnancy."

Will withdrew his hand. "I can't believe the bastard didn't have the decency to use protection. Have you been checked for STDs?"

"Will, I married him." Rebecca's tears flowed. "I didn't have access to my pills or a hospital."

"Shit. We've got to get you to a doctor."

Rebecca turned her head away and stared at the faded, cheap picture of colonial New Orleans that hung beside the TV. "I'm not ready to go to the doctor—not yet."

Shocked, Will nearly screeched, "Why not?"

"Maybe I'm not ready to deal with that decision just yet."

"Decision?" Martin moved in front of Rebecca. "Please don't tell me you would remotely consider keeping the baby of the biggest drug-dealing criminal in the country."

"It's not just *his* baby, Will. It's something that's part of me. It's growing in *me*!"

"Jeez, Rebecca. If this gets out, it could be a career killer."

"Right now, my career is the least of my worries. *My husband* will be back in New Orleans very soon, and I'm not at the plantation. I'm pretty sure that will not make him happy."

Martin dragged a rickety desk chair in front of Rebecca and attempted to fix her eyes on his.

"So, what are you thinking?"

Rebecca looked away. Had she revealed too much? Did she even care about the investigation—or LaRoux's fate? Revealing her pregnancy and her emotions had definitely not been in her plan. At this moment, she was on her own. Rebecca knew a two-sided plan had to be formulated, and quickly. "You know, he never once lived up to your profile. I never witnessed anything to convince me he was guilty of anything. And as for this trip to Colombia, he never said anything about cocaine." Martin scoffed as he rolled his eyes and drew Rebecca's full attention. "But now that I've left him, only to be put in this dump no less, I'm scared of how he might react."

"First off, I'll protect you. Secondly, he'll never find you, unless *we* decide to set something up." Rebecca displayed the cell phone LaRoux had given her. Martin took the phone and powered it down. "I'll get you a new phone today. Does he know—about the baby?"

"Yes."

Martin was unaware that LaRoux knew that Rebecca was an agent. In his ignorance, he weighed possible solutions. He glanced at the phone. "Undoubtedly, he now knows you're in this shithole as well. I'll get you moved in with Margo Carter. Since he knows Margo is NOPD and believes you're friends, he'll be a lot less likely to try anything. Tell him you need some time to think about the baby and his drug dealings. Remind him that you and Margo are good friends and that you thought staying with her was a better option than going back home. But if he pushes too hard, and if you're willing, you may need to go back to the plantation. The shipment should be here in five days or less. Once it's here, we'll take him down." Rebecca stared at the faded peach walls without replying.

Martin placed a hand on her shoulder. "I know you've been through hell and back, and it's not over yet. But once this is done, if you want, I'll take you away. I owe you that much."

Rebecca's stare remained fixed. Martin's words drifted past without consideration. Was there any logical justification for LaRoux's behavior? He could have taken her with him. He should have. The pictures did not depict a man in fear for his life.

"Rebecca?" Martin interrupted.

"Let's just get through this," she said.

Martin rose to leave, and with his hand on the doorknob, he turned back. "I never meant for it to go this far, not for anyone, but especially you. I *will* make it up somehow."

Once outside the door, Martin tugged at his zipper. He speculated LaRoux's people might be watching, and wanted to incite a mistake born out of jealousy when LaRoux resurfaced.

* * *

The photographs of LaRoux haunted her. His blatant, careless behavior was so uncharacteristic and yet orchestrated at *his* request. Maybe he was planning on turning state's evidence and the show was to incriminate San Domingo. Over and over, Rebecca tried to decipher the purpose of his actions.

A light knock at the door jarred her from her stupor. She cracked it, and her heart skipped a million beats.

"Baby, you seem surprised to see me. Are you going to invite me in?" LaRoux asked with a strained smile.

His tone was unfamiliar. Rebecca's conflicted excitement turned into hesitation. She paused before stepping away from the door.

LaRoux closed it unnecessarily hard and slid the safety chain on. As he gazed at the incriminating photos strewn across the bed, the validity of Victor Hanson's accusations were painfully confirmed.

Rebecca looked at LaRoux as he studied the collage. "Is this the reason I return home and find my wife missing?"

"I trusted you," Rebecca said tearfully.

"It would appear we were both equally foolish." LaRoux parted the curtains and studied the parking lot. "You know what really sucks worse than being played?" Rebecca's face begged for LaRoux's answer. "Knowing that you're still fucking your old boyfriend."

"I'm not—"

"Stop it, Rebecca. I know he's been here—and I know it wasn't just a social visit."

Rebecca had seen LaRoux operate in a life-or-death scenario and not lose his composure, as he had now. His tone frightened her, and she recoiled to the headboard of the bed. "David, I don't know—" Rebecca's words froze as she recognized a familiar gun and silencer.

"I gave you an out in Las Vegas, a free pass I have never offered anyone—then I gave you my world. I gave you everything."

"David, please put the gun away. I only did what you asked." Rebecca knew it was too late for words.

"Dammit, Rebecca. You should have ended this in Las Vegas when I gave you the chance. Now you know too much about the people I love and trust. You've left me with no alternative."

As LaRoux stared at the Sig in his hand, Rebecca thought she saw a tear run down his cheek. Suddenly, the door exploded open with a thunderous kick and Martin burst into the room. "Drop the gun," he screamed. He locked his gun on LaRoux.

LaRoux never flinched or looked back. He raised his hands, allowing the nine millimeter to roll from his grip until it dangled upside down from his finger. Martin moved behind LaRoux, secured the gun, and began to cuff him. Without resistance or words, LaRoux smiled strangely at Rebecca before miming a kiss.

"Are you alright, ma'am?" Martin's contorted expression begged Rebecca to play along.

"Yes," she replied, unexpectedly timid.

"Lucky for you I happened to be passing by your room when I did. From the sound of the argument, it seemed like you needed help."

With his hands cuffed behind his back, LaRoux grinned at Rebecca. "Yes, how utterly, coincidently, fucking lucky for you."

"Ma'am, I'm gonna put this guy in my car, and then I'll be back for a statement."

"Am I under arrest?" LaRoux demanded.

"From what I've heard and seen, what do you think, dipshit?" Martin led LaRoux out the door. Seconds later, he ushered him into the backseat of his rental car. "What kind of lowlife pussy pulls a gun on a defenseless woman?"

LaRoux snickered. "Hey, Dick Tracy. How 'bout putting the AC on before you get back inside? Your car stinks of dirty cop."

* * *

For the first ten minutes of the car ride, the two adversaries were silent. LaRoux watched the streets roll by until they crossed into the projects before he finally broke his silence. With his smug expression filling Martin's rearview mirror, LaRoux growled, "So, tell me, Dick, what do you plan on doing with me?"

Martin replied calmly, "I'm taking you to the precinct, asshole, where they will probably charge and arrest you." Martin's attempt at a Cajun dialect was rather poor, but he continued attempting to sound like a local. "Before you have the opportunity to make bail, your little gun will go through ballistics, and we'll see where it's been. With any luck, you'll be picking cotton for the next twenty years or so."

"Let's cut the bullshit, *Martin*. Just passing by? My ass you were. You know who I am, and I damn well know you. This is all about the night I kicked your ass." LaRoux studied Martin's changing expression in the mirror. "I beat your ass, which you justly deserved. So, you decided to come after me by tarnishing my reputation with false accusations of criminal mischief."

Martin continued to spot-check the mirror without substantiating LaRoux's allegations. Gloating internally, he was beyond pleased by LaRoux's ignorant arrogance. The prick actually believed *this* was a personal vendetta over the barroom brawl.

LaRoux began to smile as he leaned forward in the seat. "However, I suppose I should thank you for sending me that fine piece of ass. I have thoroughly enjoyed banging her every which way but loose."

"Shut your mouth, LaRoux!" Martin bellowed.

"What? Don't be so sensitive. It's not like she's ever going to let you hit *that* again."

Martin veered the car hard to the left before cutting the wheel and squealing around the corner of the nearest crossroad. The forceful turn threw LaRoux back into the seat.

"Easy now, *baby*. Don't nobody want to get hurt. I'm sorry if the lucid thought of her head between my legs is causing you anguish." In the mirror, LaRoux could see that Martin was on the brink of disaster. *Time for the kill.* "But she sure does know how to suck it good."

Martin slammed on the brakes, and LaRoux careened forward. He lunged his elbow into LaRoux's face, a move that catapulted him back into the seat. Martin snapped his head around and issued a dire threat. "Next time, I won't ask so nicely. Shut your mouth, asshole."

LaRoux buried his bloody nose into his shoulder, staining his white oxford shirt. He waited a mere three blocks before returning to his taunts. "I apologize, Agent Martin. I didn't realize you were such a sensitive man. But I guess guys like you have that tendency."

"What's that supposed to mean?"

"Well, let's see. The very first time I was fucking Agent Pearson in Las Vegas—you remember that, don't you? She came like a geyser and nearly ripped half the skin off my back. So, I had to ask her, 'When was the last time you had an orgasm, baby?' You know what she told me? This is gonna kill you. She said, 'It's been too long to remember. My last boyfriend was hung like a hamster.'"

Martin made a hard left turn. As he slammed on the brakes, he launched his elbow back again. This time LaRoux raised his forearm high enough to strike the back of Martin's head—and the momentum surged Martin forward.

"Son of a bitch," Martin screamed.

"Hey, needle dick, I didn't get this rich being stupid."

Martin turned and launched a jab at LaRoux's face. LaRoux slid to the side as Martin's fist zipped past his cheek. "Easy, daddio. You want to take these cuffs off so we can settle this like men? Then you can forget all this arrest nonsense and get on with your pathetic life. Hell, I'll even give you another shot at Rebecca, but you might want to think about buying her a big-ass dildo, because after all the damage I've done, you don't stand a chance."

Martin shoved his door open with such force, it bounced back and struck his knee as he was scrambling out of the car. As he tore the back door open, he yelled, "Come on, smart-ass." He grabbed LaRoux by his bloody collar and pulled him from the car. Thrusting his knee upward, he connected with LaRoux's groin and dropped him to the pavement. Then, with a forceful roundhouse kick, he connected with his defenseless opponent's jaw.

LaRoux laughed as he spit out a mouthful of blood. "Whoa, is that all you got, chicken shit? You fight like you fuck."

Martin looked at the empty block of scattered ramshackle houses left in the wake of Katrina. There was no need to worry about witnesses on this street. Besides, in this neighborhood, who would give a damn about one white man beating the hell out of another? Just as Martin delivered two heavy-footed kicks to the ribs, his third attempt was interrupted by the wail of a siren. An undercover patrol car had pulled up behind him.

As the two detectives hurried from the car with guns drawn, Martin threw his hands in the air and yelled, "Step down, fellas. I'm on the job."

Both cops kept their guns trained on Martin. "Show me some ID," the driver ordered.

Martin pulled his badge from his pocket and flipped it open.

The driver briefly inspected Martin's credentials, then looked down at LaRoux. "Damn! You guys don't fuck around. What's this guy's story?"

"I was meeting a CI at the Jolly Gator Motel when I heard this prick threatening a lady inside a room. When I kicked in the door, he had a nine aimed at her. I just arrived in town today, and unfortunately all they had for me was this rental car. I had him cuffed, but there really wasn't any other way to secure him in the backseat. In the process of transporting the prick, he got froggy on me."

"Bet he won't make that mistake again, Agent Martin," the driver said, handing back Martin's ID. "How 'bout we throw him in the back of our car and haul him in for you?"

Martin looked back at LaRoux, who remained curled up on the ground. "Much obliged, fellas, but I don't think that will be necessary. He'll think twice before he tries anything else."

"Actually, Agent Martin, at this point I must insist," the other cop said. He looked around at the scattered houses. "You might not see them, but they're there, like a snake in the grass—*witnesses*. You just put a beatdown on this guy. If a video should ever surface, let's say on YouTube or the nightly news—if this perp should turn up dead, and we were seen here with you—we ain't taking that hit."

The driver nodded. "Besides, unless this involves drugs, it's simple domestic violence. That's not your turf. We'll take him in. Just stop by the precinct, make a statement, and give us the info on the witness. We'll do all the dirty legwork." The driver walked over to LaRoux and helped him to his feet. "Hey, dumbass, guess you won't be trying that stupid shit again." The officer tucked LaRoux's head and ushered him into the squad car's backseat.

Martin was fuming. He could not confess that he knew LaRoux's identity to these two bone-headed cops. At this juncture, anything LaRoux had to say would be his word against Martin's. As he watched the NOPD cops pull away, the best that Martin could hope for was that LaRoux would keep his mouth shut. LaRoux had been reckless, threatening a federal agent at gunpoint. If he pressed no charges, Martin would have him released, which would set the stage for LaRoux's one final mistake, the biggest of his life. As Martin climbed back into his rental, he looked at LaRoux's gun still sitting in the passenger seat. A trip to ballistics was in order. Who knew? Maybe LaRoux's carelessness was about to catch up with him.

Meanwhile, LaRoux looked back down the street at Martin's idle car. "It's good you boys got here when you did. I was about to open up a can of whoop-ass on him," LaRoux groaned. He had called in a favor to the NOPD hours before to have Martin followed.

"For sure," the cop in the passenger seat snickered. "Captain wasn't lying, Mr. LaRoux. He said that guy's got a major boner for you. What'd you do to piss him off that bad?"

LaRoux continued to stare out the back window as he deadpanned, "It probably started with an ass kicking almost two years ago. Then I made him look like an idiot in front of his subordinates, which eventually got him demoted. Then I married his ex-girlfriend. I guess that pretty much sums it up."

Both cops turned back to LaRoux and waited for him to turn to the front. As he did, the driver chuckled. "What a dipshit. I woulda just shot you and been done with it."

LaRoux smirked through his rapidly swelling lips. "Lucky for me he ain't no good ol' Cajun boy, eh?"

CHAPTER 17

WITH HER SEDUCTIVE LEGS propped up on the balcony, Rebecca stared vacantly at the shimmering bayou while mulling what she should do. In all likelihood, if she kept the baby, her legs wouldn't look this way much longer—nor would the rest of her. If she moved forward with becoming a mom, it would not be for LaRoux's sake, but her own. She cherished the idea of being a mother. Sadly, she admired the beautiful diamond still poised on her ring finger. *To be or not to be . . .*

Margo returned with a beer and an iced tea. "You certainly look a lot more relaxed than when you got here last night." Rebecca smiled as she took the tea. Margo sat in a rocking chair beside her. "Some evenings, I'll sit out here for hours and just watch the day waste away." Margo looked up at the rhythmically swaying, slowly turning blades of the ceiling fan. "I don't know why, but just being out here somehow soothes the soul."

"It's quiet, so tranquil," Rebecca said. "Before that boat passed, all I heard was insects and birds." She felt her first real smile since LaRoux left her in New York at the airport. "Thanks for the tea and letting me stay here."

"Don't mention it." Margo took a drink, rolled her head back, and closed her eyes. "The few neighbors I have are rarely home. Out here,

I'm mostly a loner. So, it's nice, every now and then, to have some company."

"Even being a cop, I could see where it might be a little creepy at night, all alone," Rebecca said as she examined Margo's mischievous smile. "But if something, or someone, crops up, please don't hesitate to tell me to take a hike."

"I kind of doubt it will. Life out here has been pretty quiet since I've been seeing Ryan."

"Oh my God, the two of you are—"

"Off and on, but mostly on. We usually spend a couple of nights together in the city, so I'm not entertaining any other guys right now." Margo took a deep draw of beer. "At first, I was doing it to try to find out what happened to you or to get dirt on LaRoux. I've had lots worse shit assignments." Margo's smile broadened. "But Ryan is like Mr. Clean . . . I don't know, maybe they all are. Or he's the most tight-lipped man I've ever met." She sipped her beer, her focus set off across the bayou. "You know something really odd? Two weeks after Vegas, those boys settled in like it was business as usual, as if they didn't have a care in the world. There was no panic, no sense of urgency about their missing boss—or you for that matter."

"So, you believe our disappearance might have been planned?"

"If those Colombians hadn't been killed, I'd say the whole thing might have been orchestrated."

"But why?"

"That's the career-rocket mystery everyone would love to know. Until you phoned in the drug buy, everyone, except Martin, had all pretty much concluded that LaRoux was clean. His boys kept the status quo. The house and cars were kept clean and nothing at CCI changed in the least. It's almost like Vegas was meant to be some kind of exit strategy."

Rebecca scoffed. "That's what he told me he wanted—to get out— but that's all done and dirty now." She sipped on the tea as the pair sat in a moment of silence. "But you know something else? Outside of killing those Colombians, who were trying to kill us, the entire time we were gone, he never told me anything that I could use to bring charges. Even if I had been wearing a mic, there was no solid admission of anything. And when I'd ask him something point-blank, he'd say, 'Careful, Agent Pearson. You're not sounding very retired.' If Martin had not gotten those pictures of David and San Domingo, the only thing we'd have him on would be some kind of self-defense manslaughter." Rebecca shook her head. "I'd never seen anything like him when he killed those men. One minute he was beaten to a pulp, and the next he was like a ninja assassin."

"Speaking of Will, rumor has it the two of you might be an item again."

"Ha!" Rebecca nearly choked on her tea. "If I lost ninety-nine percent of my brains, had a gun held to my head, and he was the last man on earth, there is no way. That man is pure weasel, through and through."

Margo laughed. "I wasn't going to say anything, but since you opened that can of worms, he is quite the slimeball. He was hitting up on the entire team right up till the time he got demoted. But I have to admit, the man has his game tight. There were times he'd be doing his *thing*, and you wouldn't realize it until an hour later. It's a good thing you warned us about Slick in the beginning."

Too bad nobody warned me, Rebecca mused as the pair returned to silence, each reflecting on the myriad of circumstances that led up to this moment.

Finally, Margo broke the quiet. "So, tell me about LaRoux. What's he like?"

Rebecca continued her slow, methodical rocking. After several sips of tea, she replied sadly, "He said and did all the right things. It was so damn easy to fall in love with him."

"That's going to make it hard to bust him, isn't it?"

Rebecca stood and leaned on the rail, addressing the sunset. "It doesn't really matter. Officially, I'm off the case and have been ordered to stay right here until further notice. Apparently, they feel my value as a witness is more crucial than my abilities as an agent."

Margo stepped up and joined her at the rail. "That kinda sucks."

"For eight months, to do my job, all I had to do was have great sex with a delightful man who spoiled me at every opportunity. Hell, he even pretended to love me. Outside of him being a criminal and knocking me up." Rebecca raised her glass in the direction of the sunset. "But now I get to hang out here, with you." She mindlessly allowed her hand to rub her still-flat belly. "It doesn't suck all that bad."

Margo chuckled as she clinked her bottle to Rebecca's glass. *"Laissez les bon temps rouler."*

CHAPTER 18

TAZ SLOWLY PULLED UP in front of Margo Carter's condo complex and eyeballed the NOPD cruiser parked just feet away. Before he could pass it, he made a U-turn and parked his car in an adjacent lot. He decided he'd have a little fun before heading up to Margo's.

He whistled as he walked toward the marked car and said, "Evening, boys. Looking a little conspicuous tonight for undercover work."

"Sweet T," the driver acknowledged.

Taz rolled his eyes. "Roger, don't call me that. High school's been long done."

"Oh, that's right. Junior Tazwell is all grown up now," Mercer mocked. "He's making the big dollars working for the man."

"Damn, guys. Why you got to go all hater on me and bust my balls?"

"*Pardonnez-moi,*" Roger replied in his worst French accent. "Mr. *Big Money* don't want no mo' reminders of his glory days."

"You don't mean when he *used* to be one of us lowlifes, do ya?" Mercer jabbed.

"Alright guys, I get it. Jeez. I know I've blown ya'll off a bunch lately, but I've been hopping all over the place in LaRoux's absence, and now that he's back—"

"Yeah, I know," Roger interrupted. "It takes at least a half an hour to stop by and have a beer every now and then with your former partner. So, what brings Big Daddy Taz down to mingle with the common folk tonight?"

"Mr. LaRoux wants me to pick up Mrs. LaRoux and bring her to dinner."

The cops traded their best dumbfounded expressions before breaking out in thunderous laughter. "Oh my, Mr. Tazwell. I don't see how that's going to happen."

Taz stared blankly at the pair. "Seriously?"

"Oh, most seriously." Mercer chuckled. "You do understand that our purpose tonight is to keep *Agent Pearson* safe and sound."

"Come on, guys. Who are we talking about? David LaRoux is the biggest friend the New Orleans Police Department has."

"*Had*," Mercer replied. "According to one William Martin, our beloved David LaRoux is a huge drug-trafficking murderer."

"Dammit, guys. Martin just beat the shit out of my boss a few days ago. Everyone knows he's got a personal vendetta against David from some barroom brawl almost two years ago. You know LaRoux is clean."

"And where was his personal security chief when he was getting the shit beat out of him?" Roger fired back.

"Fuck you, Roger. I can't follow him when he don't want to be followed."

"Good thing a few of our boys happened across him when we did. Otherwise, you might be unemployed right now."

With his hands on his hips, Taz turned away. "Are you guys gonna bust my ass all night or let me get on with my business?" The men didn't respond, so Taz leaned his head into the cruiser. "I'm gonna go knock on the door and ask Agent Pearson to voluntarily accompany me. If she agrees, I will take her to Mr. LaRoux. When they have completed their dinner, I will personally escort her safely back home. Or I can call Mr. LaRoux and let him know he needs to get in touch with Captain Hilliard." Taz lifted his head from inside the window, disentangling himself from the cop car, and he stretched his back.

"Ease it up, daddio," Roger objected. "You used to have a sense of humor, boy." Roger and Mercer grinned slyly.

"You guys suck," Taz moaned.

"Only each other," Mercer added.

Taz shook his head. "Do me a favor. She's been avoiding Mr. LaRoux since he got back in town. Apparently, Martin told her some bullshit story about a drug deal in Colombia, and now she won't even talk to him. He just wants to explain everything, face-to-face, but she might not want to go. I'm not going to drag her, but if she thinks that maybe I did something to her protective services, she might be more inclined to go with me."

"Oh, wait. I think I've got a few ketchup packets in the glovebox. Want me to spread it on my neck, bang on the front door, and then collapse on the porch?" Mercer chuckled.

"Intimidation, Taz? That don't sound so voluntary to me. Sounds like some serious disciplinary action if something goes wrong," Roger added.

Taz sighed as he reached into his pocket. "I will keep her safe," he said. He placed five one hundred-dollar bills in Roger's lap. "Just put your heads back like you're asleep. I'll do the rest."

"Why can't LaRoux just come down here?" Roger asked as he inspected the bills.

"He ain't stepped out of the house since he got released from that false arrest. Martin did a number on him. You know, Martin and Rebecca Pearson had a relationship a few years back, and Martin has some seriously psychotic jealousy issues over Pearson marrying Mr. LaRoux. When Mr. LaRoux tried to see Pearson a few days ago, Martin nearly killed him. He is the only reason the department is keeping an eye on her. But after Mr. LaRoux speaks with her, all this nonsense will be over."

Roger leaned into the steering wheel and wrenched his back until it popped. "Okay, Sweet T. But if this goes south, Mercer and I will arrest your ass for assault and kidnapping and any other charges related to whatever should happen to Agent Pearson. We straight on that?"

"Straight as the Mississippi." Taz grinned.

"Hey," Roger called out as Taz started walking away. Holding up a Benjamin, he asked. "You got two fifties for this? Kind of hard to make an even split, unless you want to just throw in another C-note."

Taz walked back to the cruiser and tossed another bill in the car. "You guys really do suck."

In perfect harmony, the pair replied, "Only each other."

* * *

A knock at the door startled Rebecca, who jumped to her feet. It was nine thirty. She was not expecting Margo back for another hour, not that Margo would have knocked. She figured it must be one of the officers, so she opened the door without looking out the peephole. Her jaw dropped.

"Hello, Rebecca. Aren't you going to invite me in?"

Rebecca tried to peer over Taz's shoulder to check on her security detail, but her eyes could not scale his mountainous stature. The wooden screen door screeched loudly as Rebecca unlatched it and pushed it slowly open. "Hi, Taz," she said nervously.

Watching her frantic eyes seeking the status of the two officers, Taz coughed to throw her off. "Don't worry about them. They're taking a happy nap."

"What did you do?"

"Brought them coffee and doughnuts. What else you gonna bring cops on stakeout?" He looked around the condo's modest furnishings. "First time I've been here. Looks like Margo's doing alright on a cop's salary."

"Why are you here, Taz?"

"*He* wants to see you."

"Last time I saw *him*, he had a gun pointed at my head. So, I'm quite sure you'll understand if I have no desire to see him."

"He was pretty sure you'd say that. So, I'm supposed to tell you that's not an option—and that he's not mad anymore."

Rebecca looked into Taz's forest-green eyes for any trace of hesitation or mercy. "Is this *it*?"

Taz sighed. "Rebecca, you're carrying his kid. He's just trying to figure out the best way to make sure you're taken care of. But just so you know, allowing you to refuse his invitation was not an option for me either." Rebecca scanned the room, desperately seeking a remotely effective weapon. "Agent Pearson," Taz began, "I know you've received all types of defensive training from the DEA. But if you're thinking about resisting by maybe smashing my head with that lamp or maybe that wine bottle over there, I've got to tell you, it's a bad idea. Margo would not be happy with the mess you'd make, and it would only piss me off."

"Taz, I don't want to go. And kidnapping is a felony, even in Louisiana."

"Duly noted, Agent Pearson. Now, please come with me so we don't have to add assault to my growing list of crimes."

* * *

Rebecca had remained silent as she observed every turn and waited for the first sign of deception. As it began to become clear that they were headed for LaRoux's office, she felt uneasy. Her instincts were warning her that something was amiss. At the corner of Poydras and Carondelet, the fine hairs on the back of her neck jumped to attention. Two blocks short of CCI's central office, Taz pulled to the corner. Out of the shadows, a darkened silhouette appeared.

A mystery man climbed into the car, then Taz pulled away without introducing the new guy, who said nothing. Rebecca's anxiety swelled as Taz turned left on Canal Street and headed in the opposite direction of the Greater New Orleans Bridge and the LaRoux plantation.

As the car accelerated up the ramp onto I-10 East, Rebecca could no longer hold her tongue. She interrupted the low blues playing on the radio when she said firmly, "Taz, I think I'd like to go back to Margo's. I'm not feeling well."

The mystery man spoke in a thick Creole accent. "Agent Pearson," began Geno Harper, LaRoux's stateside lieutenant for drug-selling operations—the very one whom Armando had pointed to as the leak in LaRoux's operations. He turned and grinned slyly.

"It's Mrs. LaRoux," Rebecca replied indignantly.

"With all due respect, with regards to your renewed relationship with the DEA, I think you have forfeited any claims to the LaRoux family name."

So, this character works for David, Rebecca surmised. She pressed back into the rear seat and crossed her arms. "If that is how my husband feels, then I insist you take me back to Margo's."

"*Oh contraire, chérie.* You cannot go back to Margo's until this farce of a marriage has been completely dissolved. Madame Bochè must perform the ceremony of dissolution."

"Madame who?"

"Bochè—David's voodoo priestess. And yes, she is recognized by our fine state as having the authority to perform marriages, and in cases of exceptionally bad judgment, annulments. After she has undone your little marriage charade, and David is no longer bound to you, you'll be free to do as you please."

Rebecca leaned forward. "So, that's what this is all about? Some bullshit voodoo ceremony?"

"Watch that potty mouth of yours, Agent Pearson. Folks down here don't take kindly to such insults," Geno warned, amused by Rebecca's feisty attitude.

Rebecca caught Taz's prying eyes in the rearview mirror. "What about you, Taz? Are you on board with all this voodoo hogwash?"

Taz's gaze instantly abandoned the mirror and returned to the darkened road ahead as the cabin fell into silence. After a few miles, unable to hold his opinion, Taz spilled into a rant.

"You know, Rebecca, he gave you every opportunity to walk away. Why wasn't that good enough for you? I warned him, we all did, when we discovered your true intent, but he swore that wouldn't matter. He actually thought you cared about him."

"Enough, Taz," Geno interrupted.

"No, Geno, it ain't enough. All this crazy-ass bullshit David's been doing—it's fucking reckless. And it's all her fault. You know it's true. Anybody who uses love like she did—it don't get no lower."

The unexpected rage in Taz's eyes that was reflected in the mirror rekindled Rebecca's fear. "So, I'm *not* seeing David? And I'm guessing there isn't any voodoo ritual?"

"There's a ritual all right, Agent Pearson," Geno snickered.

Far from the lights of the city, Rebecca reconsidered her fate. She thought back to her protection detail. In all likelihood, they were actually dead—not drugged. Her heart remained a solitary oasis of hope, trusting LaRoux would not harm her or his unborn child. But remembering his calm fury in Vegas—the trademark of all sociopaths—reality smacked her in the face. *You do not become the biggest drug dealer in the nation by being a nice guy.*

After a stretch of dark highway, Taz killed the headlights and turned onto a gravel path that quickly turned into a bumpy root-covered dirt trail. In absolute darkness, the probability of a Good Samaritan intervening on her behalf had vanished like the lights of civilization. One final time, Rebecca turned in her desperation to the skies and road behind. There were no headlights tailing them nor helicopters—not one glimmer of salvation.

Every few hundred feet or so, the Denali slipped and sloshed through the waters of the encroaching bayou. Taz appeared to have no concern over their precarious journey, or for that matter, Rebecca, who had worked her way suspiciously close to the door. If it were only Taz, Rebecca thought she might stand a chance of negotiating a deal. But with Geno in the mix, desperation led Rebecca to slide her hand to the door handle and consider a plunge into the darkness.

Without as much as a glimpse, Geno chuckled. "You'd stand a much better chance of surviving jumping from a plane without a parachute."

Rebecca rested her hand against the door, as if Geno's warning had no merit. Five more minutes down the trail, the Denali slowed and gradually pushed its way through a veil of moss that hung from a massive cypress. Crunching their way across what appeared to be a small island, they slowly rolled to a stop. As the moonlight emerged from the scattered cloud-cover, Rebecca spied a small johnboat tied to a dilapidated dock. Suddenly, an unforeseen scenario crossed her mind: *Are they gonna keep me in some remote bayou shack until the baby is born and then kill me?*

Taz parked the Denali forty yards short of the dock. "Wait here," he ordered softly with perhaps a tinge of regret as he removed the keys.

Geno turned to Rebecca, brandishing his gun. "No need to try anything stupid out here, Agent Pearson. Stupid will get you killed really quick."

Rebecca kept her mouth shut and watched as Taz made his way to the dock, inspected the boat, and then looked about the perimeter before returning to the car. He opened Rebecca's door and extended a hand. "Okay, let's go." She refused his hand and climbed out. "To the dock, please," he said firmly.

As the moonlight danced through the moss-covered cypresses, tupelos, and twisted oaks, Rebecca was reminded of walking in the gardens with LaRoux on the night of the ball. How easily she had become smitten with his Southern gentleman's charm and that Big Easy smile. How effortless he had made it to fall in love. Even now with her life in peril, she found herself desperately wishing this were all a big mistake, that he still loved her. Lost in thought, she did not hear Taz and Geno approach from behind.

Geno gazed about uneasily, inspecting the water's edge for any signs of gators. "What now?" he asked with his gun still extended in Rebecca's direction.

"Let me see your piece," asked Taz. Without question, Geno handed over his Glock. Taz inspected the gun, then stared intently at the pair as he waited.

From out of the darkness, a voice broke into the bayou's melody of crickets, cicadas, and owls. "I suppose if Jesus Christ had his Judas, why should it surprise me that I have two?" Rebecca remained silent. She had begun to expect something more complex than just a bullet to the head—and now, here *he* was.

"David? What are you doing here?" Geno squawked.

Instantly, Taz turned the Glock on Geno and Rebecca. LaRoux approached out of the shadows as he gripped a Sig on his waist. "I told you, Geno, I *always* take care of business—*personally*."

Geno squirmed. In that moment, he *knew* LaRoux had found out he had organized the Vegas hit. Hoping an oblivious attitude might buy him some time, he replied, "David, you don't need to be here. We've got this covered."

"You know, Geno, Las Vegas was a big mistake."

"David, what the hell are you talking about?"

"Save it, Geno. I found out all about your involvement while I was in Bucaramanga a few days ago. You were trying to steal my money. Did you really believe you could conspire with Armando and get away with it?"

Geno backpedaled three steps toward the dock. "David—"

"What was it, Geno? Not enough wealth? Not enough power? I treated you like a fucking brother, Geno! I made you rich! This is how you repay my friendship, my trust?"

"Don't look at me, Geno," Taz ordered. "I ain't got no love for the usurper."

Geno cut his eyes to Rebecca.

"Don't you think for a second she's going to be of any assistance. In fact, why don't you join him, darlin'," Taz ordered with a Glock. Rebecca stared at Taz briefly before looking back at LaRoux.

"Go ahead, *chérie*, this is his show," LaRoux insisted. "Besides, we don't have all night. It won't be long till the gators sniff us out."

Rebecca moved slowly to Geno's side while LaRoux blankly studied her progress. "Now, I have a great deal . . . for only one of you," Taz said with a tinge of glee. "It's only a chance, mind you, for one of you to survive. Geno, as I have known you the longest, I'm going to give you the opportunity to call it." Taz produced a coin from his pocket and flipped it high. "Heads or tails, Geno?"

"*Da-Da-David*," Geno stuttered.

"Dammit, Geno, call it or I'll shoot you where you stand," LaRoux growled. As if summoned by LaRoux's fierce rage, a flash of distant lightning illuminated his face, casting a menacing and unforgiving image. LaRoux watched as the coin hit the ground.

"Tails." Geno's reply was timid as he struggled to see the coin in the dirt.

LaRoux snatched up the coin and showed it to Taz.

"Tails it is. Geno, it's your lucky night. You get to decide who gets to go for a boat ride. The boat has a map and enough gas to make it to Mississippi. The other unlucky soul stays here with me. Whoever stays," Taz said, waving his gun, "well, your odds ain't too good."

LaRoux stepped in. "But before you go thinking, *Damn that boat sure looks like a good deal*, know this: *If* you make it to Mississippi, you keep on going and you never come back. You forfeit everything, and I mean *everything*. The boys are already cleaning out your home, your office, and your bank account. If I ever see you or hear of you in the state of Louisiana ever again, you will die. If I hear you are in my business, you will die badly. I will feed your *fucking* heart to the gators. Am I clear enough on this?"

Geno nodded slowly.

"If you choose the honorable path and let Agent Pearson have the boat," LaRoux said as he turned to Rebecca, "then Rebecca, my dear backstabbing wife, the same holds true for you. You run away from all of this—my life, your job, everything. Whatever Geno has in his bank account, which should be substantial, I will give to you and the baby—that is, if you make it out of the bayou. But if you should try to return to the DEA, or fuck with my business, after our child is born, I swear to God, our baby will never know its mother."

The contempt in LaRoux's eyes made Rebecca quiver. Another flash of lightning highlighted his savage expression; it was unlike anything she had ever witnessed. Or was it agony?

"I'll take the boat," Geno replied without deliberation.

"Then take it, and get the hell out of my sight," LaRoux snarled.

The grief in LaRoux's voice caused Rebecca to consider the possibility that she might capitalize on his apparent strife.

Geno turned and began the solitary trek down the dilapidated pier as the timbers creaked heavily. Taz followed a safe distance behind until Geno climbed into the boat. As he tossed the bowline to Geno, he shook his head. "What the hell were you thinking, man? You had it all, you miserable piece of shit. I can't believe David is actually giving you a chance to live. I know I wouldn't."

Geno yanked the motor cord, and with a puff of smoke, the outboard sputtered. Taz shoved the boat off with his foot and pointed. "It's that way. *Bon voyage*, motherfucker."

In absolute silence, the trio watched as the johnboat sputtered around the bend and out of sight. As the hum of the boat faded, the bayou wildlife symphony echoed, filling the sky with a false sense of peace. But the turbulent rumble of encroaching thunder shattered the tranquility—a violent reminder of unfinished business.

"Taz, head back to town and make sure all traces of Geno are gone before sunrise. I don't want any reminders that he ever existed."

"David," Taz said with trepidation, "the cops know I took Rebecca."

"I've got this. You just take care of everything I've asked you to—*please*."

Rebecca's visible despair left Taz feeling distraught, and he had to look away. He shook his head in silence as he turned toward the SUV. Knowing her last hope was about to leave, Rebecca pleaded, "Taz." Utterly defeated, Rebecca watched as he climbed into the Denali and slowly drove away. As the sound of sloshing tires faded, Rebecca stared into the darkness, isolated and scared.

Rebecca finally turned and looked into LaRoux's shallow and

tired eyes. Slowly, he shook his head and lowered his gun. "I gave you everything I had, and still you betrayed me."

"I didn't, David."

"Our time together is growing short. Can you spare me the dishonesty and drop all your DEA bullshit? You owe me that much."

"My dishonesty and bullshit? You're about to kill me, and I owe you?"

A sudden splash from the shores of the river drew their attention to the end of the dock. "The boat must have stirred Big Pete. All the gators have been trained to feed at night when they hear the boat. He'll be looking for his late-night snack, so you might want to hurry up and get your story straight."

Rebecca stared in the direction of the dock. Without finding the gator, she returned her attention to LaRoux. "I never lied."

He pondered her claim as he rubbed his gun across his temple. "Okay, you didn't lie. You just sold me out while in the process of fucking your old boyfriend."

"Is that why you stormed into my motel room waving your gun? You thought I was . . . with Will?"

"I don't think, I know," LaRoux proclaimed bitterly.

"Based on what? Your inside sources at the DEA? And where did their evidence come from? An egotistical bragging liar by the name of William Martin, whose sole purpose in life is the conquest of any person with tits and a vagina."

LaRoux moved to speak, but his rebuttal was lost in a myriad of confusing thoughts.

"*You* told me exactly what to leak to the DEA, and I did, and not a single word more." Rebecca's tone began to dictate a change in circumstance and attitude.

"You left our home without so much as a word. You hid from me." Sounding more wounded than intimidating, LaRoux lowered the gun to his side.

"It's true—after you went to Colombia to meet with San Domingo,

I began to doubt my judgment and my decisions. But I never betrayed you. And I sure as hell did not sleep with Will."

As a storm gust blew across the black waters, Rebecca's hair mimicked the windblown moss hanging from the trees above. In that instant, LaRoux's angry demeanor dissipated. He searched hard in Rebecca's eyes before submitting, "Considering the way I have behaved over the last few days, this is definitely the most insane thing I've ever done." He reversed his grip and offered Rebecca the gun.

She checked to ensure the safety was off, then she pointed the gun at LaRoux with a purpose. "Where's your car?"

He nodded toward a thicket of trees.

"Get your ass over there."

He walked toward his BMW, hidden in the shadows. When LaRoux neared the driver's door, he stopped and turned to Rebecca. "You still have to kill me. I'm not letting you take me in."

The wind gusted strongly as Rebecca performed another gator check over her shoulder in the direction of the pier. Looking back at LaRoux, she found his eyes consumed with the same passion she had witnessed every time they made love.

"You are such an incredible asshole." She set the gun down forcefully on the hood and, unexpectedly, found herself delighted by LaRoux's reaction. He cringed as he followed the gun scraping across the paint, then acknowledged her satisfaction with an expression of submissive apathy. Rebecca sighed. "I should have my head examined." She reached up and began to unbutton her blouse, slowly working the buttons until her shirt hung completely open. LaRoux stared, befuddled. Rebecca reached behind her back and slowly unfastened her bra. LaRoux did not move, nor did he smile.

Agitated, Rebecca flipped off her sandals and unfastened her button-fly jeans. She pulled her denims down over her firm thighs and calves, yanked them off, and tossed them on the hood too. She was naked. Beautifully naked. She climbed on top of the hood and lay back. LaRoux still didn't move. Rebecca reached for the gun and dragged it to her side. "David LaRoux, if you don't get up here and fuck me right now, I will shoot you where you stand."

Finally, LaRoux was no longer a statue. He began to strip. Rebecca remained on the hood unfazed by sudden raindrops as they seductively began to caress her body. "You'd better already be hard, David LaRoux."

Rebecca's glistening breasts and the hint of her curved bottom sent LaRoux's body into overdrive, far ahead of his confused emotions.

CHAPTER 19

THE SOGGY RIDE BACK to town began in a deep-rooted, sexually exhausted satisfaction. Emotions and a barrage of issues to sort through nurtured a soothing silence. LaRoux had blasted the heat to diminish the chill from their saturated clothes, but now he finally turned the fan on. As it whirred, he was determined to discern Rebecca's true intentions. But he knew the risk of anything less than absolute honesty. After all the deception, there had to come a point of intolerance. He had to know whether she was on his side. He finally spoke.

"You might not believe this, but the other day at your motel—that was all scripted. Will could not have played into my plan any less perfectly."

"*Damn*," Rebecca murmured. Never once had she considered that the masterful LaRoux had been playing them. As she pivoted in her seat, her wet clothes squeaked on the black leather. "How so?"

"You had to know I knew exactly where you were, and I knew Martin and the boys were watching you. I waited until I was damn sure he knew I was coming. *Those* pictures on the bed—Glamour Shots could have just as easily taken them. We practically posed for those imbeciles. I was a little surprised you didn't trust that there was a purpose, a calculated method to my plan."

Feeling a little sheepish, Rebecca took the offensive route. "My trust? If you knew so much, then what in the hell led you to believe I was fucking Will? I told you how I felt about that ass."

Embarrassed, LaRoux cleared his throat. "Well, that may have been the culmination of bad intel and timing. There are people I trust in my organization, and a few have been very vocal about their lack of faith concerning you. When you up and moved out of *our* home and went into hiding, I was sent an audio recording of Will bragging to another agent about his renewed conquest."

"You have someone inside the DEA office?"

LaRoux spared Rebecca a *duh*, but his expression more than made up for his silence. He reached into the console. He extracted a phone and pushed play on the video. He handed it to Rebecca. "The icing."

"Son of a bitch." Rebecca watched in repulsion as Will exited her motel room tugging at his zipper with the expression of a man who had just been thoroughly satisfied. "Did it ever occur to you that he thought *you,* or somebody, might be watching?"

"No. He's not that smart."

"Apparently he's not that dumb either. And this," Rebecca said, holding the phone in front of LaRoux, "was more believable than what we shared the last eight months? I gave myself to you in so many ways."

The pain in Rebecca's voice had LaRoux pinned on the ropes. "Maybe . . ." He shook his head and paused. "Maybe jealousy clouded my judgment. I have never had to deal with that before."

"*Maybe?* You had a gun pointed at me—*again.*"

"*That* was part of the script. Even if you completely remove sex with Will from the equation, I needed him to believe I was ready to kill you." LaRoux turned to Rebecca. "But even if you had had sex with Will, or even turned against me, I could never do it. I do love you, Rebecca. And I would die before I would ever harm you."

Rebecca appeared to glean a dose of satisfaction from LaRoux's confession. "And the part where Will beat the crap out of you—I guess you planned that as well?"

LaRoux smirked. "Odd how NOPD showed up at the opportune moment, don't you think?"

"Or maybe you're the luckiest man alive."

"After what just happened on the hood of my car, is there any doubt?" He leaned over and kissed Rebecca.

She savored the moment before her inquisitiveness returned. "So, what was that whole bayou thing about?"

"It was all about ridding myself of traitors."

"So, what about Geno? How does a guy in a boat fit in with this master plan?" Rebecca pulled down the vanity mirror and studied the tangled mess her hair had become. "What happens if he goes straight to the DEA and cuts a deal?"

"Mother nature will take care of him."

"How so?"

LaRoux cast a suspicious gaze at Rebecca, then sighed. "What the hell. I seem to remember promising that I would tell you everything." He looked straight ahead and watched the wipers push the deluge from the windshield. "From the pier, there's only one route to the river. About a half mile downstream, there's an unusually heavy concentration of alligators due to a Cajun who feeds them there almost every night at about this time. They have been trained to know that when they hear the motorboat, it's dinnertime. When the johnboat pulls away from the pier, it tears away a plastic cover, exposing a water-soluble bottom. By the time the boat enters the feeding zone, it's sinking."

Rebecca jerked away against the door. "Is that how you kill your enemies?"

"Not if they are strong swimmers."

"And if they're not?"

LaRoux knew Rebecca was appalled, but business was business. "Then God decides the outcome."

Rebecca crossed her arms. "And what if Geno had decided to stay?"

"Oh, Geno was getting in that boat, regardless of his choice." LaRoux managed a smile. "But if I had let him stay, my hood wouldn't have all those scratches on it, would it now?"

Rebecca punched him in the arm. "You are such an asshole."

"If you think I'm an asshole now, wait till you get the repair bill."

"Did Colin Wells go for a boat ride?" By now, Rebecca had an inkling of what may have happened to the long-disappeared DEA agent.

"Colin was a crooked piece of shit. I'll bet you didn't know he managed to embezzle eighty grand of my money in less than a year. He tried to set me up twice for bullshit I was actually innocent of." LaRoux paused, thinking Rebecca was going to contradict his reasoning. Finally, he concluded, "But who knows, maybe he was a strong swimmer." Rebecca frowned.

"Look, baby, I know what you're thinking, and yes, it's a pretty rotten deal. But treason is unforgiveable in my organization, especially by a thieving, lying, dirty cop. And Geno, what nearly happened in Vegas, that was all his work. The gators were much kinder to him than I would have been." As Rebecca absorbed his twisted logic, LaRoux concluded his defense. "I told you I had to come home and close out my affairs. In a few more days, all of this will be behind me, and I'll never look back on this life again."

Through the torrential rain, off in the distance the silhouette of the crescent city began to take on definition. LaRoux knew he had to take Rebecca back to Margo's, though he wanted nothing else but to bring her back to the plantation.

"You know, I can't see you again until after the shipment comes in."

Rebecca frowned again. "Not even a midnight rendezvous?"

"Especially a midnight rendezvous."

"Care to share any details?"

The stakes were just too high for LaRoux to divulge his master plan. "Top secret, baby. If I told you, I'd have to kill you."

"Or you could just fuck me on the hood of your car again."

*　*　*

Will knocked twice before pulling the creaky screen door open and walking in.

"What are you doing?" Margo objected.

"I need to see her," Martin growled as he crossed the room, ignoring Margo. "Where in the hell have you been?" he demanded tersely.

Rebecca was sipping a glass of merlot when she casually looked up from the recliner and cordially smiled as if she didn't have a care in the world.

"You do understand why we have you here? What were you thinking—getting into a car with Junior Tazwell?"

Margo moved between Martin and Rebecca. "Agent Martin, do I need to remind you that you are in my house, and that I do not work for you any longer?"

Martin sidestepped Margo's blockade and fixed his irate gaze on Rebecca.

Rebecca sipped her wine. "This is *my* case! And David LaRoux is my husband—for a few days longer. *Any* other agent would still be on the job, not shoved into some dumpy motel. This is completely inappropriate gender-biased bullshit. And besides, did you honestly think I could stay hidden? LaRoux is the biggest supporter of the NOPD. There's not a cop in this city that believes he's guilty of any wrongdoing. So, is it any big surprise he knew exactly how to find me?"

"Once they see the evidence—"

"Evidence you say exists but refuse to share," Margo chided as she stepped back in front of Martin.

"I don't have to explain myself—"

"No, Will, you don't," Rebecca interjected, "which is exactly why LaRoux can continue to operate unimpeded. Without solid evidence, nobody believes you. That's why those cops outside didn't have an issue with me going with Tazwell. They've known him for years." Rebecca's stare was menacing. It forced Martin to look away. "If I felt I was in danger, I wouldn't have gone. Besides, if LaRoux wanted me dead, do you really think I'd be sitting here?"

"You *would* be dead if I hadn't saved you the other day."

Rebecca smiled slyly, edged forward, and stood. "LaRoux was never going to kill me. He was upset that I disappeared, and thanks to you, for some misguided reason, he thought I was sleeping with you. He knows a lot more than you give him credit for. This is LaRoux's town, Will. If you continue to underestimate him, you'll be damned lucky to keep your job."

Will pointed an accusatory finger but did not speak. He rolled his eyes, then looked at Margo.

"Don't look at me," Margo quipped. "It's your own fault you got pantsed in Vegas."

Will scoffed. "You two seem to forget that I was right about LaRoux. But seeing as how you have given me reason to doubt whose team the two of you are playing on, I have made alternate plans."

"Like?" Margo snapped.

"I believe you both remember Agent Turner." On cue, Sarah Turner entered from the porch.

"What the hell? Do you people think my home is a fucking Starbucks or something? Don't y'all feel the need to ask permission before barging into my home?" Margo directed her ire at Agent Turner.

Will smiled slyly. "Rebecca, you will go with Agent Turner to an undisclosed location, where you will remain until LaRoux has been arrested."

"Like hell I will."

"I thought you might disagree. But after last night's rendezvous, I'm not entirely sure of your loyalty. So, you can go voluntarily and remain sequestered until LaRoux is in custody, or I will arrest you for obstruction and you can enjoy the next two or three days in a cell."

"This is bullshit," Margo objected.

"No. But this little funhouse sorority pajama party *is* bullshit." Inferring Margo's protection detail, Martin waved his hand in a circle. "If you had done your job, Officer Carter—and believe me, your failure to do so will be in my report—none of this would be necessary. But seeing how Mr. LaRoux seems to hold sway over your department and my agent, from this point forward, we will be proceeding without the assistance from her, you, or NOPD."

Rebecca sat back and defiantly crossed her arms.

"Agent Pearson, on your feet, or the next words you hear will be your rights. Then I'll have Agent Turner cuff you and, if necessary, drag you out to the car. Your choice."

In hopes that Margo could get word to LaRoux through Ryan, Rebecca cut a glance her way.

"*Oh please,*" Martin moaned. "Do you really think I'm that stupid? Officer Carter's involvement with Ryan Patrick is *well* documented." Martin looked at Margo. "You won't be having access to a phone for the next three days either."

"I don't work for you," Margo protested.

"This might come as a complete surprise, but I don't give a fuck who you work for. This bust is so much bigger than who works for who or your trivial constitutional rights. When LaRoux goes down, the last thing anyone will worry about is two disgraced officers and how they got their feelings hurt."

Margo and Rebecca exchanged an eye check.

"That's right, ladies. It's time to go for a ride—both of you."

* * *

As Martin studied the video, he smiled broadly. Watching the contents of the shipboard cargo containers being transferred in the middle of the night, just off the coast of Playa Arimao, Cuba, he pumped his fist. "Got you, you son of a bitch." He spun in his chair and nodded in approval. "Great job, Fletcher! We would have been chasing the wrong container ship had you not put those cameras in place."

"If I hadn't got the tipoff about the switch, I never would have gotten the cameras placed on the *St. Lucia*. It was no big surprise when I found San Domingo's people in Guyana guarding the ship. Man, they had that freighter zipped up tighter than a nun's locker room."

Martin ignored the nutty analogy, and said, "You know what makes this super sweet?" Fletcher shrugged. "LaRoux went to great lengths to get us to follow his decoy to Mobile. That arrogant fucker is going to be really surprised when we show up at his Port of New Orleans warehouse." Martin dropped the shipping log on Fletcher's desk. "For some odd reason, a US Customs agent, Howard Reasons, has already flagged the *St. Lucia* for inspection. Do you know what that means?"

"Well, unless Agent Reasons has ESP and can sense what's in that container, he's LaRoux's inside man in customs."

"Exactly!" Will pounded his fist on the desk, and the clutter atop it jumped in the air. "When LaRoux's house of cards tumbles, we're going to find a nest of cockroaches in the rubble. Hell, this is going to be the biggest bust in history. And when the dust settles, I'll be sitting fat and pretty in DC running this entire dog and pony show."

CHAPTER 20

"YOU SURE YOU WANT to do this, David?" Walt asked as he checked his watch.

"Never been more sure, Walt," LaRoux replied as he scanned the refinements of his office.

"This just seems uncharacteristically risky. This guy, Martin, he's a loose cannon—and he's got a massive boner for you."

"All the more reason to do it. Besides, I've got my boys watching my back."

Walt shook his head. "I know you've taken extraordinary precautions with this shipment and the new warehouse and container switch, but if something goes wrong, with this much coke, we'll never see the light of day ever again."

"Walt, how long have we known each other?" LaRoux did not wait for a reply. "Long enough to know there's always a plan B. *If*, and I stress *if*, Martin and his band of idiots should show up—and I will be highly disappointed if they don't—it is *imperative* that you guys not engage with the DEA. I will even call them myself if they've been too stupid to follow my breadcrumbs. No matter what you think you believe about me, or all of this, you guys need to be completely unarmed." LaRoux stared long and hard at his friend. "Tell me you understand."

"You want us to lie down?"

"*Ab-so-lute-ly*. I don't want any of you guys guilty of anything."

Walt inhaled deeply as he considered if his boss had already cut some kind of deal. "Guilty of anything? Just being in the warehouse with a ton of coke—I don't know, David. Somehow, I've got to believe the feds might have an issue with that."

"You want to sit this one out, Walt?"

Walt glared at LaRoux. "David, I *have* known you a long time. Ever since you met that girl, it's like Taz, Ryan, and I have been kicked out of the loop. I don't know, David . . . you damn well nearly got yourself killed in Vegas. It seems to us that you have been living on the brink of disaster ever since you laid eyes on that agent."

"Are you referring to my wife, Rebecca?"

Walt slapped his hand on the desk and sighed in exasperation. "One year ago, would *you* have ever done business with *anyone* in this kind of relationship? *Hell no!* One year ago, with the feds sifting through the cat shit in the dumpster, you would not have taken delivery on a single gram, or especially our biggest haul ever. You're off your game, man. And this woman—she's the reason your vision is all fucked up. Tell me I'm wrong and I'll be right beside you, all the way to the federal penitentiary."

LaRoux pulled his desk drawer out and grabbed his Glock. "*If* you're coming, it's time." As he walked to his office door, he glanced back as if for the last time, then flipped the light switch.

"If I'm wrong, Walt, I promise you'll be the first to know."

Walt had not budged from standing in the dark office. "Just answer me this one question, David."

LaRoux turned and strained to see his friend's face. "Yes?"

"What in the hell are you hoping to prove from all this madness?"

"I'm not sure I know, Walt." LaRoux paused. "Perhaps that love beats the hell out of all this other insanity."

Walt scoffed as he breezed by LaRoux. "How about love tramples the shit out of common sense."

* * *

Martin checked his watch, then dialed his phone. "What's the word?"

"He's on the move," the voice reported back.

"Let me know if there's the slightest deviation from our expectations." Martin tucked his phone into his back pocket. "He's on his way," he reported to Fletcher. "Reasons sure has had that container long enough," Martin remarked as he peered through the binoculars.

"You mean long enough to unload the product." Fletcher scanned the customs warehouse with his binoculars in search of signs of movement.

"Exactly."

"So, how do we proceed, Will?"

Martin scanned across the darkened docks for any sign of strange activities. Finding the wharf suspiciously quiet, he asked, "How would you proceed, Fletch?"

Fletcher thought briefly. "With LaRoux on the roll, I've got to believe with a shipment this large, he's gonna be somewhere nearby to supervise. So, we follow LaRoux."

"If Pearson told him we're onto him, LaRoux could be a decoy."

Fletcher considered Martin's theory. "Not on an order this big. Since he personally made the buy, my money says he's gonna want to inspect the product and supervise its distribution. Pretty sure LaRoux and the shipment will make their way to Mobile pretty quickly. He's got too much riding on this one. Hell, if something goes wrong, it could bankrupt the son of a bitch."

Martin fixed his attention on an approaching semitruck. "So—"

"So, Reasons is dirty. We know that now," Fletcher proclaimed. "If he had discovered the coke, we would have already received a call. But he's not going to sit on LaRoux's shipment either. If he were to get busted in possession—" Fletcher and Martin watched as the rig backed up to the warehouse. "Reasons is not high enough up the totem pole, and he sure as hell isn't stupid enough to be ripping off LaRoux." Fletcher paused as the warehouse door began to close. "They've already switched containers, so there's no purpose behind switching again. The coke is headed for Mobile. So, I say we follow the container. LaRoux will show up soon enough."

"You don't think we should hit Reasons as soon as the rig is away?" Martin said as he continued to scan the docks with his binoculars.

"I wouldn't. There's a chance he could tip off LaRoux. Then you've got a semi full of coke, but no LaRoux." Sure of his decisions, Fletcher smiled with confidence. The pair sat in silence waiting for the semi to pull out.

As the tractor-trailer began to rumble out of the building, Martin sent a text message. *Product on the move.* Next, he dialed his phone. "What's your twenty?" Listening to the response, he sneered. "Is that so? Well enough. Maintain your position." Martin's love for superior intellect, or to prove a subordinate wrong, was renowned. "That semi is a decoy."

"Sir?"

"You were right. LaRoux can ill afford anything going wrong. He is on the way here. Reasons is sitting on the delivery."

"What about the truck? What if you're wrong and LaRoux coming here is the decoy?"

"I'm positive that truck is headed for a long road trip to nowhere. But I'll send a few guys to follow it."

Fletcher scratched his chin. "If you don't mind me asking, won't that stretch us too thin to bust LaRoux?"

"If nobody follows the truck, LaRoux will know we did not take the bait, Fletch. Then we'll lose LaRoux."

"But if the coke is in the warehouse, we'll destroy him."

"I don't give a fuck about the coke! Without busting LaRoux, he'll walk away from this. I don't just want him for the drugs. I want that motherfucker's reputation. I want to destroy him from the inside out." The veins in Martin's temples bulged.

Fletch took two steps back. "Boss, it sure sounds like this is some kind of personal vendetta."

Martin cut a menacing glare. "I know what everybody's been saying, that he kicked my ass in a bar fight two years ago and he's been fucking my ex-girlfriend, and then he got me demoted after Vegas, so this is a vendetta. But you know what?"

Fletcher shrugged, almost afraid to ask.

Martin leaned uncomfortably close into Fletcher's face. "It is."

* * *

The Denali remained uncomfortably quiet as Taz, Ryan, and Walt silently questioned their boss's intentions. As they neared the piers, Ryan was the first to break the silence.

"David, I got to tell you, I don't feel good about this. The size of this shipment alone—and we're completely unarmed like a motherfucker. You've never had us involved in your drug business before. This was always Geno's turf. I don't like this at all."

"Ryan, pull over here." The Denali slowed as it rolled onto the crunch of the gravel shoulder. Walt and Ryan turned around and focused their attention on LaRoux. "Each of you has always had specific duties, which, as you know, are sometimes exclusive unto yourselves and kept secret. You've always accepted that fact, and this is no different. Geno committed a grievous transgression and is not coming back. I expect this to be the last time we ever mention Geno. What we are about to do has virtually no risk, *if* you follow my instructions explicitly. If I had any reservations about tonight, I'd be the first to tell you to turn around. Are we all good?"

Walt was the first to turn away. Taz stared a little longer than appropriate, then huffed, "You *have* to know, *we've* already discussed tonight." Taz's declaration was met with a cordial smile from LaRoux. "But if you say we're good, then we're good."

Ryan turned and pulled back on the highway. "Shit, boss, it pisses me off not knowing what's up your sleeve. But you say jump, and I jump. Always have, always will."

LaRoux sat back and stared at the lights of the docks in the distance. He wondered if Taz, who was his only employee ever involved in disposal, had kept Geno's fate a secret. LaRoux knew his own behavior had given rise to speculation, but either way, the hour to going back had passed.

* * *

Martin checked his text. "They just pulled off the highway to make sure they weren't being followed," he reported.

Fletcher gritted his teeth as the reality of his failed assessment became increasingly obvious.

"So, how much longer?"

"Five minutes."

Fletcher prayed that Martin was wrong, that LaRoux might still be a decoy. "So, what's our play?"

Just as Martin was about to lay down the raid details, the customs office door rose and a forklift carrying a construction dumpster cautiously exited the hangar, heading in the direction of several waterfront warehouses.

"What the hell?" Fletcher moaned.

Martin chuckled. "The son of a bitch is cautious, I'll give him that much. He's splitting us three ways." Martin clicked on his walkie-talkie. "Team two, you've got the forklift. Teams one and four, hold your position. Nobody moves in until I give the green light." Martin tucked the radio back onto his belt. "We follow LaRoux. In the unlikely event *he is* the decoy, one and four will take down Reasons. If we all come up empty, team five will hit the semi last. If all of us come up empty, then Mobile has to be the delivery point. But we won't hit that, you know, make him think we don't know about it. When the coke does show, we'll be there. In any event, LaRoux's got nowhere to go."

The pair knelt behind a stack of worn pallets and watched as the forklift disappeared into a large, weathered waterfront warehouse. Just then, the Denali entered through the chain link gate on the opposite side of the terminals and headed toward the building.

"What if all of this is a decoy and the drugs are still on the ship?" Fletcher asked cautiously.

Martin turned slowly with a dumbfounded expression. "You know, Fletch, you might make a great agent one day. Wouldn't that be just like LaRoux?" Martin grabbed his radio. "Team two, pull back to the freighter and be ready to hit it hard. We'll take LaRoux and the warehouse. Time for Mr. LaRoux to come to justice," Martin boasted.

* * *

David LaRoux and his crew stared at the crates set on the dusty floor of the aged-timber waterfront warehouse. The only sign of life was a small southbound freighter quietly churning the Mississippi, the muddy waters lapping gently against its bow. The pale overhead lamps scarcely illuminated the newly deposited crates. There were no traces of the dumpster or the person who drove it in. As LaRoux and company entered, the sounds from the river evaporated amidst the confined space of stacked crates.

"That's a shitload of product, David." Ryan gawked at the crates.

"Looks like life behind bars to me," Walt moaned.

"Gentlemen, in many ways, this is the payday of a lifetime if everyone keeps their head," LaRoux explained as he turned to face his trusted employees. "Before we crack it open, just remember that I've got your backs. Just stick to my instructions."

"Dammit, David, what the hell is going on?" Walt snapped.

LaRoux ignored Walt's insubordinate tone. "Get on with it," LaRoux ordered Taz.

Taz checked his watch as Ryan looked nervously back outside. "Well, let's do this and get the hell out of here before something does go wrong." Taz hastily approached the crate, jammed the crowbar into a crack in the oak slats, and began prying the top off.

"I can't believe you'd leave this much product unguarded, David," Ryan objected as the sound of screeching nails replaced the eerie quiet.

"Oh, it's been guarded better than ever," LaRoux crowed as he spied the warehouse door.

The lid of the crate crashed to the floor, and Taz reached inside.

Without removing the metal cylindrical container, he popped the flip latches and peered into them. "Holy motherfucker," he exclaimed as he surveyed the bags of white powder.

"DEA, everybody on the floor!" Martin's voice boomed from just beyond the entrance.

Walt glared at LaRoux. "David, you set us up!"

"Steady, boys, I've got your backs," LaRoux explained softly. He smiled as he raised his hands and announced loudly, "We are unarmed."

"I said *on the floor*," Martin demanded from a safe distance, just outside the warehouse.

"Do as he says, guys, and you'll be home for breakfast. Don't worry about what I'm about to do." LaRoux watched as his team laid themselves on the ground. Shuffling two steps backward, LaRoux called out, "Is that you, Agent Martin?"

Martin stepped into the warehouse with his gun fixed on LaRoux. "David LaRoux, on the ground now!"

LaRoux winked at Walt, then turned and sprinted into the maze of crates.

"Dammit," Martin growled before he fired a warning shot. "Secure these bozos and the coke," Martin ordered Fletcher before dashing after LaRoux. In the back half of the expansive warehouse, crates were stacked and packed high and tight. His heart pounded, and he struggled to calm his breath. As he swept row to row, he regretted dispersing his team so thin.

"David LaRoux, you might as well surrender. We've got your coke and your crew. There's nowhere to go now," Martin bellowed.

LaRoux allowed a silent moment to lapse before responding, "Oh, I have somewhere to go. After I'm done with you, I'm going to Officer Carter's home to pay Agent Pearson one final visit. Oh wait, that's wrong. It's Biloxi now. Isn't that where you've taken her—to keep her safe?"

Martin cringed at the thought of LaRoux discovering the location of their new safe house so quickly.

"She *was* a pretty good fuck, wasn't she, Will? But you know what I'm going to do after I've worn her out one last time?"

Martin moved cautiously in the direction of LaRoux's voice. "Tell me, David." Martin could hear that LaRoux was close—his feet shuffling across the floor sounded just inches away. Martin quickly reversed his direction to intercept him, then pinned himself behind a stack of crates.

LaRoux knew his intentional vulgarity was inciting Martin. "After I'm finished, and my satisfaction is running down between her legs, I'm gonna slit that fucking, lying bitch's neck ear to ear."

Martin's ire was nearing a nuclear meltdown. He was confident LaRoux was right around the corner. There would be no time for second-guessing. He leaned against the ten-foot stack of crates, raised his gun to eye level, and took one last deep breath.

He spun around the corner and spotted LaRoux thirty yards away with a gun aimed at him. Without hesitation, Martin fired three rounds with lethal intent. So quickly did the explosion follow, he could not determine if any of his shots hit LaRoux. The massive shockwave and fireball consumed LaRoux and everything in its path so fast that Martin had no time to react before being catapulted fifteen feet backward from the blast. Fortunately for him, the fireball's advance dissipated a few feet in front of him, but the heat still managed to singe his hair. Dazed, he scrambled to his feet and watched as the inferno expanded skyward through the shattered roof.

Martin scrambled around the corner and found Fletcher and LaRoux's crew rising from the floor, crates toppled and debris everywhere. "Everybody out—it might blow again." The rapidly spreading fire and heat drove the agents and LaRoux's crew farther out into the yard. Speechless and dazed, they stared at the inferno.

"What the hell did you do?" Walt yelled at Martin.

Martin ignored Walt's inquisition, and, as the other agents quickly arrived, he ordered, "Cuff these guys." The agents retreated farther as several more explosions shook the terminal. Walt looked away. A tear fell as he watched the blaze reflected in the ripples of the Mississippi.

Off in the distance, the wail of sirens began to overtake the roar of the flames. Several smaller explosions rocked the earth and made the surrounding buildings and piers tremble. Fletcher grabbed Martin by the arm and pulled him away. "Half of New Orleans is about to arrive. You need to tell me what just happened back there!"

Martin cut a hostile glare at Fletcher's hand on his arm. Fletcher returned the courtesy.

"*Where* is LaRoux?"

Martin snatched his arm out of Fletcher's grip. "He had a gun. I fired three shots. One must have hit a gas tank—or a pipe, or something."

Fletcher looked back at the warehouse. "So, LaRoux is dead?"

Martin nodded. "Super-fucking-man would not have survived that one."

"God, Will, you'd better hope that evidence survives the fire, or we're going to be completely fucked on this one."

* * *

Rebecca sat on the edge of the bed and stared at the TV. Tears streamed down her cheeks, and her head reeled as if she had just been sucker punched. Sarah Turner was still clutching her cell phone, but she couldn't think of who to call. The news had already spread to Biloxi. The image of the blazing warehouse was on CNN, and the ticker scroll saying "David LaRoux killed in explosion" crawled across the bottom of the screen.

The news crawler lacked any significant details of the disaster and listed attributes of LaRoux's legacy in New Orleans. The media had already obtained quotes from the governor, mayor, and owner of the Saints. The reporter detailed LaRoux's family legacy, an intricate cog in the foundations of the French Quarter itself. But all the words fell on deaf ears. Rebecca remained focused on the flames and the bold text proclaiming LaRoux's untimely death.

Sarah watched it all in silence, not entirely sure what to say. Over the past two days, Rebecca had instilled reasonable doubt of

LaRoux's guilt. As such, his death left her conflicted by compassion for Rebecca and her duty to the DEA. The awkwardness left Sarah wishing she had any other assignment.

Her duty had grown exponentially more unpleasant. She had to keep Rebecca in Biloxi, regardless of the measures of restraint required. With LaRoux's death, retribution was sure to follow quickly. William Martin had made the consequences of any failure clear beyond all doubt.

Sarah's entire future in the DEA rested on her ability to keep Rebecca safe.

* * *

"Special Agent Martin," a deep, thick-accented Creole voice called.

Martin turned to find a wire-thin, unshaven man standing behind his back; the voice did not match the framework. The badge hanging from his neck indicated NOPD. "How can I help you?"

"I'm Chief LeSard, Agent Martin. I believe you have three of Mr. LaRoux's employees in custody. I would like to speak to them."

LeSard's Cajun drawl had Martin surmising that he was most likely dealing with a cop who was deeply entrenched in the department—a department rife with corruption. "I'm sorry, Chief LeSard. This is an ongoing federal investigation, and this crime scene is the jurisdiction of federal government agents, as are the suspects. After they have been processed, you will have full access to them."

"Agent Martin, I am behooved to seek out these men at the request of our fine governor. If I am to inform him of your lack of cooperation, I feel certain that within the next ten minutes, the president of the United States' chief of staff will be calling your boss, and it will no longer be a request when the next word reaches your ear."

Martin placed his hands on his hips and spit. He focused on the fire chief a few feet away. "Chief, how much longer?"

"Fifteen minutes, tops."

"Fletcher!" Martin barked.

Fletcher, who was jawboning with the fire chief, returned quickly. "Fletch, please escort Chief LeSard to our suspects. If any of those boys should, by chance, seize the opportunity to excuse themselves from our little party . . . well, you know what to do." Martin's half-cocked sneer telegraphed his extreme disdain to LeSard.

LeSard nodded and smiled. "Your *fuck you* is duly noted, Agent Martin."

Martin watched from a distance as LeSard held a conversation with LaRoux's crew. On several occasions, he looked back at Martin and shook his head.

LeSard had just returned to Martin when the fire chief joined them. With a bitter and harsh tone, he reported, "It's safe, Agent Martin."

Martin was beaming as he looked at Fletcher and LeSard. "Gentlemen, if you care to accompany me." Most of the timbers from the roof's collapse had burned away, leaving the stainless steel canisters visible under a small, charred pile of rubble. With great theatrics, Martin snapped his rubber gloves on. He picked up a three-gallon container and walked it back to an open space. After he set it down, he boasted, "Chief LeSard, this is what your noble David LaRoux was really all about." He unlatched and removed the airtight lid to expose a container filled with cocaine. "My only regret is that the SOB didn't live to see his day of justice."

"If you will indulge me, sir," LeSard said as he produced a lockback knife. Without waiting for Martin's permission, he stabbed the plastic seal and withdrew the blade. He ran his tongue on the edge of the blade and frowned. "That son of a bitch. I always knew he was a dirty smuggler." Martin's smile could not be contained. His moment of vindication and fame was at hand.

"Tell me, Agent Martin," LeSard growled, "with David LaRoux dead, what on earth do you plan on doing with all this flour?"

"What?" Martin shoved Fletcher from his path.

"Have a taste. I promise you won't fail any drug test with this stuff." LeSard extended the blade.

Martin swiped his finger over it, then across his tongue. He tried to conceal his acute disappointment by forcing a grin. "You didn't expect it to be so easily discovered, did you? LaRoux didn't get rich being stupid. When we get all these containers back to the lab, we'll find the coke."

"Of that, I am most positive, Agent Martin. But you'll have to excuse my skepticism. Without a trace of regret, I must inform you, I cannot allow you or your people unrestricted access to *my* evidence."

"*Your evidence?*" Martin's shriek drew the attention of everyone within earshot.

"Unless you have evidence to the contrary, I have a purchase order from Pappy Brown. That would be him, over yonder, with the scowl." LeSard pointed to a muscular middle-aged black man wearing a tight T-shirt and weathered khakis. "He oversees many of our soup kitchens in the greater New Orleans area. He arrived here with all intention of receiving a shipment of donated baking goods from Mr. David LaRoux—the same Mr. LaRoux you beat senseless a few days ago in retaliation for a barroom scuffle almost two years ago. The same man who was your rival for Agent Rebecca Pearson's affections. The same Mr. LaRoux who eventually married your former agent and girlfriend."

"I have pictures of LaRoux buying the coke from Miguel San Domingo!"

"If you're referring to Señor San Domingo, Mr. Brown will—but not so happily, I'm afraid—explain the longstanding relationship between Mr. LaRoux, San Domingo, and our soup kitchens. But I warn you, Mr. Brown may become hostile, as he has just watched a half a year's supplies go up in flames, not to mention the man who practically financed the entire program."

"Wait just a minute. Don't think I don't see what's going on here. I know LaRoux's involvement with the department—"

"Agent Martin!" LeSard boomed. "As your opinion of my department has already been well documented, I will allow one of your agents to be present during *our* lab's verification process. Lord knows, concerning your allegations about our department, we wouldn't want to corrupt the chain of evidence. But in the meantime, I have a murder, a suspect with a motive, and evidence to process. If you will do me the courtesy of surrendering your weapon," LeSard said as he motioned for two nearby officers, "I will have one of these fine gentlemen read you your rights."

"Are you fucking kidding me?" Martin screamed.

LeSard's stoic expression guaranteed that he was not. Martin leaned into Fletcher's ear. "This stinks of corruption. Move Pearson, and keep her under lock and key. As soon as you find the coke, it's our evidence again. Don't let it out of your sight." Martin turned to leave, but then he grabbed Fletcher's arm. "Oh, and call Agent Nelson. Tell him what these clowns are up to. He'll have their asses in a woodchipper before the sun comes up." LeSard held his hand out impatiently.

Begrudgingly, Martin jerked his gun from the holster and handed it over. "Enjoy your little game while it lasts, LeSard. Tomorrow, you'll be lucky if you're allowed to write parking tickets."

CHAPTER 21

THE WAKE AT THE LaRoux mansion four days later was unlike any event ever held at the plantation. Buses and limos shuttled people to the ceremony for the bulk of the morning. By two o'clock, the house and lawn were filled with dignitaries, friends, and visitors who had come to pay their respects.

The black Escalade slowly made its way up the magnolia-lined driveway and stopped in front of the marble steps. Federal agents dressed in black suits opened the door and escorted Rebecca and Sarah up the spiral stairs. Rebecca, who remained in the protective custody of the DEA, appeared worn thin from the events of the past week. She used the railing for support as she labored her way to the top. Memories of her first night at the mansion, the elegance and grandeur of the evening—and of David LaRoux—initiated a fresh stream of tears.

On the crowded back porch, the VIPs had already gathered, all prepared to offer their praise and sympathies for their fallen friend and associate. Rebecca was escorted to a fan-back, white wicker chair on the porch, just to the right of the podium. Amidst the warm breeze, suspicion and gossip whispered across the lawn. *"The nerve of that damnable woman, showing up and taking a seat of honor, no less."* Her secret's hour had long passed. Not all accusations were kept in well-mannered tones; disgraced DEA agent, gold digger, *fille de joie*—*"Well, she had a lot of nerve, indeed."*

The first speaker was the vice president, speaking on behalf of the president of the United States. He began by apologizing for the president's absence, then spoke passionately about LaRoux's legacy, not only in Louisiana but across the country too. Many environmental policies were championed by the LaRoux family, as well as trade policies and issues of social injustice.

A gentle breeze blew through the magnolias and twisted oaks, dampening the cries of many who called David LaRoux a friend. Rebecca sat dumfounded as the speeches progressed into the late afternoon. And no matter the circumstances, one thing was painfully evident—whatever the source of LaRoux's vast wealth, he had generously donated more time and assets to worthy causes than she could ever have imagined. What honestly confounded Rebecca was that through all the accusations, and even by LaRoux's own admission, not one shred of evidence of wrongdoing had surfaced.

Rebecca's tears, seemingly exhausted many times over, found new fuel as Miguel San Domingo closed out the eulogies. Was he truly LaRoux's partner in crime or a convenient scapegoat? Did LaRoux and San Domingo fabricate the entire drug lord cover just to flush out Rebecca's true ambitions? San Domingo spoke of brotherly love and commitment to friends beyond personal sacrifice. He credited LaRoux for crafting San Domingo's own life of philanthropy. He reminded the audience that LaRoux died doing the very thing he was notoriously loved for—caring for the less fortunate.

At the end of his speech, he turned to Rebecca. "Rebecca LaRoux, it is a great tragedy that we meet under these bleak circumstances. Last I spoke with David, it was evident that his love for you was insurmountable. This love my friend succumbed to *was* something to be envied—rare and precious it *was*. Having known him but too short of a lifetime, I had never seen him so dedicated to any woman.

You must be an exceptional woman indeed. I pray that you do not hold on to blame for any part of this tragedy, for justice will seek out those who are truly responsible."

As San Domingo made his way down the porch steps to the courtyard to offer condolences, his words resounded in Rebecca's mind. *Justice will seek out those who are truly responsible.*

Had he just threatened her and her fellow DEA agents in front of hundreds of witnesses?

Throughout the reception, Taz, Ryan, and Walt maintained an obvious, intentionally distant berth from Rebecca. Except for a few cordial *sorry for your loss* acknowledgments from strangers, not many people found purpose to speak with her. At every turn of her head, she saw the subtle finger-pointing. Truth be told, she knew she was responsible for LaRoux's death.

She escaped the gathering to walk the expansive porch and reminisce about the ball. LaRoux had taken her arm as they strolled around the mansion as if he already knew he loved her. Now, tears flowed freely from her shame; this newfound emptiness crushed her spirit. Through all the turmoil of their short time together, Rebecca was sure the love he had offered so freely would never find her again.

As she approached the double-hung French doors to the ballroom, which had afforded their escape from the attention of the waltz, they swung open. After Ryan's deliberate efforts to avoid Rebecca, the face-to-face encounter was uncomfortable to say the least. They stood in a brief silence before Ryan spoke. "If you gentlemen would excuse us, I would like a moment alone with Mrs. LaRoux."

The agents looked at one another, then at Rebecca. "Please, you can wait back there," she implored as she pointed to the corner of the porch. Ryan gave an appreciative nod as the agents reluctantly complied.

When they were out of earshot, he asked, "Are you wired?"

Incensed, Rebecca replied sharply, "No."

"We expected you would be. That's why nobody's talking to you. With your boss being charged with murder and everything, the DEA is desperate. They're gonna do everything they can, even manufacture evidence, to prove David was guilty and Martin justified in killing him."

"I don't believe that."

"Oh, you don't, do ya? Guess you never heard about Las Vegas after you and David disappeared."

Rebecca's brows arched. "What about Las Vegas?"

"Y'all planted two keys of coke in his room, or at least the room they thought was his. Then y'all tipped off LVPD so somebody other than the DEA could find it."

"*No!*" Rebecca's objection could be heard down the porch, causing the agents to take steps in their direction. "*I don't believe that.*"

"We're cool," Ryan called to the agents as he gestured for them to stop. His head zipped back to Rebecca, his eyes sharp. "*Oh yeah*, baby. We had you guys pegged for DEA almost from the get-go, so we wound up watching *everything* y'all did. Got some pretty revealing video footage to prove it, too. After you and David split from Vegas, Martin and company planted the drugs in the room they thought belonged to David. We were manipulating the hotel video feeds, so you guys never knew you had the wrong room." Ryan chuckled at the memory. "Some poor SOB took a free room upgrade and wound up with a lot of explaining to do to LVPD. You guys had to circle the wagons to get the guy cleared."

"I didn't know or have anything to do with any of that, and I certainly wouldn't have allowed them to frame David, or anybody for that matter."

"Your boss was unable to lay any claim to the cocaine, otherwise LVPD would have suspected his endgame. And without any proof of my boss's guilt, the entire fiasco of Martin's investigation and lost drugs became a huge waste of DEA resources, which had a lot to do with his demotion—a demotion that should have kept David safe, that is until you narced him out."

"I didn't narc out anybody. Everything I told the DEA was exactly what David told me to say, and nothing more. And whoever the ass was that told David I was sleeping with Will—" Rebecca tried to continue, but her emotions trumped her fight.

"Maybe we got it wrong." Ryan sighed, and his expression softened. "But he truly loved you, Rebecca, that much was clear." He cut his eyes to check the position of the suspicious agents. "I've got to go. Watch your back, Rebecca. They're gonna come for you."

* * *

A week later, Rebecca gazed out from the second-floor balcony of the Sunset Manor Hotel in Biloxi. She was ordered to remain in protective custody until the full extent of Martin's botched investigation could be determined. With the patchwork of evidence collected in Vegas and New Orleans, a data forensics team hopelessly sifted through all evidence to find any scrap that would warrant further investigation. But after numerous interviews with Rebecca, they were all but certain either she had no evidence to offer or was simply withholding what she knew. But she was all they had. The reality of her testimony was simple: There was not one tangible piece of evidence showing that David LaRoux had committed any crime.

Rebecca continued to claim partial responsibility for the deaths of the Colombians in Las Vegas rather than tarnish LaRoux's memory by revealing his excessive brutality. She made no mention of Geno's departure into the bayou or her knowledge of Colin Wells's fate, because she honestly didn't know what had become of either of them—nor did she care. She wondered if, perhaps, LaRoux had merely been testing her when he confessed his criminal activities. *Maybe there never were any drugs.* Three times, he had held a gun to her. Twice, he offered it freely for her to do with it as she pleased. *Was it all a test?*

He was truly a powerful man, as made evident by his list of friends at the memorial. Surely, many of them had ties to organized crime. The gaming industry and import business were certainly not the industries of angels and somewhere in the shadows, lurked her fate.

As the sun finally began to relinquish its mastery of the darkness, Rebecca returned to her room and pulled the door shut. Sarah, seated on the couch reading a book, sighed forcefully. "I really wish you would quit that," she said as she peeked over her romance novel. "Any half-ass sniper could take you down without much effort."

"Does it really matter? The only difference is if I get killed before they are done with me, the DEA loses their only witness. If it happens after Will's trial, nobody will care."

"That's not true, Rebecca." Sarah set the book on the couch and patted out a place for Rebecca to sit. "You have friends that care. I care. They were ready to reassign me, but I am here in this dump because I choose to be."

Rebecca plopped down on the far side of the sofa and sighed. "I'm sorry. I'm just tired of waiting for *it* to happen. My days are numbered. I think we all know it."

"I wouldn't be so sure. If they feel the threat is real, they'll put you in witness protection."

"Ha!" Rebecca exclaimed. "Maybe if I had some testimony that would make the case." Rebecca liked Sarah, but she also knew that if she revealed anything incriminating, it would most likely be in the DEA's ear before sunrise. "No, when this is over, they'll put me on a bus back home, end of story."

Sarah stretched her arms wide and yawned. "I don't know why I'm suddenly so tired." She stood and slowly crossed the room to the window to gaze at the remnants of a purple and orange sunset. She spoke lazily. "If David LaRoux was so damn connected as you claim, then his people on the inside will know you've given no information."

"I really don't think they give a damn about what I've said or what I might say. It's pretty evident how well insulated everyone in his organization is." Rebecca stared at the beverage-stained rug. "They blame me . . ." Rebecca said, choking on her words, ". . .for his death."

"But they all know how much he loved you. He did marry you, and you are having his child."

Rebecca dismissed Sarah's optimism. She knew there were some in LaRoux's organization who would not care; Mr. Hanson topped the list. "Why don't we go out for dinner? I'm gonna go stir-crazy if I eat one more meal in this room." Sarah turned her attention away from the sunset, took one step toward Rebecca, then stumbled back against the window.

"Sarah, what's wrong?"

Sarah's eyes glazed over as she warned weakly, "Get out." She collapsed on the floor.

Rebecca leapt from the sofa and rushed to Sarah's side. She grabbed her arm and dragged her to the door. She twisted the deadbolt, flipped the lights off, and peeked out from the corner of the room-darkening drapes. As dizziness began to set in, she realized they were being gassed. Rebecca's only hope—fresh air waiting *out* there.

As she reached for the safety chain, her vision began to blur. She flipped, pawed, and fumbled with the chain until it swung free. Just as she managed to crack the door open, her knees buckled and she collapsed. The last image she assimilated before the blackness set in was that of a large hand pulling the door shut.

* * *

Rebecca struggled to open her eyes under the opaque white orb that hovered above her head. Eventually, her eyes adjusted to the dome light, and she became cognizant of its rhythmic swaying. She realized she was in the backseat of a moving vehicle. Resigned that her time was near, she offered no resistance and allowed herself once again to fall into darkness.

Hours later, without any concept of how much time had passed, Rebecca attempted to rise. She discovered her hands and legs were bound, and she found an unexpected comfort in believing her misery was nearing an end. Perhaps shortly, she would find herself beside David once more.

As more time passed, curiosity finally got the best of Rebecca. With great difficulty, she used her forearm to rise again. The glow of the instrument cluster gave definition to a pair of menacing eyes in the mirror. The radio was low—too low to distinguish what her abductor was listening to. His eyes cut to the mirror, then back to the heavily wooded road singularly illuminated by the beacon of halogen headlights.

Rebecca did not know the stranger behind the wheel. She had hoped it was Taz or another member of David's crew. With them, she felt she could broker a quick and merciful end. If the Colombians had hired this man, Rebecca knew an *interrogation* was sure to follow.

As the miles rolled by in silence, she wondered if her sentence would be carried out like Geno's. The bayou crept into view on multiple occasions, and she knew the drill. If there was any hope of not suffering an alligator attack, she would have to dissuade this man before they reached their destination.

"Do you work for San Domingo?"

In an undistinguishable dialect, the man replied blandly, "No."

"Why didn't you just kill me at the hotel? There's no need to go through this elaborate bayou ritual. I've got no information to offer."

The driver snickered. "You should already know the reasons why I didn't kill you."

"What did you do with Sarah? Is she dead?"

The man's lips turned up into a half-baked smile. "Don't worry about Turner. They'll find her at shift change. She's going to have a headache and be really pissed off at how miserably she failed. But other than that, she'll be fine."

Rebecca pushed back against the seat. "She's not the only one who's pissed off. I'm David's wife, and he would not have approved of this at all."

The driver scowled at the notion. "*If* he had listened to me, you never would have even made that trip to Vegas, much less all of this. And he'd still be alive."

Rebecca glared into the mirror until she caught the driver's eyes peeking back. "You're Mr. Hanson, aren't you?" Hansen said nothing.

"David told me about you. He said we'd never meet, and yet here we are."

"When he told you that, he certainly hadn't planned on being dead. But he is. So yes, here we are." Hanson's eyes grew darker with what appeared to be a painful admission. "He should have listened to me about you, about all of this. But he was hell-bent on starting some kind of new life with you."

"*You*, of all people, *have* to know I did not betray David. Don't you?"

Hanson sighed. "Yes."

"Then why all of this? Why am I tied up and on the way to the bayou?" Rebecca wrestled with her restraints.

"This was the only way to save you. *They were* coming for you, and there was no way to straighten things out. And the DEA, *your* people, they sure as hell could not have protected you. So, I did."

Rebecca stopped working at her bonds long enough to lean forward. "But why all of this?"

"Do you think the DEA would have voluntarily let you go with me? And if I told you who I was, you sure as hell wouldn't have come willingly." Hanson slowed the SUV to a stop on the shoulder and turned around. "You do understand, if I wanted you dead, you would be dead?" He examined Rebecca's obstinate expression and smiled ever so slightly. "Yeah, he said you had some spunk." He twisted in his seat and continued. "David's instructions were for me to protect you with whatever measures I deemed appropriate." He produced a four-inch Emerson lockback from his pocket. "Promise you won't do anything stupid, and I'll cut your restraints."

Rebecca twisted in the seat and brought her wrist as close as possible to the knife's edge.

"If you try anything, I'll put you in the trunk," Hanson warned.

"And who is it that is supposed to be coming for me—San Domingo? David's other people?" Rebecca rubbed her wrist. Then her eyes popped wide as Hanson offered her the blade. "For your feet, nothing else," Hanson said as he squinted. "Let's be straight about one thing—I am not David's *people*. *They* are a bunch of idiots that don't even know I exist. I only answered to David, or in this case, his final instructions." Hanson held out his hand for the knife. "That Louisiana casino deal was worth billions. Only David had the connections and the funding to see it through. My guess is that somebody from the gaming industry was sending a special thank you to your former boss and the DEA. But in reality, it could be anybody. Your misguided ruse in this clusterfuck took David away and hurt a lot of people, deeply. And down here, they take *an eye for an eye* seriously."

Rebecca clung to the knife. "Then why aren't *you* killing me?"

Hanson thrust his open hand at Rebecca. "David was like a son to me. Everything he said and did, no matter how reckless, was an indication of how much he loved you—in love for the first time in his life, and wouldn't you know it, to a fucking DEA agent. All this shit—you, Martin, the DEA, San Domingo, that last shipment. We knew the game had high risks, with potentially deadly consequences, but it was his decision to play it out." Hanson pulled back. "The last thing he said to me was, 'Protect her like you've protected me all of these years, because I love her that much.'"

Rebecca sat silent as tears streamed down her cheeks. Hanson reached into the console and handed her a tissue.

"I deserve that bullet," she sniffled.

"I was about to let you keep my knife, but I can't have you going all suicidal and whatnot," he said with an unexpected reassuring smile. "Look, the fault *is* yours—and mine. Walt and that crew of idiots, you name 'em, you can blame 'em. But in reality, it falls back on David. I urged him to walk away more than once. He chose not to."

Hanson pulled back onto the road and accelerated quickly. "We've got to get moving. I need to get you to the new safe house before the sun comes up."

"Why's that?"

"I can't risk facial recognition software picking you out. When *they* realize you're gone, the feds won't be the only people looking for you."

As the miles rolled by in relative silence, Rebecca watched the moonlight dance off the water then suddenly become obscured by clouds and trees. Then, unexpectedly, it became so full and bright that it was almost blinding.

Hanson made a right turn down a surprisingly smooth gravel road. As he drove a short distance, Rebecca recognized the familiar corrugated lines of an airplane hangar, almost identical to the one in Nevada. "If I didn't know better, I'd say we were back at the hangar in Las Vegas. Should I have packed a sweater for colder climates?"

Hanson chuckled. "Even if you wanted to go back north, I wouldn't have a clue where to take you. That is unless you'd care to share the location of David's hideaway. It kind of pissed me off that I could never find the two of you." He waited for an answer, then mulled over LaRoux's ability to get one over on him. "Well, seeing as how you are rather tight lipped on that one, I'll just tell you that my primary focus is to get you somewhere where you'll be sure to stay safe."

"For how long?"

"If you live to be ninety, we might have a problem."

Rebecca wiped her cheeks briskly, then pulled herself forward until her head was literally in the front seat. "What does that mean?"

"I'm damn good at my job. There was a time that fact was close to being very bad news for you. Las Vegas, and all of this other bullshit, was a direct result of him ignoring my professional advice and choosing to chase after you. I made damn sure that he knew well in advance he was being reckless beyond my ability to protect him. As such, his game plan included a scenario where he might not survive. David paid me an obnoxious sum of money, inflation adjusted, to ensure your safety for the rest of your life, or mine, whichever should come first." He turned his face to discover Rebecca's unexpectedly close position. He leaned a little left to afford a comfortable space and said, "That is why we are leaving the Gulf Coast."

"I don't mean any disrespect, but what if I don't want you watching over me?"

"Then tonight will be the last time you will ever see me."

Rebecca huffed, surprised at his willingness to take LaRoux's money and simply go away.

"But I will always be there, watching you, keeping you as safe as my abilities allow." He pulled the SUV to a stop, killed the lights, and shut off the motor.

"I like my privacy."

Hanson grinned devilishly. "Then close your shades, and don't be naked or have sex in rooms with cameras."

Rebecca pushed away. "And how do I know which rooms those are?"

Hanson almost laughed. "It's all of them."

"I can see this relationship is going to be quite trifling. So, are you going to drug me before putting me on that plane?"

Hanson had never heard the story of LaRoux's Canadian flight, so he misinterpreted Rebecca's meaning. "Nope. At this point, if you decide you want to run all the way back to New Orleans, I'll let you. But it won't be with me driving."

"I guess you wouldn't consider selling me your keys?"

"It's a sixty-five-thousand-dollar truck. How much do you have in your purse?"

Rebecca looked at her handbag on the floor, impressed that Hanson had swiped it too. "I don't have much cash, but I do have an AMEX."

"Sorry, but I don't accept plastic, but even if I did, you *don't* have any plastic." Hanson flashed a self-congratulatory grin.

"Son of a bitch," Rebecca muttered as she shook her head and pushed her handbag away. "Would you honestly let me walk all the way back to New Orleans?"

"No, I wouldn't. You're going on the plane. The level of dignity, I'll leave up to you."

Rebecca mulled her extremely limited options. *Did Hanson fabricate the imminent purported hit? Is he planning to turn me over in Colombia to San Domingo for a reward?* She looked at the hangar, knowing there was no way to overpower him.

Sensing she was deliberating her quandary, Hanson got out of the truck and opened the passenger door. "I'll take my knife now." Once it was back in his hands, he gently guided her legs until they were pointing out of the truck. He sliced one final tie around her waist that Rebecca had not even noticed. He looked up. "I know it's a lot to process, and given my employment relationship with David, I understand you may have certain trust issues. But you're going to have to deal with that for now, because we are on a tight schedule."

Without a solitary soul to offer a hint of advice, Rebecca exited the vehicle. She felt more lost and alone than at any other time in her life. She was resigned to the notion that if they were headed to Colombia, she deserved whatever faced her there.

CHAPTER 22

AN INCESSANT RAPPING ON the door startled Martin awake. He rubbed his eyes and staggered to the door. The sun had barely been up an hour. The hangover from last night's boozing had yet to emerge. He swung the door open without checking. Agent Morris appeared impatient, his exuberant expression foretelling some great urgency.

"What the hell do you want at this hour?" Martin dragged his hands down his face.

"She's gone—Agent Pearson, that is."

Martin sighed. "Fuck her. She's worthless to me and the DEA. *All* of this shit, she's at the core of it. I'm beginning to think the bitch set me up from the get-go. I wouldn't be surprised to learn she went straight to LaRoux and tipped him off right after I brought her in on the investigation."

"So, instead of protecting her, why didn't we just arrest her as an accomplice?"

Martin rolled his eyes and began to shut the door on the agent. Stopping just short, he swung it open and walked away. "You know how a coffeemaker works, kid?"

"They don't hire you unless you do," Morris replied as he looked about the train wreck of an apartment. Empty bottles of booze, food wrappers, and clothes were strewn about. Morris made his way to the kitchen. "Mind if I make myself a cup?"

"Sure thing, kid," Martin said as he scrounged through a stack of papers on the table. "What about what's her name, the agent assigned to protect Pearson?"

Dishes clacked together as Morris search for clean cups. "Sarah Turner. According to her, she passed out. When she woke up, Pearson was gone. They think it was some type of gas."

Martin stuck his head in the kitchen. "Or so she says. If there's no trace of gas, or how it was delivered, then you should check her bank account. That fucker LaRoux has his tentacles everywhere."

"So, you think Turner might be dirty too?"

Martin saw the suspicion Morris was trying to conceal. "I know what you're thinking. But I'm telling you, that video from the warehouse was forged. I don't care what a thousand experts say— LaRoux had a gun and was about to shoot me. There's not a chance in hell I mistook his hands being raised in surrender as opposed to having a gun pointed at me. No fucking way."

"You know, if there was just some way to explain how they altered that security video that quickly, I'm sure everyone would believe you."

The penetrating glare through Martin's glassy eyes forced the young agent to look away.

"There's a Starbucks two blocks up the street. Maybe you should go get your coffee there."

Morris set the paper filter on the countertop and turned to leave. As he passed Martin, his nervousness was apparent. "I stopped by as a courtesy, Agent Martin. *Your* name came up on the list of suspects. Everybody knows you believe Pearson is partially to blame for your suspension and arrest. Talk is, you're bitter about how she rebuked your advances after your affair ended and her obvious loyalty to LaRoux, even after his death." Morris turned back at the door. "For the record, I'd like to believe you *were* on the right track. Unfortunately, outside of the attempted kidnapping, when LaRoux *and* Pearson whacked those thugs in Vegas, there's absolutely nothing to substantiate any of your claims of criminal activities against David LaRoux."

"Yeah, yeah, yeah, so I have been told. But you know what? Nobody is that innocent."

* * *

Hanson stood on the porch of the modest Sarasota, Florida beach house as he admired his security camera handiwork. "This is where we say goodbye. I must remain a ghost if I'm to do my job. You are David LaRoux's widow, and after I'm absolutely sure all risks to your safety have been neutralized, if you choose you can reemerge and become a public figure, of sorts." Hanson was comfortable with Rebecca's relocation, and his only stipulations were that she wear an oversized hat and sunglasses when she ventured out, use cash, or the credit card he had supplied. He handed her an old flip phone and the keys to the house. "This phone only calls one number. If you ever need me . . ." He turned and quietly walked down the sandstone sidewalk.

Although the beach house—another one of LaRoux's getaways—was modest, it was far nicer than anything Rebecca would have ever rented or owned on her salary. The exterior mimicked the surrounding luxury beach homes on Longboat Key, but the inside was pure Louisiana. Rebecca studied the softly lit entrance as she set the keys and phone on the foyer table. The walls were adorned with works from the same artists as LaRoux's mansion and office.

The living room appeared to be a replica of his plantation's with one exception. Instead of a view of the bayou, there was a breathtaking view of the sea.

The central focus of the great room was a startling portrait above a fireplace. Above the Tennessee stone and cypress mantel, a remarkable likeness of Rebecca in her enchanted emerald ball gown hung for all to see.

Rebecca's hands rose to her quivering lips, and her tears flowed unrestrained. Whatever doubt she had harbored, one truth was hauntingly and irrefutably evident; David LaRoux had loved her.

At that moment, life lost its purpose. The bottle of wine that followed did not ease the pain or the resounding belief she should have done something to prevent LaRoux's death. With the corkscrew in one hand and a new bottle in the other, Rebecca gazed at her portrait with disdain.

"You, Rebecca Pearson, are an asshole."

She pivoted back toward the kitchen, but her heels caught on the edge of the tweed area rug and sent her on a collision course with the floor. She and the bottle hit it with a thud. "Shit," she moaned as she watched the unbroken bottle spin and roll across the floor, far from her grasp. She crawled and flopped an arm on the sofa. "Don't think I don't see you laughing, David LaRoux. But if you were *such* a great guy, you would have bought a softer rug," Rebecca complained in slurred words as she stretched out. She rubbed her abdomen and apologized. "I know, it was only supposed to be one glass. I'll do better tomorrow."

* * *

Pain greeted Rebecca with a brutal wakeup call. Her head was reeling from too much wine, and while the morning sun soothed her body, her eyes objected to its intensity. She lay on the floor as she blamed some of her suffering on Mr. Hanson. Had he given her sandals or sneakers for her abduction, she would never have stumbled. Had he left her barefoot, like he found her, her knee and elbow would not bear the painful reminder of why she avoided wearing heels when drinking. True, his logic for choosing heels might have been solid—they did restrict her ability to flee. But at the moment, that did not soften her current opinion of him. *Hanson's an asshole too.*

As she labored up the stairs, she realized she really didn't know what she was looking for.

When she checked the first room at the top of the stairs, she discovered a converted bedroom that was now a home gym. She couldn't imagine enjoying the panoramic view of Sarasota Bay while spinning, lifting, or running. In fact, the mere thought made her head throb worse. The next room was an office of sorts. It had matching computer desks complete with iMacs, an obnoxiously large TV, and several well-stocked bookcases. Rebecca thought she'd see what types of books LaRoux had chosen for their collection, but the thought of reading made her headache worse.

The room at the end of the hall, with the sun streaming in, had to be *it*. If the portrait downstairs was any indication of LaRoux's dedication, Rebecca was sure that whatever was ahead would only increase her misery. Perhaps the living room couch would become the new master suite.

She attempted to summon the willpower to move forward, but she failed. "I can do this," she spoke softly. So, she tried again. As she balanced herself against the wall, each step she took drew her closer to another dose of reality. This room would never bear witness to passion.

"Oh God," Rebecca moaned as she stood in the doorway. If she could have designed the picture-perfect bedroom, this would be it. She remembered the pale-green walls. In Las Vegas, she had remarked how she would love to have a bedroom this color. She had admired the walnut bedroom set in a shop back in Nova Scotia. As she walked through the room she was in now, she recognized every picture—all works of art that she had admired during their time together. The SOB had not only paid attention but had also managed to purchase all this without her knowledge.

She opened the closet door to reveal an expansive space where a multitude of sundresses, jeans, and blouses all hung neatly pressed and organized in categorical order. Walnut drawers matching the bedroom furniture held all the lingerie she would ever need. Shoes sat neatly paired on two separate racks. Everything she would have ever needed for a romantic getaway was in the closet. "Too bad most of this won't fit in a few months," she muttered as she rubbed her belly.

Her spirit sank deeper as she looked at the empty racks where she surmised David's clothes had recently hung. She knew if she had any hope of surviving the morning, she had to get out of the house, and quick. The intense glare of the Gulf provided the answer.

She randomly selected a sundress, then stripped off her jeans, blouse, and bra. Standing naked, she pulled the floral teal dress over her head and enjoyed the silk fabric caressing her skin as it slid down. The sensation created a yearning to be touched, to have David's hands on her body. "I don't know where you are, David LaRoux, but goddammit, I need you now."

She found the bathroom stocked with her favorite makeup and toiletries. After a much-needed rendezvous with a toothbrush, she made her way downstairs to the patio door. A floppy hat was hanging by it and a pair of oversized shades sat on the table. She checked the clock near the fireplace. *The table clock is too damn close to that fucking portrait.*

It was five minutes to nine. Mr. Hanson had told her that a car was to pick her up at one for a critically important meeting. So, Rebecca had three hours to get lost, then found, and an hour to get dressed. Heeding his advice, she donned the hat and put on the sunglasses.

Rebecca squeezed her toes in the damp sand and savored the warm sensation of the gritty texture. It had been far too long since she strolled barefoot on a sandy beach. Off in the horizon, beyond all sight, Louisiana sat perched against these same waters. She could feel its gravitational pull; it was not about to surrender the inescapable debt she had incurred. In time, she would have to return and face the demons that remained.

But for now, this would have to do. She hiked her sundress midthigh, flopped down in the sand, and stretched her legs. She stared at the sailboats passing on the gentle breeze. Once again, memories forced the tears she thought were exhausted, but she refused to allow them to fall.

She watched as a sailboat tacked closer to shore, its bow now pointed in her direction. She closed her eyes and imagined LaRoux steering for the beach. Close enough to hear the anchor splash into the serene waters, Rebecca watched as its captain majestically dove in.

His strokes were powerful, and with purpose, every turn of his head fixed on his target.

Could it actually be him? Rebecca mused. His physique and hair all looked like LaRoux's. Rebecca's heart raced with wild, powerful thumps. She rose to her feet and staggered toward the sea.

The swimmer was now just fifty yards away. Every audible stroke drew him nearer. Rebecca waded in to her waist, and the gentle surf splashed around her. Her silk dress, now transparent, no longer concealed her wanting flesh. She reached out to LaRoux. The final stroke of his hand splashed her face.

Rebecca opened her eyes and watched as the sailboat cruelly began tacking away in a northwesterly direction. Dumbfounded in the surf, her champion faded into the reality of her hallucination.

"Oh God. I've lost my mind."

CHAPTER 23

PALMS AND HOUSES PASSED the window in a slow-motion carousel. The sunlight flickered through the car as Rebecca stared at it from behind her sunglasses. Her driver, Ben, had to remind her to bring the shades and a scarf for the ride into St. Armands Circle. Apparently, Mr. Hanson had instructed him concerning safety precautions prior to Rebecca's arrival.

They passed rows of charming shops and restaurants as they entered the center of the park. Rebecca stared blankly at it all, anesthetized to the quaintness of the village.

Ben pulled to a stop in front of a stucco two-story building, which featured a shoe boutique on the ground floor. In a distant life, Rebecca would have loved the shop. Ben stepped from the car and opened her door. "On the right side of the building, you'll find the stairs. Once you're inside, go to room 203."

"Who am I looking for?" Rebecca deadpanned.

"I don't know, ma'am. I was told somebody would be there to meet you, and they would call me when you are done."

"Thank you, Ben," Rebecca said, then she headed for the stairs without any sense of purpose.

"Ma'am," Ben began, stopping Rebecca in her tracks, "please remember to keep your scarf and sunglasses on. I was informed there are no cameras in the immediate vicinity, but my employer asked me to remind you all the same."

Rebecca nodded, then she turned back and was on her way up the stairs.

When she arrived on the second floor, she noticed the hallway lacked the luxury she had come to expect of LaRoux's associates. Musty odors accosted her as she made her way down the press and stick linoleum floor. If it were ever possible for a color to produce such a funk, Rebecca was sure these drab seafoam walls were guilty. She stared blankly at the door numbered 203. *Is this a DEA setup? Maybe Hanson's really an undercover agent.*

She breathed deeply, wishing she were back in Canada, then she turned the knob. She entered a room that matched the depressing ambiance of the hallway. A thin, elderly, white-haired man with a thick mustache and round wire-rimmed glasses sat behind a thrift-store desk. On the desk sat a straw fedora and a briefcase. On the verge of being uncomfortably warm, the room offered two windows, but sadly, both were closed.

In a deep Southern accent, the man spoke. "Mrs. LaRoux, it is so good to finally meet you. I have heard many wonderful things." He rose from his chair and met Rebecca halfway between the desk and door. He ushered her to a chair.

Rebecca thought briefly before replying softly, "It's Ms. Pearson."

"Oh, is that so? I was under the impression you were the wife of the late David LaRoux. Has there been some misunderstanding I am unaware of?"

"I am a federal agent. In the course of my investigation, I married Mr. LaRoux while in Canada. Due to the deceptive circumstances of our relationship, I'm not certain if I am legally entitled to claim spousal privileges. For that matter, I don't even know if it was a real priest who married us. I also heard several rumors at David's funeral inferring he had gotten an annulment when we returned to Louisiana."

"Please sit." The gentleman helped Rebecca into a creaking wooden chair. "Please allow me to introduce myself. My name is Adam Fletcher. I've been David's counselor, advisor, and friend for many years, and his parents' as well." Fletcher sat in the chair opposite Rebecca and snapped his briefcase open. "After conferring with David and examining your marriage documents, rest assured, you are his wife." Fletcher slid the marriage certificate across the desk.

"*Were!*" Rebecca leaned forward and briefly examined the document. "Peachy."

"Now, now, Mrs. LaRoux. I understand you are going through some rather harsh emotional struggles. This turmoil will pass, I promise you. In the meantime, there is the matter of David's estate, which I must disclose to you at this time."

"Should I have an attorney present?"

"Why, Mrs. LaRoux, I would rather hope that you will find it in your heart to trust me as the LaRoux family has done for over fifty years."

Rebecca nodded for Fletcher to continue.

"In the matter of physical property, all real estate assets are listed in exhibit 7B. As there are numerous minor properties listed, I will cover the major assets verbally. They are the LaRoux estate in Louisiana, CCI headquarters, two properties in Manhattan, the beach house here, a villa in Marseille, France, and another in Vienna. As I mentioned, the complete listing is rather extensive and is here on 7B," Fletcher said as he turned the page.

Rebecca gazed over the documents that he handed to her.

"Now, as to the matter of business interests, exhibit nine and all sub-schedules list all of the businesses and their applicable assets. Mr. LaRoux left advanced directives for how the businesses were to be managed until the time it is determined that you should play a larger role in the management of these entities. Crescent City Imports, naturally, will remain under Mr. Terrell's supervision for the immediate future. However, the current financial structures will remain in place. That being said, you will continue to draw David's full compensation from all enterprises until a change is warranted."

"And who makes that decision?"

"David had an advisory board, of which I am majordomo. If you deem it appropriate, I will continue to serve you in that capacity."

"Is this some kind of joke?"

Fletcher scooted his chair forward. "Mrs. LaRoux, may I call you Rebecca?"

She scanned the room for anything out of the ordinary. Suspicious of this entire performance, she delayed her reply. Maybe LaRoux's people had set this up to test her intentions. Had she seen Fletcher somewhere before? Maybe he was at LaRoux's ball, or was it somewhere in a DEA office? She stood from her chair and meandered about the room to discreetly scan for any electronic devices. "You may."

Fletcher studied her progress with great curiosity. As she completed her sweep, she returned to her chair. "I understand your concerns, Rebecca. You are fearful of David's associates or perhaps even your former employer. But I promise you, everything I offer is genuine. You only need to call *your* home in Louisiana. Walter Allen will confirm the terms of David's decree."

"I believe the last time I saw Mr. Allen, given the opportunity, he would have put a bullet right here." Rebecca pointed directly between her eyes.

"Oh no, my dear. They were devastated by the loss of our dear friend. But given your relationship with David, you *never* were at risk. I can assure you that Mr. Allen, as well as Mr. Patrick and Mr. Tazwell, all have been given a thorough briefing of your new position and their *potential* roles—that is, if you choose to retain their services. I think you will find them apologetic and eager to resume protective services for you."

"*They* were all with David when he died. I'm not altogether sure I can afford their level of competence."

Fletcher cleared his throat and adjusted his bow tie. "Trust me, Rebecca. On behalf of the board, I personally conducted an in-depth investigation concerning the events leading up to David's murder. There was *nothing* they, or you for that matter, could have done differently to change the outcome."

Rebecca sighed and closed her eyes briefly. "There were only two DEA agents present, and three of them. They could have shot the—"

"Mrs. LaRoux!" Appalled, Mr. Fletcher dramatically pushed back from his desk and stood. "To suggest any employee of CCI—"

"Save it, Mr. Fletcher. I'm only proving a point. David is dead because his own security people did not take necessary precautions to protect him. Things could have been done differently. There are always options."

"David specifically instructed them not to engage—"

"According to them," Rebecca objected sharply.

Fletcher sighed and dusted his shirt before sitting. After he collected his composure, he continued. "Indeed, there may have been other options, Rebecca. I believe given the nature of David's death, had they known the outcome, they would have reacted differently. Those men were loyal, and still are."

"Mr. Fletcher, you will have to excuse me if I seem a little edgy. Apparently, there are people who still want me dead or maybe even in jail. I don't sleep much, unless you count being passed out from a bottle of wine quality sleep. And now you're asking me to believe that I've just inherited David's entire empire. If I seem somewhat skeptical, or ungrateful, or whatever I appear to you, you'll just have to excuse me until I process all of this—"

"Rebecca, I do understand. Please trust me when I tell you, at this very moment, David's people are doing everything in their power to ensure your safety. The Longboat Key safe house is known only to myself and one other individual, whom David assured me was his most trusted employee. Take all these documents with you, and read them at your leisure. There are a few places for you to sign. I have indicated them with stickers. If you choose to opt out, you will find an annulment decree enclosed. It is the very last document in the package. Sign it, and all of this goes away, and you are free to do whatever you desire."

"If I sign the annulment, can I still keep the sailboat?"

Fletcher adjusted his falling spectacles. "I do not believe I saw any mention of a sailboat in any of David's documents, Rebecca."

"The house in Canada?" Rebecca stared, trying her best to intimidate Fletcher.

Despite the heat and Rebecca's best effort, Fletcher remained cool as whipped cream. "If David owned a home in Canada, he never disclosed it in any of his tax filings or asset declarations. Perhaps if you give me some details, I can perform some research into the matter."

Rebecca sat silently and considered the possibilities. LaRoux had said that *nobody* knew about the Canadian home. Logically, if it were truly his secret getaway, then the sailboat was most likely registered under an alias as well. For the first time in weeks, she felt she had a purpose. Now her mind was churning like a DEA agent's. *What else did he own or do under different identities?*

"I'm sorry, Mr. Fletcher, I *have* been rude. I will review all these documents and get back with you soon. If David trusted you for all these years, then that's good enough for me."

Mr. Fletcher reached inside his briefcase. "Here is a key for the safe in the master bedroom. Unlock it and then place your right thumb on the touchscreen. Inside you will find money, a secure phone to contact me, and instructions for car services, food, and necessities. Here is my private number, should any questions arise."

Rebecca stood, collected the papers, and stuffed them into the binder. She dangled the key before her eyes. "You said my thumbprint would open the safe?"

"Yes, after you unlock it."

"And how did that process occur without my knowledge?"

"David has owned this house for many years. Several months after the two of you disappeared from Las Vegas, he contacted me and had me arrange for various modifications to the house, one of those being the safe."

"So, he lifted my prints in Canada?"

Mr. Fletcher chuckled. "Oh no, my dear. *They* lifted everyone's prints from your mimosas at the hair salon, the day of the ball. David had you made from day one."

"Then why did he wait until Las Vegas to confront me?"

"Not about your career choice, my dear. That did not occur until later. Simply put, David knew from the first moment he saw you that he *was* going to fall in love."

CHAPTER 24

THE BOTTLE OF MERLOT was half gone, her guilt was unbearable, and her nerves were frayed. Even here, she did not believe she would survive the next seven more months. Every turn of a head, each unaccounted tick and click was surely the end. She felt the icy breath of death sending constant shivers through her body. She knew the type of people it took to run a billion-dollar empire—ruthless, vengeful, and lethal.

The phone remained on the coffee table in the same position it had been all afternoon. It was growing late, and Rebecca knew the first of several important calls had to be made. She topped off her glass, then picked up the phone and dialed. Her heart raced as she listened to it ring. "Director Cutchins, this is Rebecca Pearson."

"Agent Pearson, where in the hell have you been?"

Cutchins's tone intimidated Rebecca into a prolonged drink of wine. Suddenly, her well-rehearsed speech was lost in the director's angry inquisition. "I'm okay."

"Of course you're okay. You're on the damn phone, aren't you? I asked, where have you been?"

Rebecca drank again. With a tremor in her voice, she explained, "I'm calling to tender my resignation."

"Hold the phone one damn minute." Cutchins placed her on hold, then punched his intercom. "Get a trace on my line. I've got Pearson on the phone." He took a calming breath, collected his wits, and then clicked back to Pearson. "I'm sorry for my abruptness, but we've been looking for you nonstop for four days. Agent Turner has not gone home since your abduction. So, before you resign, I think you owe everyone at the agency an explanation."

"I don't feel as if I owe the agency anything." Rebecca paused a bit too long to collect her thoughts. "I went under deep cover for over eight months with absolutely no support. When I was able to check in, I was treated like a suspect. I have been detained, under the guise of protective custody, until it was made clear that I might be under arrest for impeding an investigation. All the while, I was denied access to legal counsel. So, now that I am free, you will forgive me if I do not agree with your assessment."

"An agent was assaulted in the process of your abduction. Like it or not, you are a witness to the crime."

Rebecca refilled her glass. "Director Cutchins, I am not a witness. I too was assaulted and remained unconscious until I awoke, all alone . . . and free."

"And where would that be?"

"Somewhere you'll never find, even with the trace you're undoubtedly running as we speak." Rebecca smirked at the thought of having been on the other side, knowing she held the technological upper hand. "I'll be back in a week or two—maybe a month—with an attorney. I'll give a full statement at that time. As I am certain you are recording our conversation, please consider this my official resignation."

Rebecca hung up and immediately set out for another bottle of wine. Her hands trembled as she applied the corkscrew and opened the bottle to allow it to breathe before pouring a glass.

Then her next and last call, if it were possible, created even more anxiety. After three rings, she said, "Walt, this is Rebecca."

"Mr. Fletcher said you might be calling soon."

"Walt, I need to explain." The tremble in Rebecca's voice returned with a vengeance.

"No, you don't. What your people did to David, there's no justification. You were one of them, and nothing will change that. But Mr. Fletcher has satisfactorily explained that everything up until the explosion was part of David's plan to publicly humiliate your former boss for attempting to destroy his reputation."

"Inasmuch as I loved David, he wasn't exactly clean."

"What do you really know? What crime did you actually witness? Outside of what happened in Vegas, which he did to protect you, he was cleared of any wrongdoing."

"He told me things."

"Personally, I don't think you know jack shit. But unfortunately, David's death wasn't in his master plan. And whether you played him or actually loved him, we'll never know. But it doesn't matter, because David loved you. And Mr. Fletcher has informed me that not only did he leave you everything but that you are carrying his child too."

As she stared at a new bottle, she wiped a tear and shook her head. "There's no way I will ever convince you, is there?" Walt's silence did not offer any hint of amnesty. "If I sign the annulment papers and leave everything to the baby, could I still raise our child at the plantation?"

Walt considered the offer for a minute. "You can do whatever you want. It's all yours. He wanted you to have it all, so that's the way it should be. Because we all loved him like a brother, it would dishonor all of us to do anything less than what he expected." Walt choked back his emotions long enough to steady his thoughts. "I'd be lying if I said everything is cool. It's not. But I promise we will give you a fair chance if you reciprocate."

Rebecca did not attempt to mute her audible sniffles. "I can't ask for any more than that. And I do appreciate your honesty, Walt. I'll be coming home in a week or so." She hung up and walked unsteadily to the kitchen with the new bottle, hunched over the sink and poured it down the drain. She filled a Solo cup with water, then raised it as she imagined that David was before her. "I promise, if we live long enough, I'll do better."

* * *

A half hour later, Rebecca reclined in a beach chair and glimpsed the surf beyond. She pulled her bikini top out just enough to inspect herself to ensure she had not begun to burn. After years in the Pacific Northwest, and almost a year in Canada, she wondered how her skin would take to so much sun. Suddenly, memories of that night in the bayou on the hood of David's car as his lips caressed her naked body replayed like a steamy movie love scene. She allowed her hand to slide over her breasts, down to her stomach, and then lightly brush sideways until it fell to her side. Beginning at her knees, her hands meandered, caressing up her thighs until they returned to her abs. As the wetness intensified between her thighs, she shuddered at the distant sensation of LaRoux sliding inside.

She rose from her chair and made her way into the surf until the warm waters reached her chest. She closed her eyes and returned to her fantasy. As it played out, her hands drifted, one to her breasts and one inside her bikini bottom. Her breathing escalated as she caressed her breasts firmly while methodically stroking between her thighs.

Quickly, the physical stimulation and the lucid visions made her climax in the emerald waters.

As she spasmed, she arched backward and submerged herself in the soothing, salty Gulf.

When she emerged, she looked around nervously, slightly embarrassed, but with a calm sense of satisfaction. Had anybody seen and surmised what she had just done? Nobody appeared to be giving her a second glance, except—

The closest beach dweller, a man in a chair, glanced periodically and then turned away. She thought she remembered his ball cap and sunglasses from a day ago when he maintained a safe distance behind her as she strolled along the beach. Yes, she had passed him as she reached the limit of her walk and turned back for the beach house. Oversized sunglasses concealed much of his face. Outside of a scruffy beard, she had not paid much attention to his details.

She returned to her chair. Reclining in it fully, she rolled to her stomach and turned so she could spy on her would-be shadow. From this distance, as best as she could tell, his body looked pretty solid, not altogether different from LaRoux's. With only one chair on the beach, it appeared that he was alone. In her mind, she knew what this mysterious stalker wanted. After all, he was a man. He probably had determined she was alone, not that that would stop most men. Her body *was* still pretty darn desirable, at least for another month or two. *But who is he—a wanton lover, an assassin, a cop? Perhaps an assistant to Mr. Hanson.* Knowing he was most likely just the product of her fearful and suspicious mind, Rebecca decided it best to maintain a sharper eye going forward.

* * *

Many hours, and glasses of wine later, after Rebecca had turned in for the night, the sound of a sliding glass door roused her awake. She lay perfectly still in bed and listened for any other trace of sound other than the rolling tide. After minutes of absolute silence, just as she was about to doze off again, she heard what sounded like a desk drawer softly close.

Her heart began to race, and she gently groped in the dark for the phone on the nightstand.

Once she located it, she pulled the covers over her head and pushed the call button.

"Someone's in the house."

"That's impossible," Hanson's groggy voice replied. "I checked the alarm myself."

"I've heard several sounds."

Hanson snapped out of his sleep stupor and immediately delivered instructions. "Rebecca, as quietly as possible, I want you to lock your bedroom door and then go into the bathroom and lock it as well. Without pulling the knob on the medicine cabinet, turn the knob a quarter turn clockwise, then pull. You will find a nine millimeter behind the cabinet. Get it, and sit in the shower until you hear from me again."

Rebecca followed his instructions, but even though she moved as silently as possible, the floor still randomly creaked. She knew the intruder had to have heard her footsteps, and with that knowledge, she felt her face go pale. Once she was in the shower, she sat on the floor trembling and pointed the gun toward the door.

Within minutes, she heard furniture crashing and glass breaking. She curled tightly in morbid fear. She kept her shaking gun aimed at the door.

* * *

"Rebecca?" She did not respond. "Rebecca, it's Victor. Are you alright?" She rose from the shower floor and moved cautiously to the door.

"Rebecca, it's Victor Hanson. It's alright to open the door now."

This man did not sound like Victor Hanson. Maybe this was all in her imagination. She kept the gun high and slowly turned the knob. As she peered through the crack in the door, blood drained from her head and her world began to spin. Rebecca's gun fell to the floor as she uttered, "David," before her knees buckled and she collapsed.

In a churning sea of mist and confusion, Rebecca struggled against the waves pulling her under. On the horizon, she could see LaRoux sailing for her, but the distance between them never closed. When she could fight no more, her muscles seized, and with her love still so far away, the might of the sea pulled her down.

There she remained until the caress of his hand on her face roused her senses. With so little light, his features remained unclear. His smile did not greet her eyes, nor a scowl, just a blank, emotionless face. "David?" Rebecca forced his name.

His hand touched hers. She trembled. "Why did you have to die?"

"I had to die to be free, so that we could be together."

"Together? Unless I'm dead too, talking with you will get me committed. If you really want me to be free, would you be upset if I asked you to go away . . . forever?"

"How about if I stay and love you for the rest of our lives?"

Rebecca's lips turned up almost to a smile, an expression missing since the news of LaRoux's death. Then she faded back into the darkness.

* * *

The radiant sun warmed Rebecca. Her eyes parted and were greeted by a carousel ride of the spinning room about her. She raised her hand to her head to discover a well-rounded knob just above her hairline. "Oh God. I have completely lost my mind."

Although the tender mound was real, the fantastic events of last night seemed a very distant memory. Ever since arriving in Longboat Key, her dreams had been filled with surrealist fantasies of LaRoux, both real and imagined. Lying in bed, bits of last night's menagerie replayed in nonsequential order. "I dropped a loaded gun," Rebecca whispered as she sat up to see if it remained in the bathroom.

It was gone from sight, and the medicine cabinet door was closed. Her miniscule hope that something from last night had been real instantly slammed shut.

Just as her eyes closed, allowing respite from the glow of the morning sun, the sound of a pan rattling in the kitchen jarred her to reality. *Somebody is in the house.* If it was Mr. Hanson, then the events of last night were real. And, of course, *he* must have been the one to tidy up after she, or somebody, hit her head.

Rebecca, wearing only a button-up shirt she had confiscated from LaRoux's wardrobe months ago, absentmindedly padded down the hall. At the base of the stairs, she turned the corner and froze in shock. The vision before her was making it impossible for her to decide whether she remained in some inebriated or concussion-induced dream or had managed to somehow reach the afterlife. Cautiously proceeding, she braced herself against the kitchen table, where she watched as the vision methodically prepared breakfast on the stove. With great apprehension, she moved into the doorway, fearful to confront reality. Suddenly, memories of her final, delirious conversation from last night returned.

"*David*?"

The man twitched and almost spilled the meal he was preparing. With a jerk, he turned and flashed an unfamiliar smile. "Oh, Rebecca, there you are. So sorry, I didn't mean to startle you," he explained in a peculiar British accent. "I'm Robert—Robert LaRoux. Are you hungry?"

This man was the spitting image of David, in every detail, except for an almost tropical tan.

And his smile was all wrong—and the accent and his hair. But everything else was identical.

"Who let you in?"

"I'm sorry. I arrived so late last night. I didn't want to wake you, though I seemed to have had a bit of a tussle with your security man."

"How did you get in?"

"I have a key and an alarm code. David sent it to me. I tried to call your cell phone, but apparently your security man has taken possession of it." Robert waited for her reaction, but lacking any, he continued. "Look, if I don't finish this omelet, it won't be fit to eat. Why don't you go get out of your skivvies, find some proper clothing, and we can talk over breakfast."

Rebecca continued to stare until he shooed her away with a "go on." She returned to the bedroom and looked in the mirror. Her breasts were barely covered by the two buttons she had managed to fasten. She decided a bra might be a good addition to help recover from her trampish first impression. And everything else? *Good Lord*, skivvies was a generous description. She pulled on some khaki capris and brushed her teeth. Her hair was hopeless, and scrunching it only moved the disaster from one side to the other.

She returned to the kitchen table to find Robert patiently sitting as if he didn't have a care in the world. Two plates of omelets and fresh fruit were waiting, as well as tea. "Are we out of coffee?" Rebecca moaned as she sat down. "You certainly seem to know your way around *my* kitchen."

With that awkward smile, he replied, "It's not my first time staying here." He took a bite of his breakfast, then dabbed his napkin on his lips before setting his fork down. "I should explain, I am David's twin brother."

"David didn't have any siblings, much less a twin brother," Rebecca objected.

"No, I suppose it would be some time before he divulged the complete LaRoux family history. First and foremost, David asked me, should anything happen to him, to come to America and offer you any assistance that I could. Although I have never been involved with the family import business, there is nothing that I don't know. David shared everything with me, including his love for you."

Rebecca stared, unable to eat, or much more, fathom the reality before her eyes.

"You should eat. It will make you feel much better."

"I don't need any help," Rebecca objected.

"My dear Rebecca, judging by the empty bottles of wine in the wastebasket, you will need assistance just delivering your refuse to the curb."

Embarrassed, Rebecca snapped, "Those weren't all mine—I had a party."

"Indeed. And what a party it must have been." Robert took another bite of omelet.

Rebecca did not appreciate his sarcasm. She pressed for his story. "You were saying you are David's twin."

"Ah yes. David and I *are* twins. Our mother, Emily, who I never knew, had an older sister, Gwen. Gwen and her husband, Charles, who I lovingly refer to as *my* mother and father, were infertile. When Emily discovered that she carried twins, she and our father, Carter, made an enormous sacrifice and decided to allow Gwen and Charles to adopt me. I was raised in England and lived there and in France my entire life. It wasn't until Emily and Carter were murdered that I learned of the truth of my biological parents and that I had a brother. Quite the scuttlebutt ensued. You see, Gwen and Charles wanted David to come live with us, but Carter's instructions were explicit concerning David's future. My life had been kept a secret because Carter knew the dangers of the family business. They believed, if they all were to perish, that through me, the LaRoux bloodline would remain safe. My entire existence is one of the family's greatest secrets."

Rebecca stared at Robert as she slowly chewed her first bite. "Robert, you'll have to forgive me if I seem skeptical. Naturally, any documentation you could provide proving any of this would be greatly appreciated." She turned her attention to her food and took another bite. "This is quite delicious," she said.

"I promise you, Rebecca, I am completely prepared to provide whatever documentation you, or anyone else, might require. I am quite certain my appearance in New Orleans will be scandalous to say the least."

"New Orleans?" Rebecca startled as if she had been shocked.

"Yes. As per David's instructions, I am to make sure your business in New Orleans goes smoothly."

Rebecca set her fork on her plate and stared at the man before her. "I suppose you'll be wanting to see the dispersion of David's estate?"

Robert chuckled. "Oh heavens no, dear." He cocked his head to the side. "Is this the root of your attitude? I'm not here for one pound of my family's estate. After our parents passed, David shared his abundant family wealth equally. I have enjoyed wealth beyond our means, thanks to my biological parents and brother. What David left behind is truly yours. I am merely here to lend my support until you are comfortable with your assets."

Rebecca looked around the room. "I am quite comfortable with my assets already."

Robert smiled again as he looked at a half-empty bottle of wine on the end table across the room. "Indeed."

Rebecca followed his gaze until she found the source of his sarcasm. Looking back, she was greeted by that damned crooked smile. "What's wrong with your smile? Did you break your jaw or something?"

"Yes. Apparently, David was quite the rambunctious wombmate. As a result, I was born with a dislodged jaw."

"With all that LaRoux money, I'd think you might want to get it fixed."

"Most women have said they find it rather charming, rather like Harrison Ford's smile." Robert's attitude was playfully light as he covered his lips. "Heavens, do you suppose those women were lying to get at my money?"

"I'm sorry, Robert. I hope you understand how hard it is for me to sit across from the *ghost* of my husband."

"Oh, I understand completely. It is not so different from my beleaguered situation. Thanks to David, I had the privilege of knowing you well before you knew me. You see, I had already seen the beauty that made my brother swoon, and I know in time I will suffer your charms as well. My brother's taste for love is not unlike my own. And that, my dear Rebecca, may prove to be a tragedy of an altogether different sort."

CHAPTER 25

THE SHORT FLIGHT BACK to New Orleans proved much less stressful than the limo ride into the city. As Robert recounted tales of growing up in London and his travels through France, Rebecca probed for a nick in his story. He claimed many things, including that he was a barrister of sorts. He told Rebecca that he was prepared to offer legal counsel to her in regards to CCI and the DEA. Not only did he want to help her, but he was charming, polite, and humorous. Despite these positive attributes, she resented his remarkable physical characteristics. For all practical purposes, she had spent the last three days with an understudy version of David LaRoux. It was downright cruel to suffer the company of a man so amazingly like her lost love.

As downtown New Orleans appeared, Rebecca's stomach knotted, and Robert grew uncharacteristically quiet. The silence riled her internal storm, so she grasped for a thread of conversation. "I never realized you could get such a great tan in England."

"When I learned of my brother's death, I flew to America via Miami, with the intention of coming to my brother's funeral. But then I considered how much consternation my sudden appearance would create, how it might be disruptive to his memorial and his friends, and especially you. So, much against my personal desire,

I stayed in Miami. Once I learned you were headed to Florida, I decided to give you a few days to settle in."

Rebecca digested his explanation without reply. She had asked Walt to assemble David's inner circle at the plantation. Preferring to temporarily distance herself from the business side of *her* empire, she thought the mansion would be the best setting to address the crew, yet it would be one of her biggest emotional hurdles. Although it was not completely clear at this point, she wanted to define her expectations and introduce Robert LaRoux to David's people.

After crossing the Mississippi and what seemed like not nearly enough time, the limo turned onto the familiar oyster-shell- and twisted-oak-lined drive. As the mansion came into view, Rebecca cried. She grabbed Robert's forearm and sniffled, "Oh God. I don't think I can do this."

"There, there, Rebecca." Robert patted her hand. "You *can* do this, you'll see. I'll be there as David's spokesperson and your shoulder to lean on if needed."

Minutes later, as Rebecca climbed the spiral, marble steps, memories of the effort it took to climb them in her ball gown replayed in her mind. Then at the door, an employee greeted her and Robert with a look of utter bewilderment, and though he was unable to keep his eyes from dancing with questions, he ushered them to David's second-floor office. There, Rebecca and Robert found Ryan, Taz, and Walt mired in a jovial conversation.

Ryan was the only one facing the door and reacted to Robert immediately. "David? What the hell?" Taz and Walt spun around instantly, and their jaws dropped.

Rebecca was prepared for the kneejerk reaction and fully expected it would diffuse whatever strategy the three had concocted. "No," she relied forcefully. "This is David's twin brother, Robert. I assume you have heard mention of a brother."

Walt was the first to approach, followed by Ryan and Taz. "We have, although David never said he was a twin."

"We were told many years ago," Ryan began, "as a matter of knowledge not to be shared or discussed." Ryan stepped around Walt to improve his inspection.

"Robert LaRoux," Robert said as he extended his hand. "It's a pleasure to finally meet all of you."

As Rebecca began explaining Robert's sudden appearance and her future plans, David's crew surprisingly appeared to settle in without objections. Their grand inquisition of Robert was not unlike Rebecca's archeological dig into his past. Patient and courteous, Robert explained every detail until David's crew had exhausted their interrogation.

"Gentlemen, I must say that I am not accustomed to being on this side of the witness stand, mind you, twice now in a single week," said Robert, who explained he practiced law in his native country. "I appreciate your diligence, and I am confident that once I have returned to England, Rebecca will be in the best of hands."

"She will," Taz proclaimed. Uncharacteristically quiet throughout much of the visit, he was ready to make his opinion known, loud and proud. He turned to Rebecca and added, "There won't be any more of David's cowboy nonsense. That's what got him killed. We're gonna take care of you and the baby."

"So, what are your immediate plans?" Ryan asked Rebecca.

"Robert and I, and hopefully one of you, are going to pay a visit to the DEA office. I need to formally resign and explain Robert's presence. We wouldn't want Will Martin to get a murder pass because everyone thinks David is still alive, would we?"

"Hell no," Ryan agreed. "If you don't mind, I think we'd all like to tag along."

"I'd like that," Rebecca said with a smile.

* * *

The hush that fell over the office was unnerving. Rebecca walked with a purpose, not slowing for the gawking eyes or whispers that surely were about to commence. Robert trailed in a more casual manner, sipping at his coffee and smiling cordially as he passed through the sea of astonished agents. Without knocking, Rebecca blew into Director Cutchins's office like a spring thunderstorm. Her fury quickly dissipated when she discovered Will Martin seated against the wall. He was sorting through documents.

"What the hell is he doing here?" Rebecca scolded.

Cutchins got an eyeful of Robert LaRoux. "Who the hell is this?"

"Jesus, Rebecca, are you fucking kidding me?" Martin chimed.

It took several seconds for Rebecca to regain her composure. Once she felt her heartbeat slow down, she began to explain. "This is my attorney, Robert LaRoux. He is David's brother."

"Brother my ass," Martin exclaimed as he surged forward. "Do you know how many weeks I've spent in *your* shitty jails, thanks to *your* corrupt judges, you miserable son of a bitch?" Just as Martin began to reach for Robert's collar, Robert fired a jab into his throat and dropped him to the floor. Director Cutchins opened his desk drawer and reached for his gun. Robert threw his hands up and bellowed, "That man just assaulted me. And if you are considering to further threaten my safety, I will be forced to press charges."

The fracas drew the attention of the entire squad room, with numerous agents beginning to swarm toward the director's office. Martin remained on his knees, gasping for breath while Cutchins hesitantly closed his drawer. Robert moved away from Martin and approached the director. "I insist that you remove that man from your office immediately. He is a criminal and a detriment to the nature of our business today."

Seething, Martin looked at the director for support. But Cutchins nodded, signaling for Martin to leave the office. Rebecca watched as her former boyfriend gathered his documents.

She ascertained they all concerned the case against David. As Martin began to depart, he cut a malicious glare at Rebecca, and remaining outside of Robert LaRoux's striking distance, he struggled to growl, "This isn't over, LaRoux."

Once Martin was gone, Robert closed the door. "I'm truly sorry about my behavior, Director Cutchins. But given William Martins's history of aggravated assault against my brother, and his slanderous accusations against my family enterprise, I am sure you will understand my fearful reaction."

Cutchins nodded as he studied Robert's mannerisms.

"May we sit?"

Again, Cutchins nodded.

Robert pulled a second chair to Cutchins's desk and waited for Rebecca to sit before he did. Now in a chair, he opened his satchel and cleared his throat. "As I will be acting as counsel on Mrs. LaRoux's behalf, and representing my brother's estate, I have prepared several documents for your department. The first and most critical document, which I assure you has been properly filed, is a restraining order to keep that animal," Robert said, pointing toward the squad room, "away from Mrs. LaRoux, CCI employees, and all properties and business interests." He handed over the small stack of documents. "I trust that you will make sure *he* is duly warned. As to his violent nature, if he trespasses or violates any of these orders, our security forces have been instructed to apply appropriate measures to protect our people."

Cutchins placed the documents on his desk without as much as a glimpse.

"Secondly, although we have no obligation at this time to divulge this information, here is a video we have obtained of William Martin assaulting my brother when he was in Martin's custody." As Robert placed the thumb drive on Cutchins's desk, the director cut his eyes to the device before returning his blank stare to Robert. "I believe it will be in the DEA's best interest to distance yourselves from William Martin. After you have viewed the video, I think you will agree. Next packet is Rebecca LaRoux's official letter of resignation, along with a complete debriefing concerning her opinions and observations concerning this case. Any further request for information should be directed to me. I trust after you have examined it, you will restore all monies and benefits lawfully due." Again, Cutchins ignored the documents as they were placed on his desk.

"Finally, as I know there may be some suspicion concerning my appearance, I have included enough documentation to verify my identity." Robert placed the last folder down. "I will remain in New Orleans until William Martin has been convicted and is safely incarcerated. You will find sufficient contact information inside the folder, if you should have any need to speak with Mrs. LaRoux. And now, unless you have any further business to discuss, I think this should conclude our interview."

Cutchins sneered at Rebecca, who returned the courtesy. His list of interrogation questions seemed somewhat pointless as Rebecca's resignation eliminated any leverage he once held. "I'll be in touch." Considering the mountain of paperwork before him, that was the best counter he could manage.

Robert set down his coffee cup on Cutchins's desk and turned to leave. "Former Agent Martin is a disgrace to all law enforcement. In the future, I certainly hope you will make better choices of the people you allow in your service. Good day, sir."

As Rebecca passed Martin, she noticed that practically any evidence of his once devilish charm had vanished. The man had finally received his just rewards. Once out on the sidewalk, she turned to Robert and hugged him. "Thank you for taking care of that for me."

"Anything less would be a disservice to my brother's name."

* * *

Martin barged back into Cutchins's office. "I can't believe you allowed that cocksucker to walk right out of the office, especially after he assaulted me. That *is* fucking David LaRoux!"

Cutchins stared at Martin, his anger tempered by years of experience. "What would you have me do, Will? Waterboard him right here in my office until he confessed? The man has handed over a stack of documents that I need to examine before I do a damn thing. I, for one, have seen more than enough results from half-cocked vendetta-driven investigations. *If* there is a play to be made, it will be a slam dunk before I lace up my sneakers. But enough of *my* investigation, let's talk about you."

Martin appeared befuddled as Cutchins thumbed through the stack of paperwork Robert LaRoux had deposited. Cutchins pulled the thumb drive from the first envelope, then he placed it on the desk and tapped it with his finger. "The day you arrested LaRoux—would you care to revise your version of the scuffle?"

Martin looked at the thumb drive and hesitated. "Let me guess—a video has surfaced. Ain't that a big fucking surprise? Yeah, it might appear that I put a beatdown on him in the streets, but he assaulted me in the car. That fucker must have set that up as well."

Cutchins sighed. "In the event that this recording, or any other that might surface, reveals contradictory evidence, I need to know all of the details, minus the bullshit."

Martin gritted his teeth. "He disrespected Agent Pearson and myself. He threatened her life."

"You dragged a handcuffed man from your car and beat him over verbal threats and insults?" Cutchins was no longer able to hide his wrath. "Will, go home before *I* have you arrested."

"Wait just a fu—"

"No, Will. You're done." Cutchins waved a stack of documents in front of Martin's face. "Additionally, Robert LaRoux has acquired restraining orders—against you. You are not to approach Rebecca LaRoux, or LaRoux's employees, or trespass on any of their property." Cutchins slammed the paperwork on his desk. "I have consented to allow LaRoux's people to shoot you should you violate the terms of these orders. Understand? Now, go park your ass on the bench out there. I will have Lorraine bring you a copy of the orders."

Martin stared at Cutchins with utter contempt. Cutchins stood with his white-knuckled fist pressed firmly into the desk. "*Now* would be the time to get the hell out of my sight."

As Martin stormed from the office, Cutchins punched the intercom on his desk. "Lorraine, send Truman in. And have him bring an evidence bag, please."

Cutchins stared out into the squad room, wishing he had gone fishing today. *Three more years of this shit,* he mused. Truman entered, interrupting his thoughts. Cutchins carefully extracted the restraining orders from the envelope. "Bag that coffee cup and this envelope. I want prints and DNA." He handed Truman the court orders. "Have Lorraine make copies of these, then give a set to Martin. Then please get that dipshit out of my sight."

CHAPTER 26

"YOU HANDLE THE BOAT quite well," Rebecca remarked as Robert navigated through the river.

Turning abruptly up a narrow stream, he quickly killed the motor and the Chris-Craft slowed to a drift, its wake swamping up behind the boat. As the water settled, Robert turned to Rebecca. "I own a boat in the British Virgin Islands. Not as nice as this, mind you, but it serves the purpose."

"I'd like to go there one day," Rebecca smiled.

"My dear, with all your money, you can do whatever you want."

"I suppose, but it just won't be the same without David." She made no attempt to conceal her lingering sadness.

"*Tsk, tsk*, now there. This is no time for that long face. In fact, it is a time for celebration." Robert reached into the cooler and extracted a bottle of Southern Belle wine.

Rebecca watched as he poured two glasses. As he handed her a glass with barely enough to even call a taste, he winked. "An exception, for a very special occasion," he said as he raised his glass.

"Hmm, I haven't had a glass since we left Florida. You're not trying to get me tipsy, are you?" Rebecca tried to nurse the glass, but after the first sip, there was nothing left. "And what exactly are we celebrating?"

"Well, as you know, they never found a single shred of evidence against David or his associates for any criminal activity. Based on your testimony concerning Las Vegas, they found no guilt in his actions concerning the death of the three Colombians. And thanks to William Martin's obsessive behavior, they found no reason to pursue any charges concerning your abduction and disappearance. My brother's fine name has been exonerated. Lastly, as my fingerprints and DNA prove my identity, they have been forced to accept that Martin killed my brother without just cause. With all the hurdles cleared, William Martin will now receive whatever punishment your criminal justice system deems appropriate. And you, Rebecca, are free to go and do whatever your heart desires."

Rebecca smiled tepidly. "It's kind of sad. I know how wealthy I am, but I really don't want any of it. I love the plantation, but it's so empty without David." She rubbed her visibly growing belly. "I know I need to raise our child there, but being there without him is just so damn depressing. And Canada? As much as I adored our home, I don't think I can ever go back there again." She studied Robert's fixed expression of concern. Not wanting to be completely self-centered, she asked, "So, what about you? What do you want from all of this mess?"

He contemplated her question for a moment as he took pleasure in the afternoon sun. "That would depend on what you want. Do you want this to be a weekend fling or something more?"

The words sent a shock wave through her memory. Instantly, she recognized that this was the precise bend in the river where David had posed the same question nearly a year ago. "What did you just say?"

"I said I had to die to be free, so that we could be together." He smiled *that* smile.

* * *

Just as he had mysteriously appeared, Robert had vanished, leaving Rebecca trembling and glassy-eyed. "Before you decide to hate me forever, please let me explain—"

"Oh God. It can't be—David?" Tears flowed freely as Rebecca lunged into his arms. She kissed his face repeatedly, then stopped suddenly with a look of dire concern. "Please tell me this is real, that I'm not kissing Robert."

"Oh, this is real."

Rebecca hugged him again, as if she might never have the opportunity to do so another time.

Then she pulled away and sniffled, "Okay, mister, you've got a lot of explaining to do."

LaRoux wiped her tears gently. "First and foremost, I'm so sorry I had to deceive you. But if I couldn't convince you, I knew I'd never stand a chance of convincing everyone else. David LaRoux had to die to make a clean break from this business."

"I don't understand. Are you or are you not in the drug business?"

"I told you pretty much from day one that I was. And the only way to put an end to it was to put an end to me. Dying was the only way to get out."

Rebecca appeared confused. "But the explosion, your body? All of the evidence?"

David smiled briefly. "Yes, all of that. Ever since I met you, I've been devising a way out. My death was well orchestrated, with several possible scenarios. It just so happened that Will played into my hands like he was auditioning for the part. That day in your motel, and then the warehouse, I could not have scripted a better reaction."

"But I saw him shoot you in the security footage, and then there was the explosion."

"I began having that set built many months ago. When you saw the video of me getting shot, you were actually watching a projection. If Martin's shot had not ruptured the gas tanks, Mr. Hanson's shot would have. The crates that burned were filled with the same fabric as the screen, so nobody ever questioned the screen fabric's residue after the fire. The gas tanks arrived four weeks prior and were scheduled to be shipped the week after. Everything in that warehouse was there by design and had a legitimate purpose."

"But your body, the DNA?"

"I had the coke delivery scheduled for when there would be a fresh cadaver. We found a Mr. Smith, who was dying. I scheduled our departure from Canada, based on my best guestimate of when that would occur. With several months of planning, I had more than enough time to have someone collect Mr. Smith's dental records and insert it into my medical history.

"Wait. Are you telling me that while we were in Canada, getting married, and making a baby, you were plotting this entire production?"

"I know, it sucks. But I did not want to risk allowing your opinions to influence my master plan. Imagine if you had known about my plans at the warehouse. What would you have said or done? It was bad enough I broke my jaw during the explosion, but I couldn't have you there, like I know you would have insisted, and have to deal with your safety as well."

Rebecca took LaRoux's wineglass, refilled it, and then leaned back. "That stupid crooked smile? It's because you broke your jaw?"

"Yes. I haven't had it fixed properly, so I can pretty much dislocate it at will." LaRoux smiled, demonstrating his accidental disguise.

"Oh, stop that. Now that I know why, that kind of makes me queasy. It's not natural." She took a baby sip of her wine as she stared at LaRoux. "So, what happens when the DEA starts looking deeper into Robert LaRoux?"

"Oh, they've already dug deep. But I didn't accomplish this all on my own. My meticulous planning was ingrained in my DNA. My ancestors perfected generations of multiple identities long before I was born. It is true—my aunt and uncle live in England, and my uncle is sterile. They wanted a child and were not wealthy. So, they did the in vitro thing with my father being the donor. So, in truth, I do have a half brother, who does look a hell of a lot like me. A very generous financial arrangement was devised where my aunt and uncle would take new identities and relocate should the need ever arise, and my family could assume theirs. Other surrogates exist, but hopefully with this life behind me, I will never need them."

"But what happens if Cutchins digs really deep into Robert's childhood?"

"Not that I *think* Cutchins will waste any further resources on Martin, but if so, I gave him all the evidence he'll ever need to confirm my identity. The fingerprints on the envelope and the DNA from the coffee cup I intentionally left behind will all match my half brother's records back in England. I have an employee, much like Mr. Hanson, whose sole purpose is to make sure all of the surrogate's information would match if ever needed. And as I said, as for the body the DEA discovered after the fire, my medical records were altered to match his. The inferno was designed to incinerate DNA, leaving bones and dental fragments as the only reliable evidence. All of *this* was put into motion right after we arrived in Canada. I was merely waiting for my Mr. Smith to die."

Rebecca frowned. "That's sad."

"For my brother or my body?" LaRoux chuckled. "My brother has hardly worked a day in his life. After law school, he has lived the life of a playboy and he understands precisely who pays his salary. As for my Mr. Smith, we've taken good care of his family."

"You scare me, David," Rebecca stated as she tensed. "I knew you were meticulous, but *wow*, it scares the hell out of me what you're capable of."

LaRoux leaned forward and stroked his hand up Rebecca's leg until it landed on her belly. "What I am capable of, Rebecca LaRoux, is doing whatever it is I have to do to safely spend the rest of our lives together—the three of us."

Rebecca's posture had yet to relax. She hid behind her glass to conceal a fresh volley of tears. "You were such an ass to watch me suffer through all of this. I don't know how I'm supposed to heal from these scars, David."

LaRoux pulled the wineglass away and carefully wiped her tears. "That's why you have to bury David LaRoux. And who knows, maybe in time, you may find yourself falling in love with Robert. Perhaps you'll even marry the bloke one day."

"What if I don't?" Rebecca sniffled through her tears. "Will I be sent back to the bayou?"

LaRoux chuckled. "Robert will be very sad and quite lonely—and broke—for the rest of his life." LaRoux swung his hand from one end of the horizon to the other. "You own everything, my dear . . . including my heart."

Rebecca surveyed the radiant sun streaking through the moss-covered cypresses and then across the entire splendor of the bayou. She sighed with absolute satisfaction. "You know, *if* I were to marry Robert, I think he would need a higher stature in society. A lowly barrister will never do." Rebecca thought briefly, then smiled brightly. "I've got it. Robert LaRoux, I crown you Lord of the Bayou."